Escaping Fate, Embracing Destiny

Beverly L. Anderson

Second edition 2024

Escaping Fate, Embracing Destiny is dedicated to my mom. She was a strong woman who influenced everything I've ever done in my life, and since this is the first story I ever penned, I want to dedicate this to her. She may no longer be here, but she is always in my heart.

Acknowledgements

I want to thank my family and friends for putting up with my bookish pursuits over the years. From writing random poems to asking them to read a chapter here and there, these people have been with me through everything. I couldn't have made it without you all.

A huge thank you to Wrey for helping me with a few things about this volume. Without him, I don't know what I would have done.

Introduction

This book was first conceived when I was around eleven years old. I'll never forget how it came about. My grandmother was in the hospital and my mom took us to Sam's Club. At the time, you had to own a business to get into Sam's, and my parents owned a little café in our small Texas town. While there, she let me buy a massive pack of spiral notebooks. They were all different colors, I remember. But there was one that I picked out, especially because there was something I wanted to do. It was a purple cover. I remember that, and I started a work called Escape. Back then, it was missing a few current elements, and CJ was slightly different than he became. But then, time changed me, so it only makes sense that the main character would evolve and change along with me.

My grandmother died shortly after that, and perhaps it was her death that influenced me more than anything to start writing whenever I could. My mom let me use her old typewriter with the automatic carriage return. I wanted a "word processor," which was all the rage right then.

In school, I learned to type correctly and use a computer, and I found myself transferring so many random thoughts onto paper for the first time. It started with poetry, so I have two books of 150 poems each and have started working on a third one. But always, I had this book as an idea. That was my very first idea. No matter what I did, it wouldn't leave me alone over the years, and now, I'm finally able to share it with the world. I hope you enjoy my interpretation of the modern world with a dose of fantasy added for good measure.

Over the last few years, I've written over three million words in fan fiction alone. It will always be something relaxing I enjoy doing. As much as I love other people's characters and twisting them to my desires, my characters have a special place in my heart. They all represent some aspect of myself, and I put my soul into them.

In this book, CJ is about my struggle with gender identity over the last few years, and he represents, by the end, how I came to terms with who I was finally. Though not a big sports person, I wanted Michael to be a character with the hobby no one expects him to have as a jock type. It's often fun to mess with expectations, I find.

I know this includes some graphic violence and sexual assault, but this is the way I've always envisioned this story. This is more about the after-effects than the actual event, and I want people to understand that the healing afterward and how CJ and Michael deal with it is the primary thing.

Most of all, I want you to come along on the ride with them to realize their true selves despite the constraints of fate and destiny. What the world has in mind for them doesn't have to be, and they are out to prove it in any way possible.

Anyway, thank you for reading my ramblings. I hope you enjoy the story presented in this volume.

Trigger Warnings:

The following trigger warnings apply to this work. Please note I cannot account for all possible triggers.
These are the most prominent and the triggers that I believe most people would be affected by.

Kidnapping
Sexual Assault/Rape
Non-Consensual Bondage
Non-Consensual Drug Use
Physical Assault
Homophobia/Sexism/Bigotry

Prologue

To Escape Their Fate

CJ Kim rolled over in bed, fighting the sheets and covers wrapped around him. He was deeply asleep as the dim light filtered through the windows in his St. Peters, Missouri, home. Turning again, images unfolded in his mind that were equally fantastic and horrible—there was no in between. He whined in his sleep and tossed once again, watching events play out.

In the pool at the river's end stood a virgin beauty like no other in existence. His eyes feasted upon her purity and newness like one would feast on the greatest offering of the gods. Her hair was midnight black and ran in perfect straightness to a point well past her knees. From where he stood, he could not see her eyes, but he knew they were very dark and large. Her skin was unblemished ebony. She was straight and still in all her beauty in the sacred bathing pool.

She stood with her head slightly bent, her hair falling over her ebon shoulders in the black night. Another maiden waded around her and cleansed her slowly with an ornate sponge. The beauty moved not one bit; the maiden instead positioned her body where it needed to be. She would wash her with steady hands and then reposition her body once more to clean a different area. The beauty looked like one drugged.

The maiden finished the ritual bathing and walked her up the riverbank on bronze steps to a disk upon which she now stood, her feet never touching the ground, thus preserving her cleanliness and integrity. Next, the maiden began applying perfumes and lotions to her. After this, she placed a white garment over her nude body, moving her arms and head as needed. The garment was edged in yellow and fell to her knees. The maiden pulled her hair from inside the back of the garment and pulled it upon the top of her head. She then began putting on ceremonial robes. They were white and accented with gold.

The dress was fine white cloth. Over this, there was a sleeveless robe. The robe was made from fine fabric and heavily jeweled with all manner of gems. Then the maiden released her hair from its confines and let it cascade around her. The maiden pulled the hair away from her face with an ornate clip. She then led her to a glimmering chair above the golden disk and the bathing pool. She then turned and left the beauty alone to wait. There should be no one to bother the beauty at this hour, and many guards were stationed along the approach. But, of course, the riverside of the approach could have been more well-guarded. No one believed anyone would come up the rocky inclines from the life-giving river.

Waiting in anticipation for the maiden to leave, he was silent and still. This was the moment he would never have again, the only opportunity he would have to be near this beauty of mind and soul. Pulling himself from his hidden place, he approached her. Kneeling at her bare, perfect feet, his lips hovered above her toes, but he dared not touch them. He looked up, expecting her to have her eyes focused on the distance as they always were, the dazed, drugged look they always carried. They were not. Her dark eyes stared into his own as though she was attempting to see into his very soul. And she probably did see that far.

"Priestess," he whispered in a shaking voice. "Allow me the pleasure of seeing your beauty without fear of death...."

His heart rose to his throat as she nodded her head in a slow-drugged way. He smiled and lowered his head, and then stood and turned to leave.

"You have been watching me for a while now," she stated, causing him to jump. He did not expect her to have a voice...

He turned, though he dared not fully face her, and nodded. She nodded back, still slowly. "I knew you were there tonight as well, watching what no mortal man should ever be allowed to see."

He bowed his head. "How did you know, oh great priestess?" he asked in a shaking voice. "And why was I not killed immediately for infringing on the rights that only the gods have?"

Her voice was like bells in the wind as she spoke to him. "I knew you were there and were not killed because I chose not to have you killed. Those are the only answers that you shall require about this."

Her voice echoed on and on in his mind. He looked up at her if only to reassure himself that this was the virgin high priestess of the secret sect of Albeme, the highest of Brishna's favor. It was she that he gazed upon.

Her eyes were not dazed any longer, but alive. "Priestess, why do you not move on your own? Can you move?" he asked timidly.

She smiled, actually smiled, at him. He nearly fainted with excitement. "I can move just fine," she said, lifting first one arm, then the other, and then each leg. "It is the ritual for the high priestess to be as such in the presence of mortal men and women." She spoke so boldly and honestly that his eyes widened a bit.

"And why do you move and speak now?" he asked, turning fully to face her.

Again, she smiled, not only with her lips but her eyes as well. "Because I know who you are, and you are no ordinary mortal."

He looked up and cocked his head. "I'm not?" he whispered. She leaned forward and shook her head.

"No, you're not," she whispered back. "Go now; my maiden returns."

She returned to her former position, and he turned and left her with the maiden. It would be the last time he saw her until the sacrifice later that night.

The priestess stood alone next to the flames of eternity. She stood with her head slightly bent and her black hair cascading about her body, a vision of rare beauty. She raised her arms suddenly and then dropped to her knees before the flames. Her hands were folded in front of her like one in prayer. She had closed her eyes and chanted softly. The high priest mounted the long stairs to the top of the altar and stood beside the priestess. He looked out on the people.

"Tonight is the Night of the Sacrifice of Purity!" he announced. "The high priestess has prepared for this day her entire life, and now is the time," he exclaimed, gesturing to the priestess.

From the back of the stairs came a procession of girls dressed in white from the town.

The voyeur cocked his head to the side from his perch on the edge of the altar. Only the upper class was allowed near enough to the temple to see. He had to hide there until the time of the Sacrifice. He did not, however, understand what the procession of girls was for. In the line, he saw Khepri and Safiya. He wrinkled his brow. Khepri was his sister, and Safiya was his betrothed. Though both were the same age, both had been betrothed since birth. Khepri's wedding was ten suns away, and Safiya's was five suns away. Both were fourteen summers of age. There were other young girls he recognized, a total of eleven. All were dressed in white with a yellow cord tied about their waist.

The priest spoke again, hands upraised. "The time of Sacrifice has come. Upon each tolling of the bell, a maiden from the town will be given in sacrifice. Upon the tolling of the twelfth bell, the high priestess will give her life in the manner of blood into the fire as well." His eyes widened from the hiding place. They were going to kill his Safiya and his sister, Khepri. They could not! He thought madly.

He stood and began the descent and climbed to the altar as the bells started to ring. No! He moved faster. With the first bell, he heard the first scream as the girl was thrown into the flames. He was sickened. And another screaming bell resounded in his ears, followed by another and another and another. Would they never end? Finally, he hoisted himself upon the platform and then to the altar. "Stop!" he yelled as the priest grabbed his sister. The priestess looked at him in a way only he understood.

The priest looked so shocked that he stepped back to where Safiya stood, holding his sister. "Jabari..." his sister whispered his name as she held onto the priest's cruel arm.

"Young one, you displease the gods. You will pay with your life..." the priest said low, so only Jabari would hear. "This is the Sacrifice! You need not concern yourself with what happens here!"

Jabari stared at him. "It is not right to take young lives like this. These girls have not lived. So why do they die?" he said.

The priest snarled at him. "It is the way of things, boy; you have interrupted the ceremony." He turned to the guards holding the remaining young women.

"Guardians, kill him," he said, and those who held the young women released them and lunged toward the young man. Safiya and his sister Khepri grasped each other. They were all that remained.

The high priestess sat, hands folded in front of her at the fire. She did not move. She did not speak even as the other maidens were burned alive. The smell of burned hair and flesh permeated the air. The High Priestess sat still, her eyes closed.

Jabari dodged blows from the Guardians of the Flame, ducking behind beautifully etched pillars with signs of their faith. Chunks of marble and stone flew as they chased the boy around, flinging great maces. The High Priest stood beside the priestess, and those in attendance sat in shocked silence. Never before had the Sacrifice been disturbed. The High Priest growled and stared at the three remaining maidens huddled together. He stepped and grasped one of them firmly by the arm, Safiya, and looked toward the boy who was ducking and weaving.

"Jabari," he said, and the boy looked, and before he could react, his betrothed was flung into the fire.

His eyes widened, and he screamed, "No!" It was too late; she screamed as she descended into the fiery pit. The bell rang for the ninth time.

"Come, no matter what you do the sacrifice will continue," he said, his dark eyes burning. Jabari could not function for a moment and said nothing, the shock and horror at seeing the girl he'd known since he was small, gone in a flash of fire.

"You take too long," he said and grasped Alisade, another girl he knew, by the arm, and the bell rang out the tenth time, and she was thrown to the fire.

Khepri stood there, her face a picture of terror; she was the last one.

"No, please, stop!" Jabari said, locking eyes with his sister. "I'll die for her!" he screamed.

The High Priest smiled. "Grab him and bring him here." One Guardian grasped him by the arm and pulled him toward the high priest, holding his hands behind his back. He smiled.

"Too bad the sacrifice is set in the stones as being young maidens." He nodded, and Jabari watched as his sister was pitched into the flame by the tolling of the eleventh bell.

"No!" he choked, tears running down his face.

The High priest smiled at him. "Don't worry, your death shall come swiftly, as well, though by blade rather than flame..." he whispered.

The High Priestess stood. She looked up, moving on her own, and all in attendance, the aristocracy's best gasped. Never had they seen the high priestess move on her own. The bell chimed a twelfth time.

"I will take the boy with me," she said, staring into the flames.

The high priest looked up in shock. "Is this the decree of our Mother?" he asked.

The priestess turned and fired him with a dark stare, her eyes livid. "I speak, and you dare question me?" she said, and Jabari's very soul quaked. The high priest stepped back, and the Guardians released the boy.

"You will come with me, boy. I told you; you are not mortal, nor am I."

Jabari's eyes widened as he heard a voice in his mind. He could not resist it, so he walked with mechanical steps to her side.

She looked deeply into the boy's eyes. "Yes, you and I, we know each other. The fire will show everyone," she whispered, then kissed his face deeply. A gasp resounded. The high priestess was the purest of any. She was raised not to know anything of love and lust. Yet she stood before them, embracing the boy passionately, making the oldest among them gape.

She released him and turned to face those who stood before her. He stood small and weak at her side, his blue eyes shifting around him.

"I am the High Priestess of the Great Mother, She Who Creates, She Who Destroys, the Goddess Brishna. I face the Flames of Eternity, but I do not face them alone. The Gods know no rectitude, for they live and love as you do. I face the flames with my beloved, Krineshaw, the Father, my mate. Now, we stand here, and I must ask that the sacrifice be ended."

She turned to the high priest. "I will return—we will return—and this place will be sundered," she whispered.

Suddenly, there was a noise as an old man mounted the platform. It was the great Seer, Tambel. He looked to the high priest, locking eyes with him. "This cannot be allowed."

The high priest looked up. Tambel was the oldest and most respected person. His word was as near to the law of the land as that of their leader. He looked with blind eyes at the two, clutching each other. She was sure stepping into the fire with him would bring them eternal life, and his visions confirmed it would be such.

"Kill them with the blade of Iman."

At his words, the priestess tried to leap into the fire with the boy. Instead, the Guardians of the Flame grabbed her.

"You can't do this!" she screamed. "I must die by the flames with the boy at my side so we may ascend!"

The high priest laughed, pulling the long, thin dagger from a sheath. The blade of Iman was used for executions because it was said that the god Iman himself had cursed it to make those killed with it be eternally returned to the earth. "You shall not ascend, priestess. Or should I say Brishna and Krineshaw?"

The priestess tensed. Jabari was clueless as he looked from the beauty before him to the flames. Was she going to pull him into the fire? Was she going to kill him? He wasn't sure he knew what was going on now. The high priest held the knife against her throat.

"You will be trapped in mortality for all time. Your fate will be to live again and again and always be separated from your dear Krineshaw. You'll never break the curse of Iman."

With that, he cut her palm and then cut Jabari's. The blood dripped into a cup as the Guardians held their hands above it. He smiled and swirled the blood in it. He then dropped a packet of herbs and stirred it with the dagger.

"Open their mouths," he said, and they were forced to do so as the substance dripped. Both resisted, but it was of no use.

The high priest then kissed the high priestess passionately. "I will claim you," he whispered in her ear as he wiped their blood from his lips, and she saw that his palm was bandaged. He had cursed himself...

"You will not erase our destiny!" she screamed as he slit Jabari's throat deftly. He dropped, his eyes blurring as he felt his life drain from him.

"No, but I can bind you forever in this fate..." he said, cutting her throat in one stroke. She, too, felt the drain of life, but more than that, it felt as if her very soul had been shackled...

CJ awoke in a cold sweat from the dream. This was the fifth time the images had assaulted his mind this week. He got out of bed and stumbled to the bathroom to drench his face in the water. *Gaesaekki*, he thought to himself as he looked in the mirror. His dark eyes were red, and the whites were bloodshot. Lack of sleep, he thought. He rubbed his eyes again and ran a bit more water for a drink. That dream left him drained. He glanced at the red digital numbers on the alarm clock as they flashed over to 3:04. Wow, it was still too early to even think of getting out of bed.

"CJ?" his mom's voice came from the door.

He looked up sleepily. "Yeah, Mom?"

"Are you okay, dear?" she asked softly, her blonde hair pulled back in a tight bun she wore when she slept.

"Yeah, I just had another weird dream. I'm okay, though," he answered, pushing his black hair out of his face. "I'm going back to sleep now, though."

She came into the room and kissed him on the head gently and whispered good night and sweet dreams. *Sweet dreams, indeed,* CJ thought as she left the room. He snuggled down into the soft black of his pillowcase and wondered who this Brishna was he kept dreaming about in various ways. And these strange people's lives he seemed to live in his dreams...

Chapter One

Opening Moves

CJ sat in the stands with his book, only looking like he was reading. In the afternoons, he didn't have any classes; he came by and watched the baseball team practice. He didn't even have courses on the South Campus; he just came here to watch them. But, of course, he was only watching one person on the team. He caught sight of the mop of shaggy, curly, sandy blond hair and stared again. Michael Heights had no idea CJ existed. He looked resplendent in the warm St. Louis sun, and CJ had to force himself to stop staring so openly. He heard giggles from down the stands farther.

"Michael! Hit one for me!" a girl yelled, and CJ sighed.

He knew it was too much to ask for Michael Heights to be gay. The chances the well-built blond was into other guys were slim, especially considering how much attention he paid the girls who followed him around. He supposed he was an excellent baseball player. He was the team's ace pitcher, after all. CJ adjusted the bag at his feet and tried to read again. With Michael on the field, he couldn't concentrate, however. Chaucer had no claim to his attention right then. He sighed again, put the book in his overfull bag, and watched for a while. It wasn't like he had to worry about being noticed. No one noticed him.

CJ was an unassuming five foot and seven inches, which wasn't that short until he considered so many of the guys he knew on campus were close to six feet tall. He looked a lot like his Korean father, only shorter and thinner. He got it from his mother, he guessed because she was only five foot three. His eyes were golden brown, though they were obscured mostly behind the simple oval glasses he wore. He had long, black hair, which he kept pulled back in a tail most of the time. His mother had been after him to cut it, but he liked it that way. It made him look girly.

That was another reason he was different. He'd been exploring his gender lately, and he was finding he wasn't exactly just male. He wanted to be feminine sometimes, but not like the drag queen feminine, though he wouldn't mind dressing up like one sometimes. His hair was the only thing he'd changed, but he found himself drawn to the women's section in the store and wanted desperately to try out some of the cute skirts and dresses they had. He didn't feel like it all the time, just enough of the time. Vaguely, he wondered if his tendency to dream about being a woman had something to do with it. He shook the thought away. It didn't matter; he was a guy and had to act like one.

Resting his chin on his fist, he watched wistfully as Michael approached batting practice. CJ did not know about baseball's terms and rules; honestly, he didn't care to learn more about the sport than he knew. He would have watched Michael walk across the hall if he could. It still surprised him that they were practicing during finals, but it looked like they had just gathered whoever was free to have some practice time before the end of the semester. Of course, Michael had been the one to gather them.

"All right, great practice, guys!" Michael yelled as he put down the bat, and everyone in the stands ran down to the fence as the players came off the field.

CJ watched Michael wave to the girls yelling at him, and his heart sank a little more. There wasn't a shot in hell for him with a guy like Michael. But, of course, if he wanted to know for sure, he should approach him and find out. There was zero chance of it happening, however. There was no way he could walk up to the star pitcher of the Triton's baseball team and ask if he was gay or not. He blushed just thinking about it. That was something he could never do in a million years.

After everyone had cleared out, he got up, slinging his heavy bag across his body, and walked back to his car. He fumbled with his pocket to get the keys out, almost knocking his phone to the asphalt.

"Oof, that was close," he muttered, clutching the device against him. It was the only place he had pictures of Michael, which he'd sneaked during practices.

He brushed his hand over his sweaty forehead. How the hell was it so hot at the start of May? It was Missouri, that's how. Stupid weather. Today was the hottest day so far this year. He'd seen in the weather that it was supposed to get up to ninety. And it wasn't even June or July yet!

He pressed the unlock button and sighed. At least the parking lot was deserted because of finals, so no one saw him struggling to balance his bag, phone, and keys. South Campus wasn't all that busy most of the time, anyway. Usually, only the optometry students spent much time there.

He opened the door, swung his bag into the car, and tossed it to the passenger seat. It landed with a thump. In doing so, though, he knocked his phone out of his other hand.

"*Ssibal*!" he exclaimed as it hit the ground and skidded under the car.

He hoped it hadn't broken. But he had a good case, so he thought it would survive that drop.

He leaned in and started the car up so the AC could run while he grabbed the phone. He got out and looked under to see it was just out of his reach, so he had to lie down and reach for it.

That was why he didn't pay much attention when a van pulled up in the next spot. People came and went all the time, and he wasn't thinking in the empty parking lot, there was little reason to pull up right beside another car. He glanced to the side and noted it, but that was all. When the door slid open behind him, he didn't think anything of it then because there were a lot of non-traditional students there, so a mom bringing a kid with her wouldn't be strange.

He grabbed the phone and stood up with it. There were no cracks when he turned it over. He let out a sigh of relief. His pictures of Michael were safe. He turned around and nearly ran into a large man standing right behind him.

"Can I help you?" he asked, looking him over. He was tall, easily over six feet five inches, heavily built, and with thick muscles. His heart skipped a beat. He towered over him.

He didn't say anything for a moment, only stared at him, his nearly black eyes flat and lifeless. Then, finally, he spoke in a deep voice, "Yer Don Kim's kid, aren't you?"

CJ was a little startled but slowly nodded. The guy must have noted the resemblance between him and his dad. But what were the chances of running into someone randomly who knew his father?

"That's good," the taller man muttered, turning back toward his van.

CJ thought this was all strange, but just as he was about to get into his car, he felt a sharp pain in his arm. He looked in time to see this strange man pulling a needle out of him and blinked in surprise. This guy just stabbed him with a needle. What?

"Why did you do that?" he muttered as he tried to back away.

The man's hand shot out and grabbed him by the bicep and yanked him close. CJ did not know what to do. It wasn't like he was prepared for some guy to kidnap him. But wait, was that what was happening? Was he being kidnapped? He didn't know how long he had before whatever he gave him took effect, but he yanked away from him, feeling the man's nails cut grooves in his arm as he did so. He tried to take off and run, but just as he got both feet under him, a wave of dizziness hit him, sending him to the ground. As his phone hit the asphalt, he heard a clatter. He hoped that didn't break it either, he thought, despite the situation. Somehow, his glasses stayed on his face.

The man walked over to him calmly and prodded him with his foot. "Just like yer dad," he growled, grabbed him up under his arms, and dragged him back to the van's open door. The world spun, and a second later, he realized he was on the floor in a cargo van, not a minivan. He reached out, but the door slammed shut. The world rocked a little, and the last vestiges of consciousness finally left him.

"Mara, has CJ come home yet?" Donald Kim yelled from the foyer as he entered the house.

Mara stuck her head out of the door to the kitchen. "No, was he staying late today?"

Don thought for a second. "He shouldn't be because it's finals week. Remember, he said he'd be home early to watch Alex and Allie while we went grocery shopping."

Two pint-sized creatures came running past Mara and into their dad's arms. "Hey there, kiddos," he said as he hefted the twins up against him. They were almost four now and getting heavy for him, even as much as he worked out. Their birthday was coming up fast, June 6th. It would be quite the celebration with the party they had planned.

The doorbell interrupted their hugging, and Mara headed over to answer it. Don tickled his twins mercilessly, sending them both into giggling fits until they were out of breath. He sat back on the floor, out of breath, and wondered who was at the door keeping Mara so long.

He looked up as Mara returned to the kitchen, blanched paler than he thought possible. Her blonde hair made her look paler, and her freckles seemed drained. Behind her was a pair of city police officers. One was a darker-skinned man with striking features and close-cropped dark brown hair framing light brown eyes. The other was a shorter, tanned woman with long, strawberry-blonde hair pulled up in a bun on her head and piercing green eyes. Both looked very serious.

"Dear, what's wrong?" he asked, standing slowly.

The twins had frozen, grabbing onto their father and staring at the strangers that had come into their house. Don felt his heart start beating harder in his chest. Why were the police at his house?

She swallowed hard. "They found CJ's car at the school. His books and bag were thrown into it. His phone was on the ground next to it. The keys were in the ignition, and it was running with the air conditioner up."

Don looked between the officers, Alex and Allie hanging on his legs as he did so. Had something happened to CJ? His mind was racing with possibilities. Why would he have left the car running? He couldn't imagine a scenario where CJ would leave his car with it running. Well, he could imagine one, but it was not one with a favorable outcome, especially after the call he'd gotten the day before.

"I'm Officer Vernon Miller, and this is Officer Patty Brown. We were first on the scene at the school when the security officer called to report the situation. But, unfortunately, all we found that might be a clue is this," the male officer said, handing Don a plastic bag, which was sealed.

"Oh," Don said, seeing inside the evidence bag was a note addressed to him that read, "I've come back for you, old friend."

"Do you know what this might be about?" Officer Brown asked, pulling out a notepad from her pocket.

"Daddy, play with me!" Alex whined, pulling on Don's sleeve, apparently tiring of waiting for the officers to leave the room. Meanwhile, her sister was hiding behind Don's leg.

"Sure, just a minute, honey," he told the black-haired little girl. Mara reached down, picked her up, and pulled her twin to the side. Neither child enjoyed being separated from their dad right then.

"There is a man from my days in the army. He might hold a grudge against me enough to do something like this," he said, handing the plastic evidence bag back to Officer Miller.

"What can you tell us?" Officer Brown asked, making notes as they talked.

Don contemplated what he could possibly reveal to them without permission. He mulled it over for a few minutes, feeling everyone's eyes on him. He had to give them something. His son was missing, and he was in a lot of trouble right now.

"Well, that I can't go into much because you'll need to contact Agent Richard Pearson with the FBI. He was the one I worked with almost 30 years ago," Don said, picking his words carefully. "He can handle coordinating things, I would think. All I can say, though, is you're looking for a man, around six feet five inches in height, black hair, brown eyes, around two hundred fifty pounds when I last saw him."

The officers nodded, making notes. "Is there anything else you can tell us now that might be helpful?" Officer Miller asked as Officer Brown made notes on the case.

"Just that the man who I think is at fault is a dangerous man and should not be approached at all until the FBI can do something," he explained.

After a few more minutes of asking questions Don couldn't answer, the two police officers left. Don stood silently for a few minutes. Then, he looked over at Mara who was standing there with the two kids clinging to her.

"I'm calling Randy," he said, returning to the kitchen.

He picked up the house phone and dialed the number from memory, knowing Randy wouldn't have changed it since the last time they'd contacted each other. So, he waited, and he answered within a few rings.

"Hello?" came Randy's voice over the phone.

"Randy. He's back."

There was a long pause. "They called to say he broke out of prison."

"He's got my son," Don told him and tried very hard not to fall into tears himself.

"He won't kill him. Not him; he wants to get to you. If he kills him, it would be detrimental to his plan. So, he'll keep him alive," Randy assured him.

"But at what cost?" Don asked. "Alive, yes, but hurt? You know as well as I do; he knows how to torture someone and keep them alive."

Another pause. "I'll tell Terri. We'll be over at your place tomorrow afternoon."

"Keep an eye on your kids, Randy. Both of them. The twins aren't leaving the house until this is over," he said.

"I can try, but both are old enough to have some autonomy. I can only keep them so safe at their ages," he exhaled.

"I know." Don sighed to himself. "Try to be safe. I'll talk to you both tomorrow."

Don hung up the phone and looked at Mara, still holding Alex in her arms while Allie kept pulling at her sleeve. She had tears in her eyes.

"It really is him, isn't it?" she whispered.

"I'm afraid so," he answered, not wanting to look at her.

"And he has CJ." Her voice was strained, and she held back tears.

"He won't kill him. That won't get him what he wants," Don tried to assure her.

"What he wants? All that man wants is revenge for you and Randy putting him away! You don't know what he plans to do to him!" she exclaimed, clutching Alex tightly against her.

"Look, I have to contact Pearson. He needs to know what's going on," he said, pulling his cell phone out of his pocket.

Mara nodded and let the tears fall from her eyes. "Mommy?" Allie asked from the floor. "Why are you crying, Mommy?"

"Nothing you need to worry about, baby," she said, wiping her eyes with her free hand as she sat Alex back down on the floor.

Don found the contact and made the call. "Connect me to Agent Rich Pearson," he told the receptionist that answered the call.

A few moments passed tensely with the only sound of Mara's quiet sniffles. "Agent Pearson here," came the response.

"Rich, I hate to bother you, but we have a situation," Don began.

It was as though swimming through the mud to wake up again. Whatever he'd given him was effective, and he couldn't shake the lethargic feeling that came with it. His eyes fluttered, and he opened them to see absolutely nothing. It was pitch black wherever he was. He pulled on his arms and found them tied to what felt like chair arms. He yanked a little harder and felt the ropes bite into his skin.

"Hello?" he yelled. "Is anyone there?"

Only silence answered him. He licked his lips and tried to see anything, but there was just no light in this place at all. Was he underground or something? His heart pounded in his chest even harder. What was going on? Some guy kidnapped him; he knew that had happened. This wasn't some movie where things like this happened; this was real life. Did people really get kidnapped in real life like that? They did because it just happened to him.

The sound of an opening door got his attention and he turned toward it. In the open doorway, he saw the silhouette of the man who had taken him. In the dim light, he could tell it was a basement.

"H-hey! What's going on?" he stammered out, trying to quell his fear. "Who are you? Why have you kidnapped me?" He wanted to sound bold and sure of himself, instead it came out as barely audible in the quiet room.

The man came down the stairs slowly, and CJ's breath quickened. Fear was something that he was familiar with in his dreams, but in real life he'd never imagined feeling this way. He couldn't say anything else, and his mind wandered to what this guy had planned. What did this guy want? Why would he do something like this? Was he going to murder him?

"CJ Kim. Aren't you a pretty little boy?" he said in the same gruff voice as before. "Why am I not surprised Don would have such an... effeminate boy?"

"I'm not effeminate!" CJ stated finally, knowing it was the opposite of true, considering how much he'd been leaning toward the feminine side of things lately, but, unfortunately, it looked like this guy wasn't too fond of that sort of thing.

"With the hair and those features? You don't even try to make up for it. Long hair, pretty little face like your momma. You a faggot, too?" he asked, coming closer and standing before him. "You look like one."

"Wh-what are you talking about?" CJ stuttered.

He snorted. "What I thought. Won't even deny it, will you?"

"Look, I don't know what you think you're talking about, but I'm not—" Pain lanced through his cheek as his head snapped to the side. He gasped as he turned back, seeing his eyes gleaming with enjoyment at backhanding him.

"Shut the fuck up," he growled. "You are nothing, do you understand? You are nothing but a convenient pawn in my game. That's it. Just know I'll take special care of you since you look like the type that likes it rough, too."

CJ licked the blood off his lip and stared at him. "P-please, don't—"

"I said, shut up!" he snapped, backhanding him again.

Breathing heavily, CJ closed his eyes, trying to make this whole situation one of his dreams. When he opened his eyes, he was still looking at the enormous man who had taken him. He ran his tongue over the split in his lip and said nothing. He didn't want to be hurt if he could avoid it. Maybe this guy was going to ask for a ransom? That would be fine because his father was a doctor; surely, he could afford a ransom. If it were a ransom, he wouldn't hurt him. He couldn't.

"You're going to be a problem just like your fucking father, aren't you?" he said, grabbing CJ by the chin and twisting his head to the side.

His father? What did this have to do with his father?

"If you want anyone to blame for your situation, blame him. He's the one that put your ass in this position."

CJ tried to be silent again, breaths coming fast, almost to the point of hyperventilating. But he had to know. "What'd my father do to you?" he managed.

"What did your father do to me?" he said, snapping his head to the side and letting go of him finally. "He got me thrown in a hellhole, that's what. He and Randy. They stood in front of the court and told them what I'd done when I thought they'd have my back. But they didn't, and now they're gonna pay for it. In their blood." He smiled. "Rather your blood. But you're that fairy mother fucker's son, so it's his blood too."

"My father's not gay!" he snapped suddenly, frowning at the accusation.

He arched a brow at him. "How do you know what happened out there in the desert, you little bitch? We spent a long time without seeing a woman, and I just bet your dad was the one to lie down and spread his legs for Randy. That's why they fuckin' stuck together."

"Who is Randy?" CJ couldn't help but ask. He'd never heard of anyone named Randy.

"None of your fuckin' business!" he snapped, reaching out and grabbing CJ by the back of the hair and pulling his head backward.

For a second, everything stopped, and CJ wasn't staring at this guy. Instead, he was staring at Iman from his dream. The same feeling of horror and knowledge rolled over him at the sudden realization of what this man was to him. He was death. Without warning, he leaned forward and licked a stripe up the side of CJ's neck, making him shiver and gasp out, trying to squirm away from him.

He stood up and glared at him for a moment. CJ didn't know what to think as he felt the dampness drying on his neck. Why did he do that? Why would he if he hated him so much? He let out a shaky breath and bit down on his split lip, sending a sharp pain through him. It kept him grounded, though, and the image of this man didn't turn into the dream villain again.

"Huh, you're a fuckin' fairy bitch like your AIDS-lovin' father," he said, and CJ swore he had a look on his face that didn't match his words. "But you got one more, don't you? You wanna be a girl so bad you can taste it, don't you?"

CJ's eyes widened a bit, and he just wanted this man to stop and go away. He just wanted to be left alone. He tried to deny what he was saying but couldn't lie. The words stuck in his throat as he tried to say something, anything. "That-that's not—"

He smiled then. "Oh, I think I've struck a chord, haven't I?"

"Please," he whispered, looking up wide-eyed at him. "Just don't—"

He laughed then, leaning over suddenly, grabbing him at the wrist where they were tied down. Moving closer to CJ's face, almost nose to nose, he growled out, "Tell me, does your dad have all the Boy George and George Michaels albums? Maybe even arranged back to front so they can buttfuck each other, hmm?"

CJ had no idea who Boy George and George Michaels were, so he just ended up looking more confused than before. This man thought the fact that it confused him was apparently amusing, because he had an incredibly smug look on his face.

"That's what I thought," he said, standing back up suddenly.

CJ had no clue what this guy wanted. He had gathered that his dad had done something to him, so he guessed it must have been when he was in the military or something as a medic. His dad never talked about that time in his life, saying it was a bad time for everyone, and no one wants to listen to old war stories, anyway. So, all CJ knew was that he'd been in Desert Storm and spent a lot of time overseas before he was born. That had been after he served in the Korean military for his two years, of course, but he'd always been a doctor.

"Fuckin' faggots, what you all are," he mumbled, glaring at him, and there was just enough light that CJ could see a scar that ran near one of his eyes. It looked like he'd nearly lost the eye.

He snorted, reached into his shirt pocket, and pulled out a syringe. He uncapped it and grabbed hold of CJ's arm. CJ jerked his arm a bit, and he only squeezed harder.

"Be fuckin' still before I just jab it in your fucking face."

CJ froze, watching as he slid the needle into him and pushed the plunger down. He winced at the slight pain it caused and breathed a few times deeply. Then, he looked up at him and saw him observing.

"That should take care of you until the bitch gets here," he mumbled.

He took the empty syringe, turned around, and headed back up the stairs. As he left, the world faded around the edges of CJ's vision. He felt good, though, as the drug hit his system.

He nodded his head forward, and if it hadn't been for the ropes holding him in the chair, he would have slid out of it.

Chapter Two

The King's Move

"Michael! It's time to get going; you'll be late for your last final! You have graduation to worry about; you don't need to flunk a class at the last minute!"

Michael Heights rolled out of bed. He hated mornings, so when he could, he slept through it like he'd done today. His final wasn't until 12:30, and the drive into St. Louis wouldn't take that long, even with traffic. His mom was right, however. It was his last final, and he couldn't take the chance of missing it for any reason. It was even in his major class, senior psychology. Graduation depended on this last class.

Sighing, he yelled, "All right, Mom, I'm going, I'm going."

He pulled on his jeans and a T-shirt, then looked in the mirror. Bedhead. Hum. He ran a hand through the blond mess it had become during the night and winced as he hit the tangles. Ah, screw it, he thought. Everyone at the university was used to seeing him with messy hair. Bedhead or hat hair, it was always a mess. He grabbed his baseball cap off the desk and put it on. There, he thought. That would take care of it. He headed downstairs, stopping in the kitchen to grab some pop tarts and a glass of juice.

"Michael, did you see the news about the school yet?" his mom asked as he chugged the orange juice.

Michael tossed the glass in the sink. "Is it closed?" he asked hopefully.

"No, son," his mom replied. "Look, there it is again."

His mom turned up the kitchen TV. It was on the St. Louis news channel. The female newscaster, a tall brunette with too much makeup who always looked utterly disinterested in the news she was reporting, was talking. Michael found her incredibly monotone voice annoying to the extreme, but his ears perked up at her first words.

"There are still no new developments in the University kidnapping yesterday. The victim, whose name is now withheld, was a young man in his sophomore year. The only information the police have released has stated that his car was found in the parking lot on UMSL South Campus. The car was open and running, so the police theorized he was abducted as he tried to enter the vehicle. The police are asking that if there are any witnesses to the abduction, please come forward. Again, we still have no new developments in the UMSL kidnapping of yesterday. We will relay any news as it comes in."

Michael's mom turned the volume down again and shook her head. "Huh," Michael said. "I was at the baseball field yesterday around noon. Wonder what time it happened?"

His mom smiled slightly. "I hate it when this stuff happens in St. Louis. At times like these, I wish I worked dispatch for the city."

Michael shook his head. "Mom, you can't work everywhere, you know. Besides, you'd get a hundred times more crazy calls than you do now here in St. Charles." He paused and picked up his bag from beside the door. "You work the late shift tonight?"

She smiled, her dark eyes sparkling. "Yeah, I'm there till 12. After that, I get all the fun calls. Your dad's cooking tonight."

"Good, because I have to work!" he said, grinning.

His mom smiled and shook her head. "Go on, get out of here before you're late for your final."

"Mike!" yelled the short, red-haired girl who ran up beside him.

Michael looked up from his book as she came running and sighed, running a hand through his shaggy blond hair. She was a nice girl, but this tagging around with him had to stop. She was his sister's best friend, not his girlfriend. He glanced around and saw his sister, Aileen, walking behind her with a disgusted look. She found it horribly disgusting that anyone should have a crush on her older brother, least of all her best friend. It was embarrassing enough to be picked up from school by your big brother, but to have your best friend drool over him was another thing altogether.

"Hey, Kay. You two ready to go home?" he asked, smiling. She just grinned at him.

Aileen walked up and rolled her eyes at him. "Come on, let's just go."

"Well, come on, ladies, your chariot awaits."

As usual, he opened the passenger door of his blue two-door coupe, and his sister had to crawl in the back because Kay wanted to sit up front by him. She pushed the seat back and hopped in, belting herself in as Michael did the same. He'd drop her off first and then take his sister home, and then he had to be back for a workout before work tonight. He turned up the music so he could ignore Kay ogling him; blasting out some Ozzy always relaxed him. Finally, they pulled up in front of Kay's small two-bedroom house, and she hopped out, waving with a goofy grin. Aileen shook her head as she sat in the front seat and turned down the music as usual.

"I don't understand what she looks at you like that for."

Of course, she knew exactly why she did it. But how embarrassing it is to have your best friend think your older brother is hot.

Michael shook his head. "It's just a phase. She'll get over it once she gets a boyfriend of her own. I'm the sexy older man, you know. You should be flattered to be my little sis."

Aileen sighed as loud as she could, getting both Kay and Michael's attention. She rolled her eyes and stared out the window. Her brother shrugged and backed out again to head home. He turned his tunes back up until they stopped in front of their house.

"You gonna be home for dinner?"

Michael shook his head. "Nah, got work tonight. Tell dad not to wait up; I'm heading to the movies with Jeremy. Horror flick, nothing you'd want to see."

Aileen just rolled her eyes again and headed into the house. Michael shook his head. Teenagers, these days, he thought, then laughed at the irony of his thinking. He had just graduated high school four years ago...and already, there was a considerable gap between him and his fifteen-year-old sister. Well, that was the way things worked.

He took off, heading to the gym for an hour or so before work at six. He couldn't slack off even though school was out for the summer. Maintaining his routine was extremely important to ensure he stayed on top of his game. The pitcher wasn't an easy position to play, and plenty of other guys were vying for the spot if he looked like he couldn't handle it anymore.

"Yo, Michael, what's up?" Jonathan Small, the front desk worker, asked him as he came up.

"Nothing much, just here to grab a quick workout before I go to work. Gotta keep in shape for the team!" he said as he was waved into the gym.

He spent the next hour working mainly on the treadmill and stair climber to get some cardio in. Tomorrow would be a weights day. He enjoyed the gym and gave him time to think as the sounds of the old rock and metal filled his ears. Today, though, his thoughts were focused on the missing student. He'd heard it happened between noon and two o'clock and on South Campus too. He could have been there when he was kidnapped. Of course, there was a theory in the news that the guy had just run away. Somehow, Michael doubted it.

After he finished his workout, he showered and changed into his work clothes. It was a simple uniform: a polo shirt with the pizza place's logo, a pair of jeans, and a cap with the logo. Finally, he walked out, waving to Jonathan again and returning to his car.

His phone rang right as he pulled up in front of the pizza place. His dad's contact info lit up the screen. He checked the time. He still had about five minutes, so he answered it.

"Hey, dad, what's up?" he asked. "I was just about to go to work; I don't have much time."

"Yeah, Michael, I know, but something's come up. Can you come home instead of going to work?"

Michael frowned. "Why would I do that? Is it an emergency? Is Aileen all right? Did something happen to Mom?" he asked, a little nervously.

"No, nothing like that. I have a friend coming by, and we can explain to you what's going on. I don't think you should work tonight," his father told him.

"Dad, I can't call off work for no real reason. I'll get fired!" he exclaimed.

"I know, son, but this is important, and I'd really like it if you could—" his dad started.

"Look, Dad, I know you worry about me at this job and driving to strangers' houses, but I've been doing this for almost two years. I can handle it. I'll be home after the movie at around two in the morning. I love you; I have to go," he said and quickly hung up.

He stared at the phone and shook his head. That was odd, he thought to himself. He couldn't just leave work unless it was a real emergency. Besides, he was already dressed and here for his shift. It was probably just more of his dad worrying nonstop about the type of job he was doing. Who would be coming by? The phone rang again, and he silenced it this time. He had to get to work.

At least it was a short shift today, six to eleven, he thought as he walked into the building. Hopefully, his tips would make the evening worth it. Making enough tips to pay for the movie and popcorn would be awesome.

As he returned from a run, he noticed a van driving slowly past. He discounted it. Probably some old guy who didn't like to drive at night. He went in and picked up the next batch of orders and grinned because one was at his friend Jeremy's place. Two large pepperoni and cheese pizzas and three two-liters of Dr. Pepper. He snickered. Game night, he thought as he headed off. He didn't note the same van waiting in the alley between the pizza joint and the house next door to it.

Before long, he was getting out of the car in front of Jeremy's place, holding the two large pizzas in one hand and the bag with the sodas in the other. He knocked on the door and a voice yelled to come in. He pushed the door open and stepped over the black and white cat, who never moved when the door opened. Jazz had caused many trips in her time.

"Damn!" Jeremy's girlfriend, Elle Peterson, spat just as he entered the sparse dining room.

In fact, the only furniture was the large table and chairs Jeremy and Elle had picked up at a garage sale. It was a good thing it had leaves, so it got smaller because the thing was massive when it was put together. But it made the perfect game table.

Elle waved at him as he sat the pizza down on a bare spot on the table. She looked like she was fuming. "Bad night, Elle?" he asked.

She shook her head and rolled her eyes. "Theo is after me with a vengeance tonight."

Sitting at the end of the table behind his fortress of a screen, Theo snickered. "Not true; the dice hate you tonight. It's not my fault you keep fumbling."

She stuck her tongue out at him. "He's just mad because I killed his plot NPC, who was supposed to be our ally. I don't believe that it's my fault you made him suck. So now he's making up for it by trying very hard to kill me every chance he's got. But he can't do it, much to his irritation. Sadima is too hard to kill."

Michael shook his head as Jeremy kissed her cheek gently, and Danny, the redhead at the table's far side, giggled. "Well, I'd rather be here than working, but I gotta make money to buy books for our games. We still on for tomorrow's FR game, Dan?"

"Oh, yeah, man, sure. Seven, you good for it?" Danny asked, digging into one of the pizza boxes.

"No problem. With the semester over, I won't have baseball practice so often," he said as Jeremy handed him his money. So, do you want me to meet you at work or here for the midnight showing?"

Jeremy shrugged. "Let's just meet here so we don't have to return and get my car after the movie since it'll be like two am."

Michael nodded. "Sounds good, my man. All right, I gotta get a move on. Don't die too much, Elle. I'll be there tomorrow to protect you for Danny's game. I'll bring soda if I make enough tips tonight. But I won't get any more if I stand here chatting for much longer."

The others waved, and Jeremy walked him to the door. Michael waved back and shook his head.

"Man, you're so lucky. Elle is awesome and a gamer chick. You know how hard that is to find?" he said.

Jeremy grinned. "I know, believe me, I know."

"Later, man!" he called out as he got into the car parked across the street from the house.

He watched Jeremy disappear back into the house, and he filed the money into his money box carefully. He never left his cash out just in case someone tried to rob him. The file box had slots for the money, and it was locked with an electronic lock only the manager back at the store could open. He thought it was a good safety feature and was quite glad his manager had invested in them for the drivers. His mom was certainly happier since they had started using them. His head shot up as someone tapped on his window. He looked up to see someone with a flashlight looking at him. He looked like a cop of some kind, but the uniform was somehow wrong. He rolled down the window.

"Can I help you, sir?" he asked. It was hard to see the guy's appearance with the light on his face.

"Son, what are you doing sitting here?" he said sternly.

"Oh, I just delivered pizza to this house. Trying to be safe and put away my money before I take off, sir. What kind of officer are you? I don't recognize your uniform," he said, trying to shield his eyes from the light.

He shifted his weight to the other leg and put one hand on his hip. "Don't be smart; what's your name?"

Not wanting to end up in jail for sassing an officer of the law, Michael squinted and pulled out his driver's license. "Eh, Michael Heights, sir," he stammered.

The officer took his license and stared at it for a moment. "Your dad Randy Heights?" he asked, and Michael breathed an internal sigh of relief. Maybe he knew his dad and would quit giving him grief and let him get back to work. His dad was a private eye; after all, many cops knew him.

"Yes, sir!" he answered.

"Get out of the car," the man responded, and Michael's heart sank. Or maybe not.

Michael slowly unbuckled his seat belt and opened the door. He didn't see any lights or even a car, which was odd, but he didn't want to question authority because the last thing he needed was trouble with the cops right now. So, he slowly stepped out of the car and stood, trying not to provoke him. Michael didn't notice that he pulled something out of his pocket as he backed away from the car. It wasn't an unusual action for a police officer to back out in case the person in the car was armed or going to try to run from them.

"Sir, is there something wrong? I don't—" he started and then felt a sharp pain in his arm.

He turned and saw the cop holding a syringe in his hand. He blinked in confusion. The guy was smiling; his dark eyes were almost malicious.

"What the hell...did...you..." he muttered as his knees folded under him. Then, finally, he hit the ground, dropping his keys and setting off the panic alarm on his car.

"Son of a bitch," the dark man muttered among the noise of the klaxon and hefted Michael up around the waist before he'd even fallen unconscious.

"Let...me...go..." Michael said, trying his hardest to fight off the big man, kicking and beating on him as hard as he could, hoping to strike something vital, though he was quickly losing the ability to stay awake. His eyes just wanted to close, but he wouldn't let them.

He lifted his head as the door to Jeremy's house opened, and Elle's face poked out.

"What the hell is all the noise—Michael!" she screamed at the end.

The big man spun around, sending Michael's head into a spin, and dropped, flopping down hard onto his side for a moment before scrambling onto his hands and knees. He looked to see the man draw a gun and aim it toward the house. But, instead, he fell again, his arms giving out this time, and face planted on the pavement. He tasted the copper taste of blood flooding his mouth as Elle started to run out to him, but then he heard the distinct crack of a gunshot. He'd never heard a gunshot before, and he had to admit, it was a lot louder than he had imagined it. They always sounded like a loud pop on TV, but this was an ear-splitting sound.

Elle screamed, and he lifted his head enough to see the splinters from the door go flying and Elle scrambling to get back into the house. Jeremy was behind her, and Michael caught the horrified look on his face.

"Leave her alone!" he tried to yell and lunged at the man's knees.

He intended to take them from under him, but whatever he'd drugged him with was taking hold, and he hugged his leg more than anything. He heard more voices, but they were getting softer, and his head was spinning more and more. Then, finally, he only vaguely felt the sharp kick to his face before the world lurched into sick, silent blackness.

"He was tall, and I think he had dark hair and eyes, but the porch light's been burned out for a while," Jeremy said, his eyes hollow and face pale. Beside him, Elle shared a similar look.

"There was blood everywhere," she whispered. "He dropped him, and he fell on his face, and it exploded in blood...."

"Shh, Elle," Danny said, his arm around her.

"Okay, so you heard his car alarm go off. You came to the door to find this tall, dark man with your friend, right, ma'am?" the officer with blonde hair verified.

Elle nodded.

"Then he saw you and dropped your friend to the ground, and you tried to run out to him, but the assailant pulled a gun and shot at you?"

Elle nodded. "He shot wide, though, like he wanted to scare me, and he did. So, I ran back in the house, and when I looked back, he kicked Michael in the face, and he just rolled onto his back." She took a breath.

"By then, I had come to the door and pulled Elle into the house. The guy put his gun back in the holster, picked Michael up like he weighed nothing, and took off to a van parked over there a little further down. But I was afraid to leave because he was armed, sir."

The other officer, an older cop with dark-colored skin and not a stitch of hair upon his head, nodded. "You did the right thing, son. Did you see anything about it? Color or anything?"

Jeremy shrugged. "I know it was light colored, maybe white or pale yellow or something. But it was so dark...."

"Officer Sheller!" a voice yelled across the caution tapes. The older officer looked up. "The Heights are here!"

He waved them over, and Terri and Randy Heights made their way through the people standing around Jeremy and the officers.

"Terri, Randy," Officer Sheller said, nodding to them. "Did Binder brief you?"

Randy, a private investigator in the area, was very familiar with all these police procedures, and the police were very friendly with him. His wife, Terri, was a police dispatcher and had been working when the call came in for Jeremy's house. She'd been allowed to leave and head over as soon as they passed the news along to her. They'd been told everything they knew. Randy was regretting now that he hadn't insisted Michael come back home, job on the line or not. At least, if he'd been home, they might have been able to better keep an eye on him.

"Ben," he said, sighing and hugging his weeping wife. "I think I know who it is because it's the same person that took the Kim's son yesterday, and this is someone who's after Don and me. Did you find a note or anything like Don's kid?"

Ben shook his head. "There may not have been time; these kids interrupted the abduction."

"Sir!" yelled one of the CSI guys. He jogged over, holding the spent syringe in a plastic bag.

Ben turned and looked at Randy Heights. "Okay, Randy, I'm listening."

Randy shook his head. "Not here and not now; I've arranged for Don to meet us at the St. Louis FBI office to meet with an agent. This is a little more serious than you might think."

Ben looked at him for a moment. "Are you sure, Randy? You don't want to get this taken care of here and now?"

Randy shook his head. "If what I think is going on is true, we've got nothing but time. The longer this gets drawn out, the happier he'll be because he's after vengeance and nothing else. He can't hurt them because they're his pawns now, and we'll have to play a very intricate chess game to get them out alive. If we're not careful, he'll kill them and disappear, so we'll have to wait for him to set the rules of the game. Once he does that, we figure out how to cheat and get our kids out without getting them killed. For him, the game is the most important part of this."

Ben nodded, not understanding but respecting Randy's wishes. Since St. Louis police were already hard at work on the Kim boy's abduction, it wouldn't matter tonight. If Don and Randy were sure it was the same man, they would have already been on track. He glanced down at his watch as the hands clicked onto midnight. It had been a long day, and he needed sleep before the next day dawned.

Chapter Three

In Black and White

The following day, Officer Ben Sellers arrived at the St. Louis FBI office to make contact with Agent Richard Pearson. He found out when he got there that there was someone from the St. Louis police department as well to represent someone on the other kidnapping case, Officer Vernon Miller. Ben found his way to the conference room, dominated by the large table in the middle surrounded by rather comfortable chairs. He recognized the Heights of course, but there was another couple he assumed was the Kim family.

The blond-haired man at the head of the table, wearing a black business suit and tie, stood up, extending a hand toward Ben. His hair was pulled back in a ponytail at the base of his neck. "Officer Sellers," he said, flashing a toothy grin at him. "I'm Agent Richard Pearson, please don't call me Dick. Welcome to the meeting." He removed his glasses and stuck them in his jacket pocket while looking around the room.

"Ah, yes, good to meet you." He turned and nodded toward the other people in the room.

"All right, I think everyone is here," Pearson said, gesturing for everyone to be seated. Once everyone was ready, he cleared his throat. "First, a round of introductions. First, we have Terri and Randy Heights from St. Peters, who are the parents to Michael Heights, who was kidnapped last night," he said, pointing to the couple Ben was quite familiar with. "Randy works as a private investigator, and Terri works as a St. Peters' dispatcher." He turned toward the other couple. "And this is Mara and Donald Kim from St. Charles. Parents to CJ Kim, who was kidnapped Thursday. Donald is a Barnes-Jewish St. Peters Hospital doctor, and Mara is a homemaker." He indicated Ben and introduced him. "And this is Officer Sellars from St. Peters PD and Officer Miller from St. Charles PD." He gestured last to the dark-haired man in the uniform seated on the side of the table.

Pearson sat down and turned toward the screen behind him, which came on with the picture of a rough-looking man in his forties or fifties. He had dark black eyes and a head of buzz-cut dark brown hair. His face was marked with several scars, including one which looked like it had nearly blinded him.

"As the Heights and Kims are familiar with, this is whom we believe to be the culprit of these kidnappings. Joseph Keith Jackson. Joe, as he is known, recently escaped from a military prison in an undisclosed location. He was being held for a life sentence for murder and a few other charges," Pearson explained.

"How does this man fit in with the families, and what makes you so sure the kidnapper is the same guy?" Ben asked, looking over at the two couples.

"The note he left for me makes me believe it was him," Donald said with a sigh. "And the timing fits."

Randy sighed. "We can't get into details, Officer Sellars. Most of it is classified. What I can tell you is this guy is dangerous and angry. Don, Joe, and I were on an elite squad during the time with two other guys. We were a five-man team, and we'd been together since basic training. Joe did something which cost us our mates, Maverick and Cole. What he did was not only illegal but also detrimental to our team's security. Randy and I convinced him we were on his side in the matter. Our plan, of course, was to turn him in and see him punished for his actions. We did just that, and at first, Joe thought we were caught as well."

Donald sipped a coke the secretary had brought him. "During the court-martial, we were required to take the stand. At that point, everything was revealed, and Joe vowed to make us pay for betraying him. He was sentenced to life in a military prison, but it appears somehow he broke out."

"This is his declassified profile," Pearson said and handed Ben a file folder. "He escaped a maximum-security lockup. They're currently investigating how, but it is believed he did so by outside aid, bribes, and blackmail. We already have two MPs in custody for aiding him from the inside, but they haven't spilled who they're working for yet. He has had contact with several illicit organizations since his escape and has made himself untraceable. We had tabs on him through contacts until one week ago, when he disappeared off the radar. We know for a fact at least two organizations are looking for him because of what he was supposed to do for them once he escaped. Our theory is these organizations helped organize the escape, and now he has decided to pursue his own interests and abandoned the contracts he's made with these groups," Pearson said..

On the screen behind him, a picture of a woman appeared. She had platinum blonde hair and bright blue eyes. She wore a lot of makeup and appeared to be looking nearly at the camera when the picture was taken. "We know this woman; her name is Sheila Roberts, but we're not one hundred percent certain she's the same woman that's with him now. Sheila Roberts was working at a St. Louis hospital until about a week ago when she, and a quantity of drugs, disappeared. She was caught on the security cameras, but it appeared she wasn't trying to be stealthy about it. She is also rumored to be the daughter of Maxim Sokolov, head of a group of Russian affiliated mobsters who are under FBI surveillance."

There was a silent moment between them. "So, he has someone with medical know-how. That explains the syringe with traces of diazepam in it," Ben said.

"We didn't find any syringe at the Kim boy's disappearance," Officer Miller said. "How can we be sure they are connected if we don't have consistency between the two crime scenes?"

Pearson nodded. "There are too many coincidences for this to be anything else. The scene at South Campus was not interrupted by anyone like the scene at the Heights boy's abduction. He may have been in a rush and dropped the syringe."

"Can something like that actually knock someone out? I mean, this isn't a movie," Ben commented, looking between Officer Miller and the FBI agent.

"With a high enough dosage injected into a major muscle, diazepam can work in between one and five minutes. We know Michael wasn't quite unconscious but stumbling by the time his friends heard the alarm go off. If he was using a large dose, it is quite possible to take effect that fast," Pearson said with a sigh. "I worry what other drugs they might be using. There were several sedatives including Propofol in the drugs taken from the hospital."

"And what does that do?" Officer Miller asked, looking over at him.

"Used in surgery as a type of anesthesia," Donald provided from the end of the table. "It isn't often used recreationally, but it can keep someone out for a while. We can only hope they are careful enough to avoid overdosing them with these kinds of drugs."

Ben looked over the folders and then back to the FBI man. "So, what do we do?"

Richard looked at each of them, shaking his head. "Not a damn thing until he makes a move. Until then, we chill, my friends."

Ben looked at him and nodded. "Do what you need to, Agent Pearson. Let me know if my people can do anything for you."

Richard nodded, glancing at the Kim's and the Heights. "Until he makes a move, kiddies, we're stuck."

The world was incredibly foggy. Something was wrong; he could see her running through a field of vibrant green grass. She turned her head to look behind, a wild shock of bright red hair slapping her in the face. Her loose summer robe fluttered around her legs as they pumped harder than ever to get to him. He stood just behind one of the monolithic stones on the inside of the circle. As usual, the temperature dropped as she neared the stone circle. Finally, she went through the deep ditch around the outer rim and scrambled quickly inside the circle of what she hoped was protection.

"Caoimhe, come closer, will you?" his deep voice announced.

"Oh yes, it's me, my love. They're coming this time. This is our last meeting, Junius," she cried. "They found out about us..."

Junius, who'd removed his usual Roman armor, dropped his head. The last time they met, they were wed by Roman laws, but not her people's laws. The natives here in the isles had very different ideas. And her father had forbidden him from entering their lands at all, and to find they had been secretly meeting at the great stone circle for several months now and after that, they had been wed there to seal Junius's death. If only that were the consequence, but it would also seal the fate of Caoimhe, for she would likely be stoned to death with her own family at the forefront. He could not take her with him, and her kind would not be accepted by the Romans as equals.

He took her into his arms as she wept. "How long until they find us?" he asked.

She shook her head against his chest. "I don't know; my brother must have followed us and viewed the ceremony. He...he...told our father, and he went into a rage like I have never seen, and then..." she sobbed, stopping to heave a shaking breath. "He t-told me...told me..."

Junius held her tighter. "What?"

"He'd kill ye and...th-then deal with me...I'm scared Junius, I don't know why Sean would...would do this..." she said gasping for breath through the tears that still fell.

"I would do this to protect our family, Caoimhe," Sean's voice came from behind another stone within the circle. The young Celt's dark eyes lit with something his sister had never seen before.

"Sean!" she gasped, pulling Junius closer to her. "What are ye doing here? Why have ye done this?!"

The young man walked closer, a clay-more swaying behind him. Junius eased his much shorter Roman short sword from the leather hilt where it lay on a rock beside them.

"Don't do this Sean; I'm one of Rome's finest soldiers. Your barbaric fighting is no match for me, and I do not wish to harm you, for Caoimhe's sake," Junius said, holding the sword before him to protect himself and Caoimhe from Sean.

Sean stopped, pulling the clay-more from the scabbard. "That's nae sure because there is one difference twixt ye and me, Junius. Honor and duty aren't the most important thing to me."

Junius felt a sudden, sharp stinging sensation between his shoulders. He turned to see Marcus, one of his fellow soldiers, holding a bloody knife. The man was his friend, or was he? He heard Caoimhe's scream of horror and fear as he dropped to his knees, blood flowing freely down his back. Caoimhe dropped beside him, screaming for her brother to stop and leave them alone.

"I'm sorry; Junius, but we can't have someone as weak as you in our ranks. You fell for her tricks, and now you have to die...and so does she. I wish I'd never let her in that night when she was hurt near the baths. Then it would not have come to this. I will not let you stain Rome's honor by one of these barbaric people," Marcus said, sheathing his sword and turning away.

To his own horror, however, Marcus felt the sting of a blade in his own back. He turned to see the fiery red-haired Celt holding the sword Junius had dropped. His face held a smile of malice unlike anything he had seen. "And ye ken, Marcus, I cannae let you live."

Marcus dropped within a moment, the strike true and to the heart, leaving Sean to wipe the blood onto the dead man's cloak. He then turned to his sister and her "husband".

"As for you, my sister, you cannae live, either," he said and in one deft swipe, sliced through the front of her throat, leaving her to die with a look of shock on her face.

Junius screamed as she convulsed in his arms, dying before a word could escape her lips. His own lifeblood was draining fast away, though. Sean calmly took his own clay-more and forced it through the front of Marcus's still body, bringing it out bloodied. Then, he took his sword and placed it against the ground to brace it at one end, and leaned upon it at the chest, burying the point there. He looked up, seeing Junius staring at him, and he winked, and something otherworldly flashed through the Roman's mind. Something... and then the Celt forced the sword through his own chest, a feat he should not have been able to do and dropping upon the body of Marcus. Why...why all the show...

Junius finally fell forward, unable to sit holding Caoimhe's body, his arms wrapped about her in a lover's embrace, as close to lovers as they had ever gotten. He wanted it to look like

Marcus killed us, he thought, his vision blurring at the edges softly. He wanted to look like he'd died in a fight with him afterward, taking vengeance for his sister's demise, for he so loved his family that he would not appear to have betrayed them, even in death. He so loved them: he killed and then died for them. Tears escaped the Roman's eyes as he stared into Caoimhe's lifeless green eyes until the world went black.

Michael's eyes fluttered, seeing only darkness for a long time. The effects of the strange dream had left him somewhat disorientated, and for a moment, he thought he was still in the dream. Then he remembered the man with the gun. His head was pounding, and he knew the room was spinning even though he couldn't see it. He swallowed, his mouth feeling as though it was filled with cotton. Whatever the bastard had drugged him with had a hangover effect, like two gallons of cheap whiskey. Shaking his head, he tried to move, stand, anything and found he couldn't. The sensation of ropes around him straining as he pulled against them was strong. After a few seconds, pain shot through his ribs and face as he struggled, reminding him keenly of the beating he'd gotten. Slowly, between the pain and the confinement, he realized there was no escape for him. He forced his breathing under control, and then he heard it. There was another person's breathing in the room.

"Hello?" he said. "Hello, is someone else there?"

There was no answer, but the breathing continued, slow and steady. Whoever it was, they were asleep or unconscious. Had they been kidnapped, too? He gasped. The boy that was kidnapped yesterday? He shook his head and waited.

Thousands of thoughts ran through his head. Who did this and why? His mind ran through the reasons for kidnapping people. None of them were good. Murder. Torture. Ransom. He couldn't imagine it being ransom. His dad wasn't rich. He was just a private investigator, and though he was good, he didn't make a lot of money. He thought hard for a second. Why else would someone abduct a person if not for money? His heart skipped a beat as the horror stories he'd seen on TV and in movies ran through his mind. Nah, that shit didn't really happen. People really didn't abduct people just to get their kicks by torturing and murdering them. He swallowed hard. He knew better because he knew it could happen and had happened. But why him? Surely it had to be something else...

The breathing to his left was replaced by a low moan. It sounded like another guy. The fact it was another guy did not increase his confidence in his idea that this was something besides a torture murder plot. And it confirmed his idea that it was the boy who had been kidnapped the day before. What were the chances there were other people kidnapped too, though?

"Wh-where..." the other, rough voice said. "Where am I? Is anyone there?"

Michael wasn't sure what to say, but he had to say something. "Yeah. Are you tied up too?"

He heard him clear his throat and the distinct rustle of him pulling at ropes. "Seems like it," he said, his voice somewhat hoarse and slurred. "What's happened? Do you know?"

"Nah, this dude nabbed me in front of my buddy's house while I delivered pizza to 'em. Dunno who the dude is, but he beat the shit outta me in the process, and then stabbed me with a damn syringe..." he said, sighing. "What 'bout you?"

He paused for a long while. "The guy pulled up by me at the school and asked me if I was Don Kim's kid, and I told him yes, then he stabbed me with a needle too..."

The two sat there quietly for a while before Michael finally spoke up. "My name's Michael Heights, I guess introductions are in order since we're apparently stuck here together."

Michael heard a sharp intake of breath from the other guy. "Um, yeah, my name's CJ Kim. Glad to meet you, Michael," he answered. His voice still sounded off, like he was not completely out of whatever drug they'd been under, though somewhat familiar as if he'd heard it somewhere before.

They were flooded with garish light as four naked bulbs flared into existence around the windowless room. Michael blinked, getting his bearings. He saw two doors, one in the back and one directly in front of them at the top of a set of stairs. The one in front of them was wood banded with steel. He blinked a few more times to be sure. A door with reinforced steel? He looked down and found the floor to be yellow-painted concrete with a rough blue area rug under them. He saw two beds when he craned his neck behind him, each a mattress and box with a pile of bedclothes in the middle of each, a couple of chairs and tables, and a larger dining-type table with a couple of chairs. What the hell was this?

"CJ, are you seeing this?" he whispered, turning his head toward him.

Sitting with long black hair falling in front of his face, he was wearing a black T-shirt hiked up around his ribs with a pair of worn jeans. He was barefoot and had been sitting in position long enough that his wrists and waist were both rubbed bright red from the ropes.

"CJ..." he asked again. "CJ how long have you been down here?"

He turned his head toward him; his eyes dilated more than they should have been in the bright light behind his askew glasses and shook his head. "I don't know... I've woken up and yelled for help once or twice and he came...and he gave me a shot...feels like it was a few minutes ago, though."

Michael realized he himself was also barefoot and tied in the exact way CJ was. He felt the ropes around his waist biting into his skin, but his shirt had slid down over them once more. He heard a noise above them. A basement? They were in a basement? It sounded like something falling. Was it the guy who took them? There was no one else...unless he was just a hired hit man to do the deed for the maniac who was going to hack them to pieces. Michael swallowed again. Fucking horror movies, he thought, letting out a shuddering breath. There was a scraping, creaking sound. They heard the noise much clearer then.

"Jesus fucking Christ, Sheila! What the fuck are you doing still messing around? Get your ass in gear and get their food to them. Dead kids don't do nothing for me," came from the other side of the door, incredibly clear.

The yelling voice, which both CJ and Michael recognized as the man who had abducted them, was answered by a muffled voice, obviously female. They couldn't make out any of the words she spoke, however. Michael's heart slipped into his throat. Maybe now they'd find out what was going on? He both wanted to know and didn't want to know. If they were going to be kept alive for ransom, there was no way his dad could come up with the money in a million years. Of course, it could be so he could torture and kill them at his leisure. At the thought, his heart thrummed harder in his chest. Oh, my God, he thought. I don't want to know.

He looked at CJ again, and he still sat with his head down. Jesus, he was doped up higher than a kite. If Michael was right, he'd been the one who was kidnapped at the school. That meant he'd been down here almost two whole days. By the state he was in, Michael guessed he'd been drugged to keep him quiet. He swore he'd seen him before though. Michael squinted, scrutinizing him, trying to place him.

"Oh, I'm so hungry," CJ whispered. "It feels like I haven't eaten in days."

"That's because it's been since Thursday morning since you ate, hon," a female voice said from the now open door. "It's Saturday afternoon now."

Michael looked up, amazed he hadn't noticed the door opening at the top of the stairs. A tall, thin woman stood there, her hair platinum blonde, but not the kind that came out of a bottle. Her skin was extremely pale, and her body gaunt, which only accented what had to be one of the most piercing set of blue eyes he'd ever seen. She looked to be in her mid-thirties, but with women, it was hard for him to tell. Her dress was simple, a pair of jean shorts and a white V-neck T-shirt, but without shoes. She carried a steaming tray over to the dining sized tables and sat it down. Michael could smell food and realized he was starving as well. As she moved around behind him, he twisted his wrist around to see his watch, realizing she was right. It was the next day, and well after noon now.

The woman came back and deftly untied Michael. He rubbed his wrists thoughtfully as he watched her with a furrowed brow. She smiled, and it was pretty, yet haggard, as though she'd seen a lot in her life, perhaps too much.

"There you go, bub. I'm Sheila, and I'll be taking care of you while you're here. I don't know anything about what's going on, so don't bother with the questions. I do what I'm told and that's it. I'm here to make your food, make sure you're healthy, and keep him away from you at his request. He doesn't want to do anything he'd regret before it's all over. I don't know what 'it' is, so don't bother asking.

"The Bathroom is back there. There's a first aid kit in the cabinet. If anything happens to you, don't worry—I'm a Nurse Practitioner. I checked over your wounds when you came in, but neither of you had anything serious. If you feel ill, let me know. I'm also keeping an eye on what he gives you. So, you have to let me know if anything feels odd.

"As far as that goes, you are being kept slightly sedated to reduce the risk of hurting yourselves or trying to do anything stupid. You can't get out, so don't even try. You're basically in an underground vault, not a normal basement. This is an old bomb shelter that has been converted into a 'basement' for the house above. You can't dig out, you can't get through the door, and you can't be heard upstairs once the two doors have been closed. If you need me, there's a button by the doorway connected to an intercom upstairs in the phone. I will know it's you because the phone has a separate ring."

She stood there momentarily and watched as Michael rubbed his wrists and stared. How do you respond to something like this? he thought.

"Any questions I can answer?" she asked, arching a brow.

Michael nodded. "Yeah, what's wrong with him?"

She approached CJ, lifted his chin, and looked at his eyes. "He's coming out of the effects of the drug. It was not the best thing for what he was looking for, but no one said Joe was smart about stuff like this; he probably grabbed the first syringe; in my case, he saw that it had a name he knew. He'll be fine in an hour or two. Alright, I'll deliver food at mealtimes, and if you need something in between, buzz me."

She turned on her heel and went up the steps to the large metal door. She knocked on it, and it opened. Michael tried to see what was on the other side, but all he saw was the silhouette of a large person, probably this "Joe" she mentioned. That must have been the name of the man from last night. He got up, went over to CJ, and started untying him carefully. He's been tied up for almost two days, he thought. He had no idea how long these drugs lasted, and he didn't know how long CJ was going to be out of it. It was a safe bet that CJ would need help.

"Hey, CJ, she brought food. Can you walk?" he asked as he knelt before him after untying his ankles.

His eyes were still bleary, but he nodded. "Yeah, I've gotta eat something," he said in a slow, drugged way as Michael stood up.

He stood up and took an unsteady step. Michael could tell immediately he was going to fall. He watched CJ's knees wobble for a second, and he collapsed into Michael's waiting arms. CJ blinked and looked up, his face less than an inch from Michael's, staring into his eyes for a second. A wave of déjà vu washed over Michael. Both were as still as death for a moment and then CJ cleared his throat.

"Yeah, so can you help me get over to the table? I'm still starving," he said slowly.

Michael was startled and smiled. "Yeah, me too."

He helped him to the chair, and they both sat down. They dove into the food, leaving nothing but the dishes on the tray.

Chapter Four

Moving Pawns

Sheila washed the dishes mechanically. How the hell did she get herself into these things? Her entire life was one mess after another. She sighed as she placed the plates into the dish drainer. It was the only time she could really think. Most people thought it was odd she liked washing dishes so much. It was a mind-numbing experience she didn't have to think about doing. Her body took over and she could just forget about everything. Or, like today, she could devote her mind to her current predicament and the two kids below.

Outside, a bright day had dawned, and she eyed it with a wistful look. It was going to be warm again, but she'd be stuck inside no matter what. At least there was a nice view from all the windows. They were at least an hour's drive from any real civilization, and the dense trees and shrubs surrounding the place only confirmed it. When she'd driven here the day before, she had wondered what he was up to. He'd disappeared completely, and for a week Sheila had been dodging questions from her father about what had happened to him. Then she'd gotten the call that was nothing but coordinates. She knew it was him. Of course, when she got here, he was furious with her because she hadn't come soon enough. As she thought of it, she rubbed her ribs, wincing still at the pain from the bruises that were just starting to turn purple.

She felt horrible now that she knew why he wanted her. Those poor kids, stuck down there with nothing until she got here. Joe didn't want any part of them except to nab them. He told her he would kill them if he got too close to them because of his anger at their parents. Sheila didn't know why it wasn't enough for him to simply be free from prison. She thought getting out would be enough for him. She also thought he was getting out for her. For the last three years, they'd communicated with each other and made plans for his escape. She coordinated with her father for him, and now that he'd escaped, he'd backed out on the deals she had made for him. Perhaps she ran to him when he called because she was ultimately more afraid of her father.

Sheila started putting away the clean dishes. Had it really been all her life she'd spent afraid of one person or another? As she slid the last plate into the cabinet, she shook her head. Knowing what Joe had planned for the kids, she knew she couldn't get attached. Maybe she could have warned them of his game, but she lied instead, too afraid to cross Joe.

That was why she oversaw the kids. He didn't want to tip his hand too soon.

She bit her lip and went to the living area where Joe had his equipment set up. The living room was an array of black boxes and wiring littering the floor. The computer he sat at ran its wires through one of these mysterious black boxes. He was keeping track of something, but that was all she knew. She didn't know the specifics, and she didn't dare ask.

"You get the brats fed?" he asked gruffly as she entered.

"Yeah, sure did," she answered, picking up the newspaper from the coffee table. "After starving for a couple of days, they're making sure they don't miss a meal. Of course, I wouldn't either were I in their position."

He snorted. "Good. Still giving them the meds?"

Sheila didn't like keeping them drugged up. "Yeah. Why do we have to do that? They can't get out, and no one is around for miles...I don't see—"

"No, you don't fucking see, Sheila," he said, turning around. His eyes flashed dangerously, and she caught her breath.

She backpedaled toward the kitchen. "Yeah, okay, you're right, I shouldn't..."

He stood up slowly and stepped toward her. "This is my fuckin' plan, you nosy bitch. Don't push me. I already told you when you got here that I have no room for mistakes. You're going to damn well do what I say, when I fuckin' say it, or I'm gonna teach you a lesson in not listening to me. Do you really want me to send you back to your daddy? I'm sure it would be a good homecoming after everything you had him do for you recently."

"Joe, it was for you, all of it, you know that!" she stammered, clutching the newspaper to her chest, her heart thrumming in fear. She couldn't go back to her father anymore, not after everything that had happened.

He snorted and stepped in front of her, grabbing her by the shoulders and shoving her against the wall. "Maybe so, but it cost him a shit-ton of money to do his little girl a favor when she asked, even if it was to my benefit. You honestly think he would forgive you when you come back and say your lover has run off and refused to hold up the bargain you made for him?"

Sheila swallowed. He was right, of course. Her father had funded Joe's escape. He'd paid the bribes and arranged the blackmail, and it was his resources that allowed Joe places to hide and ways to disappear. In return, she'd struck a bargain with her own father that Joe would be a part of his organization, putting his skills to use there in St. Louis. Then he disappears, leaving her father high and dry and out of a lot of money. Before she'd skipped town at Joe's request, he was already getting more enraged. He'd already called one of his men to find him, but Sheila knew when Joe wanted to disappear, he did so very well. This, of course, was a source of even more anger for her father. When he couldn't have him located, it made him all the angrier with Sheila.

"Please, Joe, I'm doing all I can...I'm just thinking of what's best f-for them. I know what I-I'm talking about, Joe. You can't k-keep giving them..." she stammered.

Joe's eyes flashed again, and Sheila sucked in a breath and steeled herself for the coming blow. The next thing she knew, she was picking herself off the floor, staunching the blood from her lip with the back of her hand. Tears squeezed from her eyes from the sharp, stinging pain.

"Do not question me," he said, looking over her as she stood up. "You may know something about these drugs, but so do I, and I won't be questioned by a know-it-all slut like you. I want them addicted, Sheila. Don't presume I don't know what they do. You know as well as I do they're not going to fucking live to deal with it. They're a part of this game as long as it's convenient for me. Then, like any other pawn, they'll be sacrificed."

He returned to his seat. "Get the hell out of here; I don't want to see your face until you can learn not to question me."

Sheila headed to the bathroom to clean up without another word. Why did she do these things? She knew better than to question him. She was so stupid. Why didn't she ever learn to control her mouth? Ever since she was small, she'd done things like this. Talking back to her father or mother, questioning or not doing what she should, was her lot in life. She wouldn't be punished if she did what she was supposed to. She flushed the bloody toilet paper and watched it spin. Swallowing hard, she looked in the mirror, her lower lip already swelling and turning purple. She should be used to it. It felt like most of her life had been spent with a busted lip or nose. Pulling a bottle of Valium out of the cabinet, she stared at it for a while, then popped one in her mouth, dry swallowing it. As she put the bottle back, she looked over the assorted drug bottles, all of which she'd stolen before she left the hospital. She turned and headed to the bedroom and threw herself across the bed, trying to forget about everything, if only for a little while.

"Mara?" Don swallowed a heavy knot in his throat as he called from the doorway.

Mara's red-rimmed, puffy eyes rose from the laundry basket. "What is it, Don?" Her voice was barely above a whisper.

The twins sat on the floor at the end of the bed playing with their ball, too young to know what was going on. They'd asked for their 'bro' several times since CJ's disappearance, but Mara and Don could only tell them he was away. It appeared to satisfy them, but they'd been extremely quiet.

"I just got a call from Rich. They don't think he's working locally. There just isn't anywhere in the close area he could be hiding them. The police have searched all the possible areas but there was no sign of him. The Highway Patrol is on alert for any cars matching the description we got from the Truman boy and his girlfriend, but so far, all the stops have come up to nothing," Don relayed, sighing.

Mara nodded slowly. "He still hasn't contacted anyone."

Don's face fell as he grimaced. "I know. I know what he's doing. He's making us wait. He wants us to worry that he's already done something to them. Unfortunately, we have nothing to go on until he tries to make contact. At least then we can try to trace him."

Mara dropped the shirt she was holding and looked at him with hollow eyes. "You know as well as I do, it won't work."

Don swallowed and turned away. "I know. I know."

Don remembered all too well what happened when Joe escaped after the court martial. That was part of the classified file. He'd broken free, killing several MPs in the process and taking several more people hostage. They'd managed to bring him down, but not before he'd killed the hostages he took. He couldn't contain his rage. He hadn't always been like that. When they were training together, Joe had been the mildest and the calmest among the unit. In fact, Randy had been the hot headed one out of all of them. But something had happened to Joe over there, something that twisted him.

It happened one day when they were performing a recon mission. It was simple, just scouting some buildings in the area close to their station point. Joe was on the front with Maverick and Cole. Don and Randy had taken up points outside. Don, who was the medic of the group, rarely ever went at the front, and Randy, who was the team leader, usually watched the other guys' backs. That was how they'd always done things, mainly because they were always on their while on their missions. It worked. As long as it worked, the military never questioned it or imposed any other rules on them. They got the job done.

But something had happened in the ancient building they'd come across. Things were normal; contact was held via the radios they carried just fine until they heard Joe whisper, "No, leave me alone..."

A burst of static ensued, confusing Don. The signal was fine. There was no reason it should have gone to static. The guys came out as they should have if contact were lost, and when asked, Joe didn't know what they were talking about. He claimed never to have said anything that it must have been interference. But after that, Joe was never the same. He wasn't the calm, easy-going guy he'd always been. He was quick to anger and even quicker to violence. He was unreasonably touchy with both Randy and Don. Neither of them could figure out why. It was as though he was holding back barely restrained rage.

It wasn't long after that incident that Cole and Maverick died. Joe, without anyone knowing, had gotten into some drug trading. He had been doing it for a while, and the others suspected him of doing something illegal by the way he was acting. Still, they couldn't ever catch him at anything. Then, while on maneuvers, they were ambushed by a group of drug runners who were after Joe. Cole and Maverick died immediately when they came across an IED. Both Randy and Don had nearly lost their lives, but they survived the bomb and the subsequent gun attack. Joe managed to take out the gunmen, and to this day, Don still wasn't sure exactly how he'd done it.

At first, they thought they'd just been hit by random attackers. Then the truth came out that they had been targeted because of the drug running. As things came to light, Don and Randy did everything they could to appear on Joe's side out of uncertainty about what he would do if he knew they were against him. When Joe was arrested, both of them were taken in, too. Don and Randy, though, cooperated, helped them find evidence against Joe and testified against him at the court-martial. He swore to have revenge against the two of them, no matter how long it took him.

He shook his head, clearing it of memories of the past, and headed back to the living room to wait for a call. He'd turned off Fur Elise and changed it to the annoying regular ringtone. He wasn't in the mood for music.

Aileen poked at the food on her plate, head propped on her left hand. Her mom sat across from her, and her dad at the head of the table, like usual. All three of them were conscious of the empty seat. There was a great silence, and no one wanted to break it. Each one of them glanced at the empty seat now and then. And so, the silence grew, and the emptiness expanded to cover everyone at the table.

"Don't play with your food, dear," Terri said gently to her daughter after some time.

Aileen looked up. "What else am I supposed to do with it? I'm not hungry."

Randy sighed. "You should eat, Aileen. It's not going to do any good for you to lose your strength by not eating."

Aileen pushed her mashed potatoes into a mountain on the Corelle white plate. She stared at the difference between the color of the dinnerware and the potatoes. How many times had Michael broken one of these "break resistant" plates? That's why her mom had bought this Corelle stuff. She could easily replace the broken pieces. Hell, they sold it at the local super center now. True, he broke less of these than the old stoneware plates her mom used to buy, but somehow, he could still manage to break them. She snorted. She couldn't take the silence anymore. The silence around Michael's disappearance was strangling her.

"I'm going to my room," she said, nearly knocking over the chair before she stalked off.

Randy laid his fork down on his plate and dropped his head into his hands, rubbing his face. He ran his hands over his short, blonde hair and sighed again. The waiting was killing him. It was killing them all. Like Don and Mara, the Heights knew exactly what Joe was going to do. They knew how he'd handled the last hostages he'd taken just as well as the others had. He'd gone in with the assault team. He'd found the bodies of the hostages. He maybe knew even better than Don what Joe could do.

"She's upset," his wife said slowly, standing and collecting the plates. "I should have kept her home from band practice today. All she did was answer questions about what happened since someone leaked it to the news yesterday."

Randy nodded. He wished he could get his hands on whoever had leaked the information. But there were too many sources in the police or dispatch department who could have done it. Luckily for Don, his two younger kids were still at home. Aileen was a sophomore, and very active in several activities, including the concert band. They had an end-of-year concert soon, and they'd had practice on Sunday instead of Saturday because of a parade they had attended Saturday afternoon.

"Should we keep her out of school tomorrow?" he asked as Terri picked up the last of the plates and put them on the counter.

She turned back, putting a hand on her hip and thinking. "Does it really matter?"

Randy nodded. "I guess not. It's a waiting game now. He's got us right where he wants us, truth be told."

A game, indeed. That's what the whole thing was to Joe Jackson. These weren't real lives he was playing with, not to him. These were pawns in a giant game that he was trying to win. For him, winning was everything. Unlike Don and Randy, Joe had nothing to lose, and everything to gain in this game. Randy watched as his wife went to the kitchen, wondering if there was any way to beat this man at his own game.

Michael stared at the nondescript ceiling again. There wasn't much else to do. It had been a silent day, really. Both of them felt strange, somewhat drugged. Sheila said they were being given sedatives. How lovely, he thought. It was stupid; it wasn't like they could get out anyway. He turned his head to the right to see CJ laying on the bed staring at the ceiling as well. Whatever they were being given affected him more.

"CJ?" he asked quietly.

"Yeah?" he answered.

Michael cleared his throat and resumed staring at the ceiling. "Did you notice Sheila's lip today?"

CJ snorted. "How could I miss it? It looked like a purple Christmas bulb on her mouth when she brought lunch, and not much better at dinner. You think this Joe guy hits her?"

Michael thought for a minute. "Yeah, I think he does. Kinda dude he is, all fists and fury. I wouldn't doubt it. He bagged you quite like, right? See, mine didn't go as planned, which is why my face looks like road pizza."

CJ kind of giggled, stifling it with his hand.

Michael propped himself up and looked at him. "What's so funny?"

He propped himself up and looked at him. "It's just, ah, never mind," he said, flopping back onto the bed.

"Hey, wait a minute, you can't just do that to me!" he exclaimed. "What is it?"

He turned his head to the side again and gave him a gentle smile. "It's just the way you put things. No matter how shitty things are, you're always upbeat. It makes me smile."

Michael smiled to himself and laid back down, putting his hands under the back of his head. "Well, at least I'm good for something."

It was silent for a long while. CJ wasn't sure what to do with him. He felt something, like a strange pull towards him. It was more than the previous infatuation he'd had with him from afar. This was different, and stronger than he expected. He'd never imagined he'd talk to the guy, let alone be kidnapped by the same person.

"So, you got a girlfriend worried about you?" he asked, trying to sound casual. He might as well find out now before he got his heart set on anything.

Michael snickered. "Nah, haven't met the right one yet. Most of them can't stand my addiction."

He turned his head and looked at him. "Your addiction? Like drugs or alcohol or something?"

Michael met his gaze with a serious look. Then his face split into a wide grin. "Nah, nothing like that. I like games."

He thought for a moment. "Games? Like you're on the baseball team, I know."

He watched him shift, obviously uncomfortable suddenly. "Nah, they're called RPGs. Um, you know. Tabletop games."

Suddenly, realization dawned on him. "You mean like Dungeons and Dragons?"

Michael sat up so fast he nearly fell off the bed. "Um, well yeah. Do you play it?"

He smiled. "I've played a couple times. My dad used to play when he was younger. Still got all these old books he pulls out now and then tells me all the cool stuff he did with his buddies. Slaying orcs, saving maiden elves, killing dragons, and all that stuff. He used to let me read in his books and showed me a couple times how to play it, but never known anyone else who did it."

Michael was suddenly dumbfounded. He sat stunned for a moment. He actually got stuck in a basement with another guy who knew about D&D, and he didn't know him already.

"Yeah, so no girlfriend. Most girls really get put off by it."

He sat up and looked at him. "Why is that?"

Michael fidgeted again, a little uncomfortable. "Well, the few girlfriends I've ever had think it's either stupid or they get jealous. They feel like I should be devoting my time to them, and not to some game. But I don't like watching stupid movies or playing baseball all the time. I like to really get away from reality, you know, where I can be whatever I want, and do whatever I want. Just have fun."

He realized CJ was propped up on one elbow, staring at him with a slight smile on his face. "What? What is it now?" he asked.

He blinked a couple of times. "Oh nothing, I was just thinking how dumb those girls have been. I mean come on, other guys go out drinking and doping up when they aren't with their girls, at least they knew where to find you... I've never had a significant other before," he said and blushed slightly.

If Michael noticed he used "significant other" instead of girlfriend, he didn't say anything. CJ swallowed and looked away from him. "Um, goodnight," he said.

Michael yawned. "Yeah, whatever they're giving us makes me sleepy."

Within moments, he was asleep. CJ stared for a few minutes before he turned off the light. Maybe his head was fuzzier than he thought. He curled up against the wall and slept, though tonight, it wouldn't be quite the dreamless sleep he was hoping for.

"Milady! Milady!" the handmaiden yelled as she ran through the hallways of the castle toward her mistress's chamber.

Turning slowly, her long brown hair fell in cascades down her back. She was half dressed, her corset not tightened yet, and her hair still undone. She looked at her handmaiden's face and realized this was indeed something serious.

"Julie, whatever is wrong?" she asked gently, putting the brush down.

Julie heaved a couple of breaths and then spoke. "Milady, I'm so sorry, but it is...Jared..."

She turned around fully, her eyes alert and aware now. "What about Jared? Julie, what is it?"

Julie started wringing her hands. "Your Lord has taken him...to the block, Lady Farrah."

Before the sentence was even out of Julie's mouth, Farrah had started running to the town where the executioner's square was. Tears poured from her eyes. He had done nothing but fall in love with her when she was above his station. He did not deserve to die for her. Had she not agreed to marry Lord Delvin? Why would he kill Jared?

The posted guards yelled out as she ran from the castle. She ignored them, though there were many more voices added as the townsfolk watched her run through them in her corset and under-dressings. She didn't care. Her dark hair flew wildly about her paler face and her dark eyes streamed tears.

She ran full speed up the stairs to the platform. "Stop!" she screamed.

Everyone, including the hooded executioner who held his axe over her beloved's head, stopped and stared at her. Jared, with his hands tied behind his back and head on the block, let out a sigh of relief. He wasn't completely in the clear, but at least since she knew what was happening, he had a better chance of making it out alive.

"Farrah," he breathed. "Thank God."

She stood there, her hair a dark corona around her face. "Let him go," she pronounced.

The executioner stepped back a couple of feet and stared from his eye holes at her. She knew who was under the hood. Everybody knew. It was a joke that he even wore it. There was no hiding who he was. The reason behind disguising the executioner was to protect him, but where was this reason when he took so much pride in meting out the justice of the kingdom that everyone knew who he was? But faced with the Lord of the land's daughter, he was clueless as to what to do.

Jared sat up slowly and settled on his knees. "Untie him," she pronounced, and the executioner did just that.

Jared didn't take his eyes off her as he stood and ran to her. They embraced as tears poured down her face. He didn't know what to tell her. He had done nothing wrong. They had come for him during the night in his father's little shoemaker shop and dragged him out before Lord Delvin. Lord Delvin, Lady Farrah's betrothed husband, told him he was to be executed for interfering with the affairs of the kingdom, in other words, treason.

"So, my blushing bride, you could not stand by, could you?" a rumbling voice came from the crowd. Jared and Farrah turned to see Lord Delvin mounting the steps.

Farrah released the embrace and stood tall, facing him. "Delvin, there is no reason to execute him. Our wedding is set, and I have sworn off any contact with the shoemaker's son."

Delvin nodded slowly. "This is true, but the shoemaker's son, as you refer to him as, has something more valuable to me than all the king's gold, and it rightfully belongs to me."

"I have nothing!" Jared exclaimed, a horrified look crossing his face. "How dare you accuse me of having anything which belongs to you? I am no thief!"

Delvin turned, smiling. "Oh, but you are a thief. You are a thief of the worst kind. What you have stolen is not tangible, and not something I can simply take from you."

Delvin walked, his hands behind his back, around the perimeter of the platform. He didn't look directly at either of them, huddled together in the corner farthest from the point he entered the platform. He held to her with a grip born of love, something Delvin could never have. And now, he realized, even if Jared died, he would have nothing but her hatred. That left only one solution to the problem.

"You've stolen my lady's heart," he said, growing closer with each step. "There is nothing I can do to reclaim it while you live, and now I see you hold her heart in an inescapable grip, and not even death will separate it."

Farrah breathed a small sigh of relief. Delvin understood she could never love anyone but Jared. And even if he killed him and married her, there would be no love between them. It would be a matter of show. He stood before them now, his dark eyes staring into Farrah's. A moment passed, and something rose to the surface of her mind. His eyes...they weren't supposed to be that dark. Delvin's eyes were gray...

Suddenly, she felt a sharp, searing pain in her stomach. She looked down to see red blood blooming over her corset. She looked to Delvin's hand, holding a dagger. He smiled.

"I cannot separate you any other way. I will separate you both from your life."

Farrah dropped to her knees. Jared yelled something unintelligible and rolled out of the way of Delvin's strike. Delvin was a noble, not a fighter, but Jared was more than just a shoemaker's son. His vocation over the years had turned somewhat illicit. He made a dash for the dumbfounded executioner and snatched away his axe from a slack hand. He then ran at Delvin with a fury born of pure hatred.

Delvin turned and parried it with a long sword he carried on his hip. "You think you threaten me, boy?"

Jared circled around him. "I think I can separate you from your life quite easily."

Delvin laughed heartily. "You assume I play fair."

Jared felt a stinging sensation go off on several points in his back. He reached his hand behind him. Arrows, he thought madly, as he felt the wooden shafts. Searching his back, his hand came back bloody. Four archers perched atop the nearby buildings. He turned back to Delvin. He'd planned this. He knew Farrah would try to stop it. The axe fell heavily from his hand which could no longer bear the weight. He dropped to one knee, heaving slow breaths.

"You bastard," he whispered, wavering on his feet. "You never intended to marry Farrah and let me be."

Delvin walked slowly toward Jared, stopping and looking down on his kneeling form. "Of course not. Who do you think sent the girl to tell Farrah of your execution this morning? I knew all along her death would be the only satisfaction I would earn. Your death was inevitable."

Jared looked up suddenly, a grin splitting his bloodied face as crimson flowed from his mouth. His eyes were different, now...almost green.

"You too," he whispered and leaped to his feet and grasped Delvin's left shoulder, punching forward with his right fist. He fell to his hands and knees from the action.

Delvin was forced back a step and stared incredulously at the object protruding from his chest. It looked like some sort of dagger, but spring loaded somehow. He'd had it all the time, hidden inside the bracers he wore. The guards hadn't removed all his clothes, so they hadn't seen it. They were idiots. Delvin fell to his knees and had time to look upon Jared with gray eyes filled with shock before he fell dully to the planks.

Jared crawled toward Farrah, slowly, slowly. He finally reached her. She'd fallen to her back on the ground, her eyes staring at the sky. He dropped on her, one arm over her body and searched her face. Blood flecked her mouth, and she turned to look at him, smiling. Her mouth moved, but no sound issued, and her eyes turned dead. Jared felt the tears falling, but he could do nothing else as his own soul fled his body.

[Hideout - 11:00 PM]

Michael gasped and sat bolt upright in the small bed, his breath heavy and heaving. He ran his hands down his body, making certain there were no holes in it. Swallowing the cotton in his mouth, he stood up and headed into the small bathroom. He flipped on the fluorescent light as he pulled the door shut. His reflection stared at him from the mirror. His eyes were red and puffy. He didn't even know what time it was. The bastard hadn't even given them a clock. With no windows, it was impossible to guess the time. The only way they even knew the time was when Sheila brought them food. He rubbed his eyes. Dammit, his contacts were bothering him. He sighed, blinking.

He hoped they got out of here before it really bothered him because he couldn't see a damn thing without them.

He picked up the plastic cup and filled it with water. He sipped it, watching himself. Just what the hell was he supposed to do to get out of this place? It was already too long. What the hell did this guy want from them? Dammit all, he'd been a gamer for so many years, he had come out of so many role-playing situations, it all had to be good for something. He had to think. He had the skills necessary to figure this out. He knew a lot about getting out of tough situations, but he never had his life depend on it. Well, now it did. He put the plastic cup back and shut off the light. He opened the door and headed back to the bed.

In the bed next to him, CJ didn't speak, but his mind was filled with the faces of people long ago that he'd never heard of.

Chapter Five

The Board is Set

"Get up," Sheila announced.

Sheila stood over him, shaking him hard. "What?" he asked, snapping to full wakefulness.

"Now. You have ten minutes. Get him up, too. Joe's making the calls today," she said, her voice and eyes distant.

She turned away and headed out. Michael sat up and went to CJ's bed, shaking his shoulder to wake him. He looked up with groggy eyes.

"Hurry, we've got ten minutes before they get down here again to call our folks from the sound of it."

He headed into the bathroom so CJ could wake up. Michael splashed water on his face, rushing through his somewhat normal routine, before leaving to give CJ a chance. CJ also only took a few moments before he exited the bathroom. CJ took a moment and pulled his hair back up into a tail. Michael glanced over and froze, staring at the few inches of exposed tawny beige midriff. He averted his gaze. Why was he staring at his stomach right now? Now was not the time for such thoughts. When the door opened and Sheila appeared, he pushed those thoughts aside. She pulled two chairs from the table and sat them side by side.

"Sit," she instructed. Michael and CJ exchanged glances but did as she said.

She started tying them to the chairs. Michael glanced at her with a confused look, but her face was stoic. She obviously wasn't in the mood to talk about what was happening. She jerked the ropes tight across Michael's waist and belly, making him grunt. She then wrapped them around his ankles. She then did the same thing to CJ.

"Are you finished yet?" a familiar voice boomed from the open door.

Sheila blinked slowly and sighed. "Yeah, ready for you, dear," she called and headed up the stairs.

Joe descended. He wore a black T-shirt and a pair of dark jeans. His black hair was close cropped in a buzz cut, and his face was bright. Excitement shone through the stoic expression, and an uneasy weight settled in Michael's chest. He hadn't been this near his abductor since the night of his kidnapping. He held three pairs of handcuffs. Silently, he snapped a pair onto Michael's right wrist and then to the chair arm. Then he did the same to CJ's left arm. Lastly, he took a pair and handcuffed Michael's left wrist to CJ's right wrist. All along, he said nothing, nor showed any emotion.

"Is it ready?" he yelled.

"Yeah, got a good shot, foot to head. Do you want me to pull it back so you can stand behind them?" Sheila called from upstairs.

"Not yet. First, I'll talk into the camera without them in the shot. Then I want you to pan to them, then pull back when I walk around behind them. The scrambler is still connected?" he asked, frowning.

"I haven't touched anything, Joe. It's just like you left it."

"Good. Alright."

He yanked on the ropes Sheila had tied. "Watch it," Michael grunted as he felt them cinch against his stomach.

"Shut the hell up," Joe growled at him, turning his eyes on him. Michael realized how dark they were.

He then went to CJ and did the same, but Michael watched as his hands lingered around his stomach. He saw CJ's eyes following him. CJ swallowed hard. Joe didn't say anything, though, and then stepped in front of them.

"Alright. Initialize the connection," Joe demanded, and they heard a ringing sound.

After a couple of rings, the phone connected. CJ's ears heard the distinct sound of his mother's voice. "Hello?"

"Put on the speakerphone and the video feed, dear. It's the call you've been expecting," Joe said, a superior sound to his voice.

There was a loud clicking sound and they could hear talking over the phone. "We have visual," a strange voice said in the background.

"Hello dear friends," Joe said, voice dripping with sarcasm. "I suppose you're done sweating, at least enough for my tastes. I hope all the things you know I'm capable of have been touring your little brains. Oh, the fun I could have with these two little kids of yours. But that's beside the point."

"What do you want?" asked a voice CJ was unfamiliar with, but Michael knew well: his father.

Joe thought for a moment. "I want what I deserved to get a long time ago. I want money. Lots of it. And I know you can get it. So, I want two million in a Swiss bank account that I'll transmit the number of when the time is right. Then, I'm leaving the country, heading somewhere I can be left alone, without threat of being put into another hell hole."

There was a long silence. "That's not easy. You know that, Joe, it takes time..." Don answered with deathly calm.

"I know that, Don. I'm not fucking stupid. You've got the time you need. But while you're getting your ducks in a row,

I've got your sons. And I'm warning you now, make sure things move forward quickly," he answered, smiling.

There was a sound of muffled talking. "Let me see CJ!" came Mara's voice over the phone. "You son of a bitch, let me see him!"

"Mara, please," Don whispered.

"No!" she responded.

Joe walked around behind them. "She's right, Don. I will let you see them. I'm less likely to get my money if you think they've been killed."

Joe came around behind them, dropping a hand on each of their shoulders. On the phone, they could hear both their parents' voices in a flood of emotional outpouring.

"CJ! CJ are you alright? Has he hurt you?" Mara sobbed.

Joe squeezed his shoulder hard. "I'm fine, I want to go home," he stated, looking around for the camera which he spotted mounted to the wall. He wondered why he'd never noticed it there before.

"We're both fine," Michael said as Joe squeezed his shoulder hard as well. "How is Aileen?"

"She's okay, Michael, she's okay," his mom answered. He could hear her voice straining to stay calm. "She misses you."

"Now you've seen that they're fine. But I'm warning you, they won't be that way for long if you screw up," Joe said, squeezing hard on both of their shoulders. This time, neither one could hide the grimace that came to their faces.

"What the hell do you mean, Joe?" Randy asked, his voice heightened. "You said you'd give us time."

Joe smiled. "The money isn't the only thing, boys. If I find out you're nosing around where you shouldn't, the deal is forfeit. I will kill them and ship their bodies to you piece by piece. Only after I get done torturing them and recording it for your entertainment pleasure."

He then leaned over and grasped CJ by the face with his right hand and jerked it to the side.

"I'm not sure your son wants to be a little boy. He looks like a fag to me with his hair like this, Don. Maybe he needs someone to teach him how to be a man," he purred, stroking his hand up and down his thigh. "Or maybe he just needs to be treated like a bitch."

"You fucking bastard, I'll kill you if you lay a hand on him—" Don screamed, and they heard voices trying to calm him down and pulling him away. CJ could hear his father's muffled voice in the background. He tried to keep his breath calm despite what he was saying.

Randy's voice chimed in. "Joe, you bastard, don't do anything to them or you'll never get your money," he said tersely.

Joe stood up suddenly and smiled. "Don't worry. It won't come to that, as long as you don't do anything to piss me off. I know you already got the feds and cops involved, and they better back the fuck off. I better see you day after day working on my money. Believe me, I've got eyes all over town, and I know who you're seeing and where you're going. I've got surveillance in a hell of a lot of places you don't know about and can't even fathom. You won't find me, because I won't be found. I'll contact you in three days to see how things are progressing."

There was a click as the line was closed. He then walked up the stairs and left them to sit there. CJ and Michael weren't sure what to do. Soon enough, though, Sheila came down and started untying them. She unlocked the cuffs and took them with her. She didn't say a word the whole time. CJ and Michael got up and found a box of pop tarts sitting on the table. They guessed that was breakfast this morning...

Agent Richard Pearson sat at his desk, watching the security camera footage from the school. There was no mistaking the man on the tape. He was sure, even more so now, that the man on the tape and this Joe Jackson were the same individual. Of course, the images were grainy and long distance, but the body type matched the description given both at the Heights boy's kidnapping scene and what they had on file.

He stood up and went into the next room to lean over his tech agent.

"Anything?" Rich asked.

The young, blond-haired agent looked up at him with a sheepish grin. "I'm sorry, sir; I've not seen something like this in a long time. He's either got someone helping him or he knows a helluva lot about masking and bouncing..."

"Don't get into the techno-babble. Just put it in terms I can understand, kid."

Simon Davenport gave a superior smile, which said more than words ever could. "Okay, sir, it's like this. He knows how to hide. It's possible he learned these techniques from the military, but I'm just guessing here without the file on what he's been trained in. He's got access to some sort of tech I've never seen."

Rich nodded. "So, you're saying he knows how to make sure we can't find him?" The younger man nodded. "Can you trace him at all, Simon?"

Simon smiled, again a superior smile. "Of course, it just takes a lot of time to trace this back to the source. I can't tell you how long, boss, but I can try. And there may be unforeseen delays, too."

Rich cocked an eyebrow at the scrawny kid. He was relatively new to the department, but he was fantastic at what he did. "What do you mean?"

"Let's just say there are ways to cause me to trace the wrong direction, and if he used them, I'll have to do things several times to find the right source of the signal."

Rich inclined his head. "Do what you can, Simon."

He left the young agent with the resources of the department at his hands, hoping he could trace the signal back to where it came from. Until then, he'd have to rely on good old police work to make the difference. He headed to talk to Brandee Schneck, the head of their crime lab. He hoped she'd found something on the tape.

"Hi, Agent Pearson, what's up?" asked Brandee as he walked into the room.

"Have you got anything for me?" he asked, stepping behind her where she was working on the video from the morning before.

She shook her head. "As you know, I've been going through this since this morning. I haven't found much useful yet. The place is some sort of basement or interior room because, as you can see, there are no windows or areas of exterior light entering the room. There are some unusual features of the room, however..." she replied, moving the images frame by frame.

Rich leaned closer, keeping his face clear of the bushel of her red curls. "What have you found?"

She turned and winked one green eye at him. "Look at this," she pointed to the back wall. "I don't think this is a normal basement or building. I can't quite put my finger on it, but there's something different about this room. There are no traces of water, so it isn't a leaky basement like so many around here are. Also, if it were the interior of a building, it would be a wood construction. They've obviously left the constructed walls up, whatever they're made of, and haven't even bothered to paint over them. But it's not easy to figure out what it is from just a video of the room."

Rich sighed. "Do what you can," he said, squeezing her shoulder gently.

He headed off into the conference room, where Randy and Don were both waiting for him. After receiving the call at Don's house, both had come into St. Louis to wait and see if they could be of any assistance and if they found anything out.

"Got anything, Rich?" Randy asked as he entered.

He shook his head. "Simon is working the trace, and Brandee's still at work on the videotape from this morning. But so far, neither one of them has had anything substantial to report."

Randy nodded. "You know how good he is, Rich. And there's no telling what he learned in lock up. He was never supposed to get out of there. No one is. But that's the problem, because he was surrounded by some of the most notorious military offenders."

Rich poured a cup of coffee, dropping two spoons of sugar in and stirring it in slow circles. "How are you doing with this, Don?"

Don sighed. "I'm worried for CJ. He's in a lot of danger if he's already figured out he's not straight," he said. "I mean, it isn't something CJ's ever said, but a father knows these sorts of things. And I know how Joe feels about anyone like that. We saw it overseas."

"You did?" Rich asked.

"See, after Joe changed, but before he got our teammates killed, we were still taking our orders and doing what we were supposed to do, just like good little soldiers." Randy's face was suddenly devoid of all emotion. "Don was with him on a recon mission to an area we were going to set up camp in for a few days. It was supposed to be clear of all civilians. But it wasn't. Don heard screaming from one of the old houses, where Joe had gone into. Thinking the worst, he went running in, calling for help as he did. We headed in as quickly as we could.

"Don got there first, of course. He found Joe with this boy he'd found in the building. Apparently, he'd had a gun, and threatened him with it. He'd gotten the gun away from him, beating him pretty good in the process." Randy stopped, sipping his coffee for a second. "He said he 'looked at him funny' and was 'probably a fag' so he deserved it."

Don nodded beside Randy. "I tried to save the kid, but I couldn't. He went far beyond subduing someone with a gun."

Rich sighed. "The man's a monster."

Randy arched a brow and gave a curt nod. Finishing the coffee, he stared into the depths of the cup as though it were an ocean emptied. "But the thing is, he wasn't always like that. He changed, and when it happened, we never saw our friend again. He was someone none of us knew any longer."

Terri sat at the head of the table, sipping a cup of green tea. Across from her, Mara sipped a similarly steaming cup.

"So, we just wait?" Terri said with a lethargic tone.

Mara nodded. "It would seem. There really isn't anything else to do."

"Where are the guys now?" Terri asked, looking up.

"I sent them to pick up lunch, fast food. I didn't feel like cooking," she answered, looking up, her eyes red.

Allie and Alex came running into the room, chasing each other and laughing. Mara looked as they ran through the room and out and burst into tears. Terri stood and enclosed her arms around her old friend.

"Hey, you remember the night we met?" Terri asked as she sat back down again.

Mara sniffed. "Yeah. It was at the garden party thrown by Missy Truman."

"Remember the awful yellow sundress I wore?" She smiled.

"Oh yes," Mara told her, wiping her eyes. "I remember. I was in that hideous salmon colored apron dress," she said.

"And Missy wore that obnoxious green colored suit she thought so much of because her husband brought it back from overseas." Terri grinned. "She was so proud of that one."

Mara nodded. "Yeah, she was. I wonder what happened to her?"

"I heard Daryl died not long after we left the base," Terri said sadly. "She was pregnant at the time."

"At least our husbands came back," Mara added. "So many of them didn't."

They were silent for a while, listening as the twins laughed and played in the living room in front of the TV. "It's weird not having CJ here." Mara sighed. "He was always good with the babies."

Terri nodded. "Aileen is having trouble adjusting to Michael being gone."

Mara sipped her tea as the back door opened. Both women turned to see their husbands coming in with fast food. Alex and Allie came running into the kitchen squealing because they rarely get chicken nuggets from the fast-food place.

"Nuggets! Nuggets!" Alex yelled, jumping up and down.

"Calm down, Alex," Don scolded as he sat down everything on the kitchen table. "Just a second."

He quickly got the twins their food and sat them both down at the coffee table with their drinks. He came back as Randy was distributing the sodas. Neither of them commented on their red-eyed wives.

"We were talking about meeting each other at Missy's garden party," Terri said as she picked up the teacups to take to the sink.

Randy stopped as he unwrapped his hamburger. "Oh gosh, that was Daryl's wife, wasn't it?"

Don set down his soda and nodded. "Yeah, I remember them."

"Wonder whatever happened to her after Daryl died," Randy commented, taking a bite of his food.

Mara sighed, staring at her burger and fries. "I can't imagine losing your husband while pregnant."

"I'm sure she found her own way," Don assured, patting Mara on the back.

"What does Rich think?" Terri asked as she ate fries one at a time.

"He's still working on the tech aspect of things. He has someone working on the video feed from the call and someone trying to work on the trace, but you know he set things up to make it difficult to find him."

Mara picked at her burger. "I don't know why I was hoping for something different, knowing what he's capable of."

"I wonder how they're getting along with each other?" Terri said suddenly, looking between them. "I think Michael was four the last time they saw each other."

"What kind of things does Michael do?" Don asked, crumbling his wrapper and laying it on the table.

"He does this tabletop gaming thing, and he plays baseball for the school team," Randy said with a grin. "A pitcher. He's pretty good."

"Baseball?" Mara frowned. "Wasn't that what CJ was reading about the other day when he came home early? He even watched a game on TV."

Don looked over at her. "Come to think of it, you're right. He was watching baseball the other day. I thought he hated sports?"

"He usually does," Mara admitted. "Curious. Why would he suddenly start watching baseball?"

Randy and Don exchanged a look. "Wasn't he on South Campus when he was kidnapped too?" Terri asked. "Because Michael was there that day, he was practicing at the ball field."

"Come to think of it, why was CJ at South Campus? He doesn't have any classes there," Don asked. With everything that had gone on, he hadn't really thought about the fact CJ didn't even have classes at South Campus.

"You don't think...." Mara started. "Was he watching someone play?"

Don nodded. "He had to have been."

No one said anything, lost in their own thoughts. Mara and Terri didn't know how much hatred Joe had for anyone different from him.

"CJ, want to play a game?" Michael asked, sighing.

He snorted, turning over on the bed. "What do you mean? There's nothing here we can play a game with. We haven't even got playing cards."

Michael sat up quickly. "Don't need anything, my dear CJ." He tapped his head. "All you need to have a game is up here.

"Oh, you're talking about the whole role-playing thing," he said, nodding. "You have to have books, dice and all sorts of stuff for that."

Michael smiled. "I think we could come up with something to pass the time."

The door opened just then, and Sheila came down with a tray of food. Some chicken nuggets, fries and corn on the cob. It smelled delicious.

"Sheila, you are an awesome cook," Michael breathed as he came to the table.

She blushed. "You really think so? This is all just zap it stuff, you know."

"No, really Sheila. I know zap it stuff, and the stuff you fix at night is far from zap it stuff." Michael smiled.

CJ nodded, sitting down beside him. "Yeah, Sheila, you have a way with food."

She smiled at them. "I'm glad you like it. Makes me feel good to know I'm doing something right after all."

CJ and Michael exchanged glances. Sheila was sporting at least one new bruise today on her forearm. She was wearing jeans and a dark T-shirt, so they couldn't see much else. It was becoming increasingly obvious, though Joe abused more than just his helpless prisoners.

"Sheila, can I ask you something?" CJ asked quietly, sipping the glass of grape soda she'd brought him.

She looked at him. "Well, I guess so," she said. As the days passed, both noticed Sheila had become increasingly quieter.

"He hits you, doesn't he?" he asked.

Suddenly, Sheila's eyes flared, and her face tightened. "That's none of your damn business."

Sheila turned and left, heading back upstairs, but both CJ and Michael knew the answer to the question. Over the past few days, they'd both noted the changes. Neither of them understood what exactly was going on. But then, neither of them had ever dealt with an abused woman like Sheila before.

Sheila closed the door behind her quietly. She breathed deeply and sighed. Why could she not admit it? The part of her mind that understood the fact they were right screamed at her to just walk out the door, go to the police, and lead them back. That was the logical, easy part. But Sheila also knew what would happen if she did. The two of them would be lucky to survive the hours it took her to get there and return with help. Despite herself, they were growing on her. So young and innocent compared to her now. They hadn't seen the hard life she had, and now they were getting a taste of it. For nothing but Joe's perverse pleasure.

She cleaned the stove, clearing the pans as she wiped it up. Joe wasn't there; he was off on one of his "recon" missions to make sure things were going the way he wanted them to go. She walked into the small living room and stared out the window. Not another house in sight in either direction. Where would she go even if she left? She would have to drive to St. Louis before she found anyone she knew, and that was quite a drive. Who knew if she'd be safe, even there?

She could see the small barn building where her car was hidden. She could take them and go, she thought, but then shook her head. No. He'd find her and kill her, and no one could stop him. It was best she went along with his plan. She was having trouble swallowing his reasoning now, though. She was watching everything, and nothing made sense. Joe wasn't quite the victim he claimed to be, and these kids were the ones who were going to pay the price. He had no intention of letting them go. This was all a game to him. All of this was being played out according to his detailed plan. She glanced over at the table where his notebook was sitting. That was his planning book. One of the things she was forbidden from even touching. She picked it up slowly, ready to drop it, when she heard his key in the door. She ran her fingers over the smooth and worn green cover. It was just a cheap spiral-bound notebook from Wal-Mart, but still, what was inside...

She opened it to the first page of notes. It was all scribbled plans for the kidnappings. Then, several pages in, she found a neat, lined sheet with a timetable. The first four lines were crossed off, being already accomplished.

"~~Day 1—Kidnapping Kim~~.

"~~Day 2—Kidnapping Heights~~.

"~~Day 3 and 4—Waiting~~.

"~~Day 5—Ransoms.~~

"Day 6 and 7 – Waiting.

"Day 8 – check progress on money

"Day 9 or after – Have money wired to the account.

"Make arrangements to be picked up by helicopter, dump corpses from the helicopter, jet to Cambodia."

Sheila heard the key in the door, and she jumped, knocking the notebook to the floor. She quickly grabbed it to put it back on the coffee table.

"What are you doing?" his voice boomed from behind her. She turned around quickly.

"Nothing, Joe. I was resting and knocked your book off the table when I put my feet down," she told him, pushing the notebook back onto the table.

Joe stared at her for a second. "I told you not to touch any of that."

She sucked in a breath slowly. "I know, I'm sorry, I didn't mean to..."

Joe didn't say anything else. He didn't need to. As usual, he let his fists speak for him. She spent the next twenty minutes in the bathroom, trying not to throw up everything she'd eaten for lunch. She pulled down the med kit she had in the cabinet and studiously taped her ribs. From what she could tell, they were bruised, but she feared one was broken. Well, there wasn't much else she could do besides tape it. She reached into the box and dropped a couple of pills in her palm. She didn't need to be conscious for a few hours, at least not until dinner time. Adding Valium to the pain pill, she downed them with a glass of water. Stumbling, she made it to the bed and got under the cover before she passed out completely.

Chapter Six

Gameplay

"So, you're saying all we have to do is visualize these 'characters' and we interact with each other and 'play' things out vocally?" CJ said, sitting across the table from Michael.

He smiled. "Yeah, yeah, it's like acting, kinda. All the action takes place in your head. You become the character you're playing, and I'll run the game, so I'll be everyone else."

He thought about it. "You'll be everyone else?"

"Yeah, everyone you meet. I play the NPCs, or non-player characters. We'll start out really simple, come up with a background story for your character based on the setting I'll put you in. And the one I know the most about is this one called Scarred Lands. It's really cool and has a lot of cool things in it. They don't publish it any more, though, which makes me kinda sad, but that's how it goes, right?" he said, and CJ thought his face was going to split from the grin.

"Okay, okay, but it would be easier with some paper or something to write on," he admitted.

Michael nodded. "Maybe Sheila could get us some."

CJ arched a brow. "She was so helpful yesterday," he said coyly.

"Well," Michael began, but the door opened. Lunch time.

Neither one of them could avoid noticing the fact Sheila's face looked pale; she moved carefully as she navigated the stairs with the tray. She placed their plates in front of them with a grimace. It looked like cheeseburger helper and mixed veggies. And it smelled great.

"Are you okay, Sheila?" CJ asked quietly.

She stood up, holding the tray against her stomach, and smiled. "I'm fine. Do you guys need anything?"

Michael took a bite of the veggies and smiled. "This is awesome, I don't even like vegetables. But yeah, you think you could get us some paper and pens or something? We really don't have anything to do. Or some board games, cards, dice, anything...a TV and some DVDs would be great as well, but I know that's a tall order."

Sheila nodded. "I'll see what I can do."

She turned and walked away. CJ and Michael dove into their food, avoiding the subject that was foremost in their mind. She was in a lot of pain, and it was more than physical pain. But what could they do about it? She was the one in power over them.

They ate their lunch in silence, and CJ thought about this gaming thing. Maybe it would be fun, and something a little more interesting than talking about baseball. He was rather glad that so far, the subject of sports hadn't come up.

"Um, I didn't expect you to be into something like gaming," CJ said as they each sat on their beds. It was about the only place to relax in the basement, since there wasn't a couch or anything like that.

"What's that mean? We just met. How did you expect something?" Michael asked, turning over on the bed and staring at CJ.

CJ's face heated immediately. "Um, just that, I've heard of you, and I knew you were on the baseball team."

"Really? You've heard of me? Do you like baseball?" he asked, grinning again.

CJ bit his lip. "I'm not really into sports much, so I just know a little bit. I-I was watching practice the day I got kidnapped. That's why I was on South Campus."

"Why were you watching baseball players practice if you aren't into baseball?" Michael asked, confused by CJ's admission.

"Ah, well, you see, I just like to watch one person on the baseball team play," he whispered finally, face going completely red.

Michael looked at him for a moment. "Oh. Oh!" he exclaimed, finally getting what CJ was talking about. "So, you're like that?"

CJ nodded slowly. "That Joe guy knows already, and he's scary about it. He doesn't like me."

Michael nodded. "Yeah, noticed that. What he said about your hair and all that. I didn't want to bring it up, but I was wondering."

CJ flopped on his back and put an arm over his eyes. "If he knew the truth, I'd be in really deep trouble with him," he muttered.

"The truth?" Michael asked, getting up and coming to sit down on the side of CJ's bed. Michael reached over and pulled his arm off his eyes. "What's that mean?"

"Th-that he's right. I sometimes like girl things," he said slowly, not sure how Michael was going to take the admission. "Th-that I'm not only gay, I'm kinda confused about gender and might not quite be a guy, at least not all the way, if that makes sense."

Michael cocked his head to the side and looked at him for a minute. "Well, I mean, I've never known anyone like that, but it isn't like it's a bad thing. What does it matter anyway? You're who you are, no matter what you are."

CJ's breath was getting short from Michael's proximity. He was so close. "It was you," he blurted and then covered his face with both hands. His face was so hot he could feel it in his hands.

"Huh?" Michael asked, reaching for CJ's hands again, but this time he didn't let him move them.

"It was you. You're who I was watching at the baseball field."

When Michael didn't say anything, CJ didn't move, sure he would be revolted to know someone like him had been watching him. He probably thought he was a creep now. He felt his gentle touch on his hands, pulling on them to move them from his face. This time, he let him and stared at him, getting lost in the blue of his eyes.

"You're probably grossed out to know a guy has a crush on you," CJ mumbled finally.

Michael smiled and reached a hand out to cup CJ's face gently. CJ took a shaky breath and didn't move. "Why would I be grossed out?"

"B-because you have all the girls, and you said you couldn't keep a girlfriend because of gaming, and I just... You're straight, so why would you not be grossed out by it?"

Now Michael smirked. "Who said I was straight?"

CJ's face felt like it was on fire, and he knew Michael had to feel it where he was touching his face. "W-what?" he finally stammered.

"I never said that. You just assumed it," Michael commented softly, eyes staring into CJ's brown ones.

"B-but... the girls..." he whispered.

"The girls are nice. But I never said I was only interested in girls," Michael told him, and CJ thought his head was going to explode. He was bi?

There was something there between them, something almost tangible. It was heavy and pulled at their hearts in a way nothing had ever done so before. It was like a sense of déjà vu where Michael touched his face, as though there were something connecting them in a way neither of them understood.

CJ sat up suddenly, running a hand through his hair and pushing it back out of his face. "I can't wrap my head around this!" he exclaimed.

Michael looked at him. "You totally convinced yourself there was no way I could return your interest, huh?"

"Well, of course! The way the girls hang on you, what else could I have thought?!" he exclaimed, looking over at Michael sharply.

"I'm used to it. Those girls never work out. Like I said, they have an issue with my gaming habit. They're fine with the baseball, in fact, they love the baseball part. But when they find out what else I do in my spare time, they run for the hills. Never have gotten one to stay and play with us. Never had anyone interested in learning about it. Until now," he told CJ, sliding a hand over and putting it on CJ's where it lay on the bed.

CJ just stared at his hand for a minute, unsure of what to do. Michael Heights was touching him. After months of watching him from afar, he was actually touching him. And he wasn't put off by the fact he liked him at all like he thought he would be. He twisted his hand around and intertwined his fingers with Michael, breath still quick in his chest.

"I want to learn about what you're interested in. I want—" CJ was interrupted by the sound of the door opening. Both turned to look, CJ snatching his hand back, afraid it might be Joe.

To their relief, it was Sheila carrying a small box. She brought it in and sat it on the table. Both Michael and CJ got up to see what was in it. CJ had a moment of dizziness he was getting used to now. He looked to see some spiral notebooks, a box of colored pencils, some playing cards, and a couple of loose pens.

"This is all I could find," Sheila told them.

Michael picked up a spiral and smiled. "This will be just fine. I think I can keep us busy with this for a while," he said, opening the notebook and fanning the pages.

Sheila nodded. "Okay. Just don't make too much noise. Joe doesn't like to be reminded you're here." She turned and walked back up the stairs, leaving them alone.

Michael picked up a pen and sat down at the table. "Here, I'll show you how you draw up a character sheet," he said.

CJ nodded, taking the chair and moving it over beside him. If he was a little closer than necessary, Michael didn't say anything about it.

Mara answered the door mechanically. It had been another day with no news. Every time the phone rang, her heart hammered in her chest; every time the doorbell rang, she rushed to answer it. The disappointment when she answered the phone or opened the door was almost too much to bear. They hadn't been found; they weren't okay. And every morning when she opened her eyes to the light filtering into the bedroom, she hoped it was a nightmare.

It wasn't.

It was wishful thinking.

"Jeena," she said, smiling at CJ's friend.

"Ms. Kim," she answered, bowing slightly. "I came to see if there had been any word yet?"

Mara ushered the girl in. She was the same age as CJ, and as long as they'd lived here, the two had been inseparable. Then again, there were few of Korean heritage in the town, so it made sense they would become fast friends. They were of common roots, and there were not a lot of diverse individuals here. It had been a difficult adjustment for her as well as CJ when they first moved to St. Peters.

"I'm sorry, Jeena, but there hasn't been anything since yesterday."

She nodded and walked to the kitchen. "Let me take care of the dishes for you, Ms. Kim. I know it's tough right now."

"You don't have to..." she began.

"Nonsense, it's the least I can do. And I can be here in case you get a call. I'll fix dinner if you don't mind my cooking."

Mara considered arguing but then sighed. "It's just fine, Jeena."

She headed to the living room and sat down. Other than the clinking of dishes, it was quiet. Don had taken Alex and Allie to the park. They had to get out of the house for a while; they were getting all wound up. With the kids gone, Mara had nothing but her detrimental thoughts.

Her eyes fell on CJ's phone. It had been returned from the crime scene. She picked it up and turned it over. It still had some battery left. She opened it, and it asked for a PIN. She smiled, typing in "72499". He always used his birthday as a PIN, which was a horrible habit. She wondered what he'd been taking pictures of lately. She opened the gallery and saw there were an awful lot of photos that looked like they were taken at the same place. She frowned, opening them up and scrolling through to see if she could figure out what he was taking pictures of. It was of a baseball field, she realized. So, he was going to watch someone play baseball. She realized there were a lot of photos of one player, though. A blond boy who was the pitcher. Wait, she thought. Wasn't Michael the pitcher for the team? Was that him? She reached over and grabbed one of the file folders Pearson had left behind. She opened it to find the two pictures clipped to the top. CJ and Michael's senior pictures.

She looked at the blond in the shots CJ had taken and thought it could be the same person. What were the chances CJ had already known Michael? Did he remember from when they were little? There was no way he could remember that. It was just not possible. Right? But how could she explain this connection?

Laying down CJ's phone, she wondered exactly how something like this could possibly happen. Was it all just chance and coincidence?

Their move to St. Peters had been partially motivated by knowing Terri and Randy were living near St. Louis. Even though they'd been separated by Randy and Don's assignments, Mara had kept email contact with Terri. It wasn't like they talked every day, but now and then, they would email each other. Mara knew Don and Randy had also kept in loose contact similarly. So, it was no surprise they were near each other when they moved to the area. They maintained their contact through the internet, mostly just mundane things like sharing recipes or asking how each other's kids were, but nothing specific. With Don and Randy's military past, neither woman would reveal too much information in a forum like email.

They'd talked about meeting and introducing their kids to each other, but the timing was never right, and they didn't have a chance. Mara knew Michael had gone to UMSL like CJ did, but it was the most likely school for kids in the area to end up at. CJ had briefly considered Lindenwood, but the cost was too high for him. He could have gone there but opted for the cheaper state school instead.

"I'm done with the dishes, Ms. Kim," Jeena said as she came out of the kitchen.

"Jeena, did CJ ever mention being interested in someone?" she asked, looking at her seriously.

Jeena's face changed, and she looked like she didn't know if she was supposed to answer that or not. Mara smiled gently. "I thought so. The boy on the baseball team."

"How do you know about that?" Jeena asked suddenly. Then she covered her mouth with both hands. "I shouldn't have said that."

"It's okay. I kind of finally put two and two together and came up with what he was doing. He's got pictures of a baseball player on his phone, and he's apparently been hanging out at South Campus. That's where he was when he was taken," Mara confided.

"He was afraid you'd be disappointed in him," she sighed. "I told him I thought you and his dad would be okay with it, the whole him being gay thing."

Mara was quiet for a second. "I'm sad he thought I'd be disappointed in him for being his true self. But I understand the fear. How long has he been interested in this boy?" she asked. She left off her suspicion that she knew who it was specifically.

Jeena shrugged. "I don't know for sure, but at least this year I know he's been going over to South Campus to catch them practicing when he can." She paused and gave Mara a slight smile. "He's always been afraid to approach him, though, no matter how much I encourage him to do so. He's convinced he's straight and would get angry if he said anything to him."

"Thank you," Mara said, standing up and hugging Jeena tightly. "For everything."

Aileen picked at the food on her plate. Mr. Jameson didn't say anything; in fact, no one said anything. Aileen was spending the night with Kay. She thought maybe it would take her mind off Michael. Instead, she thought about him more. Aileen barely noticed when the Jameson family started talking.

"Kay, how was school today?" her mother asked.

Kay smiled. "Great, since it's the end of the year. Getting things wrapped up. It's weird though since Aileen isn't in class."

Kay's brother, younger by six years, piped up. "It's funny to hear everyone talk about you, Aileen!"

"Hush, Eddie," his mother chided.

Aileen smirked. "It's okay; I'm used to it by now. You mind if I head up to Kay's room? I'm not very hungry."

"Go ahead, dear, if you get hungry later, there's plenty in the pantry and fridge," Kay's mom said gently.

Eddie watched her leave and frowned at his mother. "But Moooom, you told me if I didn't eat dinner, I couldn't have no snacks."

"Any snacks, Eddie, and yes, I did. And that's the rule in this house. Aileen is in a lot of pain right now," his father told him.

Eddie made a face. "She's no hurt anywhere. Why's she so special?"

"Honey, it's complicated. But her pain is on the inside. She misses her brother, and is afraid he won't come back alive," his mother said, pushing back her own plate.

Eddie nodded and looked at his mom, his face extremely serious. "Well, how else would he come back? The only way he can come back is alive..."

His mom took a breath to explain things but stopped, letting it out slowly, because he was, of course, right. If he wasn't alive, he wouldn't come back at all, and that's what they all feared more than anything.

The sands blew into his face, searing his skin with their force. A sandstorm was blowing in. He would have to find shelter soon, or he'd be buried alive in the moving sands of the desert. But he couldn't stop. There was no way he could stop. Ahead, he saw a building, a shoddy building, but a building, nonetheless. He trudged through the sand. His mount had died days ago; he'd ridden it to death. It was no matter. He had to get to her before he made her his fourth wife. He would not allow it. He loved her beyond all else. But he was confident Allah would not allow him to have her.

He waited out the storm in the shoddy structure. When it was done, he continued. If he was right, he should be close to his destination. It didn't take long for the buildings to appear in the distance. He trudged on. The tents were pitched on the outer edge of the area and the sturdier structures toward the middle, where he would find him, and her.

People tried to stop and ask him if he needed aid. He said nothing, only plodded toward where he would find them. He knew he'd wait for him. Finally, he threw back the flap on the largest, most elaborate tent in the place. Several women sat, veiled and covered, and he sat among them.

"Haidar. I had heard the Lion was among us," he said with a smile.

"Jamila is mine in Allah's name. How dare you take her from me, Khalid," Haidar said, stepping forward menacingly.

Khalid stood. "Come forward, my beauties."

Five women stepped forward slowly, their covered heads down. Khalid opened his arms. "Choose your woman. Choose Jamila, and I'll let you ride off into the desert sunset together. Choose my daughter, and I will allow you to leave with her. Choose one of my wives, and I will kill you."

Haidar caught his breath. He could not tell which one was Jamila. They were nothing but covered figures. "I cannot tell anything save their shape. At least give me their eyes."

Khalid turned and looked upon the five women. He nodded and motioned for them to lift their heads. Haidar's heart nearly stopped. Their eyes were similar. Apparently, he chose his wives with similar features. This was going to be more difficult than he thought. He looked at the third woman.

"That is your first wife, the third in the row," he said.

Khalid smiled and dismissed her from the tent. She bowed and left. Haidar stared at the eyes. How would he choose his love? It was impossible. The first woman had been old, he could tell easily. Now it would get more difficult. The second, she had eyes too large for Jamila. Much too large, and wrinkles belied an age above Jamila's. He nodded at her. Khalid dismissed her as well.

"You do well, choosing my second wife next," Khalid said, obviously quite amused by this little game he had invented to play with Haidar.

One more woman stood between him and his life. The third wife, younger than the others, would be harder to distinguish by age. Haidar stared back and forth between the three remaining sets of eyes. He pointed at the last one. Khalid smiled and dismissed her.

"Correctly, you have chosen to dismiss my three wives. You are left with my daughter, In'am, and your precious Jamila. Now, choose your lover," Khalid said with a superior tone. "You see, I win either way. My daughter is married to you, and I forged an alliance with you. And if you choose Jamila, I have had my time with her already, and she is worth nothing to you."

One of the women closed her eyes, and when they opened again, Haidar swore they appeared to be brilliant blue for a second. He swallowed. That was her, his Jamila. But if she had been spoiled already, he could not marry her, and there would be no hope for them. He stared at the eyes of In'am, so similar to Jamila's own eyes. It did not matter. He would have Jamila. He motioned to In'am to leave, and she did so slowly. Khalid's face showed his displeasure.

"Take your whore," he said sourly, throwing her at him.

Haidar caught her in his arms, feeling her warm body against him. But then, she suddenly sucked in a harsh breath. He looked up at her eyes, tears squeezing from the corner of her eyes.

She whispered softly, "I am no whore; I am for you alone, my love."

"Jamila?" he whispered, his hands so warm...warm and wet.

He raised one hand over her back and saw the velvet coating of scarlet dripping from his fingers. He looked up at Khalid, who stood, his eyes satisfied. Haidar quickly passed his hand down her back and found the dagger's hilt. She slumped slowly in his arms, her life fleeing her body. He frowned. His Jamila...the lion would follow her.

"Why?" he moaned, lowering her lifeless form to the ground at his feet.

Khalid snorted, hefting another throwing dagger. In one smooth move, he tossed it at Haidar. Haidar ducked the first one, but the second buried itself in his right shoulder. He grunted but lunged forward. He avoided another of the deadly implements, but a second planted itself deep in his upper thigh. A wash of warmth flooded down his left leg. Dizziness overtook him, and he stopped for a second to collect himself. He stared at the smug Khalid.

"Just die, Lion. Just die. I've won. I've taken your woman, and now I've taken your life," he said in a haughty tone. "I will lay claim to your land, claiming victory in combat against you, and everything works in my favor."

Haidar knew he could stand no longer. He fell to his knees. But as he did, he saw motion behind his nemesis. Black clothes and a veiled face.

"What?" Khalid said and turned to see his daughter's face.

Haidar smiled to himself as he fell onto his hands, the blood pooling around him. He knew he was bleeding to death. In'am was indeed her father's daughter, Haidar thought as the gurgling sound of Khalid's dying filled his ears. He felt someone over him as the daughter of Khalid slowly pushed the killing dagger into Haidar's hand. She leaned over and whispered in his ear.

"The Lion has won the day, and Khalid has died in shame because he murdered your wife...go to Allah's grace, great Lion, your name will be spoken with honor, while Khalid's will be spat upon."

She leaned over and kissed him gently on the cheek. "Jamila was your first wife, and now I claim the part of second wife and lay claim to your lands."

He turned slowly and saw the eyes of Jamila, dead and flat, staring into his own. Only death would bring them closer. It was Allah's wish...

Michael awoke with a start, blinking rapidly. His breath was fast and heavy in his throat. Good God, he thought. These dreams were getting more and more intense. He didn't even know what they meant; he only knew they left him feeling as though he'd run a marathon. There was a theme, though, that ran through all these dreams, and that was his and the other person's death. Whether he was a man or a woman (and he'd been both in his dreams), they always died. And it was always at the hand of the same person. That same, dark-eyed man that caused their death. He swallowed, calming his heart.

He turned his head to see CJ staring at him, his eyes wide and brilliant blue in the dim light. That color, that blue... It was gone as quickly as he'd seen it. His eyes were their normal honey brown color.

"CJ?" he asked hesitantly. "Do you..."

"Dream?" he finished.

Michael didn't say anything for a bit. CJ's eyes answered for him. "Yeah. Me too."

CJ was quiet for a time. It was like he was contemplating how to say what he was about to say, as though it were extremely important. "It's not just my imagination, I know that now. I've always dreamed other lives, you know, but since I've been here with you, it...it's different somehow. More real, more...I don't know. More."

"Yeah… I just always chalked it up to my gaming habit, the reason I dreamed up these weird people and places…" he whispered. "They're just so vivid though, and I remember every detail."

CJ smiled at him. "And I just assumed it was my overactive imagination and my love of writing…but it isn't, is it, Michael?"

Michael shook his head. "I…I don't think so, CJ, I really don't."

"You dream of them, don't you?" CJ continued.

"Them? You mean the goddess and god that started it all?" Michael assumed that's what he meant. If they were dreaming the same thing, surely he meant that.

"Brishna and Krineshaw," CJ whispered in the dark.

Michael's heart clenched, and he didn't know what to say. How would CJ know those names? How would anyone know them if they were a product of his imagination? No, something more was happening, something beyond them. He just didn't know what to do about it. He didn't know what to say for the longest time.

"And Iman."

Again, silence descended on them. Iman. The one that destroyed them every time they came to life. The one that was in the way. The one that separated them out of envy and hatred. The one that wanted Brishna as his lover, despite her constant refusal. The one that didn't want them to be together.

"It's weird," CJ continued. "In my dreams, I love so totally and completely that I don't mind dying if there is a chance I can be with my love again."

"Death doesn't end us," Michael muttered, almost to himself. "Death brings us back together again."

CJ seemed to have heard him though, because he stared for a moment. "Do you think this is possible? That we're the people in our dreams?"

"Anything's possible, I guess," Michael said, thinking. "But don't tell anyone else. We'll end up in a psych ward."

He was in psychology, after all. None of this would be looked on kindly by anyone else. He was supposed to be an atheist, yet here he was thinking he was possibly the reincarnation of a god?

The night encroached on and covered them in silence as they lay there under the dim light emanating from the small fish light in the bathroom. Michael had forgotten to shut the door, as usual. But there was something comforting in its soft orange glow.

Chapter Seven

The Queen and the Knight

"Okay, I don't know if I'm doing this right or not," CJ said as he stared at the paper. The statistics and things looked similar to what he'd seen in his dad's old stuff, but it was different, too.

"Look, since we don't have dice or other players, we just have to do the role-playing portion, not the combat stuff. When we get out of here, I'll teach you how to do the rest. But the most important thing is to role-play properly. The mechanics and all the crunchy stuff can wait," Michael assured as he sat across the table from him.

CJ tilted his head to the side. "Crunchy stuff?"

"Um, the bits like rolling dice and stuff like that. Mechanics, you know. The actual numbers and what they mean. Everything else is fluff." He grinned, pointing to the numbers on the sheet he'd written. "Now, tell me about the character you came up with."

"Ah, okay. But this is kind of embarrassing. Maybe I should change it..." he muttered, wondering whether he should pursue his idea.

Michael shook his head. "Nah, just go with what you got! I'm sure it will be cool."

CJ was more nervous about this than he wanted to admit. "Oh, okay. Well, her name is Serna. And she's a wood elf. Her mother was a ranger—that's the one with the bows, right?"

"You got it. Go on," he encouraged him with a smile.

"Alright, ah, let's see. She's got copper-colored hair and bright green eyes. She wears her hair shaved on the sides and long in the middle." He motioned with his hands as he spoke, showing on his own head where the shaving was. She's tall and muscular but not bulky. She's really good at acrobatics as well as anything that takes dexterity—that was the stat, right?"

"You're doing fine. You're catching on really fast," Michael assured him. "Now, tell me what she wants to do?"

"I don't know?" he said tentatively, staring at the paper and then looking up at Michael.

"Well, I can't tell you. Serna is your character. So, it's up to you. Is she a good person? Or is she free-spirited? And what makes her tick?" Michael put his chin on his hands on the table and watched CJ as he figured things out in his head.

CJ sat for a moment and thought about it. "Well, she's a good person, but she doesn't like unfair rules, so she won't tolerate them. She wants to help others, and she knows good people exist in the world, sometimes the good has to be discovered in people. Um, I guess she's into guys..."

"She can be into whatever you want her to be into," Michael said with a slight smile. "Do you want her to be into something besides guys?"

He thought for a minute. "No, I think she's into guys."

Michael looked at him for a minute. "Are you just into guys?"

CJ immediately flushed red and covered his face. "I dunno," he mumbled behind his hands. "I think so."

"You know, you're cute the way you blush so easily," Michael commented, reaching over and pulling his hands off his face.

Now, CJ really felt his face heat. He just stared at Michael for a minute. "Um, about the game..."

Michael smirked. "Yeah, the game," he whispered, looking down at the notes he'd been taking.

"So, you tell me where I am, right?" CJ asked, trying to get his face to cool.

"Yeah, you're gonna start out in a place called Savan at a tavern and inn called The Rested Wench," he explained as he drew on a piece of paper a rough map. "It looks kinda like this. It's pretty small, and you've just come into town. You've got 100 gold pieces on you."

"Did you make all that up?" CJ wondered as he watched Michael sketch out the town.

"Actually, no, an old DM, er, Dungeon Master, of mine came up with the town and tavern. I think it's cool and a neat place to start off characters. It's a small town and lots of interesting NPCs. Of course, my NPCs aren't the same as his NPCs. But that's okay. See, here I'll keep track of the people I make for you to meet." Michael showed CJ another piece of paper with small characters drawn up in the space.

CJ nodded and looked at his paper again. "Okay, I think I understand. So, now I just...do what?"

"Up to you. You're in the town and can do whatever you want. You see the inn I mentioned, a blacksmith, a general store, and a few nicer houses. Whatever you want to do," Michael told him with a grin.

"Alright, I guess I'll go to the inn. I'll need somewhere to sleep tonight, right?"

"Sure. When you get inside, you see it's pretty empty besides a few patrons. A man in the corner with a hood looking like a wannabe Strider and a dwarf sitting at the bar in full plate armor drinking an ale." Michael pointed to each point on the map as he spoke.

"Uh, okay. I guess I'll go up to the bar, then," CJ said as he nervously twisted his fingers. He had no idea if what he was doing was right or not.

Michael smiled encouragingly again. "Okay, a woman comes up and asks you, 'What'll it be?'"

CJ froze for a second, not sure what to say. He looked a little like a trapped animal at the question. Michael just continued instead.

"She says, 'Are you gonna stay the night or you just want a drink?' She's wearing an apron and cleaning a glass with a rag."

"I tell her, um, that I want to stay the night, and I'll take a drink. Some wine?" CJ asked without being too sure if it was the right way to answer the question.

Michael nodded. "You got it. You're doing fine." He winked at him. The action caused another blush to rise to CJ's cheeks. "The woman nods to you, then turns around and gets a glass. She fills it with red wine and sits it in front of you. 'That'll be 2 silver for the wine, and a gold for the bed.'"

"Oh, okay, I'll give it to her," CJ told him with a nod, feeling a little surer of himself.

"She takes it and turns back to the dwarf who is asking for another ale. You notice the man with the hood keeps watching you." Michael pointed to the position on the map of the tavern again.

CJ wondered if he was supposed to do something about this person. Michael had mentioned him twice, so was he important? Or was he just someone in the background? "I glance over at him and try to ignore him after that. Is he doing anything else?"

"Just watching you. You wear leather armor and carry a bow strapped to your back. And you notice no one else in here has a weapon," Michael explained. "And—"

The door came open, and they both looked up to see Sheila coming down with the lunch tray. She didn't look too bad today, so that was good. They really didn't like the fact that this Joe apparently hit her too.

"Sheila, do you know what's happening out there?" Michael asked as he picked up one of the ham sandwiches off the tray.

She shook her head, hair loose about her face today. "No, I'm in the dark, too. I only know what little he tells me. And that's not much," she explained, handing the other sandwich over to CJ.

"How long do we have to wait?" CJ wondered, taking a slow bite of the food.

Sheila shrugged. "I'm not sure. He said three days from when he called your parents. So, I hope they have what he wants by then, or he might do something bad. He—" She stopped abruptly and swallowed. "I don't know," she said finally and turned to leave the room.

CJ and Michael watched her go, again wondering if there was a way to reach her. CJ could tell she wanted to help them. He just knew it. Deep down inside, she hated what she was doing. But CJ was a lot like the character he was playing for Michael. He believed there was good in everyone, except maybe Joe. He was thoroughly evil.

"I wonder what her story is," Michael said as he ate, careful to keep the food off his papers.

CJ shook his head. "I doubt we'll ever know. Do you think they'll really get the money for him like he wants?"

"They'll try. My father's a private eye, so I don't think they're going to have access to much money." Michael sighed.

"Mine's a doctor, but that is a lot of money even though we're well off," CJ admitted, chewing thoughtfully on his lip for a minute.

"Yeah, it's a lot of money, that's for sure," Michael agreed.

"Our fathers know each other, apparently," CJ said, picking at the potato chips on the plate. "It had to be from when my dad was in the military. Was your dad in the military too?"

"Yeah," Michael sighed. "He never likes to talk about it. He doesn't like to be reminded of it, even on Veteran's Day or something. He'd rather forget."

CJ looked at Michael and felt that same tug at his heart. All he wanted to do was put his arms around him. The sensation of Michael being familiar was stuck with him still. He knew it was because of the dreams.

"Are you always a guy in your dreams?" CJ asked suddenly, changing the subject entirely.

Michael looked at him for a second. "Ah, well, not all the time. I've dreamed of being a woman before. What about you?" he asked, shifting. "It was weird being a woman."

"Sometimes I wonder if that's why I'm like I am, because of the dreams. I'm usually a woman in them," CJ admitted with a sigh. "I couldn't just be normal."

"You're normal." Michael frowned. "There's nothing wrong with the way you are now," he said and pushed the plate back on the table. "There's no reason you should feel bad for being yourself."

CJ looked up at him with tearful eyes. "You don't think there's something wrong with me?"

"Why would there be something wrong with you?" Michael asked as he got up and moved to sit beside CJ. "There's not a thing wrong with you."

He felt the tears before he could stop them. He sniffed and wiped his eyes slowly. "I don't know. I just feel like I'm different from everyone else, and the only explanation I have is the dreams. Like the one where I'm a priestess and there's this sacrifice going on—"

"And there's someone there, a guy that's been watching from the shadows," Michael whispered with a bit of awe in his voice.

"Wait, that's exactly the dream," CJ said with a frown. "How can we both have the same dream?"

"Well, what else do you dream about?" Michael asked, putting an arm around CJ's shoulders.

He thought for a moment. "Um, there's one that's like in a desert, and one where there's some kind of execution, and one where there's this man chasing me, and more...it doesn't matter what is going on, I always die and the person I love dies with me."

Michael was silent for a minute. "Wow, that's what I dream, basically. Every time, I'm dying somehow horribly, and there's always someone that is there every time. And he's always trying to kill me and the other person in the dream, and he always does it."

"But it doesn't feel like a regular dream. I can remember it just fine when I wake up. And they always repeat, exactly the same. If they were real dreams, they'd change some, but they don't change at all," CJ said, wiping a stray tear away from his eye. He felt comforted with Michael so close. There was something right about it, and he couldn't identify why it would feel this way. He just didn't want him to move for a long time.

"It's weird. When I met you, I felt like I knew you already," Michael murmured, turning and nuzzling a little at CJ's hair along his neck.

A shiver went through CJ. "I feel that way, too," he answered, not sure what to do with Michael touching him like this. His heart was beating fast, though. "Like I've known you for my whole life."

"Well, you were spying on me," Michael said, moving his arm, reaching out and pushing CJ's hair back over his shoulder. "I'm flattered, you know, to have caught your attention so readily."

"You always looked good in your uniform," CJ admitted, blushing again as he trembled a little. He could feel Michael's breath on his neck.

Michael smirked and leaned in to kiss at the side of his neck gently. CJ practically came undone right then, so he stood up quickly.

"Game. We should play a game."

Michael looked at him, a little confused. "Uh, yeah, sure. You want to continue what we were doing or play some cards?"

"Cards, cards are good," he said, a little breathless still.

Michael retrieved the cards and sat back down, glancing at CJ. CJ's heart was in his throat as his face morphed into the ones from his dreams. Were they more than dreams?

Tears could not describe her grief. So close, yet unable to touch. So near, yet unable to speak. An eternity of separation had only let her longing grow. It had been her own hubris which had put her in this place, locked away in a mortal coil that was never ending. Every time, every single time, they were torn apart before the curse could be sundered. He constantly foiled their love, and she constantly refused to bend to his will. She would have her one and only love, her Krineshaw. And Iman would not be granted the satisfaction of taking her willingly. If only their souls could touch, the curse could end...

All of this would end if she bent to Iman's will. The cosmos would be hers again, but to do that would betray everything she had ever been. And Krineshaw would be doomed to an eternity of mortality with no hope of redemption.

All you have to do is accept my offer, Brishna, the voice whispered. *Accept me and abandon your dear Krineshaw to a fate of mortality and this will end. The cosmos will be yours to inhabit, and you will only answer to me. You will no longer suffer, and neither will Krineshaw. Once he is mortal, he will forget, and no more will you be in pain, and no more will he be in pain.*

The offer tempted her as always. He made her the offer each time. But each time she refused, and when she did, the mortal life would end, and she would be spiraled into a new life, the mortals around her dying. But she would not give up her consort. She refused to do so. She would not bend to Iman. She would fight him until time itself ended.

No.

Somewhere inside herself, she knew the offer would bring no peace. It would only bring greater pain to herself, to Krineshaw, and most of all to the mortals. They died with and around her, it was true, but if Iman were given power, it was untold what he would do with it. She could not allow it. Not only for herself, or for Krineshaw, but for the mortals in the world. No, she could not do it. It was not selfish, it was not...

You know the consequence. I am the one in power over you, as always. I will make certain you suffer, and the mortals will also suffer because of your selfishness. One day, for their sake, I hope you tire of this game.

There was silence, and in that silence, Brishna wept tears of longing.

Rich wasn't sure what direction to take things. He had no new information, and everything was unsure. So far as they knew, Jackson was in the area somewhere close enough to get to by vehicle. That narrowed the search parameters down significantly, but still not enough to be sure of finding him. Since he claimed to be watching them, the FBI had taken a covert approach to anything to do with the case. The Kims and the Heights put together enough money despite the FBI telling them not to do so. They were sure if they failed to follow through, their kids were dead. Rich was sure those kids were dead no matter what they did unless they found them and freed them.

"Sir, Randy Heights and Don Kim are here to see you," the receptionist called from the doorway.

"Can you send them down?" he asked, leaning back in his seat, wondering what they would be thinking this time.

A few seconds later, the two disheveled-looking men came into the office and took a seat across from him. Rich didn't say anything; he just turned and poured a cup of coffee for each of them and sat it down in front of them.

"How are you today?" he asked as he sat back down at his desk.

"It would be better if we knew more," Randy said, stirring his coffee with the stir stick and taking the sugar offered.

"I've got my best people on the video feed he sent us." Rich reached over and picked up a file with printouts of various stills they had captured from the video. He pushed it across the desk.

Don put the coffee down and picked it up, going through the images with a grimace on his face now and then. Rich couldn't blame him. Seeing his kid in this situation had to be difficult. He knew not much else could be done yet, but he still felt like he should try and do more. He didn't know what or how.

"He's hiding close by, I bet," Randy mentioned, taking the stills from Don. "He wouldn't be far away from us."

"But he had to have found someplace out of the way," Don added, picking up his coffee. "But there's so much open area in and around St. Louis, it's hard to figure out where he might be."

"We know he's within driving distance, but that could be as much as six or seven hours away, depending on where he's located. He could be in mid-Missouri, or even in Illinois for that matter," Rich pointed out, sighing.

Randy put the folder back down on the desk and picked up his own cup of coffee. "I don't think he's that far away."

"What makes you say that?" Rich asked, frowning a little.

"Just knowing him, he wouldn't put that much distance between him and a major city," Randy continued. "He wants money and a way to get away with that money. The chances of that increase in the city."

Don let out a long sigh, downing his cup of coffee and setting the cup down gently. "I don't think it's about the money."

"What makes you say that?" Rich asked, wondering what was on Don's mind now.

"This is about revenge, pure and simple. The money is an excuse to string us along and possibly give him an exit strategy. I honestly don't think he intends to return those boys at all. I think he's planning to kill both of them when this is over," Don said slowly, without emotion on his face.

Randy turned toward him. "But why all the show? Why the video feed and promising to release them if we cooperate?" He was surprised at his willingness to see things as they really were.

"It's a game to him, that's what I think," Don explained. "He's playing a game with us and using our kids as pieces in this game. We're nothing but pawns to him in this."

Randy didn't say anything for a minute. "I don't want to admit it, but I think Don's right. I don't think he has any intention of returning them. He's keeping them alive long enough to further his game. If we give him his money, he'll kill them. If we don't get his money, he'll kill them."

"We're left with one choice: find them." Rich stood up from the desk. "I'll double the efforts of our people on getting a trace. We have until he calls tomorrow. What have you two decided in regard to the money he's asked for?"

Don shook his head. "Stall for time. That's all we can do. It's our best shot to make sure CJ and Michael get out of this alive. Maybe not unharmed, but alive."

"Will he buy it if you stall him?" Rich asked, frowning.

"We'll have to hope," Don responded, leaning back in the chair. "We have to put him off and say we couldn't get that kind of money yet. Somehow, we have to make him believe it. I don't know for sure how to do that, though," he said sadly.

A long silence spread between them. Rich sighed and stood up to look out on the rest of the room where his people were steadily working. He had as many people on the case as he could spare. There was no more he could do.

"He's supposed to call again tomorrow. What's the likelihood that your people can trace it this time?" Randy asked, standing up and moving beside Rich where he stood in the window.

"I don't know. The kid that's on tech is good. He nearly got a trace last time, but it was just too fast for him to get it down. Simon will get him, though. I know it," Rich told him.

Just as he was about to continue, Brandee knocked on the door. "Agent Pearson?"

"Yes, Miss Schneck?" He turned to face her.

"I have something you might find interesting from the video," she said, smiling at him. "It's not much, but it might be something."

"Alright. Don, Randy, wait here, and I'll check this out. Have some more coffee," Rich told them as he left the office with the redheaded agent.

Brandee led Rich out to her desk and sat down. "I've noticed a few things in the basement. Just subtle things, and if we weren't looking for anything unusual, I wouldn't have even seen it."

Rich leaned over her desk and nodded. "Show me what you have."

"Well, the basement they're in looks different. Weird. Something isn't quite right about it. I noticed immediately, but I couldn't put my finger on what was wrong with it. I think I know, now." She punched up something on her computer and a zoomed in picture from the video feed came up. She pointed to it. "See there, the seams in the wall. Those aren't brick and mortar construction, or even a roughed out basement. The walls are smooth and joined here, and here," she noted, pointing it out. "But see, it's metal, not Sheetrock or any other building material."

"So, the walls are metal. What does that do to help us?" Rich asked.

"Well, I don't know for sure, but I think this might be an underground bunker, not just a regular basement," she said, zooming back out from the walls. "It might explain why we lost the signal so quickly if he's got the equipment in a shielded area."

Rich stood up slowly. "A bunker. Do we have possible locations on bunkers in the area?"

"That's what I'm trying to figure out now. I've started a search for any buildings in a hundred-mile radius from the center of St. Louis city," Brandee told him as she brought up another screen. "I haven't had any luck yet, but there's a chance it isn't on the records, as well."

"Why wouldn't it be in the records?" Rich wondered aloud.

"Well, there is the possibility of some old cold war bunkers being constructed without proper records being kept, or of course, them being lost along the way. It's a long shot, I know, but it's the only one I've come up with so far." She sighed.

Rich patted her on the back. "Keep it up and let me know if you find anything else. Even if it's just a way to narrow down the search."

"Sir!" he heard and turned around to see Simon waving at him from his desk.

Rich made his way over to his desk. "Please tell me you have something for me."

"I have narrowed down the radius to less than two hundred fifty miles," he said proudly.

Rich looked at him for a second. "Two hundred fifty miles?"

"I know it's not much, but it's better than all of the surrounding area," Simon pointed out to him.

"That's true," Rich admitted. "Keep working. Tomorrow, we'll have another chance to do a trace."

Rich headed back to his office, where Don and Randy had settled down and were talking. They both looked up at him as he entered.

"Any good news?" Don asked, putting his coffee cup back on the desk.

"Nothing substantial," Rich told them as he went around and sat back down at his desk. "Narrowed down the search area some, but not nearly enough. And we've got a possible way to identify the building. It's taking time, but we're going as fast as we can," he assured.

Don and Randy both nodded. "We better get back home." Don stood up. "We have to get back to the kids."

"I understand." Rich nodded.

Randy also stood, setting his cup down on the desk beside Don's. "Aileen isn't dealing the best with her brother being gone."

"I'm just glad Alex and Allie are too small to know CJ is gone." Don sighed deeply.

"You two take care of yourselves," Rich reminded him.

Rich watched them go and stared after them for a few minutes. He couldn't imagine the turmoil they were going through. Sighing, he opened the file and looked at the stills again, settling on one in particular. Both boys were facing the camera, their eyes begging him to find them. He had to get those two out of danger. Snapping the folder shut, he knew he had to deal with Jackson once and for all.

Chapter Eight

One Square at a Time

Joe sat at the breakfast table as Sheila served food. He was looking at his phone, another burner he'd picked up before coming to the house full-time. Today, he would call and check to see how his old friends were coming along with the money. He smiled to himself, wondering what their next move was going to be. If they turned over the money, it would end the game, though. And Joe wasn't sure he wanted this little game to end just yet. He'd given them three days, and he knew they would try to stall for time today. If they were smart, they would realize the chances of those kids getting out alive were nonexistent. Of course, he didn't think they were that smart.

"What time do you want to make the call today?" Sheila asked as she sat down on the opposite side of the table.

He glared at her. She was such a nosy bitch sometimes, always wanting to know the plans and what was going to happen. He told her everything she needed to know. She was here for one reason, and that was to keep those kids alive until they no longer served a purpose. He was hoping this game would be more entertaining than it was, but then, he'd just started.

"What does it fuckin' matter to you?" he growled, eating slowly and noticing Sheila had put more work into breakfast this morning.

Of course, the fresh ingredients they had would be used up first. After a week, they were getting through most of the fruits, vegetables, and milk products. He didn't intend to go back into St. Louis again, so this was what they had until the game was over.

"No reason. I was just wondering," she muttered, ducking her head. He wondered if he needed to remind her of her place again.

"Well, keep wonderin'. You don't need to know anything until it's time to know something," he told her as he finished eating. "Go feed those fuckin' kids."

He stood up and went into the living room. Set out was an array of technological gadgets he knew how to use but didn't necessarily know how they worked. He didn't care how they worked, though, only that they did. He bought most of the stuff with the money he got from Sheila's Russian mobster father. He smiled to himself, amused he'd gotten one over on the old bastard so easily. He'd been extremely easy to manipulate when his little girl said please. Of course, he was pretty sure they both had hits out on them by now. It didn't matter. What did matter was what was happening now. Everything depended on this.

Joe couldn't remember when the pure obsession with revenge against Don and Randy started. He thought it started before they'd done anything wrong. It was like they set off some deep-seated hatred he didn't even know existed suddenly. They had been his friends at one time. So, what could have changed so drastically to make them his enemies? He discounted it. They had turned on him and put him away, and now they had to suffer for it. And the best way to get at someone was through their heart. But that wasn't all there was to it. Just being around those two kids set him on edge so much he didn't want to be around them more than necessary.

Especially the little bitch, CJ. For whatever reason, he wanted to do things to him. He wanted to hurt him and make him suffer in the worst ways before he was done with him. He'd never seen another man he wanted to defile and break so badly in his entire life. Sure, he knew of those things while he was in the military, and he knew they happened in the prison where he'd been, though he'd never participated. He was always on top of the pecking order, so he never had to worry about anyone coming after him. He was quite happy to put them down right quick if they tried because he was not a fucking fairy.

But CJ made him want to grab him by the back of his long hair and hold him down until he was begging for mercy he wouldn't give. He'd never fantasized about such things before, and a little rough sex with Sheila usually relieved any pent-up stress. But the longer he was locked in this house with those two, the more his mind went there. He shook the thoughts away again and concentrated on what he was doing.

He would make the call as soon as the two brats were done with their breakfast. They had to eat because that was how he was keeping them doped up. It wasn't a lot, but it was enough that if they tried to run, they wouldn't get far, and it made them sleep more than normal. That was fine with him. He looked up as Sheila came back into the living room.

"When ya go down and pick up the dishes, take the rope and set them up in front of the camera. I'll make the call as soon as yer ready down there," he told her, figuring that having her do the tying up would be better than doing it himself. He didn't trust himself around those two at all.

After about fifteen minutes, Sheila went downstairs to do as he asked. He had to give her one thing: she followed orders well. He guessed listening to her daddy over the years had helped with that. She came back up after a little while.

"Do you want to use the handcuffs this time, or just have them tied up?" she asked.

"Go ahead and handcuff them like I did before, each one to the chair and to each other," Joe told her, handing her the three sets of handcuffs. He didn't even want to go downstairs to do that much with them.

She nodded, taking the handcuffs downstairs. He set up the call, and the equipment to foil any attempts to trace him. It rang through on Don's number. He figured if they were smart, they'd be waiting for it. And of course, he expected the FBI to be involved and try to trace him. He had the best equipment he could buy, though, and unless he was on for too long, they weren't going to get a trace.

"Hello," came Don's voice.

"Open your video feed, there Don," he demanded and clicked the button to transfer to the camera down in the basement.

He walked down the stairs, seeing Sheila had done just as he asked and tied them both to the chairs and then handcuffed them. He stepped in front of them and stared at the camera.

"Good morning." He smirked.

"You know good and well that we haven't got everything in order by now," Randy said gruffly.

"Oh, is that a fact?" Joe asked, having expected the answer. "I said three days and today is the third day. Do I start sending you pieces of them?"

"No! You ask for too much! There's no way we can possibly have that kind of money available in three days, and you know it," Don exclaimed.

"I think you need more incentive to get this done, old pals," Joe told them and walked around behind his two bound captives.

"Don't you touch them, Joe, or you won't see a dime of the money!" Randy warned. Joe had to wonder how many people were around them listening into the conversation.

Joe reached over and grabbed CJ by the back of his hair, twisting his neck to the side harshly, getting a gasping yelp out of him.

"Leave him alone!" Michael shouted, glaring at him. Joe smirked, liking the kid's spunk. Too bad it was misplaced.

"Stop, Joe, please!" Don said over the line, sounding desperate. Good, that was just the way he wanted him to sound. Desperate and willing to do anything.

"You aren't taking me seriously enough," Joe said in a low tone as he leaned over CJ's shoulder where his neck was bared. He could see the quickness of his pulse from the angle and knew he was scared of him. That was good. He should be scared of him. "I have your little boy. Or is he really a little girl?" he said as he twisted his head more to the side. "I think he wants to be a girl. I mean, look what he's wearing? And what good boy his age lets his hair grow out like this? The answer is none of them unless they're little bitches. See, I can understand the pitcher, y'know. But the catcher? Hmm, why would anyone choose that?"

"Leave him alone!" Michael growled again, yanking hard on the handcuffs. "He hasn't done anything!"

Joe turned toward Michael and smiled. "You're awful protective, why's that? Did you make him your bitch? I couldn't blame you; I mean, I never went for it when I was locked up, but never faulted the guys who did."

Michael looked flushed and angry enough at the statement that Joe knew there was something going on between these two, whether they knew it or not. Well, he couldn't have that, now could he? He couldn't separate them, though. So, he had to scare them into being afraid of him.

"Joe! Stop this! You'll get your money, then you can release them, just like you said!" Randy insisted across the phone and Joe blinked because he'd been so distracted, he wasn't watching the time.

He stood up, pulling CJ's head all the way back until he was looking straight up at the ceiling. "Yeah, my money for their lives. That was the deal. But not just that. A safe exit, and once I'm safe, I release them."

"You never said that before!" Don exclaimed.

"Well, I just added it to the deal. I won't have my money and not be able to get away with it. That would be foolish of me," he growled, not moving to let go of CJ's hair at all.

"Alright, you have your deal! Now, give us enough time to actually put it together this time!" Randy said.

Joe smiled. "You have a week. That's it. I put a bullet in their brains one week from today if I'm not safe in a non-extradition country. It's that simple."

"Alright!" Don yelled. "Just don't hurt them!"

Joe finally let go of CJ's hair and CJ put his head back up, breathing heavily as he stared at the camera. "I'll do whatever I want in the next week, so I suggest you hurry things along. The sooner you have things squared away, the sooner you can have your crotch fruit back. I can't guarantee I'll keep my hands off them. I'll try, but you know what a temper I have."

"We know, now please, just let them be until we can get everything—" Don started.

"Time's up, boys. Now, you have a good day, okay?" he exclaimed and moved around to turn off the camera.

He turned around after he was done and stared at CJ and Michael. "Yer fuckin' lucky I need you twerps alive for a little while longer," he growled out and then headed up the stairs once more.

He checked the equipment and turned everything off. His head was full of very graphic things he wanted to do to those two downstairs, and he didn't know how to handle it. Whatever happened, he knew he planned to kill both of them. So, what did it matter if he had a little fun beforehand?

"You don't think he'll do something before we can get this set up, do you?" Don asked, more worried now than he was before the call.

"He can't lose his leverage," Rich reminded them as he watched Simon working on the trace with the portable equipment he'd brought to the house this morning.

They had managed to get Mara and Terri to take the twins and go over to Terri and Randy's place this morning so they wouldn't be there for the phone call. Both had tried to argue it, but they listened to reason after a while. It would do no good and would only upset them further without cause.

"He can still hurt them; he just can't kill them," Randy pointed out.

Simon let out a pleased whoop, causing everyone to look at him. He looked up and grinned. "I got it down further to a fifty-mile radius!"

"Fifty miles?" Don frowned. "That's still a lot of ground to cover."

"Yeah, but I wouldn't have gotten it if he hadn't gotten distracted during the call. He lost track of time, I think, and let the call go on longer than it should have. But at least now we have a smaller circle to work with. He's within fifty miles of here," he said, pointing to a map on the tablet screen where a circle was drawn. "It's not far, so he's closer than we anticipated."

Rich nodded. "Good work, Simon. Keep on it and see if you can't do anything else with it," he told him before he turned back to Randy and Don. "Believe it or not, this is good. Between this information, and Brandee working the bunker angle, we've got a better position than we had before. We have one week, at least. It makes me wonder why he gave us three days the first time, anyway."

"It's all a game to him," Don said, rubbing a hand through his dark hair. "Nothing but a game. The more he can string us along, the more he's entertained. That's all there is to it."

Rich sighed and nodded. There really wasn't much else to be done. They were already sweeping the area and looking for buildings which would house a bunker type basement, but the records were sparse. Now, they had a smaller radius to work with, so it was a good thing. Still, it wasn't enough. Now, they'd been given another week, but at what cost to those two kids? The way he was obviously manhandling them in the video was concerning.

"You don't think he'd take things out on CJ, do you?" Don said softly.

Randy looked at him with a sad look. "Don't try to think about it."

"I can't help it. You know as well as I do what he's capable of doing. He doesn't have to kill them to make them suffer." He ran a hand through his hair again.

"He hasn't hurt them yet. Seems to me he's intent on scaring them and us. He's had them a week, so it's a good sign they're not injured," Randy told him with a soft smile. "Just try and keep that in mind. He can't play this game with broken pawns."

"But now he can, can't he? He's given us a week, but he won't release them until after he's safe. You know as well as I do, there's a very good chance he has no intention of releasing them at all," Don pointed out.

Rich put a hand on Don's shoulder. "We just have to keep going and try to find them first. A week is a good amount of time for us to get a breakthrough. Just stay positive and keep your chin up. They wouldn't want you being so upset all the time."

Don and Randy both nodded. "So, we're back to waiting again." Don sighed deeply.

"Waiting and working. We only need a small break, and we'll be able to find them," Rich said with a definitive nod.

Rich and Simon packed up all the equipment to get out of Don's house so they could be alone. It was a tough situation for all of them to be in and having them still there was a stark reminder of what was going on. He was glad the wives had been absent this time. It was going to be bad enough letting them watch the video feed and seeing how he acted toward CJ. Rich worried about that. He appeared to have a special level of hatred toward the boy. He could only assume Randy and Don were right, and it was severe homophobia which was driving his cruelty. That didn't look good for CJ, though. The question became how long Jackson could hold himself back before actually hurting him.

After they were packed up, he told Don and Randy goodbye and drove him and Simon back to the office. His head was on the case, though, and he was looking forward to seeing if Brandee could get anything else off the new video feed.

"Hey, CJ, you still awake?" Michael whispered, blinking wearily at the ceiling. He realized he'd left the light on in the bathroom and the glow illuminated the room.

"Yeah. I'm having trouble sleeping after today," he admitted quietly.

"Have you noticed you haven't been feeling as foggy?" he asked. "I wonder if Sheila stopped dosing our food as much as she was."

"Maybe. I don't know." CJ's voice was tight and sounded strained.

"You okay, CJ? You're not letting that shit he said this morning get to you, are you?" Michael said and rolled over to where he could see CJ's bed. He was facing the wall that the bed sat up against.

"No..." he trailed off.

Michael sighed and sat up, facing his back now. "Hey, don't do that. He's an asshole, alright?"

"I know, but still. I feel weird when he touches me and I don't like it," he said in that tight voice again.

Michael got up and sat down on CJ's bed, reaching a hand over to take one of his. "Hey, he's not going to do anything to you. I won't let him."

CJ turned over on his back, searching Michael's face for a few moments. "How are you going to do anything to stop him?"

"I dunno, I'll find a way," Michael assured him, taking CJ's hand and interlacing his fingers with his.

"Why are you doing this?" he whispered.

"Doing what?" Michael asked as he pulled CJ's hand into his lap.

"This. Touching my hand like that. Why did you kiss my neck yesterday?" CJ asked, voice trembling a bit.

Michael smiled gently at him. "Because I wanted to, and I want to." He squeezed his hand and then picked it up to lay a kiss on the knuckles.

He noticed CJ's breath had kicked up a notch, and he was breathing through his mouth a little. "Does it excite you a little?"

CJ's face reddened, and he turned his face away. "I don't know what you mean."

"Come on, you said yourself you had been watching me. Did you ever just want to walk up to me and ask me if I was interested?" Michael asked, a smirk still fixed on his face.

"How could I do something like that?" CJ gasped. "You were always surrounded by those girls and the guys from the team, and how would it look if some weird guy came up and confessed his love?"

"Love?" Michael asked, arching both brows.

CJ covered his face with his free hand and turned away again. "Oh my god," he whispered. "Did I just say that?"

Michael's smile spread across his face. "No taking it back; you already let it slip."

"I don't even know you that well! How can I have feelings for someone so quickly?" CJ asked, frowning.

"How long have you been watching me?" Michael wondered, taking his other hand and brushing CJ's hair back from his face.

CJ thought for a second. "About a year or more," he mumbled, almost too low for Michael to hear.

"So, I wouldn't call it quick," Michael told him.

"But you don't know much about me," CJ told him, staring at his hand where Michael still held it.

"I know enough. I know a lot about you from watching you play your character, Serna. I think she's a lot like you, and the way you want to be," he said with a soft grin now. "I know you're cute, and I'm attracted to you. Isn't that enough?"

"Enough for what?" CJ asked, looking up at him sharply.

"Enough to do this," he said and leaned forward, bringing his lips close to CJ's. "Can I?" he whispered against his lips.

Michael could tell CJ didn't know what to do, but he nodded slightly and let him press forward. His lips touched CJ's, and he flicked his tongue out to brush across the seam of his lips. CJ opened tentatively, and Michael pressed forward, caressing CJ's tongue with his own in slow and gentle strokes. CJ gasped a little and then took a breath through his nose. Michael thought CJ's lips were softer than most girls' he'd kissed. CJ seemed to like the feeling because he grabbed onto Michael's shoulders and pulled him closer.

"Whoa, easy," Michael whispered. "I'm not going anywhere."

He leaned down and captured his lips again, but this time, Michael slid his hand up under CJ's shirt, rubbing against his stomach and then his chest. He hummed into the kiss, probing his mouth as deeply as he could as his fingers found his left nipple and pinched it.

"Ah!" CJ said, breaking their kiss. "What are you doing?"

"Does it feel good?" he asked, continuing to roll his nipple between his fingers.

"It feels different!" he squirmed a little under Michael's touch.

Michael hummed and leaned forward to occupy his mouth again, not letting him get his breath properly. CJ couldn't help but react strongly and honestly to everything Michael did to him. He gasped a little as Michael let go of his nipple and slipped his hand down to press at his crotch, rubbing gently to find he was definitely aroused. He couldn't say much because he was painfully hard in his own jeans just from kissing him like this. He'd never gotten so worked up from a little kissing before, but here he was.

"Wh-what are you doing now?!" CJ asked suddenly, eyes a little wide.

"Hmm, you seem to like it," he mumbled, stroking him through his pants. "We can stop if you want. Kissing is nice enough if you aren't ready to go any further," Michael said as he kissed his lips softly again.

"But I don't want to stop!" CJ exclaimed suddenly, face going immediately two shades darker.

"Oh, ho." Michael smirked. "You do like it."

CJ turned his head to the side, covering his face with his hand. "It feels good," he admitted, just barely loud enough to be heard.

Michael unbuttoned CJ's pants, sliding one hand inside to grip at him gently. CJ sucked in a deep breath and let it out again. "Look at you. You're getting all wet down here. We better take off these pants before you soil them."

CJ leaned up on his elbows and watched as Michael slipped his pants and boxers down over his hips, sliding them down his legs very slowly. "What if someone comes down here?" he whispered.

"No one will come down here. We're on our own by now. They're probably asleep already, or busy themselves," Michael assured him. "It's okay, I'll get undressed too, so I don't make a mess either."

CJ's breath stuttered in his chest, and he watched Michael stand up and strip off his pants and boxers. Michael had no doubt that CJ was into this, his arousal blatant. CJ reached out and touched him gingerly, as though afraid to do it. Michael got closer and took his hand to place it on him. CJ looked up at him.

"I've never touched anyone else..." he said softly.

"I've never touched another guy, but I know what feels good to me, so it can't be that different," Michael said as he reached down and covered CJ's hand with his own. "Want to do something fun?"

CJ looked at him, eyes wide again. "Something fun?"

"Well, I don't want to make a mess, so there's one way to make sure we don't," Michael told him with a smirk spreading over his face.

"What are you talking about?" CJ asked, breath coming faster.

"You use your mouth on me, then I do the same for you. Don't you think that'll be nice?" he asked, leaning over and stroking CJ. Michael felt him twitch in his hand. "I think you like that idea."

"But I've never—" CJ started.

"It's easy. Here," Michael said as he sat down on the side of the bed. "Come here."

CJ looked unsure as he crawled out of bed and stood in front of Michael. Michael reached out and stroked him firmly a few times, noticing he was leaking profusely.

"Now, just get on your knees here," he said and spread his legs out a little.

Swallowing, CJ nodded and dropped between his knees. He stared at him for a moment and Michael thrust his hips forward a little. He moved and put his hand on CJ's head and pushed him forward. "Just open and take as much in as you can. It won't be a lot before it hits the back of your throat, but it will still feel amazing."

CJ nodded, opening his mouth and first sticking his tongue out, licking at the tip where liquid glistened. He frowned, obviously having never tasted something like it before. Michael was quiet, letting him go at his own pace. He leaned forward a little, taking the head into his mouth, getting a pleased moan out of Michael.

"That's it. You're doing fine," Michael told him as he tightened his hold on his hair. "Just like that. Use your tongue under the tip; that feels really good."

Taking his advice, CJ rolled his tongue and slid it under the tip. He rubbed it for a few seconds and Michael squeezed his hand in his hair. Michael was trying his best not to thrust into him, but the desire caused him to push deeper. CJ was accepting though, and it didn't take much longer before he felt the orgasm rushing him. He'd never gone off so fast before, so he guessed it was a matter of the right partner.

Michael gasped and, without warning, pressed CJ's head down harder and deeper. CJ struggled against him as his throat tried to reject the intrusion, but Michael was already coming. He let go as soon as he could, and CJ came up coughing a little with tears in his eyes.

"Oh, I'm sorry, got a little over-enthused," Michael said, reaching over and cupping his face. "But I'll make it up to you."

CJ nodded, clearing his throat. Michael felt bad because he hadn't meant to choke him. CJ smiled up at him.

"Here, lay down up here," he told him and patted the bed.

CJ got up on the bed, obviously anticipating what he was going to do. He looked at him as he scooted down further. "Here, open your legs. I wanna do something."

Michael knew CJ had no idea what he was talking about, but he did as he asked, letting him get between his legs. Michael leaned up, crawling on top of him and pressing his fingers at CJ's lips. He had a smirk on his face again. CJ frowned but sucked on his fingers, not sure what he was doing. After a few seconds, Michael pulled his hand back and knelt between CJ's legs again.

"I'm going to finger you," Michael explained. "Let me know if you want me to stop," he said as he slipped his hand underneath him.

Michael knew that he didn't get what he meant to do, not really. CJ blinked as he watched him lean over and lick at the head softly. It was a first for him, tasting another man, but he found the taste salty and slippery, though not bad. Just different. Michael smiled and traced a finger down and rubbed at his entrance.

"Ah!" CJ said with a gasp, his body tensing.

"Shh, just relax. It won't hurt," Michael told him as he rubbed more against him. "I'm going to put a finger inside you. If you don't like it, tell me, okay?"

CJ nodded to him, watching as he sucked on the head and began pushing into him. He gasped out again. Pushing deeper, Michael knew he was doing something he liked because he was making little whimpering sounds. He smiled around him and took more of him into his mouth. He made another choked sound, and he plunged his finger the rest of the way into him. He felt him constrict on him, and he leaked a sudden bunch of fluid into Michael's mouth. Michael wondered if he could get both fingers into him as he pushed at him with two now that he was pulling back and pushing forward. He pulled back and then worked two into him. It was tight, but CJ wasn't tensing at all as he pushed back in.

"There, you're doing good, CJ," Michael said as he came up off him for a second. "You like how it feels?"

"Uh huh," CJ managed, writhing on the bed.

"Imagine what sex feels like," Michael said as he went down on him again.

"Oh, I'm close, I'm close!" CJ gasped out, hands buried in his own hair.

Michael nodded and worked his fingers as deep as he could, trying to find the spot... He felt something different in texture. He stroked the spot, noting it felt spongy and a little firm to the touch. CJ arched his back and made a loud noise in his throat. Michael smiled around him as he swallowed against him, feeling him at the back of his throat. CJ gasped out, and Michael felt him stiffen and his cock pulse as he came, his body getting incredibly tight on his fingers.

Michael came up, wiping his mouth with the back of his hand and slipping his fingers out of him. CJ was panting openly and staring down at him. Michael crawled up over him, leaning in to kiss him deeply again. CJ responded, reaching around him and hugging him tightly against him. Michael had to be careful because if he wasn't, he was going to get hard again. He leaned back and kissed his nose quickly.

"There now. You seemed to enjoy it. It was very good, wasn't it?" he asked.

"Yeah," CJ said, still gawking at him.

"We should get dressed, unfortunately," Michael said, moving back and getting off the bed.

He found his pants and boxers and put them back on as CJ did the same. CJ then sat down on the bed and looked up at Michael. Michael reached out and cupped his face with a smile. He could see tears glistening in the corners of his eyes.

"Are you okay?" he asked, concerned.

"Yeah, I just feel a lot of things," CJ replied, smiling weakly.

Michael nodded. He leaned forward and kissed his forehead gently. "I'll sleep in this bed with you. I usually wake up early enough to move before Sheila catches us," he said and smiled at him.

CJ nodded, kind of glad for Michael right then. They snuggled down into the twin bed together, clutching each other tightly and fell asleep before long. Of course, their night wasn't void of dreams.

Chapter Nine

Vulnerabilities

Rich was in the office early to see if he couldn't get a start on things. They had seven days to find those kids before they were most likely murdered. Of course, now that they had seen them again, there was no telling what would happen to them. Jackson had made no promises to contact them again before the seven days were up. There were no guarantees that they would be safe, so speed was of the utmost concern.

"Ms. Schneck?" Rich said as he came over to her desk. "Anything?"

"Simon might have something on the tech he's using. It's cutting edge, nothing like we've ever seen," she answered, staring at her computer screen where the video was queued up as she worked on it.

Rich nodded, heading to their technophile's desk. "Brandee said you might have something?"

"Yeah, this tech; I don't know where he got it, but this stuff is secret military grade technology. Usually, doing a trace takes a few minutes at most, depending on the equipment, but this..." Simon gave a low whistle. "Well, I'd love to get my hands on it and examine it. I have put in calls to the higher ups for more information about it, but I've been told that access to that information is restricted. This has to be something the military doesn't want most people knowing about."

"Someone knows about it then," Rich said, frowning. "I'll see if I can't get you access to more information on it. Maybe if they have the technology, they also know how to trace the technology," he said hopefully.

"Maybe, sir. I hope you have better luck. Let me know if you can get anything because I really want to get my hands on whatever tech he's using," Simon said with a hopeful look on his face.

Rich smiled and patted him on the back. "I'll see what I can do."

He headed back to his office and sat down. He hated requesting classified information because it was always such a hassle. But, if it would lead them to these kids, he would do it. Any amount of time was worth it in the end if it led them to find those two before something bad happened. He was afraid that no matter what they did, something bad was going to take place.

After a couple of hours, he'd filled out all the necessary requests and forms, and sent them off. He just hoped they moved faster than the speed the government usually moved with. He headed back out to see if Simon had gotten anywhere with his attempts to get through whatever this technology was.

"Anything, Simon?" Rich asked as he came up to his desk again.

"Nothing, sir. Um, but I do have a rather...unconventional thought," Simon said, looking up sheepishly at Rich.

Rich frowned and tilted his head to the side. "What's that?"

"See, I know this person that might be able to help, but what they do isn't exactly, well, legal."

"Simon, what are you talking about?" Rich asked.

"Well, I was just thinking, I can't break through this tech he's using. I just can't crack it. And if it takes the higher ups a while to release the information down to us, it might be too late. You know how long it can take to go through all that red tape," Simon told him.

Rich wanted to tell him no. He really did. But he couldn't because he knew as well as Simon that the chances of the military releasing classified information in a timely manner were next to none. "We're up against the clock, Simon. We'll do what we have to. Can you get a hold of this person quickly?"

"They go by Chaz. I'll have to contact them through the chat server I know them on, one for techno geeks like me that I belong to. They've posted a few things and I've talked to them privately about some stuff. They don't know I work for the FBI, though. They might be reluctant to work with us," Simon admitted.

"Offer complete immunity to what they do and let them know we can classify them as an informant from here on out if they agree to it," Rich said. "Just get on it. We needed help yesterday."

"Got it, sir," Simon said and pulled his phone out of his pocket and started texting. Rich sighed, walking away and hoping that this person could help. And that they lived close enough to be of use.

Aurelia ran as hard as she could because she had to get there before the inevitable happened. She couldn't let her die. Not after everything they'd been through. She just couldn't! She ran through the streets of Constantinople to get to the old temple where they usually met. Maximina would be worried if she was late or didn't show up at all, and to know that they'd been found out was terrifying. She wasn't sure what she thought she would do once she got there, other than warn Maximina about what she'd found out.

For months, Aurelia and Maximina had been meeting outside the city in an old, rundown temple from before Christianity became the official religion. No one went there anymore, and it was a safe place for the two women to meet in secret.

At least it had been.

Now, they'd been found out by one of the priests, a man named Viator. Viator had followed Maximina to the temple grounds and saw them kissing each other, and now was intent on putting a stop to their love. Two women weren't permitted to be together, and they knew it. It was against God himself, but neither woman could hide from the absolute joy the other ignited in their heart.

"Maximina!" she called as she came into the broken temple. "Maximina! Where are you?"

"Aurelia?" came Maximina's voice as the other woman came out from behind a broken pillar.

"I got here in time!" Aurelia gasped, breathing heavily.

"In time? For what?" Maximina wondered, brows meshing in confusion.

"For me to arrive," another voice spoke from beside them.

Both women turned to see Father Viator and a retinue of at least ten armed men standing there. Aurelia stepped closer to Maximina and clutched her hand. Maximina, too, realized what was happening because she squeezed Aurelia's hand in return.

"I don't care what you say, Viator. We're in love, and that's the only thing that matters," Aurelia said, back straightening significantly.

"You know such things are not permitted under the eyes of God," Viator said, not moving from where he stood.

"We don't care about your God!" Maximina blurted. Aurelia didn't say anything, but she figured they were in trouble already, so being called on their heresy wouldn't matter.

"You would blaspheme as well? Your sins are many!" Viator growled out. "Take them!"

The soldiers moved forward and grabbed the two women in vice-like grips. They both struggled, feeling the strong hands squeezing their arms, and knowing there was nothing they could do. They had been condemned from the moment they saw each other for the first time.

"Kill us, it won't matter! We'll be together in the afterlife!" Aurelia yelled, leaning forward as far as the soldier holding her would allow.

Viator came over, snarled at her, and shook his head. "No, you shall descend to hell for lying with another woman. How vile!"

"Do whatever you like." Maximina sighed, resigned to her fate. "I would rather die than live without her."

"Oh, die you shall," he growled and backhanded Maximina fiercely.

Maximina spit blood at his feet and glared at him. "Then kill us and be done with it."

"Yes, I will get to that," Viator told them, turning to one of the soldiers. "A dagger." The soldier handed over a dagger to him without a word.

"There is nothing wrong with our love," Aurelia said staunchly as she stood straighter. If she was going to die, she was going to die with her dignity. "Your God has no right to judge us."

"Oh, He may not judge you, but I have," Viator said, stepping forward, and with a flick of his wrist, he cut Maximina's throat.

Aurelia gasped, her composure faltering as Maximina's lifeblood flowed down her front, and soon, the only thing keeping her standing was the soldier that held her limp body from behind.

"Maximina!" she cried out, heartbreaking as she spoke.

"Yes, cry for your dead lover. But you shall follow her soon and meet her in hell. There is little doubt in my mind that you will go there for your deeds and heresy. You dare decry the Lord God! It is your ending," he said, taking the still-bloody dagger and holding it to Aurelia's throat. "You wish to say anything?"

Aurelia, tears streaming down her face, took a breath and, with all of her might, spit into Viator's face. The priest wiped his face casually and moved the dagger, choosing instead to bury it in her stomach.

"Die slowly. Leave them here for the carrion birds," he said, handing the bloodied dagger to the soldier he'd taken it from.

Aurelia pulled herself to Maximina's body. She cradled her in her arms and despite the pain of the wound in her own stomach, great wracking sobs shook her body. Her own lifeblood flowed from her, but she didn't care. Her precious Maximina was gone. She had no reason to live any longer, so it did not matter what pain her own body felt. She was confident that she would be with her on the other side, whatever was on that other side.

Michael's eyes flew open, and he heaved a breath. That was an unusual dream. He usually wasn't a woman in the dreams, but he had them before. He sat up, forgetting that he was in bed with CJ for a moment until he felt him move beside him. He looked down and smiled, because he was still sound asleep. He reached out and brushed the dark strands of his hair off of his face. He was cute; he had to admit. He never really thought about dating a guy, but he'd never been opposed to it, either. The opportunity had never presented itself.

Now that he was really looking at him closely, he had a soft face. CJ had lush, plump lips and a cute little nose that wasn't too big. On his rounded ears, he wore earrings; he realized for the first time. They were small ruby studs. He hadn't really noticed that before, but he hadn't been paying attention to details like that. With what they'd done last night, he should. He'd initiated, and it had been a first time for him as well, but it turned out research was worth it. That was something his friends wouldn't ever find out about unless they went deep into his search history. He never thought he'd date a guy, but he'd certainly seen his share of videos and knew exactly what to do.

He sighed and stood up, stretching as he did so. It felt like he hadn't moved all night. He made his way into the small bathroom and noticed he'd never turned off the light last night. Last night... He wondered how CJ was going to feel about what had happened? He hoped he didn't regret it. Michael certainly didn't. But he figured he had more experience in sex than CJ did. He'd at least slept with girls a couple of times. But the girls hadn't been as much fun as CJ. He smiled, using the bathroom and coming back out in time to see Sheila coming down the stairs.

"Good morning," Michael told her as he walked over to the table.

She smiled slightly at him. "Good morning. Is CJ still sleeping?"

Michael glanced back over to see CJ was still curled up. "Um, yeah, he hasn't gotten up yet."

"Well, you should wake him up before breakfast gets cold. I'll be back to get the dishes," she said and headed back up the stairs.

Michael looked to see they had waffles and syrup with orange juice. They were just frozen waffles, but that was okay. Going over to CJ, he sat down and shook him gently. He really didn't want him missing meals.

"CJ, time to wake up. Breakfast is here," he murmured.

CJ's eyes opened and then he stared at him blearily. "Michael?" he mumbled.

"Yeah, come on, time to get up and eat something," Michael said, standing back up.

Immediately, CJ's face pinked, and Michael guessed he was thinking about the night before. Michael couldn't help the smirk that spread across his face as he, too, thought about the night before. CJ swallowed, looking nervous as he sat up.

"Don't be so shy," Michael said, reaching out and putting his hand against CJ's face. "I plan to do more than that with you, you know."

CJ turned a shade darker and ducked his head. Michael thought it was incredibly cute, and he liked teasing him already. He turned his honey-colored eyes on him again, and Michael's breath caught a little. There was just something there between them, something he could not explain, and sometimes it felt so strong. It was as though he was looking into the eyes of someone he'd loved for all of his life. Or perhaps it was lives, if their dreams were any indication.

"I don't know how you act after something like last night," CJ mumbled, but turned his head into Michael's hand.

"Just act normal," Michael said, reaching a hand out to help him up. "Nothing's changed except we're acting on our desires. And I plan to act on them more."

CJ was still red in the face when he took Michael's hand and let him help him stand. "How much more can you do?"

Michael pulled CJ suddenly over into him and wrapped his arms around him. "All the way, you know."

CJ's eyes widened a bit. "But can you do that? Will that work?"

"There's a bottle of conditioner in the shower. It'll work," he said with a glint in his eye.

"You can do that?" CJ asked, staring at him with such a serious look.

Michael smiled and leaned forward, kissing his lips quickly. "Sometimes you have to make do with what you have at hand. I've seen it used in videos."

CJ looked away and stammered, "You've seen videos of that?"

"Uh huh, I've seen all kinds of videos online. When we get out of here, I'm going to show you some of them," he told him, still smirking at him.

CJ swallowed, then glanced over at the table. "We should eat, though," he said.

"Oh, yeah, it'll get cold," Michael said, releasing him to head back over to the table with him. "She looked to be doing okay today."

"That's good," CJ said as he slowly ate the waffles.

Michael noticed they had already gone cold, but he was hungry, so it didn't really matter. He'd been having too much fun teasing CJ.

A few minutes after they finished eating, Sheila came down and retrieved the plates without a word. She barely looked at them as she did it. It felt so surreal, Michael thought as she left. His head was a little fuzzy, so obviously they were still being drugged.

"I wish she'd stop dosing our food with whatever this is," CJ commented as he stood up shakily.

"Yeah, but not much choice but to eat what we're given if we want a chance to escape," Michael responded.

CJ dropped onto his bed and sighed. "Will we escape?"

"We have to. You heard this guy. Do you honestly think he's going to give us back to our parents?" Michael stood up and went to sit on the bed next to CJ.

CJ shook his head. "No, I don't think he intends to let us live. We're only alive now so he can play this game with our parents. He must really hate them to do this."

Frowning, Michael looked at CJ. "But it's more than that. It's like I know him."

"I know the feeling. Every time he gets close to me, I feel like I'm looking at someone else. But I just can't see who it is. It's like just out of focus, you know?" CJ ran a hand through his hair, as it had come loose.

Michael reached out and slipped a hand around his shoulders and pulled him in close. "We'll make it. We have to. It's just the way it is from now on. We've got a lot to do outside this basement together."

CJ looked up at him and blinked for a second. "Outside of this basement? You mean, you'd be with me, out there?"

"Of course!" Michael said, squeezing him close again. He wished that CJ would have a little more confidence in him over this, but he understood why he didn't.

"I guess I never thought about it, you know, having something like this," CJ said softly, snuggling his head into Michael's shoulder.

Michael placed his hand on CJ's face, then turned him to face him. They were inches apart, and he could feel CJ's breath warm on his lips. He cracked a smile and leaned forward, brushing against him to see how he responded. When CJ opened the door immediately for him, he went in and deepened the kiss. CJ was growing used to it, Michael noticed. His tongue pressed against him, twisting and sliding back and forth. He pulled away to get his breath, seeing CJ had flushed again.

"You seem to like that," he said, brushing a hand through CJ's black hair.

"Yeah," CJ breathed. "I mean, of course, I do. It's you," he said quietly. He cleared his throat and sat back. "Uh, so, you have a sister?"

Michael blinked in surprise at the sudden change of topic, but he guessed CJ was growing a little uncomfortable with all the sex talk. He nodded.

"Yeah, Aileen. What about you?" he asked.

"Alex and Allie are twins. They're almost four," CJ said. "I guess I'm just missing my family right now a lot. I wish I could introduce you to them more than anything."

Michael smiled and reached out to cup CJ's face. "Don't worry. We're going to get out of here."

CJ was silent for a moment. "I don't know about that."

Joe stood in the sporting goods store and looked around. He'd had to leave the hideout because being there alone with those kids was giving him ideas, and he wanted to go down the stairs and enact them. He couldn't. Not just yet. So, he'd left and gone to one of the few places he found solace. It calmed him down for the most part.

"Looking for a new gun?" asked the man behind the counter.

Joe smirked. "I just like to see the ones for sale. Got plenty of my own," Joe told him.

The man's name tag read "Bill." Bill nodded. "Need some ammo while you're here, then?"

"Just window shopping, Bill," he said, staring now at the survival knives in the case. There were some decent ones, but nothing like he had from his military days.

Bill wandered off, obviously getting the hint that Joe wasn't all that interested in sales pitches. Joe bet he could outdo Bill at his job of selling weapons, and he also bet that the weapons he had would make the ones sold in the store pale in comparison. Shelia's father had gotten him all the tools he needed to do this work. Sighing, he thought he needed a drink, and it was already late in the day.

He found himself in a dive bar, downing whiskey on the rocks, when he saw a woman staring at him. She was dark-haired with a red dress on. The slit went up her hip. He downed his drink and walked over to where she was sitting.

"Staring at me, and not saying anything, now that's not nice," he commented.

She smiled, her teeth not perfect in the least, and spoke up. "Oh, I'm sorry. I was just admiring your physique and wondering if there was any way to see more of it."

"Not without asking," Joe commented, flagging the bartender down and pointing to them both as he pulled himself onto the stool beside her.

"Well, I guess this is me asking," she said, eyes also large and dark.

Joe looked her over with an appraising eye. Good breasts, probably a push-up bra, though. Good amount of cleavage. The slit on her skirt revealed nothing underneath it, so likely she wasn't wearing much in the way of underwear. She wore a pair of black heels and carried a shiny leather purse.

"Let's get out of here and find somewhere quiet," he said, draining the drink and getting the bartender's attention to close his tab. Of course, it was a card in an assumed name.

"What's your name, big guy?" she asked with a smirk, her red lips pulling taunt.

"Joe. You?" he asked.

"Selena. You have a place?" she asked.

"Nah, from out of town. You got a pad?"

"Yeah, we can go there," she responded and got up. "Just follow me, sweetheart."

Joe followed her to her car, and she drove them to an apartment complex. He frowned. That meant he couldn't get too rough with her. She might scream too much and alert the neighbors. They got inside and he grabbed her, throwing her against the door and crushing her mouth in a fierce kiss. She responded, obviously liking the force. She rubbed her leg against his.

"Let's get comfortable." She smiled and took him by the hand, leading him to the bedroom.

She turned and presented her back with the zipper to him. He got the idea and unzipped the dress from the neck down her back, staring at the pale flesh as he went. He kept imagining what bruises and marks would look like on that flesh. He watched as she dropped the dress down and he saw she was wearing a white string thong underneath it. She turned around, breath heaving a bit as she looked him over. He stepped out of his shoes and watched her for a minute.

"You gonna take that off?" She smiled a little.

Joe nodded, pulling his shirt over his head quickly. She cooed a little and moved closer, placing her hands on his toned muscles, and then kissed his chest. He didn't like feeling out of control, though, so he grabbed her and started biting at the chord of her throat. She made some remark about him being an animal, and he grunted in response, not really caring what she said.

She went for his jean button, and he knocked her hands away, walking her back to the bed and shoving her down on it. Again, she remarked about how rough he was being, something about not wanting to end up with bruises, but he shook the thoughts away and undid his jeans and stepped out of them, showing her what he had.

"Oh..." she whispered as she looked him over. "So, that's what you're packing in those pants. I'm not disappointed."

"Of course you aren't," he responded and crawled on top of her, ready to just fuck her and get on with it. He'd never been one for foreplay.

"Can we go a bit slower, though?" she asked.

Joe internally groaned. They always wanted to go slower because it was always about what they needed. Well, Joe thought, he needed a good fuck he could do whatever he wanted with. He snorted, looking down at her naked body.

"Anal?" he asked.

Her large, dark eyes went a little wide. "Well, I've never done that, so I don't think it's a good idea. Let's just stick to the regular thing, okay?"

Joe was annoyed at that. The answer was always the same. He'd had to prod Shelia into doing it, too, and it took several attempts before she quit whining about it. Of course, he knew it was easier if you used stuff like lube, but he really didn't care about her comfort when it came to their sex. And he didn't care about this woman either. In fact, he'd already forgotten her name.

He positioned himself between her thighs and thrust into her quickly, despite her pleas to slow down. He didn't even bother taking her thong off, just moving it to the side. She moaned like the whore she was, liking it no matter how much she complained. He was going to get what he wanted, though. So, he pumped his cock in her pussy a few times, then pulled out and slammed into her ass. She screeched, but he was ready and leaned over and clamped his hand over her mouth, silencing any further protests.

It felt good, just like he wanted, though she was fighting him now, trying to get him off her. That was getting on his nerves, too, so he leaned up and wrapped his hands around her neck, cutting off her air and crushing her throat. He got a little heavy with the thrusting, and then he heard the pop. She went limp immediately, but he wasn't quite done yet, so he finished up and pulled out, using her covers to wipe the blood off his cock before he got his clothes. It had only taken a short time, and now he needed a cigarette, so he searched her nightstand and found a pack with a lighter and lit up one.

He glanced over at her naked body and thought it was an alright body. He noticed the c-section scar, so someone was going to miss her. Maybe. Unless she was one of those mothers that ran out on her kids. It wasn't like he cared either way. She'd satisfied his needs, and that's all that mattered to him. He sighed, crushing out the cigarette on the side table and put his shoes on. He grabbed her purse and pulled out her keys, taking a moment to see if she had any cash. She didn't, but she had several credit cards. He took them and walked out, remembering to lock the door behind him.

He got in her car, a shitty coupe, and took off back to the bar where he'd left the van parked far away from the building. It was early in the morning, and he didn't want any hassles with being seen on security cameras, even though he honestly didn't care if they caught sight of him. He'd just left his DNA and fingerprints all over a murder scene, so it wasn't going to be too hard to connect him to what had just happened. He got out and into the van and left to go back to the hideout. It was a bit of a drive, but he used the time to go over the plan again and again in his mind. But he kept coming back to the little bitch CJ.

Just thinking about him gave him a hard on, and he didn't understand why. He'd just nutted in that bitch, so why was this happening? He didn't know. He just knew that little slut was tempting him, and he didn't know how long he could keep his hands off him. He wanted to take him and fuck him raw right in front of Randy's bastard child. He smiled. Yeah, that would be the ideal setup.

Chapter Ten

Queen's Heart

Shelia was up earlier than normal for a Saturday because she had to take care of the kids. The night before, Joe had been in a foul mood and ended up getting way too rough in bed. He'd come home at three am and woke her up, insisting on sex right then. It wasn't like she could say no when he was like that, so she'd agreed. Now, she was aching in her hips and her shoulders. Lately, he was always like that, and she hated it. She sighed, pulling down two bowls and pouring the cereal into each one. She poured a pitcher of milk and two glasses of orange juice. She sprinkled a dose of the drugs in each of the glasses and stirred them.

She took it down to the basement to find CJ asleep and Michael sitting on his bed. He got up when she sat the tray down on the table.

"Um, Shelia, we've been here like a week, and we don't have clean clothes. Is there any way to get our clothes washed or something?" Michael asked as he looked at what she'd brought down for breakfast.

"I can see if I can find some sweats for you two. There's a washer upstairs, but I'll just have to find you a change."

"You okay this morning, Shelia?" he asked her.

She turned to him and gave him a small smile. "Yeah, I'm fine. I'll see about the clothes. I imagine you're feeling grimy in the same clothes for a week."

She headed back upstairs and closed the door, careful to seal and lock it. She had to do something. He was going to kill those kids. He couldn't keep his hands off them forever. She knew her purpose was to keep them alive as long as she could, but what would happen when she couldn't stop him? She couldn't even stop him from practically killing her daily, so what was she supposed to do to stop him from killing someone else? If he wanted those kids dead, he would kill them.

So, that left one option. She had to get them out of there the next time Joe disappeared for a while. He typically disappeared for hours at a time, and if she hurried, she could get them out before he returned. She swallowed, went to the bathroom, and found she was either starting her period, or he'd done more damage the night before than she thought. Neither option was good. Just in case, she went to her med case she'd stolen and dug out some Keflex and took some. It would at least help with any infection if it was his treatment of her the night before. At least he hadn't wanted to do it the other way... She was always sore for days after that.

She passed the living room and saw him sitting at the little headquarters he'd set up. He was doing something on the computer, and she wasn't about to ask him what it was.

"The fuck you doing there?" he snapped, looking up at her suddenly.

"Nothing, sorry, was just thinking."

"Go fucking think somewhere else, bitch. I don't want to be disturbed, especially not by you," he growled.

She nodded and went back to the kitchen. She didn't understand how he could be so hateful to her now. After all the things he'd said in the letters, and later in the phone calls, she had a hard time recognizing the man she fell in love with. It had been stupid. If she hadn't picked up the mail that day, things would never have started. She'd taken the mail to her father, and he'd taken it, but tossed one letter in the trash without opening it. She shouldn't have done it. She picked it up and opened it to find it was from a Joe Jackson looking for information. She just wanted to tell him that her father wasn't interested, and that was it.

Then, he wrote back to her, saying that was fine, but would she be interested in writing him? He had no one to talk to and it would be nice to have a pen pal. She hesitated at first, not wanting to get involved. This was a guy locked up, so what was he going to do, though? It wasn't like he was going to walk out and look for her. So, she started writing to him. After almost two years, the letters got more and more personal, and she was telling him everything that went on in her life.

The thing was, though, he listened when no one else would. He didn't tell her, "Shut up, Sheila. You're in this Family. Act like it." He didn't tell her she couldn't do things because of her father. He encouraged her to go to school and become a nurse, and she did it, despite her father's misgivings. And more than that, she was good at it.

Now, she knew, it had all been to benefit Joe. If she became a nurse, then she could help him when he needed it. And her father was someone who could help him escape.

After that, they started phoning using the limited privileges he earned in the prison. She didn't know it, but he was already bribing officers and had his group of insiders building slowly. He was a natural leader, even though he didn't enjoy doing it. He was capable. He had charisma to spare. And she loved him for it.

Then, she presented her father with his offer. Help to escape for his services from then on. He'd also promised to marry Sheila and become a permanent member of the Family, which was a big deal to her father. So, things had been arranged, and everything went off without a hitch. Except Joe had never intended to follow through on his plans with her father. He had his own plans, and he dragged her along.

She couldn't go back, so her only choice was to go to the police. She had to take the kids and run. That was her only option at this point. Her father would probably have her killed if she returned to him without Joe to fulfill the arrangement she'd made for him. He was a father, but he was a leader first and foremost, and he wouldn't hesitate to make an example of his daughter.

Rich wasn't sure what time this Chaz was supposed to arrive at the office, but he was expecting their arrival greatly. He hadn't gotten anywhere with military intelligence yet because they said everything was classified and he had to be given proper clearance. He understood the need to be careful, but they weren't considering the situation at all. It was very frustrating. But there was not much that he could do to change the speed of bureaucracy.

Simon knocked on the door to his office and he looked up to see that Chaz had arrived. Chaz was shorter than Simon, maybe five feet three or four, and had bright green hair shaved on one side and long on the other. Their eyes were obscure behind a pair of thick, chunky framed glasses in bright pink. They were wearing a band T-shirt and old, worn jeans and carrying a purple plaid backpack. On the strap to the bag was one of those pride flag buttons, with black, purple, white, and yellow with the words "They/Them" printed on it.

"Chaz, this is Agent Richard Pearson," Simon introduced.

"Yo. Agent Dick, huh?" Chaz said with a smirk.

"Rich, actually," he said, trying to smile despite hating being referred to by Dick.

"Yeah, so whatcha wantin' me to look at for ya?" they said, adjusting the bag and looking at the room. "Techguru, er, sorry, guess yer real name is Simon. Anyways, he told me ya had a tough nut ta crack and wanted ta give me a chance to try my magic on it."

"Yeah, let's go to Simon's desk and he can show you what we're dealing with. It's a technology that we've got no experience with. I've tried putting in with the higher-ups to get information, but that sort of request takes time. And we honestly don't know how much time we have before things go bad," Rich told them as he led them over to Simon's desk.

Chaz slid into the office chair and looked at the computer. "Anti-tracking tech, eh?" they muttered.

"Yeah, like I told you on the server, we're looking at something that can mask the location of where the signal source is coming from. It's cutting-edge and classified tech. Just like you like," Simon told them.

Chaz reached into their pocket and pulled out a hair tie and tied back their hair and adjusted the seat. They cracked their knuckles and smiled.

"Let's play, boys," they started typing in the program rapidly, barely pausing.

Chaz's incredible typing speed impressed him. He did not know what was going on, though. Everything was just flashes on the screen of text and boxes popping up here and there. He crossed his arms and watched until it was obvious this was going to take a while, so he went back to his office to see if there was anything from the military yet. Of course, there was nothing. He expected to get a response well after everything was over and done with.

After a solid two hours, Simon came running over to the door and knocked on it.

"Sir! We've got something!" he said, excited by whatever they had found.

"Great!" Rich said, getting up and following Simon back to his desk. Chaz looked up as they got there, smiling.

"So, this tech is major tough to break." They shook their head as they spoke. "But I broke the bitch."

Rich liked this kid. "All right, what did you figure out?"

"Well, I can't do much without a live signal. I've done what I can ta the program, though. I've set up something that we can use that should find the signal no matter what tech he's using to protect those two he's kidnapped." Chaz looked quite proud of what they'd done so far.

"Wait, how do you know about the kidnapping?" Rich asked, glaring at Simon.

"I didn't tell them!" Simon said, putting up both hands.

"Don't worry about it. Hacked yer system on the case. Sorry, couldn't resist it. Had ta know what was goin' on with it. But ya said I had immunity, so I figure I'd use it." They winked at Rich and Rich wanted to say something, but what could he say? They were doing the FBI a favor, as it was.

"All right, just don't go digging into anything else while you're here. I don't know how far I can make that promise of immunity stretch if you push the boundaries too hard." Rich sighed.

"Cool, cool," they said and pointed to the screen. "But the main thing is that next time yer boy calls in, if ya get in on the call immediately, it should trace back to him with the code I wrote up to breech the tech he's usin'."

"Can Simon use this, or do you need to be here to do it?" Rich asked, wondering how long it would even be before Joe called back again.

Chaz narrowed their eyes at Simon and then shook their head. "I don't know for sure. I can try and show Simon how ta use it the right way, but it would be better if I were here ta do it."

"Are you able to stick around in the area?" Rich didn't know what else to do. He had to make sure that this person was here for it when Joe contacted them again.

"I'm stayin' with Simon right now. I can stick around. I ain't got nothin' ta do right now. I brought my laptop, and that's all I really need to do what I do," they said, patting the backpack sitting on the floor at their feet.

"All right. I'll get you temporary credentials so you can come and go easier with Simon while we wait for the next call. We don't know when it will come in, so you'll need to be ready for it whenever it happens."

"Sounds great, Agent Rich." Chaz stood up and stretched their arms over their head. "Got a break room? I could go for a soda or somethin'." They reached down and picked up their bag as they spoke.

"Yeah, sure, Simon. Show them to the break room and then come back here. I'll work on getting the temporary creds for Chaz," Rich told them and watched as they took off to the back room.

Rich took care of everything immediately with the office assistant. The only thing left was for them to get their picture taken for the badge. He just had to hope that this only took a few more days to resolve. He didn't know how much time those two had, and who knew what kind of hell they were being put through so far?

Sheila came down and took away the plates from dinner, leaving them to themselves. It was a little lonely since there wasn't a lot to do. But tonight, Michael had an idea and CJ wasn't sure what he thought about it.

Michael wanted to play strip poker.

"I've never done anything like that!" CJ gasped.

"We'll, not only strip poker, but a special strip poker. Where when you lose, you draw from the hat." Michael smiled and held up a hat that he'd acquired from Sheila.

"What's in the hat?" CJ asked, curious.

"I made little pieces of paper with instructions on them while you were napping earlier. They have fun stuff on them. We'll each have to draw from the hat when we lose, so it's not going to just be you doing it. But we have to be quiet. We don't want Sheila and Joe coming down here to see what's going on, especially after I beat you and you're naked."

CJ narrowed his eyes at Michael. "Who said you were going to beat me?"

Michael smirked. "We'll see how you do." He began shuffling the cards.

CJ didn't know what to do at first. He wanted to make Michael happy. He really did, but it also embarrassed him at the same time. Could he strip if he lost? It wasn't like Michael hadn't seen him naked already. So, he got up from the bed and sat down across from him.

"Deal," he said, eyeing Michael.

Michael dropped a wink and dealt the cards. CJ's first hand was horrible. He had one ace, though, an ace of diamonds. But the rest were nothing much, and not even another diamond to go with the ace.

"Five-card draw," Michael said.

CJ lost the hand. He sighed as he stripped off his shirt. Michael held out the hat. "Not done yet!" he said.

"Yeah, yeah," CJ muttered, drawing a piece of paper from the hat.

He opened it and blinked. It said, "Kiss me on the cheek" and that was it. He frowned and showed him, and Michael leaned over and pointed to his cheek. CJ was a little embarrassed, even though it was no big deal, and kissed him gently on the cheek.

"Next round!" Michael said and handed the cards to CJ to shuffle and deal.

Over the next three hours, they went through several hands. CJ was definitely at a disadvantage because it became apparent that Michael knew what he was doing. It left him utterly naked, hands folded in his lap, while Michael still had his pants and undershorts on. The little slips of paper had been undeniably cute, reading things like "kiss my nose" and "kiss my hand." Michael could have easily made it more degrading to the loser, but he hadn't.

"You're blushing," Michael said as he shuffled the cards.

"I'm naked. Of course, I'm blushing!" CJ frowned and looked away from him.

Michael got up and came over. "You're naked and I have a problem," he said in a husky tone.

CJ turned back toward him to see he had pulled himself out of his pants and was holding his cock in his hand. CJ gasped and looked up at his face, seeing his blue eyes hooded with lust.

"Ah, okay." CJ wasn't sure what to say.

"I want to show you how much fun this is. I've never done it with a guy, but I've heard you need lube. We can use that conditioner, but I really want to fuck you right now," Michael said, breath heaving a little.

CJ stared at him. "You mean, put that... there?" he said.

"Um hmm. It'll feel good for both of us," Michael said.

"How do you know if you've never done it?" CJ narrowed his eyes and stared at him. He was hiding a growing erection, though, just at the thought of doing it with Michael.

"I've had sex with a girl before, and this isn't much different. If you don't want to, I'm not going to make you or anything. It's up to you," Michael said. "I just know I think we could make each other feel really good, and besides, we've got the time."

CJ swallowed and sighed a little. He wanted to do it, but he was scared. Wouldn't it hurt? He thought about when he'd fingered him. It had felt a little strange, but not bad. It felt nice, and he had to wonder what it felt like to go all the way. Especially with Michael.

"Okay," he said, nodding and looking down into his lap. "I want to do it with you."

Michael came closer and reached out a hand to him. "Come on, over on the bed. I'll do you from behind; it's easier for the first time like that, from what I've seen on videos."

"Videos?" CJ said as he stood up, still shielding his arousal from Michael's sight.

"I've seen a few," Michael said, nodding as he led him to the small cot. "Lay on your stomach. I'll grab that conditioner."

CJ did as he asked but was still unsure about the whole thing. He crushed the pillow to his chest and, a few moments later, jerked as he felt Michael's hands on his hips and ass.

"God, CJ. You're so beautiful," Michael breathed. "I think of you all the time, you know. Just seeing your body writhe under me is going to fill my head for days."

CJ nodded into the pillow he was hugging. He felt Michael's hand slide down and probe at him. He swallowed and gasped a little as his finger breached him, unnaturally slick. It felt nice, and his finger slid in and out quickly. A second later, he slipped a second finger into him, which stretched him, but it wasn't painful. He swallowed as he thrust those two fingers back and forth a few times.

"I think you're ready," Michael said in a strained voice. "I can't go any longer; I gotta do it," he added, and the bed moved as he got on and pressed in between CJ's legs.

Squeezing his eyes shut, CJ had no idea that tensing was bad. He soon felt what he knew was Michael's cock pressing at him. He swallowed a ball of fear in the back of his throat and gasped a little as Michael began pushing forward.

"I don't know about this," CJ said quietly. "I don't know if it'll fit in me!"

"Don't worry, CJ, it'll fit."

Michael pressed forward, and CJ gasped again a bit. "It kinda does hurt!"

"Relax, you're tensing up. I can feel it. It will hurt if you don't relax," Michael said, pressing forward more.

CJ tried to relax, but it was easier said than done. He felt like he was being pried open, and it was at the same time strange and erotic, and he didn't know why. Images began flying through his head about other times and places when, in his dreams, he'd lie with the one he loved. And that made the pain less important.

"I'm in all the way, CJ. You okay?" Michael said.

Pressing back a little, CJ could feel Michael's body against him. He could also feel his cock throbbing inside him, filling him up and making him feel strangely complete. He swallowed the fear that tried to bubble up his throat. Instead, all he wanted was for Michael to move.

"Move," he muttered, bucking his hips back against Michael.

"Hmm, yeah, baby," Michael said softly, slowly pulling out and pushing back in.

CJ couldn't help the moan that escaped his lips as Michael began thrusting deep and slow into him. It felt good, if a little painful at first. He had experienced nothing like it before, but being in this position with Michael was fulfilling. Michael thrust faster and hit a spot that made things go white for a second, making CJ gasp out loud and moan louder.

"I think I've got an angle on your sweet spot, baby," Michael said, seeming to aim for that same spot again.

After a few more thrusts, tears streamed down CJ's face, and he was in a constant state of moaning and pleading with Michael to go faster or deeper. Michael complied, thrusting deep and fast, making the small cot rock a bit as he did. CJ had never felt anything like it. It was initially uncomfortable, but it felt amazing as it continued. He'd never had this kind of sensation in his body. It was almost electric.

Michael then leaned over, moving one hand in front of CJ, and gripped him, sliding his hand up and down CJ's dripping shaft. CJ let out a long, low moan then, feeling the internal and external stimuli simultaneously. It was too much, and he felt the toe-curling sensation of an orgasm rushing toward him faster than he expected.

"Mikey!" he gasped. "Mikey, I'm coming!"

"Mikey?" Michael murmured but continued his ministrations, stroking CJ's cock as he thrust down into him harder and faster.

"I can't wait!" CJ said between moans.

"Don't wait. Come, baby, come for me," Michael said with a smile in his voice.

CJ didn't need much encouragement as he felt the orgasm slam into him, cascading through his body like a flow of water. Michael grunted and thrust a few more times, and then CJ felt him throbbing inside him as he came. Michael held his position, panting over CJ's back, clutching him to his chest.

"Oh my God, CJ, that was amazing," he gasped out. "Baby, that's the best sex I've ever had."

CJ clutched the pillow, coming down off the high sensation himself. "I've never felt so good," he whispered in confirmation.

[A Place Unnamed—A Time Unknown]

Brishna wept tears of ecstasy into the void of silence. The reunion with her beloved had occurred, and she was once again whole. Though she feared. The evil one would try to do everything to separate them, and he would do anything to claim Brishna for himself. There was nothing Brishna could do, though, for she could not act while contained within the vessel.

Only Iman's death would break the cycle. She didn't know how, but it would have to happen, so she and Krineshaw could be one together.

Chapter Eleven

The Pawn's Escape

Sheila washed the dishes numbly, losing herself in her mind. She was still sore and the bruises on her body reminded her of each day. Joe was on his computer again, mumbling about making sure no one could trace it when he called them the next day, and Sheila knew things were going to happen. She had to do something, and soon. She couldn't make a move with him there, though. There was no way. Even when he was sleeping, it was too dangerous to do something. She had to wait for him to leave.

"You feed those fucking kids?" he growled, turning up in the doorway.

She turned to him. "Yeah, they're fed. And drugged. Just like you wanted."

"They better fucking be," he continued, and she wondered if he was going to strike her again.

He turned and returned to the living room, and she breathed a sigh. She swallowed against a sore throat. After the abuse it had taken the night before, it was no wonder. She didn't have much to say about it, though. It was her place. She chose it.

But did she really choose anything? She guessed she had. When Joe told her to steal the medicine, she could have denied him. She could have denied him when he told her to come here via coordinates. She could have just gone to her father and given him those coordinates, and he would have cared for Joe without a second thought. But her heart had gotten in the way. She thought she loved him more than life and did anything for him.

And she had. She looked out the window and exhaled.

"What do I do?" she whispered to herself.

Chaz chugged their soda and stared across the table at Simon. They smiled at him.

"So, Simon, tell me a bit about yourself. Techguru, indeed?" Chaz smirked.

Simon blushed a little. "Ah, my life isn't interesting at all," he said. "I mean, I picked up forensics in college and combined it with my technology experience, and when I graduated, I caught the eye of an FBI recruiter. That's really all there was to it."

Chaz ran a hand through their green hair. They'd removed the hair tie so the non-shaved side flowed down over their shoulder. "I never got ta go to school."

Simon looked up from his chips and frowned. "What?" he asked. "How did you learn so much tech stuff?"

"My friend was in a cybercrime group. Well, I thought he was more than a friend. Spent a lot of time on my back, just to learn the stuff I wanted to learn. Didn't think of it at tha time that I was tradin' sex for trainin' but ya know, what can ya do?"

Simon was quiet as he sipped the cola he had. Chaz guessed it disgusted him. "That's terrible that he took advantage of you like that. I mean, how old were you even?"

Chaz looked up and blinked. He wasn't disgusted. "I guess fourteen."

"And how old was this guy?"

Chaz shifted uncomfortably with that question. But what could they do? "I guess about twenty-five."

Simon let out a low whistle. "That fucker's lucky he never got caught."

Shrugging, Chaz looked toward the window. "Well, I made the choice."

"You were a kid. You didn't really make a choice," Simon said with a great deal of venom in his normally placid voice.

Chaz turned back because of that. "Well, I mean, I knew better. I just wanted to know more about computers, and there was no way I was going to school. How could you say I didn't choose? Even then, I knew it was wrong."

"You weren't even eighteen," Simon tried to tell them. "I can bet he didn't treat you well, either."

Chaz swallowed hard. "I mean, well enough. I was still living with my parents. Well, technically, I was living with them. They didn't give two shits where I was really, so I just did my thing. If I didn't come home, they never noticed." Chaz shrugged. "But what else could I do? I didn't see a future coming out of a house like that. Mom drank wine on the daily, and dad was never there. So, what else was there for me?"

Simon was silent for a while, and they both ruminated on what Chaz had said. Finally, Simon cleared his throat. "Well, I could treat you better than he ever did."

Blinking, Chaz turned toward him, unsure how to respond. "Is that a half-assed way to ask me out, Techguru?"

"Well, for me, it's whole-assed, I guess." Simon was blushing again.

"You know I'm not a girl, right? Not a guy either."

"I know that. And I don't care. I really like you, and I want to show you that I do." He brushed a hand over his own head and looked back. "I've never dated anyone, though, so we'd be figuring out what to do together."

Chaz smiled. "Alright, Techguru. All right. We can try this, and we'll see what you can do outside the computer system." They winked at him, and Simon blushed again.

"I'm going out," Joe said, grabbing his wallet from the table and headed out the door.

Sheila stayed sitting for a few minutes, then felt her heartbeat hard in her chest. It was going to be now or never, and this was the only chance she was going to get before he took the step of murdering those kids downstairs. After a few minutes, she got up and went to the window, and saw the van leave the shed. Her car was in there. If she could get CJ and Michael out before Joe got back, this would all be over. She'd turn the evidence to the police, and they'd protect her.

She opened the door and rushed down the basement stairs. CJ and Michael were playing a card game and looked up as she came down.

"Get up, now," she said. "We're leaving."

CJ and Michael exchanged a look and then got up, saying nothing. She waved her hands to hurry them along, and then Sheila took them up the stairs. CJ and Michael were quick enough, and they rushed up the stairs and out into the empty kitchen. She stopped and glanced around, making sure Joe was nowhere to be found. She heaved a sigh and pushed the two of them toward the door.

Once outside, they ran to the shed where the car was. Fumbling with the keys for a moment, she unlocked it, stopping once again to look for any sign Joe had come back. She let the boys get in the back, and she got in the driver's seat and started the Chevy. For a moment, it hesitated to start, and she almost panicked. It finally turned over, and she breathed a sigh of relief.

"Be quiet and get down," she said as she pulled out of the shed.

CJ and Michael ducked down in the back seat, and she stopped to look around again. She felt so paranoid, but she had to remember, it wasn't being paranoid when what you feared was real.

She thought she would make it this way. He was gone, and there was no way he'd already have returned to the hideout. But she was mistaken because as she was about to pull onto the gravel road leading out to the main road, the van appeared from the trees. How could she have missed that? He wasn't there a moment ago! She gasped, turning the wheel to avoid crashing into it, and slammed head first into a gigantic tree.

Shaken, she turned back.

"Run," she said. "Just run down the road and turn to the left at the end of the gravel road. Then go for a house." She got out and took off, prioritizing herself over those kids. If they didn't move fast enough, she couldn't help them.

A shot rang out, exploding the dirt at her feet, but she kept running. He had a gun, and she wasn't going to get shot.

Michael couldn't believe what happened, but he rushed to get out and CJ did the same on the other side. Sheila was already gone. So, Joe would have to go after her or after them, and somehow Michael doubted Joe was going to give them up. CJ came around and Michael grabbed his hand, and they took off for the gravel road. Michael looked to the side of the road and found it lined with thorny looking bushes and other shrubs. He shook his head because they couldn't make it through that. That left the road. Unfortunately, it was open, and Joe had a clear shot to either of them. Michael was banking on him wanting them alive, though, and figured he'd chase after them.

"Fucking stop, or you're dead!" Michael heard.

He glanced back, and Joe was standing by the van, not running after them at all. Michael shook his head.

"Keep going, no matter what, CJ, don't stop!" he said as they ran.

Then, there was another loud crack and this time, pain exploded in his upper right leg. He screamed and fell immediately, pulling CJ down to the gravel with him. He'd never felt anything like it; it was like someone was ripping the muscle away from the bone and twisting at the same time. It was hot and burning and his entire leg was wet with blood.

"Michael!" CJ gasped, scrambling to get to his feet. "You can't run!"

"No, go! God dammit, just run, CJ! Get out and get help!" he said, tears forming in his eyes from the pain.

"I can't just leave you!" CJ gasped, looking back. "He's coming!"

"Run, and you're next, CJ!" Joe yelled, growing closer by the second.

There was another crack, and the ground inches from CJ exploded as the bullet impacted. "I can't run. He's gonna shoot me!"

"You can get away!" Michael encouraged and turned to look. "He's coming, just go!" he said, stumbling to stand on his one good leg. "I'll stop him!"

"CJ, if you run, I'm going to shoot your boyfriend right in the fucking face, got it?" Joe said, now only a few feet away.

"Leave him alone!" Michael said, stumbling on a leg that was screaming in pain. He couldn't put any weight on it, so he wasn't sure what he thought he was supposed to do to stop Joe from getting to CJ.

The ground at his feet exploded after another crack. CJ, instead of running, had frozen in place. Michael cursed their luck. He wondered how many times Joe had pretended to leave, just to see if Sheila would do anything like this. Obviously, he had never trusted her to start with. He had to be close to empty on bullets, right?

"Stay right there," Joe said.

CJ grabbed onto Michael's left arm, and Michael leaned into him heavily. Michael didn't let his fear show, though. He stood as straight as possible, even faced with Joe and a loaded gun. He had to at least show him he wasn't afraid, even if he was shaken to his core.

"Back to the house," he said, gesturing with the gun.

When neither of them moved, he stepped forward, flipping the gun around and slammed the butt into Michael's face, knocking his precarious balance off. Michael felt the pain radiate across his face from the blow, and nearly face planted in the gravel. CJ leaned down and helped him back up. Michael felt blood running down his cheek from the blow.

"Move, now," Joe growled.

Hobbled, Michael leaned against CJ for most of his support. The smaller man, though, was having difficulty holding him up, and Michael felt bad for being the one injured. He was supposed to save CJ, not be the one CJ saved. The pain was throbbing, but he swallowed and willed it to go away. He didn't know anything about guns and bullets, but he knew it wasn't good when someone got shot in the leg. He wasn't dead, so that meant he hadn't hit the artery.

CJ stumbled at the step, helping Michael up and into the door. They paused, and Joe grabbed CJ by the hair and yanked him backward.

"You're going to pay for what just happened. Get downstairs," he said, pushing his head forward.

CJ struggled with Michael's weight as they got downstairs, and he dropped Michael on the bed. Michael looked up at him and saw that he was crying.

"What should I do?" he whispered.

"Get b-bleeding stopped," Michael stammered as he shivered. "Wrap the w-wound. Sheet. Tie it. That's all-all we c-can do right now."

CJ pulled off the sheet and used it to tie around Michael's leg, staunching the slow flow of blood and covering the wound. He looked at Michael.

"What now?" he whispered.

"We wait," Michael said.

Shelia thanked the truck driver that had taken her back to town. He'd found her on the road leading to the interstate and offered her a ride. She hadn't been sure, but it was a hell of a long walk back to St. Louis where she was at. If she could get to somewhere with a phone, she could call a friend in St. Louis who would put her up for the night. She walked into the truck stop and looked around. If she was lucky, they'd let her use the phone.

"Hey, can I use the phone? My cell's lost and I need to get to my friend's place," she told the lady behind the counter.

She was a short, plump woman with an acne-scarred face and round glasses. But she smiled at Sheila.

"Here, use this," she said, handing over a cell phone.

Sheila thanked her and took it, dialing Beatrice. Beatrice O'Connell was a high school friend, and one of the few people she could trust completely. She just hoped she answered.

"Hello?" came Bea's voice.

"Hey, it's Sheila. Sorry for the strange number. I don't have a cell anymore," she said.

"Sheila? What's going on? You don't call for no reason."

Sheila sighed because that was true. "I need somewhere to crash. And a ride to get there."

"You know my couch is always open," Bea said. "Where are you?"

Sheila gave her the location of the truck stop and then handed the phone back to the lady behind the counter, thanking her. She then went to wait outside until Beatrice arrived.

About fifteen minutes later, the familiar green mustang pulled in and Sheila smiled. Some things never changed. That mustang was one of them. She was grateful for some sense of familiarity. She pulled open the passenger door and slid down into the seat.

"Bea, thanks for this," she said, turning to the red-headed woman.

Beatrice was a plump woman, but in the voluptuous way that made men come after her. She had a set of huge breasts and wore clothes that showed them off, and a shapely hour-glass figure with a moderate stomach. Her hips and legs went on for days, and she was always willing to show them off in short skirts. She was very much Sheila's opposite body type.

"No problem, you're my sis, after all. Let's get back. Want anything on the way to my place?" Bea asked.

"Nah, I just need somewhere to get away from everything."

As Bea drove, they listened to the local rock station and Sheila watched the world go by outside. She didn't know what had happened to CJ and Michael, and she kept dwelling on it. She'd run when given the chance, proving she was nothing but a coward. When it counted, she hadn't saved them; she hadn't even looked back even when she heard gunshots. She'd just kept going, leaving them behind. Bea wasn't safe, not by a long shot, but she was the only chance she had. She had to decide what to do now.

They pulled into the apartment complex, and Sheila followed Bea up to the fifth floor to her place. She entered and flopped onto the couch.

"So, what happened?" Bea said, sitting on the adjacent love seat.

Sheila turned to her. "Oh, all sorts of shit. Remember that guy I told you about, Joe?"

"The one in the prison that I told you not to get involved with?" Bea arched a sculpted brow at her.

Sheila sighed. "Yeah. That one."

"Is that why you look like hell?"

Sheila nodded. "Yeah, turns out he's a bad man. And not in the good way," she said, running a hand through her platinum blonde hair. "I was stuck, though. You know, I was helping him get out of his situation with my father's help. But then, he had other plans than to help my father."

"So, not only are you on the outs with this guy, you're on the outs with your father, too?" she said, looking a little unsurprised.

"Yeah, it's like that."

"What happened today?" Bea asked.

Sheila didn't want to tell her about the kidnapping. It would put her in danger if she knew the truth completely. She swallowed. "Well, just finally decided I'd had enough."

"So, you need to disappear for a while?" Bea asked.

"Probably for good. I don't want to face my father again. I can't do that. He'll kill me." Sheila knew better than anyone that he wouldn't hesitate.

CJ didn't know what to do. Michael's bleeding had stopped mostly, but it was still a terrible wound. He sat on the floor beside Michael's cot. He'd fallen into a fitful sleep, but CJ couldn't do the same at all. A feeling of dread had settled into his chest. There had been no food since they came back, and somehow, he doubted they would receive anything again since Sheila was gone now.

He wondered if they'd just starve to death down here, and then that would be it. Surely, someone would find them before that happened. Sheila would help them, wouldn't she? He swallowed. He couldn't count on that. Given the chance, she'd run, and she'd gotten away. He turned and looked at Michael. What would happen to him? A gunshot wound was nothing small, and if the bullet was still in his leg, what were they supposed to do? He put his head in his hands. He could have run, but he froze instead.

Michael's hand touched his head, and he turned to look at him.

"You okay?"

"Hurts, but I'm alive, so that's something, right?" Michael said, sighing a little.

CJ jumped as the door banged open, his heart stopping in his chest. He stared at Michael, locking eyes with him for a moment, before both turned to see Joe coming down the stairs. CJ's stomach dropped because he still had the gun. Something bad was coming.

He leveled the gun at CJ's head. "Get up."

CJ scrambled to his feet, eyes wide at the sight of the gun. They were trapped here. Why did he have the gun?

Joe held out a set of handcuffs. "Put this on Michael. Attach it to the bed frame."

CJ took the handcuffs and did what he said. He didn't have much choice in the matter, and he had no idea what was going on. Joe glared at him as he stood back up and looked at him.

"Gimme yer hands," he growled.

CJ held out his hands and Joe stepped forward, pulling a set of handcuffs out of his pocket, and slapped them onto CJ's wrists. "You ain't going anywhere," he said, narrowing his eyes at CJ.

Suddenly, Joe slapped CJ across the face. CJ gasped, pulling his hands up to hold his cheek, staring up at his dark eyes. Then

Joe smiled, reaching out his free hand. He grabbed him by the hair, twisting his head to the side.

"You've been teasing since you got here," he said, staring at him with those hard eyes.

"Wh-what do you mean?" CJ gasped, his scalp hurting from the hold on his hair.

"I mean, you want me to fuck you, don't you?" he said after a few seconds of silence.

CJ swallowed and shook his head. "No, please, don't do this."

"I'll do what I want, don't you understand that?" he growled and yanked him to the side by his hair, forcing him down onto the second cot beside Michael's. He pushed him onto his back and used the gun to make him lie down and face him.

"What are you doing?" Michael gasped, yanking hard on the handcuff. "You leave him alone, you bastard!"

Joe pointed the gun directly at CJ's head. "Keep it up, boy. I'll splatter his brains all over this bed. Is that what you want?"

Michael stared at CJ, who turned his head to the side, eyes wide and frightened. Joe took his free hand and pulled the sweats down CJ's hips slowly, exposing him to the chilly air of the room.

"P-please don't do this," CJ's eyes filled with tears from the sheer mortification of it all.

Joe flipped the gun around in his hand and struck CJ across the jaw, hard with the butt. "Fucking shut your goddamned mouth before I make it where you can't talk anymore, got it?"

CJ was quiet, blood filling his mouth and his jaw aching from the strike. He felt like something had loosened in his jaw when he hit him, and pain exploded in the side he'd hit. The lip had split and blood just kept flowing from the wound into his mouth, nearly choking him. Joe pulled the sweatpants off completely, leaving him bare from the waist down and trying to catch a desperate breath.

"You're not much to look at," Joe commented, sliding a hand down the dip of CJ's hips. He turned to Michael. "You've already had him, haven't you, faggot?"

Michael didn't say anything, but CJ glanced over to see him fighting with the desire to do so. It was obvious he wanted to say something. With the pain in his jaw, CJ didn't even know if he could talk, let alone try with the gun on him like this.

"Spread your legs for me like you do for that other fag," Joe demanded, gun pointed at CJ's head again.

CJ shook with fear and embarrassment, and he did what he said, spreading his legs open and allowing Joe to move between them. He reached down and cupped CJ's balls in his hand, then squeezed him. As Joe continued to squeeze, CJ emitted a low, painful whine. Finally, he let go of him and then slid a finger into him dry.

"Yeah, you fags have been fucking down here already," Joe said to no one in particular, roughly slipping a second finger in and plunging both back and forth painfully.

CJ was helpless as he lay there and let Joe do whatever he wanted. He didn't have much choice. He supposed he could have tried to run, but what would have been the point? Joe would still have Michael, and then what? Where would CJ even go? He whimpered as Joe pulled his fingers back.

CJ looked down as Joe pulled himself free from his jeans, and his eyes widened. Joe was a lot bigger than Michael. And he knew beyond a doubt this was going to hurt a lot. Joe pressed up between his legs and against him. Then, without warning, he thrust hard into him, sliding all the way in without hesitation.

Gasping for air, CJ arched up, wanting to do anything to get him out of his body. He heard Michael make a noise, and he wanted anything to have this be somewhere except in front of him.

"CJ, your ass is pretty tight. I think I like it," Joe said, thrusting in and out a few times. "Did it feel good when I thrust into you like that, filling your ass-pussy with my cock? What about it do you like? A real man's cock differs from a boy's," he said as he thrust back and forth harder.

CJ couldn't do anything but let the tears fall because it felt like he was tearing everything inside him apart. He was still bleeding from his lip, and it didn't feel anything like the pain from Joe's treatment. He just wanted him to finish and stop. Of course, that would have been the easy way out. Instead, Joe seemed intent on making it last as long as he could, putting his hands, even the one with the gun, on the bed by CJ's head so he could pound into him harder and rougher.

"Well, I smell blood," Joe commented. "I knew you'd bleed for me, bitch boy."

CJ turned toward Michael and saw him just staring hollowly at him, and his wrist was bleeding already from trying to get out of the handcuff. CJ looked at Joe and felt him stiffen, sliding inside and releasing, his cock throbbing as he came. He thought he was done. He had to be done.

He wasn't.

He grabbed CJ by the arm, flipped him to his stomach, and walked around to the front of the bed, presenting his flaccid member to CJ.

"Use your mouth," he said.

CJ's eyes went wide. He shook his head, but Joe pulled the gun up and pressed it to his temple. "Open. A little ass-to-mouth won't kill you."

CJ opened, and he forced himself forward. CJ didn't know a lot about this, but he felt his cock rapidly hardening in his mouth, filling it up quickly. He grabbed his head and forced it down his throat a few times, thrusting back and forth until it seemed he was satisfied. Then he pulled out of his mouth and went around behind him again, slamming his cock into him again. CJ whined loudly as he roughly fucked him, then he grabbed him by the hair, yanking his head back to his chest and making him sit up on his knees while he was inside.

"Good bitch, you make a perfect receptacle for my come. I think I'll use you until I kill you. How's that? You like that idea, being fucked by me until you're of no use? Or maybe I'll just shoot your boyfriend over there and keep you as my fuck-toy. Hmm, that might be an idea," he said as he slammed forward hard enough to make something shoot deep pain in him.

He let go of his hair and forced his head down, knocking his glasses off his face, and they hit the ground with a cracking sound. CJ looked, his vision blurry from tears and more now, as he saw his glasses had broken when they hit the ground. He only had a moment to think about it, because Joe was pressing him into the bed and fucking him hard and fast, making it hurt as much as possible. He went a little numb then, the world quieting and everything seeming unreal in that moment.

When he felt the throbbing inside him again, he crashed back to reality. He choked on tears and blood and hid his face in the bed as Joe got up, slapping CJ's ass hard as he stepped back.

"Not bad. I'll be back in the morning," he threatened and went up the stairs, leaving them both cuffed.

The door slammed, and CJ couldn't stop the tears that suddenly hit him. He started sobbing loudly into the bed, and Michael was quiet the whole time, letting him get out the tears. When they slowed, Michael whispered, "I'm sorry, CJ. I'm so sorry."

CJ turned over, sitting up, and saw his sweatpants on the floor. Despite being handcuffed, he got them on. He had to get them on. He couldn't be naked right then, not after what had just happened.

"We're going to get out of here," Michael said, but he didn't sound as sure as before.

Chapter Twelve

The Queen's Despair

Sheila woke up with the sun. She felt guilty for leaving those kids, even though she knew she had no choice. Nevertheless, what Joe would do to them was terrible, and it was her fault for trying to get them away before he killed them. She flopped over and found Bea was standing there, staring at her with a cup of coffee in her hand.

"Want a cup?" she asked.

Sheila sat up and nodded, gratefully taking the cup from her.

"Thanks," she said and sighed.

"What's wrong?" Bea said, sitting down beside her on the sofa with her own cup of coffee.

"I might have done something bad when I left, and now I don't know what to do about it. I don't want to tell you, though, because you could get in trouble for just knowing it," Sheila explained, taking a sip of the hot beverage.

Bea sighed. "Sheila, you know I'm here for you. Why don't you just tell me and get it over with? It's not like I'm gonna tell anyone," she added.

Sheila looked at her over the steaming cup. "Joe kidnapped two college kids."

"Wait, what? He did what?" Bea said, sitting the coffee on the side table slowly.

"Their names are Michael and CJ. Two boys. I think the one at least is gay or something, or maybe wants to be a girl, I dunno, but that doesn't matter. What matters is yesterday I tried to leave with them because he intends to kill them before the whole thing's done. But he caught us, and I got away. He shot one of them. I heard him go down. I don't know what else happened, but he was focused on catching them again instead of me." Sheila paused. "I don't know what to do now."

"Go to the police, Sheila! You can't just let him kill people! Not if you can stop it!" Bea exclaimed, eyes wide and staring at Sheila.

Sheila sighed again. "But they'll arrest me, too. I stole a bunch of drugs from the hospital I was working at, and they got it on camera, so I'll definitely go to jail for this."

"Jail is one thing, but can you live with two murdered kids on your conscience?"

Sheila looked away. "I guess you're right. I don't even know who to call. I think the FBI is involved."

"I'll take you to their building. I know where it is," Bea said, standing. "Come find some clean clothes and we'll go after you take a shower. You have to do this, Sheila. You can't let two boys die when you can stop it."

Sheila got up, draining the coffee from the cup first. Bea took her, and she picked out a couple things, a pair of sweatpants and a T-shirt, and then she got in the shower. It was a little after seven when she was done getting ready to go. Admittedly, she was going slow as she got showered, her mind wandering until the water went cold.

Bea had dressed while she was in the shower and nodded. "You can do this, Sheila."

"I guess I've got no choice," she whispered and followed Bea back out to the mustang.

She got in and rode in silence. Her mind was completely on those two boys now, and she couldn't think of anything else. She didn't know how this would work, but she guessed she'd find out soon enough. She followed Bea to the entry and up the elevator to the floor where the FBI office was located. They entered and Bea led her to the receptionist at the front.

"Yes, we have information on a case," Bea said confidently.

The receptionist, who had a plaque that read "Annette" looked at them curiously. "A case?"

"Yeah, Sheila, you tell her."

Sheila looked at Annette and couldn't talk for a minute. "Uh... Well, you see, I was with Joe Jackson. He kidnapped CJ Kim and Michael Heights. And I think the FBI was involved."

Annette reached for the phone. "Agent Pearson? I think you should come to the front. It's about the Kim/Heights case. Yes, sir. Thank you, sir."

"Just a moment. Have a seat over there," Annette said, indicating the chairs nearby.

Bea and Sheila took a seat and waited. After a few minutes, a man with blond hair pulled back in a low ponytail and a pair of glasses came in their direction. He approached and pulled off the glasses, placing them in his shirt pocket.

"Ladies, can I help you?" he said, but he was staring directly at Sheila.

"I guess you already know me," she mumbled.

"Sheila. Yes, we have your file. Tell me, what's happened?" he asked.

Swallowing, she crossed her arms over her chest. "I mean, it's a long story. Do you have an office?"

He nodded. "I'm Agent Richard Pearson. Please, follow me," he said.

The agent took them to a small conference room with a table and chairs and took a seat. Bea and Sheila sat down near him.

Sheila reached out and took Bea's hand suddenly as the fear of what was going to happen to her set in for real now.

"So, Sheila, give me what's happened?" Agent Pearson said, staring at her with questioning eyes.

She swallowed hard. "I left. I tried to take CJ and Michael with me, but Joe was waiting. I guess he was waiting for me to do something like that, and I crashed my car into a tree. I got out and ran. I heard the gunshots behind me, and I think one boy went down. I'm not sure though. I just ran." She chewed her lip for a moment. "I know I should have gone back, but he would have killed me this time."

"I take it Joe's the reason for the bruises," he noticed.

She nodded. "I thought I loved him. How could I love a monster like him?" she whispered.

"Can you take someone to the place where he's at?" the agent asked.

She shook her head. "I don't think I could find it again. The first time, when I drove there, I was using GPS coordinates, so I didn't pay attention to where I was going other than to follow the GPS. Then, when I ran, I had a truck driver pick me up and I don't know, I ended up on the north side of St. Louis where Bea came and got me."

"But we're dealing with the north, right?" he asked.

"I think so," she nodded. "Bea could tell you where she picked me up at."

The agent looked at Bea. Bea gave the location she'd picked Sheila up at, and he jotted it down on a notepad he pulled from the interior pocket of his jacket. He nodded.

"Okay, stay here. Someone will be in to talk to you," he said, standing.

"Um, just wondering, what'll happen to me?" she asked.

The agent sighed. "I don't know what I can do for you, but I can try to get you help. You coming and giving this information looks good for you, but considering the type of man Joe Jackson is, I don't think you'll be safe. And considering who your father is."

Sheila nodded. "I'm going to disappear, aren't I?"

"Most likely," he said and left the room.

Sheila sat holding Bea's hand for a while. "It'll be okay," she said finally. "I did what I could, right?" She turned and looked at Bea with tears in her eyes.

Bea reached her free hand out and cupped her face. "You did what you could."

CJ sat on the cot and held his knees to his chest. He hurt still. It was an ache that didn't want to go away, and it reminded him of what had happened the night before. He'd barely slept because every time he closed his eyes, he saw Joe's dark eyes boring into him. Michael had a rough time sleeping too, but he was in a lot of pain. Luckily, there was a pitcher left down there that Michael could relieve himself in if CJ held it for him. It wasn't easy with the handcuffs, but they managed.

"CJ, are you okay?" Michael asked for about the hundredth time.

"Michael, just stop asking," CJ said, barely above a whisper. "I'm fine."

"I know. I just wish I couldn't have done something. Anything."

CJ shook his head. "There's nothing to do. If we're lucky, we both live. If we aren't, we both die. Sheila's gone. We're stuck with him now, and with your injury, we can't run even if we could get away."

"You could get away," Michael said. "You could have run."

"He would have shot me," CJ said with finality. He didn't want to talk anymore.

After a few minutes of sitting in silence, the door opened. CJ's heart pounded in his chest as he looked up. Joe was standing in the doorway.

"Get yer scrawny ass up here, boy," he growled. "Fix food."

CJ got to his feet, stumbling a little as he tried to keep his balance. He walked up the stairs, and he got his first real look at the main part of the house and was shocked. When he'd been ushered through before, he hadn't noticed how perfectly normal it was. He entered a quaint little kitchen with yellow gingham curtains on the windows overlooking a wooded area. There was a stove, refrigerator, dishwasher, and trash compactor. A pantry door was nearby, and there was a bar on the other side of which was a breakfast nook with windows surrounding it.

Joe unlocked the handcuffs and put them in his pocket, then turned away and walked around the counter.

"Fix something to eat." Joe sat down at the bar and stared at him.

CJ didn't know much about cooking, but he wasn't about to say that. He went to the refrigerator and opened it up, seeing what was in it. Eggs, he noted. Okay, he thought he could cook eggs. He pulled them out and then opened the freezer on top and found some of those shredded hash browns. He thought those would be easy. They just went in the pan with some oil and that was it. He swallowed and set to cooking the eggs and the hash browns. He didn't know what else to do. He made enough for Joe and the two of them, putting it on three plates.

Joe took the plate and glared up at him. "Feed the other faggot."

CJ nodded, picking up the two plates and taking them both downstairs.

"Come clean up when yer done!" Joe called down after him.

Sitting down on the bed by Michael's good leg, CJ waited for him to sit up on the cot.

"That bastard would make you cook," Michael said as he pulled himself to sit up and took the plate from CJ.

CJ nodded, eating even though he was sick to his stomach. He had to eat, and if he didn't, Michael would worry. He didn't want Michael to worry. It was already bad enough with the leg injury. He didn't want to make Michael feel worse. They finished, and CJ took the plates back up the stairs. He didn't see Joe, but the empty plate was in the sink. He washed all the dishes and put them away. He guessed he'd just go back downstairs.

"Where the fuck are you going?" Joe demanded from the small dining room as CJ left the kitchen.

CJ jerked because he hadn't even seen him sitting in the darkened room. CJ's heart hammered in his chest.

"I-I was g-going back downstairs," he said.

"Get yer faggoty ass in here."

CJ swallowed and went into the dining room. Joe was sitting facing him and he stood up, towering over him. For some reason, he seemed so much bigger than he really was. He reached out and grabbed CJ by the back of the hair and yanked him forward, pushing him over the table. CJ's eyes went wide as he caught himself before his face hit the table. Not again, he thought, but Joe's hands were already on his hips, and he could feel him hard through his pants.

"Told you, you're my fuck-toy from now on," he said in a husky voice, sliding the sweatpants down CJ's hips. "Sheila's not here, so I'll use you. Imagine what your father would think, seeing his son bent over this table, ass bare to the world, about to be split open by his enemy's cock. It's a good look on you, this fear," he said and kicked CJ's legs further apart.

There was a pause as he pulled himself from his pants and then positioned himself against CJ and slammed forward. CJ choked on spit, because between the soreness of the night before and the fresh pain, he couldn't stand it. He let out a deep sob.

"Oh, are you crying, bitch?" Joe said, thrusting hard into him. "You feel bad because it feels good, don't you? Why don't we make it feel good, huh?"

He reached down and began playing with CJ's cock. CJ let out a moan because, despite what was happening, his cock reacted to being played with. He was mortified because it started to feel good when he stroked him.

"Look at that. You're getting hard while I'm raping your ass. What does that mean, huh? If I can make you hard? Maybe even make you come? What's that mean?" Joe wasn't letting up at all, slamming into him enough that the table was shaking and stroking him at the same time.

CJ began to sob and moan at the same time. He didn't want this at all, but his body was reacting to what he was doing. In the back of his mind, he knew he couldn't help his body's reaction to stimulation, but it didn't help. The sheer mortification of getting any pleasure out of it was almost too much for him. The more he stroked CJ, the closer he came. He panicked as his body jerked and the unwanted orgasm came.

"The fuck? Are you some kind of freak?" Joe laughed, slamming into him hard. He wiped his hand on CJ's shirt and kept going. "Coming while being raped. What kind of freak does that? Just a gay freak like you." He leaned over him and grabbed his chin, wrenching his head to the side. "Should I tell Mikey downstairs that I made you come like a bitch in heat?"

"P-please... no..." he begged, tears streaming down his face.

"You don't want me telling anyone you fucking enjoyed it, do you?" he hissed. "I bet your daddy would love to know that I made his faggot child come with my cock up his ass. Wouldn't he like that?" he growled and threw his head forward.

CJ put his head down on the table as Joe clutched his hips and sped his way to completion, finally coming and pulling out. He made sure to slap him hard.

"Get your ass back downstairs."

CJ pulled up his sweats and couldn't stop crying. He stumbled back down the stairs, unable to stop the sobs wracking his body.

"CJ!" Michael said as the door slammed upstairs. "What did he do?"

"Nothing!" CJ gasped and turned away from him. "He didn't do anything!"

"CJ, please don't lie to me!" Michael said in a hushed tone, and CJ let out a loud sob at that.

He didn't want Michael to know what had just happened, but how could he lie to him, either? He shook his head.

"He said what he wanted last night," he said after he got his tears under control. He couldn't stop them completely, though. "You know what he did."

Michael didn't say anything else, and CJ was glad. He laid down and wept bitterly for a while. He didn't think there was anything that could save them now. Joe had made his intentions clear, and he didn't doubt he'd follow through on the threats to kill Michael and leave with CJ. That, more than anything, was what CJ was afraid of.

Rich sighed. He was tired of waiting. They either needed to find more information, or Joe needed to call. They hadn't heard anything in days, and one, if not both, of those boys were wounded. Time was not on their side. He had both Simon and Chaz working on what they had already, but Chaz wasn't sure there was anything they could do until he called them again. Chaz was confident that they could trace it back to him, especially now that they had a general direction to look in. He looked up to see Don and Randy standing in the doorway.

"Anything?" Don asked.

"Nothing more than you already know," Rich said, standing up and walking around the desk. "Simon and Chaz are working.

Multiple people have interrogated Sheila, and we're sure we've gotten all the information she offers."

"How'd she get wrapped up in this, anyway?" Randy asked, frowning.

Rich shook his head. "She started talking to him by mail. And he seduced her into doing everything he wanted her to do. She was vulnerable, and he took advantage of it," Rich explained. "I feel bad for her in some ways, but she still made her own choices."

"What's going to happen to her now?" Don asked.

"Witness protection program. With her father, she's not safe. And with Joe, even if we catch him, there's no telling how many people he has working for him we're not aware of." He paused. "I don't even know if witsec will be enough to protect her."

"Sir!" came a voice from down the hall. "He's called again!"

"Keep him on as long as possible," Rich said as they all three rushed into the next room.

Chaz nodded their green head at Rich as they tapped away on the computer and Simon did likewise next to them.

"Joe?" Don said as they got nearby.

"Donny," Joe answered. "I guess the bitch ran to you."

"What do you mean, Joe?" Randy said from beside him.

"Don't play coy with me," Joe growled out. "I have your kids, remember? Oh, Don, let me tell you, your son's ass is sweet. Too bad he's wrecked, now."

Don's eyes went wide. "What the fuck did you do?"

Randy put a hand on him and shook his head. "Joe, you touch them—"

"Oh, I've done more than touch, that's for sure," he said, pride in his voice. "But no matter what happens, your bitch boy will never be the same again."

Don was shaking with rage, and Rich knew it had to be difficult for him not to lash out verbally at Joe right then. He wanted to think Joe was making up stuff to get under their skin.

But a part of him knew Joe would be more than willing to take things that far.

Randy cleared his throat and put both hands on Don's shoulders. "Dammit, Joe. Cut the bullshit. You wanted money, we got the money."

"It was never about the money, Randy," Joe said, the levity gone from his tone. "And you know that. It was always about the game. I got what I wanted. I won."

The line went dead.

Michael fought with the pain coursing through his leg. It wasn't good, but what could he do? The bullet had torn through the outside of his thigh. He didn't know if it had come out, or if it was still in there, but he knew it hurt like a bitch. Only thoughts of CJ could take his mind off the pain.

He'd curled up on the other cot, covers pulled up so that Michael could only see the black of his hair. Pulling on the cuff again, he noticed the blood on his arm had crusted. He'd fought to free himself, but what would he have done if he had? He jerked his arm again, making the cuff jangle a bit. He bit his lip mostly to stop the pricking at his eyes. He'd been helpless then, and again when CJ came back from upstairs. Joe hurt him again, and Michael couldn't do a thing.

There was a noise upstairs, and then a loud crack. A gunshot? The door snapped open, and Joe came through it. He shut it and barreled down the stairs, gun in hand. Suddenly, someone was beating on the door. What was happening?

"Fuckers," he growled, coming over and grabbing CJ by the hair and waking him.

"What?" CJ gasped, reaching to grab at the hand in his hair.

Michael sat up as much as he could, looking up the stairs and hearing the door being beaten on again. Was someone here to save them? Did Sheila actually do something good and turn Joe into the police?

Joe had CJ by the arm, gun cocked at his head as the door blew open from something loud on the other side.

"Come any closer, and he's dead!" he called.

CJ, who was still waking up, suddenly realized what was happening and looked up the stairs to see two men with guns standing there. One had long blond hair in a ponytail.

"Joe, it's over," the blond man said.

"Fuck you! You're going to let me walk out of here with this fag bitch, and if you don't, he dies," Joe said.

Michael's heart was in his throat. What were they going to do? Joe had the upper hand right now. CJ wasn't in a position to fight. Even if he could, Michael didn't think he would after what Joe had done to him.

The two men on the stairs came down slowly, guns trained on Joe. "Just give up. You're surrounded. Even if you leave this house, we'll find you again."

"I won't be found if I don't want to be found," Joe said. "Move, or he dies."

Joe jabbed the gun into CJ's temple and started walking with him toward the stairs. Michal could see CJ's brown eyes, which were wide and full of fear. Who wouldn't be frightened in that position? He was being led to the stairs, and Joe backed up them, keeping an eye on the agents in the basement. He got to the top, pulled the door closed, and disappeared. Michael gasped. Had they only brought two men?

"What are you doing? Go after him!" Michael yelled out.

"Charles, check on him. I'm going after Jackson," the blond said and took off up the stairs.

The other man, a guy with dark hair and a suit like the blond, came over and unlocked the cuff. "Just stay there. We'll get paramedics to come get you out."

"What about CJ? You can't just let him leave with CJ!" Michael said.

"There's men upstairs. They won't let him get far," Charles said, patting him on the shoulder. "Just let them do their job."

Michael swallowed, panic welling in his chest. What was going to happen now? How was CJ going to get away from Joe? Would he get away?

Chapter Thirteen

Queen in Check

CJ couldn't move. He was bound with a coil of twine that Joe had in the back of the van, wrists and ankles both tied together. Joe had forced a dirty cloth into his mouth and ripped off some of his T-shirt to make a gag. CJ had marched to the shed, gun to his temple as police shouted at him to put down the gun. Joe had yelled at them and said if anyone followed him, he'd kill CJ, and CJ had no doubt he would do exactly that. So, they let him go. He had no idea where they were going, but eventually they entered somewhere dark, and stopped. CJ couldn't count the time that passed, but he knew it had been a while.

"All right, we're here," Joe said, pulling a phone out of the glove box.

CJ could hear him dialing someone. "Yeah, I need a place to lay low. Heat is on, and I've got an insurance policy with me." There was a pause. "Oh, well, don't worry. I share."

CJ's eyes widened and suddenly he realized that as bad as his day was, it was about to get worse. He put the phone down on the seat beside him and turned around, glaring at CJ for a moment until he got out of the van. CJ's heart was pounding, and he knew there was nothing he could do.

A few moments later, the side door of the van slid open, and he blinked because a light was shining in his face.

"Well, it's a boy, I think," came another man's voice. "What's up with that? You couldn't nab a hot girl?"

"Shut up," Joe growled, reaching in and grabbing CJ to pull him out. "He's got a hole, that's all that fuckin' matters, ain't it?"

The other man, who CJ could now see, was tall, though not nearly as big as Joe. He was kind of skinny and had a drawn face. He had a cigarette resting between his lips and had ratty brown hair. CJ couldn't see his eyes too well. They were in a garage that smelled of oil and sawdust.

"I mean, yeah, though he is a pretty one. I take it you've had yer way with him already?" he said, reaching out and grabbing CJ's feet and letting Joe take him by the arms to lift him.

"What do you think? Shelia fucked off, so got no pussy to fuck. His ass is good enough."

CJ wriggled a little to see if he could get away, but he was bound up tightly. They dropped him on a dirty sofa that sat between a workbench and a wall covered in tools. He turned his head and all he could see was the dim outline of another car with the hood up beyond the van Joe had driven. He swung his head back and tried to see if there was any way out of this place.

"What's going on?" a woman's voice came from the next room. CJ couldn't see her.

"None of yer business, Jackie," the new man said. "Take the fuckin' baby and get to bed."

"Walter!" she nearly yelped. "What the fuck is goin' on here? Why's he here? And what the fuck are you doing with a kid tied up?"

"Goddammit, Jackie, stay the fuck out of it. You're gonna wake the brats! Get the fuck to bed, or I ain't picking you up any dope tomorrow!"

The woman walked away, and a door slammed nearby.

"You need to get that bitch under control," Joe said.

"Yeah, well, she's a good lay, and she's not bad when she's high. Which is most the time," Walter said and flopped on the couch beside CJ's bent legs.

"Well, I'm horny," Joe said, leering down at CJ. "How about we have some fun with this little fag."

"Oh, he's gay? Probably likes the attention, huh?" Walter said, putting a hand on CJ's hip.

"I know he does. Made the little bitch come like a whore already," Joe said proudly.

Walter chuckled, sliding a hand up and then down inside the back of CJ's pants. He slipped a finger into him and hummed.

"He's pretty tight. You bust his cherry?" Walter said, thrusting his finger back and forth a few times.

"Nah, the other faggot boy I had did that. But he's been broken in nicely by now. You know me, I like 'em raw."

"So, what's with the kidnapping, huh? I never knew you to be interested in that before," Walter said, still fingering CJ, having worked up to a couple of fingers now.

CJ felt the tears starting. He couldn't stop them. He wasn't a person anymore; he was a thing for Joe to use however he wanted. If he wanted him to have pleasure, he'd give it to him. If he wanted him to have pain, he'd give that to him too.

"Now, you got me wanting to get my dick wet," Walter said, pulling his hand out of CJ's pants. "I don't want to do the work. Can he ride?"

"No idea, but cut his legs loose and make him," Joe said.

Walter pulled a pocket knife out of his pocket and cut the twine on CJ's ankles. The relief was short-lived, though, because he grabbed the sweatpants and yanked them off, leaving him half-naked.

"Get up."

CJ managed to get up with his hands still bound and stared at the floor. Walter pulled his cock out and adjusted himself.

"Well? You know what to do, bitch boy," he growled out.

CJ hesitated a little too long because Joe whacked him on the back of the head, setting his ears to ring and nearly knocking him down to the floor. CJ got his bearings and moved up and straddled Walter's lap, feeling the hardness between his legs.

"Here, I'll help," Walter said, reaching under and positioning himself. "Do it, or I'm going to beat you."

CJ swallowed and pushed down, feeling the cock invade his body. Luckily, he was nowhere near as big as Joe. It was different with him being in control. It was even worse like this. At least when Joe had done it, CJ had just laid there. Now, he had to do it to himself.

He didn't move fast enough, and Walter backhanded him. CJ, his jaw still sore from the hit Joe had landed, whined loudly as he felt it shift. He got the idea though and began bouncing on him, trying to get him to come faster so it would end. He had no idea how long a night he had in store, because when Walter finally came, making a horrible face, Joe pulled him back by the hair.

"Not bad," Joe said into his ear. "But yer not done yet."

Joe pushed him over the back of the couch and fucked him like that. CJ just held on with his bound hands as he did whatever he wanted. Luckily, he didn't seem to want to touch him. It was better that way, CJ thought. When he finished, he pushed CJ over to the side, but didn't give him his pants back.

"I've got an idea," Walter said with a grin. "Let me grab the toy box."

Joe chuckled. "I remember that box," he said, and Walter got up and left the room.

A few minutes later, Walter came back with a small wooden box. He sat down and placed it on the coffee table. Opening it, he rummaged around and pulled out what CJ knew was a vibrator.

"Come here, boy," Walter said, pointing at him with the toy.

CJ shook his head, not wanting anything to do with what he wanted. Joe narrowed his eyes, then grabbed him by the arm and pulled him closer. Walter and Joe, together, turned him onto his belly and then pressed the vibrator against him.

"Let's see how many times he can come before he passes out," Walter said and turned it on.

If CJ hadn't been gaged, he would have screamed as the vibrator penetrated him. He pushed it far inside him, and it was hard, but it felt intense at the same time. It buzzed against that internal part that felt good when Michael had touched it. He squirmed, but Joe held him down as Walter thrust the vibrator back and forth. The orgasm was sudden and overtook him as he moaned into the gag.

"Glad I keep a sheet on the couch," Walter said, not stopping.

Joe continued to hold him down as they pulled it out and began rubbing it along his cock until he got hard again, then they pressed it back inside and forced another orgasm out of him. It took longer this time, and CJ couldn't stop it again. After they'd forced another two out of him, each one taking longer and longer, they seemed to get bored and put up the vibrator, leaving CJ lying on the sofa in a puddle of his own come. The tears never stopped streaming down his face. The humiliation was more than he could bear anymore as silent sobs wracked his frame.

"He cries a lot," Walter said.

"Yeah, he's a bitch."

"You should put the clothes on him, and I'll clean up," Walter said, getting up.

Joe pulled the sweatpants back on him and then pulled him to stand again. He grabbed him by the collar. "We're sleeping here. And I'm going to tie you up again, and you're not going anywhere, understand?"

CJ just nodded. It wasn't like he had any choice in the matter.

A steady beeping noise made its way into Michael's consciousness. It was a strange thing, because nothing beeped in the basement. Maybe it had been a dream, and he was back home with his alarm beeping? No, that was an obnoxious sound. This was steady and getting faster as he listened. Maybe CJ knew what it was. The beeping got faster as everything from the night before began spiraling through his mind, ejecting him fully from his sleep.

"CJ!"

"Son?" his dad said from beside him.

"Where's CJ?" he asked, frantic.

Randy shook his head. "They don't know yet."

"What do you mean?" Michael stared at him with wide eyes. "They have to save him!"

"They're trying, I promise. The agent in charge is working with some technology guys to track him down. They think they caught a break when he used a cell phone, but they aren't sure." Randy put a hand on Michael's shoulder. "How are you feeling?"

"What's that matter? After what CJ's gone through, I'm fine!" Michael said.

"You've been shot. That bullet did significant damage, but they think you'll heal up okay. What did he do to CJ?" Randy asked.

Michael covered his face with both hands. "It was horrible, dad. He made me watch! And he handcuffed me to the bed, so I couldn't even try to help him!"

"Son, what did he do?" Randy insisted.

Michael turned to him like he was dumb. He shook his head. "He raped him."

Randy closed his eyes and looked away. "I was afraid he wasn't lying. Did he touch you?"

"What, no! But what he did to CJ was horrible! He hurt him, dad, and he was crying so hard, and I couldn't do anything!" Michael was beside himself. He couldn't stop it from happening. And more than anything, that hurt.

Randy put his arms around his son and nodded. "I know, son. I'm just glad you aren't hurt more than you are."

Michael pushed his dad back. "You've got to help CJ! I've got to see him!"

Randy frowned. "I understand you two bonded a little while you were there, son, but they'll find CJ. It'll be okay."

Michael was getting irritated. "You don't get it. I love CJ."

Randy blinked and stared at his son. "You what?"

"I want to be with CJ from now on. I need them to find him so I can see him again!"

"Son, you've known the boy for a few days. There's no way you love him," Randy said, shaking his head. "You're interested in girls, anyway, so this doesn't make sense, son."

Michael sighed. "I've always been bisexual, dad. I just never said anything because I never was interested in another guy."

"Michael, this is trauma bonding, and it won't last," Randy said. "Once you have some time and space away from CJ, you'll see the feelings will fade."

Michael didn't know what to say to make his father understand it was more than that. He couldn't come out and say he and CJ dreamed the same dreams and were bonded on a deeper level than anyone else could understand. He couldn't tell him that.

"It's more than that. You'll see. My feelings aren't going away." He crossed his arms and looked away from him.

Randy didn't say anything for a while, and Michael stayed quiet. The door opened and his mom and sister walked into the room, excitement flashing on Aileen's face when she saw him.

"Michael!" Aileen said, running over to hug him.

"Hey, little sis," he said, hugging her back.

"I was so worried about you! You look terrible!" she exclaimed, looking him over.

"Huh, yeah, the guy that had us wasn't too nice. He liked to use the butt of his gun a lot," he said, rubbing a painful part of his face. "But they've got me on pain meds, so it's not so bad."

Aileen hugged him again, surprising him. She wasn't normally this affectionate, but from the look on his mom's face, Aileen hadn't dealt with his absence well.

Terri placed a hand on her son's shoulder, then leaned over to hug him. "We were so worried about you, Michael."

"It wasn't that bad."

"Wasn't that bad?" Aileen repeated. "You got shot and hit in the face with a gun!"

"Well, there were bad points, sure, but I found CJ, so something good came out of it." Michael smiled at the thought.

"CJ? The other boy?" Terri said, frowning and looking over at Randy.

"Michael became attached," Randy said. "He thinks they formed a relationship."

"What? In a few days? You don't even know him, Michael," his mother said, waving a hand to dismiss it.

Michael growled under his breath. "Fine, you'll all see. After they get CJ back, we'll be together, and you won't be able to stop us."

"I think it best when CJ is found that you do not see him, son," Randy said, looking at him with a serious face. "What you've been through with him is terrible, but I think seeing him will be detrimental to both of you."

"You don't want me to see him?" Michael turned and glared at Randy. "How are you going to stop me from seeing him exactly?"

"It's not a real bond, son." Randy sighed. "I know it feels that way now, but the bond you formed with him is temporary and comes out of being held together. I've seen it before in hostages.

They think they're loved by others in the hostage group. The feeling fades within a few weeks. You'll see."

Michael swallowed and shook his head. "You have no idea what happened in that basement between us." He wanted his father to understand that this bond was not going to fade.

"What happened down there?" Aileen asked, sitting beside him. "What do you mean, brother?" she asked.

Michael shook his head. "It doesn't matter what I say. They're just going to say it's trauma that binds us together. There's more than that. CJ already had a massive crush on me before we met. It was more."

"CJ's going to be different when this is over," Randy continued. "After the trauma he's gone through, he'll be a completely different person, and you're not prepared to handle that. The person you found down there when you were kidnapped is going to be gone. You may as well prepare for CJ not to want to see you after everything."

Michael shook his head. "No, none of you understand. You'll see. We'll be together."

"Chaz? Simon?" Richard said as he came in. "Anything on that phone trace?"

"We pinged several phones along the possible route Jackson took," Simon said. "We've got at least three good possibilities, all burner phones that have since been deactivated somehow."

"Yah, there's gotta be somethin' ta them," Chaz said, turning the monitor Richard's direction. "Here, here, and here." They pointed at the map they were showing him.

"Tell me how exactly you did this? I thought it was impossible?" Richard narrowed his eyes at the pair.

Chaz grinned, and Simon looked sheepish. Chaz spoke, though. “Well, ya see, it’s some new tech that just came out. It hasn’t been released ta the public yet, but the military has been usin’ it. I ran across it and learned ta use it recently.”

“Ran across it, how?” Richard was sincerely curious.

Chaz continued to grin, but Simon chimed in. “Well, just through connections. Best we not know the details, okay?”

Richard nodded, not wanting to know what illegal things Chaz had been doing. He really didn’t want to arrest them.

“Either way, we got the info,” Simon continued. “So, what do you want to do with it?”

“Well, let’s check those three locations. I’ll send out three teams, and we’ll see what’s in each location,” he said, nodding. “Send those locations to me, and I’ll get it going. The faster we find them, the better. There’s no telling what that boy’s being put through.”

CJ had been put in a bedroom. It looked like a spare room of some sort, with a dingy mattress lying on the floor. He was once again tied up, hands and feet, and they’d left the gag on him the entire time. His stomach growled, but it didn’t compare to the thirst he felt right then. He chewed on the gag and wondered if dying by dehydration was such a bad way to go.

The door opened, and he looked up, afraid it was Walter or Joe again. Instead, it was a kid. He looked to be about ten years old or so, wearing shorts and a T-shirt. He had messy brown hair and dark eyes. He just stared at CJ.

“Who are you?” he asked.

CJ mumbled behind the gag and stared back.

“You must be bad,” the kid continued. “They tied you up and won’t let you leave, so that means you must be bad.”

CJ wanted to tell him to call the police. But, of course, he couldn't do that gagged. The kid considered him for a few more minutes, then he turned and left, shutting the door.

He dropped his head on the pillow and sighed. What else was there to do? They'd left him alone all day with nothing. He wanted Michael. Tears welled just thinking about him. What would Michael do? Would he even talk to him again? If he ever got out of here, that was. Joe didn't intend to let him go. He said he'd make him his toy, and that's what he'd done so far. Why would Michael ever want him after this?

Fate was a cruel mistress, he decided. His dreams proved that. He felt destined for something greater, but he couldn't quite get there. Joe was stopping him—Joe was always stopping him, even in his dreams. Could they be connected, he wondered? Joe and the dreams?

The dreams. He hadn't had one since Michael and him had done it. Why did they stop? He frowned, though he'd pondered it before. It was becoming clearer that they really were all connected. Even Joe played his part.

Yes.

He blinked in surprise. Where had that voice come from? He lifted his head and saw the door was closed still. Had it come from inside his head? His breath came faster, and he wondered if he was going crazy. He wouldn't doubt it, after what he'd been through in the last couple days. But hearing voices? Wasn't that serious?

The door opened, and he saw Joe. He had a bottle of water in his hands, and CJ couldn't have been happier unless Michael had been at the door.

"I suppose you want something to drink," he said, staring at him.

CJ nodded furiously.

Joe came over and glared at him. "You talk, the gag goes back on, understand?"

He nodded again, not wanting to jeopardize getting some water. Joe untied the gag and pulled the wet cloth out of his mouth, throwing both on the floor. CJ worked his mouth a little, and Joe opened the water. He put it to CJ's lips and began pouring it into his mouth. CJ gulped it down as fast as he poured it, grateful for the cool liquid.

"Do you need the bathroom? I don't want to clean up piss, so if you have to go, now or never," Joe said as he pulled the nearly empty bottle away from his lips.

Again, CJ nodded. Joe reached down to his feet and undid the rope they'd used. CJ wanted his hands free, too, but he didn't know if he should ask.

"Can you let my hands go?" he said as quietly as he could.

Joe looked at him with a harsh glare. "For now," he said, reaching behind him and releasing the bindings. Feeling rushed into CJ's numb fingers once the twine was removed. He sat up, rubbing his wrists. Joe reached out and grabbed him by the arm.

"Come on," he growled and pushed him toward the door. CJ stumbled but stayed on his feet.

Joe took him to a bathroom, and he went in. He stood there for a minute, enjoying the limited freedom he had at the moment. Relieved to use the bathroom, he finished quickly, only stopping to stare at himself in the mirror. Everything was blurry without his glasses, but he could make out the bruising and crusted blood on his lip, smeared from the gag. His hair was loose and wild, and he didn't want to know what the rest of him looked like.

"Are you fuckin' done?" Joe sniped from outside the door.

CJ opened the door and Joe grabbed him, pulling him along back into the living room where Walter was sitting on the couch.

"Is it play time? The boys and the bitch are gone to their grandma's house. I told them to get the fuck out of here," Walter said, and CJ wanted to sob.

Joe chuckled. "It can be. Did you have something in mind?"

"Now that his mouth is free, let's make him use it." Walter grinned and looked at CJ. "He's got a pretty one with those thick lips of his."

CJ shivered and looked away. He wanted anything but this, and every time, Michael's face flashed in his mind. He could only be thankful that Michael had been his first. At least he had that memory to hold on to. No matter what Joe did to him, he couldn't take Michael's touch away.

"Before we tie him up, let's give him a little attention." Joe smiled and grabbed CJ by the back of the neck. "Over the coffee table."

CJ swallowed and knelt in front of the coffee table. Garbage littered the table, but Walter reached out and swept it away and shoved him forward. CJ caught himself on the table and laid on it, the side biting into him under his arms where he draped across it. Joe moved around behind him, and pulled the sweatpants off his hips, then started slapping him hard. CJ bit down on his finger to keep from crying out if he didn't stop soon.

"Nice and cherry red," Joe said after a few moments, sounding satisfied. "Looks good on you, CJ. Need to do it more often."

CJ felt the tears start because the thought was horrendous. More often. Then, he grabbed his hips and found his place, slamming hard into him. CJ groaned, still biting down on his finger. But he couldn't for long. Walter came around and pulled his head up by the hair, and presented his cock to him.

"You bite me, you'll be sorry, got it, boy?" he said.

CJ nodded, opening his mouth, and Walter shoved himself inside. CJ tried to close his eyes and imagine it was Michael in his mouth again, and for a moment, that thought was nice. Then both Joe and Walter began thrusting deeper and harder, and it was hard to keep imagining such rough treatment coming from Michael. Michael had been sweet and loving and so much more when they were together. He just couldn't put Michael's touch to what these men were doing to him.

Unable to get a proper breath, CJ felt like he was choking to death. He kept shoving deep down his throat, and no matter how much he gagged, it didn't seem to matter.

"He's got a fine mouth, Joe; you try it?" Walter said as he worked in and out.

"Of course, you don't think I'd let those lips go unfucked, do you?" Joe chuckled, ramming hard into him.

"Huh, never spit-roasted someone before. Kinda fun," Walter said.

"Yeah, well, this slut gets off on it; I bet he's hard," Joe said, reaching under him. He laughed out loud, and CJ felt more tears because he was hard. He couldn't help it, but it was still embarrassing. "Fuckin' slut bitch, I tell you," Joe added.

Despite the fact he was hard, he was thankful they didn't touch him because he didn't feel quite as bad. They both finished a few minutes later, almost at the same time. They both pulled out, leaving him feeling more disgusting than before. The grime coating his body was sticky and thick, making him feel suffocated in his skin. He hadn't bathed since they were in the basement, and that was days ago. Would they let him?

He was about to ask when a light shined through the window. It looked like a blue light, then red. Wait. Those were police cars!

Chapter Fourteen

Checkmate

"You're sure?" Richard said into the phone. "Absolutely sure it's the same van?"

Simon and Chaz were staring at him, but then he was standing in the middle of the room when the call came in.

"Stay put, I'll get reinforcements. Make sure no one leaves the place. Keep out of sight, and don't let anyone see you sneaking around the place."

"They got him," Simon guessed, as Richard hung up the phone.

Richard nodded and made another call, giving them the address and instructing them to get ready, and telling them he would be there within the hour. He hung up and looked at the others.

"It's Jackson's van. No plates. White Ford Transit van. Unknown year," Richard said, nodding at Simon and Chaz. "Good work, both of you. Without your help, we wouldn't have found them."

"Are you going to call the family?" Chaz asked, pulling their green hair back in a tail.

"Not yet. Not until we have CJ."

"Probably for the best, just in case something bad happens," Simon said, shaking his head. "With Jackson, it's hard to predict what he'll do. Why'd he even take CJ?"

Richard blinked and looked over at Simon. "Why, indeed? Convenience? Michael was locked to the cot, and CJ wasn't. Maybe that's why."

The phone in Richard's pocket buzzed, and he reached for it. It was Randy. He answered, "Yeah?"

"Rich, I just wanted to relate to you some of what Michael said." Randy's voice sounded tired.

"Hold on, let me go in my office and put you on speaker so I can record it," Richard said, taking the phone into his office and shutting the door.

He turned on the recorder and switched to the speaker. "You there?"

"Yeah," Randy said, voice clear in the quiet room.

"Now, what has Michael said?" he asked.

Randy didn't speak for a moment. "He raped CJ and made Michael watch. I think that's why he kept CJ. Michael said he wanted to make him his 'toy' and that's what he took him for."

Richard felt slightly nauseous at the thought. "Damn. I was hoping he was lying."

"He wasn't. If nothing else, Joe has been completely honest."

"Have you talked to Don?" Richard was afraid the answer was no.

Randy sighed. "No. How do I tell him what happened to his son?"

"Someone is going to have to tell him," Richard said. "And we don't know what's happened to CJ since he's been captive alone with Jackson."

"I'm afraid to think of what he's done to him since he took him. Especially with the things he said around Michael." He paused. "Richard, have you found him?"

"I'll tell you when I have something substantial, all right, Randy? I promise. You'll be the first to know after Don." Richard didn't want to get anyone's hopes up about the van being found. It wasn't certain yet.

"You're not telling me something," Randy commented.

"You know me, Randy. I won't hide what happens. Something is in the works, but we'll see if it pans out, okay?" Richard needed him to stay put. Don, too.

"Okay, look, there's something else. Michael seems to think he's in love with CJ." Randy paused. "It's ridiculous because it's nothing but trauma bonding."

Richard frowned. "I wouldn't say that to your son."

"I already have. I don't want him to see CJ again. After tonight, I'm taking him home, and they're not going to see each other again."

"And just how are you going to keep your adult son from seeing another adult?" Richard asked.

Randy was quiet. "I can insist."

"You can't. Your son is an adult and can do what he wants. You have no idea what those two went through together, and if they care for each other, why would you keep them apart?" Richard was surprised at his reaction. He shouldn't care what Randy did.

"What are you saying? I should let them be together? It's nothing but the trauma talking! They need to be kept apart." Randy seemed certain.

Richard shook his head. "You don't get it, Randy. Those kids are adults, and they'll do whatever they want. What are you going to do, watch them all the time? Your son is graduating from college soon. You can't stop him from living his life. What's the real reason you're not wanting them to see each other?"

"Look, I don't want my son with someone so damaged!" Randy exclaimed.

And there it was. "Damaged? Because he's been raped? And probably tortured? You think that he's not capable of being loved by someone else?"

Randy was silent again. "Look, I'm just looking out for my son."

"You think you are, but you're not letting him make his own decisions. You can't stand in the way of what he cares about. Of whom he cares about."

"Who knows what condition CJ will be in when this is over? He's traumatized, probably beyond help! Michael can't handle that sort of thing in his life. He shouldn't have to take care of someone like that!" Randy wasn't budging.

"Randy, listen to yourself. You've got to stop trying to control the situation. Let your son make his own mistakes. If this is even a mistake. You don't know what went on between those two. It's not up to you to stop them if they want to be together." Richard knew it wasn't his place, but he couldn't help it. If he could stop Randy from making this mistake, it was worth it—his place or not. "CJ is going to need people to help him. Maybe your son is one of those people."

"I don't want my son to be one of those people, Rich. He's supposed to get married and have a family, not be saddled with a traumatized partner who he can't even have kids with. Do you have any idea what it's like to deal with someone with PTSD like that? It's flashbacks and nightmares, and its medications and therapy, and half of it doesn't work. Michael shouldn't have to deal with that."

"But that's not your choice, Randy. That's his."

"I'm not going to allow it, and if they press the issue, Michael won't be welcome home," Randy proclaimed.

"You'd really abandon your son because he loves someone you don't approve of?" Richard was shocked. He'd never thought Randy would make such a demand of his child.

"He won't choose CJ over his family. I know that."

"You're betting on something you don't understand, Randy. There's no guarantee your son won't walk out the door and never come back. Which would you rather have, your son as he chooses to live or not have him at all?" Richard wanted him to understand. For Michael's sake.

"Look, you're not a parent. You don't understand," Randy said.

"No, but I'm a son that walked away from his family over a girl and never looked back, even when we broke up," Richard explained. "My family didn't approve and gave me an ultimatum, the girl or them. I chose the girl, and I would do it again. We didn't last, but you know what did last? My hatred for my family for making me choose."

Randy didn't seem to have anything to say to that.

"I'm trying to tell you that you can't make your child choose, or you'll lose in the end. No matter what, no one comes out on top in that situation, no matter what you think." Richard paused. "You've got to understand, Randy. Your child has to make his own choices, even if you don't like them."

"How do I watch him make a mistake like this, Rich?"

"You're there for him if it turns out to be a mistake. But you don't, can't, know if it is a mistake. I'm telling you now, you're going to lose your son if you stand between them. Trust me. It will tear your family apart."

"I don't know how to do this," Randy said in a near whisper.

"Just be there for him. That's all you have to do, Randy. Support him. Support his decisions, even if you think they're wrong. Let him make his own decisions." Richard took off his glasses and wiped away tears that had escaped just thinking about the situation.

"I'll try, Rich. I guess that's all I can do." Randy hung up then.

Richard replaced his glasses and glanced over at the corner of his desk where CJ's broken glasses were sitting. He reached over and picked them up. They had shattered and were useless now. He swallowed and hoped that they were able to save that boy from Joe Jackson. He heard a knock and looked up to see someone in his doorway.

"Yes?" he said.

"The file on the house," the intern said, a scrawny boy with rough brown hair. Richard forgot his name. Timothy or something like that.

He put down CJ's glasses and took the file, opening it. Walter and Jackie Remington. They lived there with their 10-year-old named Charles, their six-year-old named Jeremiah, and a three-month-old named Darren. They had been investigated twice by child services for suspected drug use in the house, and the police had been called for loud fighting between them on three occasions. What was the connection to Joe Jackson though?

He kept going through the file until he came to Walter's military service. It was redacted, which meant something secretive. That had to be where they connected. He put the file down. His phone vibrated again, and he picked it up.

"Richard Pearson," he answered.

"Sir, we've got the house surrounded. Will you be on point?"

"Yes, I'll be right there. Let's get CJ out of there."

Mara was cooking and trying to ignore the pain in her chest. She couldn't stand the thought that Jackson had her son while Michael was free. Even though she wanted to say a lot of things about it, she said nothing. Instead, she just kept making spaghetti. It was the third night this week they'd had it, but Alex and Allie didn't care. It was their favorite food.

Donald came into the kitchen and watched for a while. "You okay, Mara?"

She looked, tears running down her face. "No, why would you think I'd be okay? Our son is in the hands of a terrible man, alone, and Randy's boy is in the hospital."

"They'll get him, Mara. Richard's going to find him."

"Yeah, everyone says that, but he hasn't yet, has he?" She put down the spoon she was stirring the sauce with and wiped her eyes on a nearby towel.

"There's something you need to be prepared for," Donald said, his voice quiet. "I wanted to be sure, so I called Randy after some things Joe said on the phone."

Mara looked at him, face lined with confusion. "Something I need to be prepared for? What does that even mean, Don?" she asked.

Donald sighed. "He's done something to CJ, and I don't know how to tell you."

Mara blinked, turning around to face him now. "What are you talking about? Has he been shot?"

"No, not that I know of." He looked away. "Mara… He raped him."

Mara blinked, heart dropping. "What? What are you saying?"

"I'm sorry, I can't soften the blow at all. It is what it is. Joe said as much when he called, and Michael confirmed it." Donald put a hand to his mouth and shook his head. "I didn't want to tell you."

Mara stood still, tears dripping down her face. She didn't know how to react to this news. Her son, her precious boy, had been hurt so deeply. She put her hands over her mouth and rushed past Donald to the bathroom, throwing up violently as soon as she got over the toilet. Her baby. He was still her baby, and this had happened to him? She sobbed and after a couple minutes, she felt small hands on her shoulder.

"Mommy?" Alex said, blinking her big blue eyes at her. "Are you sad, mommy?"

She looked up at her little girl and the reality of the situation crashed down on her. She was sick again, throwing up. Alex went to Donald, telling him that mommy was sick. Alex wouldn't understand. No one would understand. She couldn't even understand what CJ had gone through if she tried. She'd never had anything so horrible happen to her, and she couldn't imagine how her son would deal with it. She had questions, but she knew there were no answers.

"Mara?" Donald whispered.

She swallowed the bile in her throat and turned back to him, still sitting on the floor. "How bad is this going to be?" she responded.

"I know Joe. It's not going to be good," he said after a few moments. "He's cruel. He would have taken his hatred for me out on CJ."

Mara swallowed hard again. "This is your fault."

Donald didn't say anything for a time. "I know."

"If you hadn't gotten involved with this man, our son would be safe at home. Not dealing with this."

It wasn't fair to blame him. In her heart, she knew this. It gave her some sense of control, which she desperately needed right then. She needed an answer to why something so terrible had happened to her baby.

Donald nodded. "I don't know what to say to that, Mara."

Mara stood up slowly, straightening her shirt. "I'm going to my parents with the twins. Call when CJ's found," she said, walking past him.

Going to the bedroom, she silently packed a bag for herself, and then went to the twins' room and packed one for each of them.

"Alex, Allie, we're going to grandma's," she said as she came out of their room.

"Oh yay!" Allie said, jumping. "We having dinner with her?"

"We're getting nuggets on the way. It takes a bit to get there, remember?" she said. It was an hour's drive to her mother's house.

"Okay!" Alex said, grabbing her bag from Mara.

Donald came in and watched them. "Be safe," he said at length.

Mara didn't respond. She watched as the twins said goodbye to their father, but she couldn't even look at him. Her heart hurt so much she could barely stand it, and it was because of him. Her baby was hurt, and she couldn't help him. So, all she could do was get away from Don and away from these thoughts blaming him. She hoped some distance helped, but she couldn't be sure.

"What the fuck?" Walter said, pulling his pants up and buttoning them. "Did they find you?"

Joe did the same, leaving CJ on the table and going toward the window to look out. CJ didn't move, still splayed on the table, but his eyes fell on something on the floor. Where Walter had wiped all the stuff off the table, there had been a screwdriver. Without even thinking, he reached down and grabbed it, gripping it in his fist. He then moved back and pulled the sweatpants back up and sat on the floor.

"That's impossible. There's no way they traced me here. Unless..." Joe frowned and turned and glared at CJ where he sat between the table and the sofa. "Stay there, got it?" he growled out.

CJ nodded and watched as Joe disappeared into the hallway. Walter turned and narrowed his eyes at him. "Don't think of trying shit, got it, brat?" he said.

Swallowing, CJ had the screwdriver under his shirt. He was holding it as tight as he could because it was the only thing real right then. Nothing else mattered but the screwdriver. If he could get to him and stab him, he'd be able to get away. He wasn't afraid of Walter; he wasn't like Joe. Walter, he'd just hit and leave. Joe was another story, though.

Joe came back with a gun in his hand. "Walter, would your bitch have turned on us?"

"No!" Walter exclaimed. "Why would you think Jackie would do that? She's a bitch, but she's not a narc."

"I don't know about that. Someone got information to police, and that bitch over there has been tied up all day."

"Well, they probably traced you when you called me!" Walter exclaimed.

"That's bullshit. It was a burner phone. There's no way they had access to the technology necessary to do something like that! They'd have to go through a fuckton of red tape with the military to access that kinda tech!" Joe was sure of that, from what CJ could see.

"They had to get it. It wasn't Jackie, goddammit!" Walter growled out with a narrowed glance.

"Your bitch did this! And I'll bet on it!" Joe said, pointing the gun at Walter.

"The fuck?" Walter said. "Point that somewhere else!"

"Fuck you, Walter!" he said and shot him in the chest.

CJ jerked and gasped as Walter fell to the ground. CJ had never seen someone die, but he was dead before he hit the ground, the shot straight to the heart. There was someone pounding on the door then. CJ wanted to run, but before he got to his feet, Joe had him by the arm and dragged him to the middle of the room as the door burst open.

"Joe Jackson! Put the gun down!" a man with blond hair in a ponytail said as he came in, gun leveled at Joe. He thought he'd been at the other place, too.

Joe jabbed the gun into CJ's temple. "Come closer, bastard, and he dies."

"Joe, you're surrounded. You're not getting out."

"You're going to let me out, or else!" he said. "This boy belongs to me, and we're going to leave and you're not going to follow me!"

CJ's heart was beating so hard and fast he heard it pounding in his ears. He squeezed the screwdriver and wondered if he could really kill someone. His mind flashed to dying a dozen deaths, all at the hands of the man with the black eyes. Thousands of times, he'd been in this place and lost. A million chances at destiny, and fate took it away.

No more.

CJ moved while Joe was distracted by the agent. He swung his hand with the screwdriver up and aimed right at Joe's exposed temple. With as much force as he could muster, before anyone could move, he slammed the screwdriver's pointed tip right through Joe's temple. For a moment, nothing happened, and Joe looked shocked. Then his head shook, and he stumbled to the side, crumpling to the floor after a few moments, the screwdriver buried halfway into his head. CJ eventually fell to his knees, shock settling over him. He'd just killed a person.

The agent rushed over and dropped down in front of him. "CJ?" he asked.

"I killed him," CJ whispered, tears dripping down his cheeks already. "I really killed him."

"I'm Richard, CJ. I'm an FBI agent. We're going to take you to the hospital, okay? Are you hurt anywhere I should know about?"

CJ shook his head. "I killed him," he repeated.

"He's dead, yeah, CJ. I don't know how you did that, you must have had a burst of adrenaline. That's not easy to do, CJ." He sighed. "But you did it. Can you stand?"

CJ nodded and stood up slowly with Richard's help. He seemed like a good guy. Suddenly CJ stopped. "Is Michael okay?" he asked.

"He's at the hospital. Where you're going, okay?" he said. "We're going to get you checked out and treat any wounds you have, okay?"

Richard put an arm around him and led him out of the house. CJ winced and shielded his eyes because there were a lot of lights out there. He took him to a plain looking car and opened the door for him. CJ got in without a word and sat in silence as they drove to the hospital. He was numb, really.

Things went fast from there. He was ushered through the emergency room and taken to a room where a doctor came to see him. Richard stayed with him, which was nice, he thought, because he wasn't sure what to do right then. The doctor was a kind-looking woman with glasses from what he could tell, though she was a bit blurry to him.

"CJ, right?" she said.

CJ nodded. "CJ Kim," he said.

"Okay, CJ, I'm Dr. Robertson, and I'm going to be examining you today." A nurse walked in with pink scrubs. "And this is Nurse Janie."

"Okay," CJ nodded and looked between them.

"Tell me what's happened?" she asked. "I understand you were kidnapped."

CJ nodded. "Joe kidnapped me and Michael. He wanted to get back at our parents. We were pawns in his game, though."

"Have you been hurt?" she asked.

CJ looked down at his hands and shook his head.

"CJ, this is important. It was reported he raped you. Is this true?" she asked.

CJ swallowed, not wanting to answer that question, but he knew he should. "Yes," he said softly, barely above a whisper.

"Okay, we're going to have to take an evidence kit, and I'm going to examine you for damage. It won't be comfortable, I'm afraid, but we have to know if you've been hurt from his attack."

"Walter did it, too," he said after a second.

"What? There was more than one attack?" she said, turning to him from the box she was holding.

CJ nodded. "He did it a few times." CJ was still talking very softly. "And then Walter did stuff, too. They said I was a toy."

Dr. Robertson looked over at Richard and nodded. "Alright, let's get this taken care of, okay? First, I need you to change into a gown. Do you want us to step outside?" she said.

"Yeah," CJ nodded.

She gave him a gown. "It ties in the back, okay?"

CJ took it and watched as they all stepped outside the room. He was alone for a few moments, and he wondered if he should do what she said, or if he should just ignore her and do something drastic. He shook his head and undressed, pulling off the dingy sweatpants and the dirty T-shirt he was wearing. He put on the gown and tied it around the back of his neck. He had to see Michael again, and if he did something to himself, he wouldn't.

The door opened, and they came back in. Richard, though, waited outside. Dr. Robertson spent the next hour collecting evidence and checking him over from head to toe. She combed out his hair and cleaned under his nails, and then her gentle gaze met his.

"We have to examine you, okay? So, lie down on your side, and pull your knees up on the table."

CJ felt his breath hitch. He didn't want to do it. It would expose him to her. But she was a doctor, so it should be okay, he thought. He laid down on the table and pulled his knees up a bit.

"Okay, CJ, I'm going to check you now and take evidence swabs. So, I want you to relax as much as you can. You're going to feel my finger, okay?"

CJ bit down on the inside of his lip as she felt around and then pressed a finger into him. He clenched unconsciously because he was sore.

"CJ, there's some blood, so you've had some tears internally. I'm going to give you an ointment to apply, and I'll need you to do it for a week or so, okay?" she said and removed her finger to CJ's relief. "Okay, that's over. You can sit up again," she said.

CJ sat up, still sore. "But it will get okay, right?"

"Yeah, you'll heal up just fine, I think. But no anal sexual activity for at least a month. I want you to heal completely." She nodded.

"Okay, I don't think I want to do anything like that right away," he told her.

"I'd like to keep you overnight, so I'll have you put in a room, and your father will come to see you. He's already here," she said.

"Okay," CJ crossed his arms and looked at the nurse. "I'm getting tired."

"You'll get to rest," she said, and she and the nurse left the room.

Richard came back in. "CJ, your father's waiting in the waiting room, so when you get a room, he'll come see you," Richard let him know.

"That's what Dr. Robertson said." CJ was nervous because Richard had seen him kill Joe. What must he think?

"CJ, are you okay with what happened to Jackson?" Richard asked after a few minutes of silence. "You did what you had to do."

"He wasn't going to let me go." CJ looked at him. "He was going to keep doing horrible things to me as long as he had me. I know that."

Richard put a hand on his shoulder, and they waited for the nurses to come with a wheelchair to take him to a room. Richard went with him and stayed close. CJ was glad; it was difficult to think he'd actually killed someone, even after everything Joe had done. They got him into a room, and he crawled into the bed, covering up completely. Richard patted his arm again.

“I’ll get your father.”

He left CJ alone for a little while with his thoughts, and CJ kept coming back to the image of Joe’s body crumpling to the floor. He’d done that. He’d made that happen. Still, he was having trouble believing it was over.

Chapter Fifteen

Aftermath

Michael couldn't sleep due to worrying about CJ. That, and his father's comments. How could he say it was nothing but trauma bonding? Was that even a thing? He sighed and flipped through the channels on the TV again and still didn't find anything to watch. Why would his father be so sure that there was nothing real between them? All Michael had thought about was CJ since they were separated. He couldn't imagine it being anything but real. He shut the TV off in frustration and rolled over to face the window. The door opened quietly and shut, and he assumed it was a nurse again.

"Mikey?" he heard and flipped over.

"CJ!" he gasped, seeing the beaten and bruised face. "Baby!"

CJ was already crying, and Michael couldn't stop his own tears at that sight. "I'm sorry," CJ said quietly.

"CJ, what are you sorry for?" Michael asked, wondering why he was just standing there. "Come here, I need to feel you!"

He hesitated, and that alone broke Michael's heart. But he moved, coming up beside the bed and reaching tentative arms out, and Michael grabbed him and pulled him in tight. He ran his hand through his hair and nuzzled into him, kissing his neck and cheek repeatedly.

CJ started sobbing while he held onto Michael, and Michael knew he had to let him. He just held on, consoling him. "It's gonna be okay, baby, I got you," he whispered and hugged him even tighter. "You're mine, okay? That means for good, no matter what they say."

"Even—" CJ choked out. "Even after—"

"After everything, yes, you're my baby, okay? Now and forever," Michael whispered.

CJ's tears didn't magically stop, but he held on, whispering words he hoped comforted him, and he hoped he understood that to him, what Joe had done didn't matter at all. He wanted CJ as he was, even after everything that had happened.

"He-he made me—" he gasped and couldn't continue.

"Take your time, baby, don't try to do it all now, okay?" Michael said. "Just take your time."

CJ clutched him tightly and Michael winced because the position put pressure on his wounded thigh, but he didn't care. He'd sit like this and be in pain forever if it helped CJ. Then, the door popped open, and a nurse stood there. She sighed.

"CJ," she whispered and walked forward.

CJ looked up at her. "S-sorry," he said.

"It's okay. I was worried when you weren't in your bed," the nurse said softly, reaching out and putting a hand on CJ's shoulder. "I figured after we talked, this is where you'd go."

"How'd you figure out how to find me?" Michael said as CJ let go and stood, staring at the ground.

"My father told me you were here, so I asked Angela, and she said you were here. I couldn't wait; I had to see you."

Michael sighed and reached out, taking one of CJ's hands in his. "I'm glad. I was afraid I'd lose you."

Angela looked over at Michael. "I shouldn't have said you were in this room. I'm sorry."

"No, don't be sorry. I'm glad you did it. I needed to see him," Michael said, tightening his grip on CJ's hand.

"CJ told me about you." Angela smiled as she spoke. "I thought it was very sweet of him, but he was afraid, too."

"I didn't know if you wanted to see me," CJ whispered, looking over at him, honey brown eyes shining with unshed tears.

"I—well of course I'd want to see you!" Michael said, pulling his hand to his lips and kissing his knuckles. "You're everything to me."

"But-but my father said it wasn't real. And he said that your father didn't want us to see each other. And they both agreed it was just fake. And they won't listen to me!" CJ exclaimed, looking at him with tears sliding down his face.

"CJ, baby, they don't understand us. They can't. We're gonna be together, okay? Forever." Michael kissed his hand again.

"It's not like we can trade numbers, right? I lost my phone, and I think you said you did, too. But the next few days, they'll keep us apart. I know my father will take me home tomorrow and won't let me leave. So, what I want you to do is meet me in six weeks on Sunday at the ball field, at noon. They said I should be walking by then. I'll go there and I'll pick you up. Bring your stuff that you can carry, okay?" Michael leaned over and cupped CJ's face. "We can make it that long."

"Where will we go?" CJ said, looking at him.

"I don't know. Somewhere no one can find us if we have to. It'll take time, but our families are gonna have to accept us being together. If they can't, then we make our own family, okay?" Michael hoped CJ would do it. He'd wait forever for him, though. "Do you think you can do it?"

CJ nodded. "For you, I'd give the world up."

Michael smiled. "Okay, six weeks. Sunday at noon. I'll meet you under the bleachers. And we start a new life."

CJ sat in bed and waited for his father to finish his discharge paperwork. He'd thanked Angela earlier for keeping the previous night a secret. Like she said, it wasn't like they were teenagers. They were both adults. He felt better having a plan in place with Michael. "Your mom will be home with the twins when we get there," his dad said.

"What happened? Why'd she go to grandma's?" CJ asked.

Don paused. "Just some personal things, nothing to worry about."

Dr. Robertson came in and smiled at CJ. "How are you feeling?" she asked.

"Okay," CJ answered. "I'm glad to go home."

"Just remember to use the prescription salves I've given you, one for pain and one to help heal. And take the antibiotics until they're gone. We don't want any infections setting in. The STI panel will be back in a week, so try not to dwell on that too much," she said.

"Any other advice?" Don asked.

CJ narrowed his eyes. "I got this, dad."

Donald turned to him. "I think you need some help with things, CJ. So, I'm going to ask you to stay home for a while."

"What? That doesn't make sense. I'm not hurt," he said, crossing his arms.

"I'd rather not see anything happen to you," Don said.

CJ arched a brow. "I can take care of myself."

"Son, just do what I say without arguing."

CJ frowned. "I'll do what I want," he said, sliding out of the bed and wincing as pain shot up his spine. "I'm capable of making my own decisions."

"I don't want you going into St. Louis anymore alone," he continued. "I want someone with you."

"Dad, stop." CJ straightened the T-shirt his dad had brought him this morning. "I'm not changing my life because of this. I'll be going back to school in the fall, and that's that."

"I want you to take online classes from home, CJ. I'm serious about this," he said.

CJ turned and shook his head. "No."

Don blinked in surprise. "What?"

"I said no. I'm not changing my life. Or do you have more military enemies out there I need to worry about?" he asked, knowing it would cut his dad.

"We'll discuss this further at home," Don said, taking the paperwork from the doctor.

CJ refused to speak to him all the way back to St. Peters. He sat and stared out the window, the little bag of prescriptions in his lap. He wasn't about to change his entire life because his father had become overprotective of him. And in six weeks, he and Michael were going to be together again, and that's all that mattered to him.

They got home, and he saw his mom's SUV in the driveway. He slid out of the car carefully and headed into the house without talking to his father. He found his mom and the twins in the living room.

"Brudder!" shouted Allie, and she came running and grabbed him.

CJ smiled and hugged each of them and then gave his mom a hug. She was crying.

"You have no idea how worried I've been," she said through her tears.

"I've missed you!" CJ said, stepping back. "I'm glad to be home."

"Are you feeling okay? Your face looks terrible!" she said, putting her hand against CJ's face.

"I'm okay. At least I didn't get shot like Michael," he said. "I want to call him, but I don't know the number."

"I don't think that's a good idea," Don said from where he stood in the doorway. "Randy and I talked, and I think it best you and him stay apart. What you went through was traumatizing, but being together will just make it worse."

CJ turned and glared at him. "What do you know?" he snapped. "I love Michael, and that's all there is to it."

"CJ, honey, you can't fall in love that fast," his mom said, her voice soft and slightly unsure. "You don't even know him."

"I know enough!" CJ turned his gaze on her now. "Neither of you understand, and you're not even trying. The only good thing to come out of this whole situation is that Michael and I found each other. I'm not letting it go."

"You're going to have to. Michael's housebound until he's healed, and you're not leaving either." Don spoke with finality.

"How old am I? You can't do this."

"I can, and will," Don said.

CJ looked at Mara. "You're going to allow this? I'm almost twenty, not twelve."

Mara sighed. "It's for the best, CJ. You'll see."

CJ growled and headed for the stairs, ignoring pleas from them to come back and talk about it. He wasn't going to listen. They were treating him like a child, and he wasn't going to have it. He'd gone through more in a week than they could ever imagine, and most of it he hadn't even talked about. Both the people who knew were dead, and if he never talked about it, no one would ever know. The only thing anyone knew was what Michael had told them. They didn't know about the rest, and they weren't going to know.

Michael sat on his bed with his laptop and wrote letters to CJ. That's all he'd done since he'd gotten home. He told his parents he was writing his memories of his time and journaling. They didn't need to know what he was doing. He had a calendar on the computer with a countdown to the Sunday he was going to meet CJ. His phone, the new one his mom got him today, rang. Luckily, he had kept the same number. It was Jeremy.

"What's up?" he answered.

"I can't believe you're okay, man!" Jeremy said. "We were all worried and watching the news nonstop!"

"Yeah, it was pretty weird."

"You even got shot. That's just fucking wild, man," Jeremy exclaimed. "Are you doing okay? What all happened? Can you talk about it, or is there some rule that says you can't?"

Michael smiled. "I can talk about it if I want. But there's not much to it. I just had to stay in a basement with another boy named CJ, and we got to be real close." He paused. "Like, romantic close."

"Wait, what?" Jeremy nearly yelled.

"Yeah, I didn't think much of it, but I fell in love for real this time." Michael sighed, just thinking of it.

"But you like girls?"

"So? I like boys too. Just never dated one," Michael stated.

"Whoa. So, like, did you do it with him?"

Michael shook his head. Of course, he'd ask that. "We had some fun."

"Really? Wow. So, what now?" Jeremy wondered.

"Well, our parents are both being dicks. They don't want us seeing each other. But we worked things out. I might need your help in a few weeks, though. On the down low."

Jeremy snorted. "Of course, man, of course. Whatever you need."

"Tell no one, though. Not even your girl, okay? This is between us. When I'm ready, I'll tell the others, but until then, keep your damn mouth shut, okay?" Michael insisted.

"Okay, okay, I got it," Jeremy said. "How long are you housebound?"

"About six weeks, give or take. They said to stay off my leg for a while, then there'll be physical therapy. But it's a good prognosis. The bullet tore through muscle and missed anything important. I was fuckin' lucky, man." He looked up to see his mom staring at him from the doorway. "Hey, gotta go. Talk later, okay?"

"Yeah, take care. I'll swing by this weekend and see you," Jeremy said and bid him goodbye.

"Yeah?" he asked.

"Who was that?" she asked.

"What does it matter? It was my call," he said, looking at her.

"On the phone I got you, Michael. Who was it?" Terri insisted.

"What is with you and Dad? It was Jeremy. Who do you think?" Michael frowned and stared at her.

She said nothing and turned and left, leaving Michael more than a little annoyed. They were both acting weird since he got home. It seemed to him the only way he was going to be happy was once he and CJ made a run for it. He grabbed the computer and started researching. He might as well get things in order now. He only had six weeks to make the arrangements for him and CJ. First, he had to find a job. He was officially a graduate with a Bachelor of Science in psychology. He had to find something.

After a couple hours of applying for jobs, he was exhausted. He'd only worked at the pizza place, and he hadn't ever thought about trying to support two people before, but he had a lot of good prospects. He'd found the psychiatric rehabilitation center was hiring entry level psychiatric technicians. That was something he was interested in and could do. He just wondered if they'd do an interview over the phone or online. In the notes, he'd explained his situation and hoped they would take it into consideration.

"Dinner," Aileen said from the doorway, holding a plate.

"Thanks," he said as she came in and put it on his lap. Looked like Salisbury steak tonight. Not bad, he thought.

"You know, mom and dad are acting strange. It's because of you," she said. "They won't even let me go to my friend's house because something might happen."

"Well, it's not like I chose to get abducted by some psycho from dad's past," Michael groused, stuffing mashed potatoes in his mouth.

"Yeah, well, you still caused this, and it's pissing me off." She glared at him.

"Don't blame me!" Michael said, turning to her. "They're the ones overreacting!"

She snorted and left the room, leaving Michael feeling furious. It wasn't his fault. He hadn't done anything, but everyone was treating him like he'd done this on purpose. His parents were treating him like a two-year-old, and he'd about had it. He would have gone and found CJ if he hadn't been injured.

He pulled out his phone and texted Jeremy.

About that favor.

Sure, buddy, whatcha need?

I need a place to live in St. Louis. Do you know anyone?

You don't have a good enough job. How are you going to pay for it?

I've got a couple of prospects. Just hook me up with someone if you can.

I'll send you the information of a landlord my dad knows. I don't know if he'll do anything for you.

Thanks, Jer.

After he sent the information, Michael sighed and put the phone on the charger. It was really too late to talk to a guy about a place to live, but he would do it first thing the next day. It was something he had to do. He didn't know if he could pull all this off in six weeks. It wasn't a terrible lot of time, but he had to do something. He would have CJ in his life, no matter what his parents thought about it. He put the plate on the side table and lay down to sleep.

"She's not a witch!" James said to the magistrate, standing between him and the love of his life, Anna.

"She's been seen cavorting with demons!" the magistrate said, pointing at her.

"She has not!" James growled out, leaning forward.

"She's to be burned, it's already decided!" he stated.

Around them, several men with weapons stood. They grabbed James and held him while they pulled Anna away. The magistrate turned and smiled, his eyes flashing black.

"Anna!" he screamed as they dragged her to the town square.

"Bring him, too," the magistrate said. "He can watch her burn. Then, we'll behead him for consorting with witches," he continued.

The two men holding James yanked him forward, dragging him to the town square where people were gathering. Anna, her dark hair flying about her like a corona, watched with wide eyes as wood was gathered at her feet. She'd already been lashed to the stake. There was nothing he could do. They were both going to die here.

Anna smiled at him suddenly as they continued to build the fires around her. "Don't worry, my love. We'll live yet again, and one day, he won't come between us."

James gasped because he felt her words were true and he didn't know why. It was more than a platitude. It was something real, and something that had great meaning and weight.

"I love you!" he shouted as the men held him still.

The flames had been lit around her and they were growing closer. Still, she smiled. "I'm not afraid of fire. You remember, don't you?"

Then the fires consumed her, and she screamed in agony as they burned her alive. Despite her words, the pain from the flames was too much and she could not hold in her voice. James looked away and tried not to remember that the person he loved more than anything stood in flames before him.

The magistrate came forward and smiled. "For the crime of consorting with witches, you are sentenced to die."

"You wanted her, and couldn't have her, and that's why you did this," James said, narrowing his eyes at the magistrate. "She wouldn't have you because she loved me, and you had to end her."

The magistrate smiled and pulled out a dagger. "What does it matter now?" he asked and plunged the dagger into his chest.

For a moment, James watched his life blood run, but above the fires, he saw an image of a beautiful woman, one he knew but did not know, and in the end, he smiled as he died.

CJ woke with a start. His breath was coming in quick pants. This wasn't unusual, ever since he could remember he'd woken from dreams like that, but this was the first dream since he and Michael had been together the first time. Why was he suddenly dreaming again?

Break through.

He blinked and looked around. There was no one in the bedroom. He was alone. So where did that voice come from? He swallowed hard and got up, stumbling a bit to the adjacent bathroom to get a drink.

Remember.

He nearly dropped the cup of water. He was getting dizzy. What was happening? He put the cup back after draining it of water and went back to his room before he fell. Was he hurt more than they knew? His jaw still hurt, but the doctor had said it wasn't broken. But would that cause him to hear voices? No, not unless he was losing his mind.

Sitting on the edge of the bed, he tried to gather his thoughts. Remember what? What was he supposed to remember? Was there something he was supposed to know?

An image of a rushing river in a desert came to his mind. The name was on the tip of his tongue. Who's name? Her name. His name.

Brishna.

He jerked. That name. It was from one of the dreams, the one that plagued him the most from the time he was a child. A goddess walking among mortals, fated to be with her partner, Krineshaw. But wasn't it just an overactive imagination producing these images? These things? He was a writer, so wasn't it just overdoing things? Some things felt so real, though, no matter how he looked at it.

Was he this person? This goddess?

He swallowed. He had to know for sure.

He got up and went to the computer and opened the browser. He felt ridiculous, but he typed in "past lives" and hoped he would figure this out. A wealth of information flooded his screen. There was so much! He shook his head and typed in "Brishna" and only a few things came back. Tentatively, he opened the first one.

Disbelief cascaded over him as he read an account of the dream. It was different in some ways, but the backbone of it was the same. It was the story he'd dreamed of for so long. And it was real? At least someone else knew the story, so that meant it wasn't just a dream. He knew he hadn't read it somewhere because he'd been dreaming it as long as he could remember. Since he was a child, it had invaded his sleep.

He backed up and looked at the rest of the links. Nothing substantial, just an ancient prophecy referencing a goddess in mortal form and how, only when the cycle was broken, she would return to the heavens.

What was the cycle?

That was easy. They always died. In his dreams, they always died together at the hands of a man with black eyes. If they were in fact incarnations or avatars of these gods, hadn't they broken the cycle already? Joe, the man with the black eyes that was after them, was dead. They'd done it.

Hadn't they?

They weren't together, though. They were being kept apart. Was that why the dreams continued? They hadn't broken the cycle. The cycle wasn't death, he suddenly realized. The cycle was that they were kept apart! He swallowed. So, that meant they had to break the cycle, and that meant they had to be together. Now, their families were in the way. There were only a couple of ways to be together. In all their previous lives, death was their redo, another attempt to be together. The man with black eyes was dead, and they were closer than ever. This time, death wouldn't be the answer.

No, death wasn't the answer. The answer was being together, and that was all there was to it. CJ had to trust Michael. Six weeks. Sunday. Noon. And they'd be together again.

Chapter Sixteen

A New Page

CJ was nervous. He'd had a hard time getting out of the house and, in the end, had secretly called a ride-share and sneaked out. His mom had been fixing lunch, and his father had been in the living room watching TV. The twins were sleeping, luckily. He knew they would freak out when they found out he was gone. However, at the moment, he didn't care about them.

Healing had gone well for CJ. His face and jaw were better, though sometimes his jaw would pop painfully, and the doctor thought he might have TMJ. The damage from Joe and Walter had healed, and he'd been forced to see a therapist that his father had picked out for him. He despised him, a Dr. Thompson. He was haughty and asked him invasive questions CJ refused to answer. He wanted to know the details, and CJ felt it was morbid curiosity on his part and not anything professional.

He knew he needed a therapist. He just knew he didn't want Dr. Thompson. He would find his own therapist, who he liked and got along with. Preferably a woman who understood his gender identity, too. He'd mentioned that to Dr. Thompson and commented that traumatized people sometimes felt like that. He didn't get into the fact he'd always felt that way, so he skipped talking about it.

The sun was high, and he looked at his watch. He'd left the phone his parents gave him at home. He didn't want to be found. He leaned against the support for the bleachers and waited. Michael would be here. He wouldn't forget. He wouldn't abandon him.

At 12:30, CJ started to worry. Maybe something stopped him from coming. He knew he was having trouble with his parents, too, but he didn't know what to do. He had no phone and no car, so there was nothing for him to do. All he could do was wait.

It was almost one, and he was dozing against the bleacher support when he felt someone drop a hand on his shoulder. He screamed, jerking and scrambling away, only to look up and see a worried-looking Michael.

"Mikey!" he gasped, getting to his feet.

"I'm sorry I'm late, baby. I had trouble getting out of the house without being noticed," he said, wrapping both arms around him.

CJ couldn't stop the tears from coming. "I've missed you so much!"

"I know, so have I, baby, but I got things worked out. It took a bit, but I managed," he said, smiling at him.

"What do you mean?" CJ frowned.

"Come on, did you get a bag?" he asked.

"As much as I could carry." CJ pointed to a black duffel bag sitting nearby.

Michael took his hand and grabbed the bag. He led CJ to his car and threw the bag in the back. CJ got in the front seat and buckled himself into the car. Michael got in and they took off, headed out of the parking lot.

"Where are we going?" CJ asked.

"It's a surprise." Michael smirked at him and kept his eyes on the road.

CJ wondered what it was. They eventually came to a duplex. It was not far from the school, but it looked like a nice neighborhood. Some of the ones close to the school weren't so good. Michael got out and came around to let CJ out. CJ frowned again, but Michael just took his hand, and they walked up to the front door. Instead of knocking, Michael unlocked the door. CJ looked at him and then walked into the duplex.

It was nearly empty. There was an old, beige sofa in the front room, a crate with a small TV sitting on it, and a game system of some sort. There were stairs leading up and a small kitchen with a little table and two chairs sitting in it.

"Welcome home, CJ."

CJ blinked and looked at Michael. "What?"

"I know it's not much, but they had to go with what I could afford on my new salary at the psych center. It was enough for this place. I started two weeks ago, so I don't get paid for two more weeks, so we're not going to have much yet. I borrowed a few hundred dollars from my buddy Jeremy, and he's gonna let me pay him a little at a time. I got the furniture from some people who were giving it away online, and they even brought it over when I told them the situation." He paused, grabbing CJ by the hand. "Is it okay?"

Speechless, CJ stared at him, eyes filling with tears. "It's perfect," he said at length.

Michael wrapped him up in a hug and held him as he started crying again. He cried so easily these days. He pulled back and wiped away his tears. "How'd you manage to get to work? I heard they weren't letting you leave."

"I told them it was my career, and I had to go to work. It took some convincing, but they finally agreed they couldn't stand in the way of what I went to school for. And even more than that, the place I'm working for does tuition reimbursement. So, I can keep going to school and get my master's degree in psychology while I'm working there." He smiled at CJ. "It won't be easy, but do you want to try and make it work?"

"I do! I'll get a job, too, and help out!" CJ nodded.

"I want you to finish school," Michael said, brushing a hand through CJ's long hair.

He still hadn't cut it, even though his mom had told him it was too long. Michael had liked it long, and he kept it that way. He adjusted his new glasses and sighed at Michael.

"I love you so much," he admitted.

"You have no idea how much I love you," Michael said in return. "Here, I'll show you our bedroom."

He took CJ's hand and led him up the stairs. It was a small bedroom with a closet and a bathroom. On the floor was a double mattress covered with sheets and covers. There were dark curtains on the one window in the room, and Michael flicked the light on. The only furniture was an old chest of drawers sitting against the wall. CJ walked in and looked around.

"Perfect."

The sound of the phone ringing woke CJ and Michael. Michael groaned and was tempted to send it to voicemail, but he saw it was Jeremy. He clicked the speaker.

"What? You know what time it is?" he said.

"Look, man, I've been visited by the cops twice in the last three days looking for your ass. When are you going to tell your parents where you are?" Jeremy asked.

CJ watched him, a slight frown pulling at his lips. "Well, I guess I should do something, huh?"

"Yeah, and they're asking about CJ, too. I think they know you two are together."

"What'd you tell them?" Michael asked, propping himself up on his arm.

"Just that last I heard, you were working in St. Louis full time at the rehab center. They were going to look for you there, so be ready." Jeremy paused. "But really, where are you anyway?"

"I'll send you a text," he said. "I'll call the parents. Get it over with."

"Okay, take care of it, man. Please."

Jeremy cut the line and Michael flopped on his back. "Well, we can't put it off any longer. My off days end tomorrow anyway. I'm surprised they let me take off to move, especially since I just started."

CJ was lying on his stomach, propping his head up on his hands. "We should do it."

"What?" Michael blinked. "It?"

"Sex. We should have sex again," CJ said.

Concern lined Michael's face. "CJ, are you sure you want to? It hasn't been that long. I want you to be ready for it."

"You're not him." CJ didn't look at him as he spoke. "You're not going to hurt me. I know that. And maybe I just want to have some good memories to replace the bad ones."

Michael wasn't sure about it. After what happened to CJ, he had to be bothered by the thought of sex. He couldn't be ready, could he?

"It wasn't just him," CJ said after a few moments of silence. "That other guy, Walter, the one Joe shot, he had a turn with me, too. He made me ride him. It was so degrading, being such an active part of something like that, you know."

Michael didn't know what to say. So far, CJ had not talked at all about what happened. To hear it was hard, but to say it must have been even harder. He reached over and took his hand, squeezing it to make it clear that he was there for him. CJ took a shuddering breath.

"But that wasn't the worst."

Michael didn't want to hear it, but he had to. He didn't say anything, just was there. He held tight to his hand, even though he could feel CJ shaking now.

"They made me come. They made me enjoy, and that was the worst part of it all." CJ swallowed thickly beside him. "To be forced to enjoy and feel pleasure at the hands of someone like that, I can't tell you what that was like. For a while, I thought I could never pleasure even myself again."

CJ put his head down and laid on his side to face Michael now. "Then one night, I was thinking about you and how much I wanted to see you again. I got hard, and at first, I was scared, you know, because that was the first time in a while. So, I played with myself, stroking myself and then I pressed my finger inside and thinking of you, it felt good again. So, I want to be with you again."

"Well, do you want to do that, or call our parents first?" Michael reached out and caressed his head.

"I want you," CJ whispered hoarsely.

Michael had an instant hard on at that, and he growled, petting CJ's hair a little more aggressively. He was careful, though, not wanting to be too rough.

"It's okay to be a little rough," CJ said, eyes wide and centered on Michael's. "I like that."

It didn't take much to flip the switch, because that go ahead meant he wrapped his hands in CJ's hair and pulled gently on his head, baring his throat. He leaned in and began kissing him, biting gently on his neck. CJ moaned in response and Michael reached for his T-shirt and pulled it over his head. He then began kissing his chest, pausing to suck on each of his nipples. It apparently was good, because CJ grabbed his head and moaned low in his throat.

"Lemme get somethin'," Michael said, getting up and going to the chest of drawers.

He opened the top and grabbed a bottle and brought it back. CJ smirked. "You planned this?"

"You're the one who initiated. I bought it just in case," Michael said, kneeling on the mattress.

CJ rolled onto his back, and Michael reached for his shorts, pulling them off, baring him completely. He took in his body. Perfect, he thought. Smooth, unblemished skin on his chest and stomach led down to a trail of dark hair that led down to his pubic bone. His cock was already erect, leaking pearls from the tip. Michael licked his lips and then went down on him without warning. CJ buried both hands in Michael's blond mess of hair and groaned loudly.

"Oh, oh, yes," he managed.

Michael wasn't used to doing this yet, so he wasn't the best at it, though he tried. He sucked him down as far as he could, using his tongue to swirl around the tip and under the glans. It seemed to work on CJ because he kept pressing down and mumbling under his breath. He slipped one hand down and moved to press against his entrance, waiting to see if he stopped him. Instead, he just kept moaning and encouraging him. He grabbed the lube bottle, put some on his fingers, and slipped one inside his tight, hot body.

"Please, more!" CJ begged, and Michael obliged, pushing a second finger inside and then thrusting them back and forth as he sucked him.

He found the spongy spot and began playing with it. It put CJ into a fit of mumbling that Michael realized had to be Korean, because he couldn't understand a word he was saying. He'd never heard him speak Korean before, so perhaps that was a good sign. After a little while, CJ bucked his hips, forcing his cock down further in Michael's throat. Michael suppressed his urge to gag, instead swallowing against him. CJ's groan turned into a soft scream as he exploded into Michael's mouth. Michael sucked until his cock quit throbbing and came up, wiping his mouth with his hand.

"Well, you certainly liked that," he said, mostly to himself.

CJ was staring at him, eyes hooded, and he'd drooled on himself. Michael moved up on his body and licked his face, tasting him, and then got to his mouth. He slid between his legs, pressing his own clothed erection against his body. He delved into his mouth with his tongue, and CJ responded, twining his tongue around Michael's. Michael sucked on his tongue, bringing it into his mouth, and he reached down and began stroking him.

"Do you feel good, CJ, baby?" he breathed into his mouth.

"Yeah," he answered, arching as Michael played with his cock. It was slowly coming back to life. "Please, I want you inside me," CJ begged, looking at him with teary eyes.

"Oh, god, CJ, I can't say no to that," Michael muttered, sitting up on his knees and pulling himself out of his pajama pants.

He grabbed the lube and slicked himself up, using plenty. He didn't want the first time in a while to hurt him. He looked down at CJ.

"Baby, spread your legs wide for me. Show me your need."

CJ spread open his legs, reaching down and stroking himself as he watched Michael. "Put it in, please. Make me feel you."

Positioning himself between his legs, he pressed down against his entrance, then slipped easily inside.

"Ahh..." CJ exhaled, arching a little. "More!"

Michael swallowed and leaned over him, then thrust his hips, burying his cock in all the way in one motion. CJ moaned loudly, pressing back against him. Michael leaned over him, wrapping his arms around his neck and pulling him in for a consuming kiss as he thrust slow and deep.

"Baby," he muttered against his lips. "You're so sweet and hot inside. It feels so good," he continued. "I feel you squeezing my cock hard, so I know it feels good. I want you to come while I fuck you hard and fast, okay, baby?"

"Hmm, yes, please, fuck me hard," CJ managed, hands twisting in the sheet on the mattress.

Michael thrust into him hard and fast, just like he said he would. He wasn't too rough but rougher than he thought he'd be. CJ was asking for it so that he would give it to him. He must have got a good angle because CJ started mumbling again, and there were tears in his eyes. Michael kept giving him long, deep kisses, never breaking the rhythm.

Finally, CJ gasped and came between them, tightening up on Michael so much he could barely move. He thrust a few times, feeling his own orgasm slam into him, releasing and filling CJ with his essence. After he was spent, he pulled out, rolling over and cupping CJ's face.

"Oh baby, that was amazing," he breathed.

"Uh huh," CJ said, lying on his back and staring at the ceiling. He then turned to Michael. "Thank you," he whispered.

Michael sat up and kissed him, another lingering kiss until they were out of breath. "Thank you, baby, for trusting me."

They both got showered and changed individually since the shower wasn't big enough for two. When they were done, they grabbed their phones and sat on the couch. CJ curled into the corner, pulling his legs up under him.

"You first?" he said to Michael.

"On speaker," Michael confirmed and dialed his dad's number.

"Hello?" came his father's voice.

"Dad," he answered.

"Michael! Where the hell are you? You've been missing since Sunday! You haven't even been to work!" his dad exclaimed.

"No, I haven't. I took a few days off to settle into my new place," he answered.

"New place? What are you talking about?"

"I rented a place in St. Louis. I'm working at the rehab center still, and I'm going to be living here from now on."

His dad was quiet for a time. "Don't be ridiculous, son. Come home. We miss you. Things were fine until you left."

"No, they weren't. I had to fight you to get my job, and the only reason you didn't stop that was because it's my career. You didn't want CJ and me to be together, but now we are."

CJ nodded, encouraging.

"What do you mean? You're with CJ?"

"I am. We're living together, and eventually, we're going to get married and adopt a couple of kids, and you've got a choice. You can either be in our lives or not. It's up to you."

"You can't be serious!" his dad exclaimed. "This is wrong. CJ can't handle a relationship right now, and you are too young to make this decision. You need to come home."

"I refuse," Michael said,.

"You refuse? You can't refuse! I'm your father!"

"And I'm an adult. You don't control me. I'm turning twenty-two in December of this year. I'm a college graduate with a career now. Now, are you going to accept this, or not? Because if you aren't going to accept it, I don't have to see you, no matter how much you bluster and blow."

There was silence. Michael let it go on for a while.

"You have my number. I got a phone plan of my own for CJ and me, so when you decide to talk like an adult and quit demanding, I'll be around," he said and tapped the phone off.

Michael sighed. "I guess that could have gone better," he muttered.

"I guess I'll call mine," CJ said, taking out his phone and dialing the familiar number.

Like Michael, CJ's dad answered, "Hello?"

"Dad, hi," CJ spoke quietly.

"CJ, where are you? You've been gone since Sunday! I called Richard at the FBI, and he's been looking for you! What happened?"

"You weren't being reasonable, so I left." CJ chewed his lip for a bit. "I had no choice. I wanted to be with Michael, and you kept me away from him and everything else."

"What? Michael? Are you with him? Is that where you've been?"

"Yeah. We met up and now live in a little place in St. Louis. I'm going to finish school, and he's going to work on his master's program at the place he's working."

"CJ, please, just come home. We can work this out," his dad said. "I know we were being too protective, I get it, but after what happened, can you blame us? I didn't want to see you hurt again." CJ's dad cleared his throat. "Please, son. You can't just live with a guy you've known for a week or two."

"You don't understand it, Dad. I love Michael, and we will be together, whether you agree or not. So, it's up to you. We want to have a family, and we're going to. If you want to be in our lives, you can, but you will have to accept this." CJ let a couple of tears slip. "I love you, Dad, and I want you to be in my life, but I can't leave Michael. I love him, too."

"CJ, I don't know if I can accept this."

"Either accept it, or I'm not coming home again," CJ said. "This is my new phone number. I'll let you talk to mom and think about it. But I hope you come to the conclusion that's best for everyone."

CJ cut off the phone before he could say anything else. He wiped his eyes, and Michael leaned over and hugged him.

"We don't need anyone else. We've got each other," Michael pointed out.

"I'll be out here," Michael said as CJ got up from the chair beside him.

"I know. I hope I like this one." CJ nodded to Michael and followed the nurse to the therapist's room.

CJ had canceled his appointments with Dr. Thompson. The receptionist had tried arguing with him that he wasn't allowed to cancel. CJ informed her that he was looking for another therapist, and she could go directly to hell. She hadn't liked that. CJ went through several pages of therapists in the St. Louis area and finally found one that sounded like a fit.

This therapist was a counselor, not a psychiatrist. Her name was Nadia Primrose, and she was a specialist in PTSD and was LGBTQ friendly. So far, she seemed like the type that would work with CJ's situation.

"Have a seat here. Nadia will be right with you," the nurse said, leaving the room.

A few seconds later, a woman came into the room. She was tall and wore her hair up in a bun. Her skin was darkly tanned, and her hair was black. She had big, brown eyes. She sat down and smiled at CJ.

"Hi, CJ. I'm Nadia."

CJ swallowed a ball in the back of his throat and spoke shakily. "I'm glad to meet you," he said.

"I requested records from Dr. Thompson, so I know a little bit about the situation. I understand you were kidnapped and raped?" she asked.

CJ nodded. "Well, more than that. I mean, it wasn't just once." CJ felt more comfortable with her already.

She nodded. "Tell me what happened if you're able."

CJ started at the beginning, telling her everything in one long explanation. He didn't stop once he started. He just kept going, even describing what Walter and Joe had done, and telling her about the vibrator. He expressed his shame at having received pleasure at their hands, and then he told her about how his family had acted and leaving to live with Michael.

"That's a lot, CJ," Nadia said when he was done. "I mean, to go through all that, and then have your family be against your wishes, that had to be terribly hard."

"It was," CJ said.

"What you went through was terrible," she started. "But you've come through it. And that's the important part of the story. You survived."

"I guess," he looked at her, and he didn't see judgment on her face. She appeared genuine, which Dr. Thompson had never seemed that way.

"We'll work on these things if you want to come back and see me. But I want you to work on first realizing you're not a victim." She smiled and stood up.

CJ frowned. "Not a victim?" He stood up as well.

"You're a survivor," she explained. "Keep that in mind."

CJ walked out and saw Michael waiting for him, and he smiled. It was true. He was a survivor.

Chapter Seventeen

Learning to Live Again

Almost a month had passed, and CJ would be starting school again. He had two years to go until he got his creative writing degree. Their families still hadn't come around, which saddened them. Michael had gotten a text from his sister, saying they were still angry and wouldn't talk about him. CJ had heard nothing.

Since things had happened, though, they'd improved their situation. CJ got a part-time job at a local retail place, and his extra income helped them. Michael was making a good salary at his job, and his prospects for a career at the place were excellent. They'd upgraded the bed from a mattress on the floor to a nice queen size bed. It wasn't fancy, but it was better.

Michael came in unusually excited, and CJ had made fish sticks and macaroni and cheese (one of his favorite meals). Michael couldn't wait to go to bed, and CJ guessed he wanted to have a little fun, which was okay with him. As long as it was Michael, he could stand to be touched. Other people he avoided. Even shaking hands was too much, so he didn't do it.

A few people had thought it weird, but random people didn't need to know.

Michael led him upstairs and then pulled a bag out of the drawer. "I got something today!"

CJ blinked, frowning. "What?"

"Toys! I figured it would be fun to try something new!" He was obviously very excited, but CJ's heart fell.

"T-toys?" he said.

Michael picked up on CJ's shift in mood immediately. "Baby? What's wrong? I thought you'd be as excited about this as I am. I mean, I've never had any experience with them, and you haven't either."

CJ had the decision to make, and fast. Should he reveal to Michael what had happened or not? He'd broached the subject of the toys being used on him during the kidnapping at therapy but hadn't ever told Michael about it. There was no way that Michael would have known about it, so that he couldn't blame him.

"Mikey, I can't do that," he said, looking away.

"Baby, what's wrong?" Michael put the bag down and went around the bed.

"I didn't tell you. But while they had me, um, they used toys on me, and I don't know that I can do that."

"What? Why didn't you tell me?" Michael gasped, putting his hands on CJ's shoulders. "I don't want to make you uncomfortable!"

CJ felt the tears already. "I know, and I just didn't want to talk about it."

"We don't have to do anything you don't want to do, baby, okay?" he said.

"But you don't get it!" CJ sighed. "I want to do things like that. I really do. But I can't get past the things that happened!"

Michael pulled him into a hug. "Baby, shhh, it'll be okay!"

"But it's not! It's interfering with our relationship, and I hate it!" CJ gripped him hard and couldn't stop the tears.

"Baby, baby." Michael tried soothing him, patting his back and rubbing it. "Please, don't worry about it. Maybe we can make small steps, huh?"

CJ pulled away and wiped his eyes under his glasses. "What do you mean?"

"What exactly did they do to you?" Michael looked severe now.

CJ swallowed. "Uh, they used a vibrator and made me come for them a bunch."

"Okay, so we don't use that," he said, walking over to the bag.

He rummaged inside the bag for a moment, then pulled out something. "We could do this?"

CJ came over and looked at it. It was a piece of black silicone, shaped weirdly. "What is it?"

"It's a prostate stimulator. It doesn't vibrate at all," he said.

"So, you just put it in?" CJ asked, taking it from him.

Michael nodded. "We don't have to. But if you want to try and work through it, we can take little steps and work up to a vibrator. And you can talk to your therapist about what we're doing and see what she says. So, we can wait until you talk to her if you want."

CJ didn't want to wait. He wanted to work through it like he had been doing with sex itself. He enjoyed Michael's attention, and he wanted to be okay with whatever Michael did with him. He wanted to have a good relationship and experience pleasure, as long as it was with Michael.

"I want to try it," CJ said. "I mean, I've gotten over being afraid of sex so long as you're the one involved. I don't think I could ever have sex with someone else, though." CJ blushed a little, looking down as he spoke.

Michael cupped his face and lifted it. "Baby, you don't ever have to have sex with anyone else. I don't plan to see you ever with another person."

CJ's heartbeat a little faster at that. His biggest fear was to be asked to sleep with someone else. He didn't think Michael would ever do anything like that, but he was still afraid. He wanted to do whatever Michael wanted so badly, but that was something he didn't think he could do.

"Okay, I think this is okay," he told him, handing him back the strange-looking toy.

"Are you sure? We don't have to." Michael took it and held it in his hand.

CJ swallowed hard and nodded his head. He was sure. He wanted to go forward, and that meant getting through some of these things that bothered him. If it involved Michael, he wanted to do it.

Michael nodded and patted the bed. "Get undressed for me, baby. I'm going to make you enjoy this more than you can imagine." He paused. "You took a shower earlier, right?"

CJ, as he was pulling off his shirt, stopped. "Uh, yeah?"

"Okay, just checking," Michael mumbled, mostly to himself.

CJ slipped off the linen shorts he was wearing and the briefs he wore under them. Michael was watching him intently, so he blushed as he stood there.

"Baby, you know what I want to do?" he said after staring for a few moments.

CJ frowned and shook his head. "No, what?"

"I want to buy you some pretty underwear. No one but me will see them, but I want you to have some lacy and satiny panties, so when you get undressed, I get to see them. Would you like that?"

CJ blushed even harder, but he had to admit, he loved the idea. He had been thinking of wearing more feminine clothes for a little while now, even before everything happened. He shifted uncomfortably under the intense gaze.

"Um, yeah, that'd be okay," he said, realizing Michael was waiting for him to say something.

"Good, that's the next thing I'll get for you, baby," Michael said. "Now come on, up on the bed. I want to see that gorgeous body of yours."

CJ got up on the bed, self-conscious of every move he made. He sat there and waited for Michael to tell him what else he wanted him to do.

"Lay down on your stomach, okay?" Michael said, grabbing the lube bottle and spreading it on the toy. CJ could smell the strawberry scent from the flavored lube.

CJ was nervous, but he did as he asked. He then felt the bed move as Michael got on and pulled his legs apart. He then settled between them and when CJ glanced back, he was lying on the bed behind him.

"Stop looking!" CJ said, embarrassed that Michael was looking at him with such intensity.

"Baby, it's okay. I've seen all of you already," he said, rubbing one butt cheek gently as he probed him with a lubed finger. "Besides, I like looking at you. Every inch."

CJ buried his head in his arm, completely without words for that. He jerked a little when he felt something hard pressing into him.

"I'm going to put in the toy. Tell me to stop if you can't take it, okay, baby?" Michael said.

CJ didn't want to say anything but managed a weak "Okay."

The toy slid into him smoothly, almost with no pressure. It was slick, and it didn't hurt at all. Michael seated it against him, and CJ squirmed because it pressed right into the spot that really felt good.

"How's that, baby?" Michael asked, kneading both sides of his ass.

"Ah, it's okay," he said as he moved a little, shifting it inside him.

It felt nice, and it wasn't really bothering him as much as he feared. His mind still tried to go back to that time, but he forced those thoughts and feelings away easily.

"Okay, that's enough of that," Michael said as though his patience had suddenly snapped.

"What's wrong?" CJ asked, glancing over his shoulder as he felt Michael slowly pull the toy out.

"I've got another idea, and I can't wait to try it," Michael said. "Here, lift your ass up." He pulled up on his hips.

CJ got his knees under him, thinking Michael wanted to fuck him like that. Then, Michael was shifting his position, staying behind him. Instead, he felt Michael kiss him back there. He blinked and squirmed a little. He'd never done that. It felt weird, then, he licked his balls from behind, trailing his tongue up the underside and then up farther. CJ gasped, feeling Michael's tongue drawing over his entrance, a completely new sensation.

"Wait, what are you doing? Ung..." he groaned, feeling the sensations all the way to his toes.

"Just relax, baby," Michael said before licking his way around the hole and then dipping his tongue through the tight muscle. CJ gasped and shifted, wanting to move his legs, but Michael would have to get up if he did that. He had his tongue inside him, and it felt amazing. Michael reached between his legs and began stroking his cock slowly as he licked at him. CJ felt himself already dripping, and he started moaning as Michael became more aggressive with his tongue, pressing it deeper than before. CJ didn't think he'd come like that, but it felt incredible. After a few more minutes of torturing him with his tongue, Michael pulled back, sliding two fingers inside him.

"Ah, baby, you're delicious."

CJ felt his face burning at that. "You-you're dumb! It's the lube!"

"Oh, no, it's all you," Michael said, sliding his hand up and down CJ's length. "But I've gotta sink my hard dick into you, okay? All this playing and tasting you inside and out made me painfully hard."

CJ didn't say anything, but a few seconds later, Michael sunk into him, groaning in relief. CJ moaned as Michael began a fast, hard rhythm that he could feel all the way to his toes. After all the foreplay, CJ didn't last long before he was coming.

Luckily, it was on a towel Michael had thought to put on the bed. Michael spent a couple more minutes bringing himself to completion, but soon, he was lying on the bed beside CJ, panting from the exertion.

"You okay?" Michael asked, running a hand over CJ's head.

"Oh, yeah." CJ nodded and laid on his arm as Michael pulled the covers over them.

Michael pulled him close and nuzzled into him. "You did good, though, with the toy. I'm proud of you for being so brave about it."

CJ swallowed hard. "It wasn't too bad. I don't know about anything else, though. I'll have to test it out and see what happens."

"Well, I bought a couple of little butt plugs that don't vibrate, a dildo, and a vibrator. Took a chunk of my check, but we'll take it a step at a time, okay?"

CJ nodded against him and sighed. "Thank you," he said.

"No need to thank me, baby. None at all."

"How has the week gone?" Nadia asked, looking over at CJ as he got comfortable in the big chair.

"Well, something came up unexpectedly." CJ was a little uncomfortable talking about sex with anyone, but he could talk to Nadia.

She nodded. "What's that?"

"Michael brought home toys." CJ looked over his glasses at her. "And at first, I was afraid to try anything. But he showed me something called a prostate stimulator, and we tried that."

"How'd that go?" she asked.

"Well, actually. It wasn't the vibrator, but it was still a toy, so it was a step, right?" CJ looked to her for confirmation.

"It was a big step, CJ. You have to understand that these things take time. And even then, you may never be ready to use the type of toys they used on you."

"But I want to be!" CJ insisted. "No, I will be!"

Nadia smiled gently at him. "I believe you, CJ. Just please take this slowly. You were under severe conditions before. Trying to use a vibrator too soon may trigger flashbacks."

"I know, so Michael is okay with going slow. He said we didn't have to if I didn't want to, but I wanted to try it. And it wasn't that bad. I had some thoughts, but I could push them aside."

"What were those thoughts?" she asked, leaning forward a bit.

"Just the shameful thoughts. About how they made me come, it made me feel pleasure even though I didn't want it. And for a minute, it felt like that. But I got through it, so that's good, right?" CJ looked up from his hands where he'd been staring.

She nodded. "Of course. Every step is progress, CJ. Always remember that. What else is on your mind? I don't think that's all."

CJ was always amazed at how good she was at picking up on stuff before he even said it. "I've been thinking about my gender."

"You've mentioned before that you weren't a boy or a girl."

"Yeah, I'm neither. Or both. Or something. I don't know. I think gender-queer fits the best because I'm all over the place. But I do want to wear more feminine things. Michael said he wanted to buy me pretty panties, and I really liked that idea." CJ felt his face heat at that, so he looked away from her.

"Was the idea of dressing up for him what you liked, or just being more feminine?" she wondered.

CJ thought about it. "Both, er. Can...Can I say both?"

"Of course you can," she said, smiling at him. "There's no right or wrong answer."

"Like, I want some skirts to wear and some pretty shirts. I like my hoodies and T-shirts, still, but I also want to dress in pretty clothes. And having nice underthings makes me feel good, too." His face burned hotter.

"You can be fem if you want," Nadia explained. "There's nothing that says you have to dress like a boy or dress neutral, even with a gender-queer identity. You don't have to be androgynous."

"What if I'm just a feminine boy?" he asked.

"Then that's what you are. But you said you feel like a girl some of the time, so you should listen to yourself, not just society's expectations of you. Somehow, I think this journey is just beginning for you, and that's fine." Nadia leaned back and crossed her legs. "Tell me, have your parents contacted you?"

CJ shook his head. "Nothing yet. I'm afraid they're not going to come around. What do I do if I never see them again?"

"You live your life, CJ. They were there for you when they needed to be, but it's up to them if they want to be with you now."

"I feel bad because Michael's family hasn't contacted him yet either. It's because of me, so I feel guilty." CJ hated to admit it, but it was true.

"Michael made his own choice, didn't he?" she asked.

"Well, yeah, he could have stayed home that day, but he came and got me," he said, looking up at her. "I guess you're right. I can't feel like that. It's their choice as much as it's my parents' choice. Though I miss my sisters." He sighed.

"You have to give them time," Nadia said.

"I guess you're right." He nodded.

CJ and Michael were sitting on the sofa when first CJ's phone, then Michael's phone, went off. They looked at each other and then down at their phones.

"That's odd," Michael said. "Almost the same time?"

"No one but my parents have this number, and a couple of people from work who give me rides," CJ muttered and picked his up.

"It's my dad," Michael said. "It just says, 'call me,' and that's it."

CJ looked at his phone and back at Michael. "Mine says the same thing."

"Want to call first?" Michael asked.

"Yeah," CJ said, dialing the number.

"CJ?" came the answer.

"Yeah, dad."

"Son, are you doing okay?" he asked, a little frantic sounding.

"Everything's good, dad; I didn't expect to hear from you. It's been months."

"I know, and I'm sorry. I just—I thought this would fall through and you'd come home. I see now that I was wrong, and this isn't just some dalliance."

"I love Michael, Dad, and he loves me. We're very happy together," CJ said, still wary of the whole situation.

"You stopped seeing the therapist we got you."

"I found a new one, one that I liked. I couldn't stand that other guy," he answered. "This one fits me much better, and we've talked about the whole situation. I'm working through things."

"I'm glad, CJ. Here, your mom wants to talk to you," he said.

There was a shuffle, and his mom's voice came onto the phone, sounding tearful. "CJ, honey, I've missed you so much!"

"Me, too, Mom. I wanted to hear from you. But I guess it wasn't time yet," he answered.

"Honey, please come visit. Bring Michael, and we'll get to know him, okay? I know we were hard on you, but you have to understand we were just afraid after what happened."

"I want to do that. I miss the twins and you both a lot. But are you going to realize I'm an adult and can make my own choices?" he asked her.

"I know that now, CJ. I'm so very sorry that we didn't treat you like a grown-up before. I get that you just wanted to be treated like someone capable of making their own decisions and even mistakes, if that's what they were."

"Next weekend. I go to school during the week, and Michael works during the week at his job. But we can come next weekend."

"That'd be good. We'll make lunch, and everyone will have a chance to get to know each other. What day?"

CJ looked at Michael, who shrugged. "Probably Saturday at noon." Michael nodded, and CJ smiled at him.

"Okay, so we'll see you then. I love you, honey," she said.

"Give Alex and Allie a kiss for me, and I'll see you all next weekend."

"Bye," she said, and the line went off.

CJ frowned. "They talked to each other, I bet. That's why we both got texts at the same time."

Michael nodded. "Has to be. Well, let's see what my old man has to say," he said and dialed his phone.

"Michael?" came his dad's voice.

"Michael!" He heard his mom as well, so it was on speaker.

"Mom, Dad, hey there," he said.

"Son, please, are you sure you won't come home?" his dad asked.

"Dad, I told you. I have my own place. I have a job that's turning into a career. And I have CJ. I've got all I need."

"That's okay," his mom said. "It really is. We just wanted to ensure you were in a good place good for you."

"Well, we don't have much stuff, but what we do have is enough," Michael told them.

"Son, we really want to see you again. Can you at least come to visit?" his dad asked.

"With CJ?" Michael wasn't going if CJ wasn't invited; CJ knew already.

There was silence. "Of course, son. CJ's your significant other. And it's time we understood that," his dad said slowly. "I can't say I agree, but it's your life, not mine. If it turns out to be a mistake, it's your mistake to make. I can't protect you from the world any longer. You're a grown man, now."

"We're going to St. Peters to see CJ's parents Saturday for lunch. Then, we can come to see you for dinner," Michael said.

"That sounds fine," his mom said. "I'll make lasagna, just like you like," she added.

"Sounds wonderful. We'll see you Saturday at about four then," Michael said, nodding at CJ. He nodded back.

"Goodbye, son, we love you," his mom said.

"I love you guys too," Michael said, and the line went dead.

"Well, looks like we have visits this week," CJ said.

"Looks that way." Michael nodded. "How do you think your parents will like me?"

CJ shook his head. "I have no idea. First, they have to get past the whole me being more girly than they remember and then accept that I've got a man in my life."

"Mine have to get past that, too," Michael nodded. "They didn't expect me to bring home a boy. But that's okay. We'll get through this."

Michael reached over, took CJ's hand, and kissed the back of it. "I love you, baby," he said with a grin.

"And I love you, too, Mikey," CJ responded, blushing a little as he looked at his hand.

Chapter Eighteen

Reuniting

"Are you nervous, baby?" Michael asked as he drove to CJ's parents' house.

"Of course. How are you not?" CJ turned and glared at him. "This is like the first time seeing them in months, and we both just snuck out of their lives. Why wouldn't I be nervous?"

Michael nodded, eyes on the road. "I know, but it'll be okay. You'll see."

"What if they don't like me?" CJ asked, fiddling with the ring Michael had gotten him. It was just a cheap silver promise ring, but he wore it on his ring finger anyway.

"My folks? Don't worry. They'll like you. What's not to like?" he said. "Is this it?" he asked, glancing down the side of the road at the houses.

"The blue one, with the gray awnings," CJ said as they pulled in beside the car CJ used to drive.

CJ breathed deeply for a couple of seconds. "Okay." He nodded and got out.

Michael got out and came around to where he was standing, staring at the house. He nodded at him and took his hand.

"They're your parents. They love you," Michael said.

"Even though I left like I did?" CJ asked, turning toward him.

"Even though you left. Now, let's go," he said.

CJ opened the door, clutching Michael's hand in his left as he did it. The door opened, and immediately, he was flooded with the scent of Jjajangmyeon and Kimchi. His mouth immediately watered as he walked into the dining room. His father was sitting there and stood up.

"CJ!" he said.

"Brudder!" called one of the twins, and they both came running from the living room.

CJ knelt and hugged them both as they grabbed onto him. He held back the tears. He wasn't going to cry in front of his sisters. They let go and CJ stood up, ruffling Alex's hair.

"Hey, how are you two?" he asked.

"Good," Allie said. "Who's that?" she said, pointing to Michael.

"Um, this is Michael. My boyfriend."

"Boys don't get boyfriends!" Alex frowned as she stared at Michael.

"Yeah, boys get girlfriends!" Allie agreed, crossing her arms and glaring at Michael.

CJ's dad came around. "Now, girls. Anyone can have a boyfriend, and anyone can have a girlfriend."

"You mean I can have a girlfriend, daddy?" Alex said, turning to her father.

"If you want when you're old enough," Don said, patting her head.

"Okay, I'll get a girlfriend. Boys are icky," she said and left, returning to the living room, followed by her sister.

Don shook his head. "Um, hi, Michael," he said, extending a hand to Michael.

Michael took it and shook his hand. "Good to meet you, Mr. Kim."

"Don, please. We don't stand on formality when it comes to family," he said, glancing over at CJ, who was holding onto Michael's hand again.

"Okay, Don then," Michael said.

CJ's mom came out of the kitchen. "CJ! You're here!" She rushed around and grabbed him up into a hug. "I missed you!"

When she released him, CJ smiled, a little stiff and unsure about being touched. "Mom, this is Michael."

She turned to him and for a second, she almost made a face, but she didn't. She instead nodded. "Good to meet you. And it's Mara," she said.

"Thank you for letting me come with CJ. I really wanted to know his family," Michael said, looking between them.

"He didn't give us much choice," Mara muttered, almost too low to hear, but she smiled at him. CJ had heard, though.

"Come, let's sit down while your mom finishes the noodles. We got fresh kimchi just for today, but I'm not sure how Michael will like your favorite foods, CJ," he said, sitting down at the head of the table.

Michael and CJ sat on one side next to each other, and CJ grabbed Michael's hand and pulled it into his lap. Only holding Michael's hand helped slow his trembling fingers. His mom brought out all the food and placed the noodles, the side dishes, and the bowls on the turntable in the center of everyone.

"You take what you want," CJ explained to Michael. "The noodles are my favorite. They're not spicy or anything, just a noodle with black bean sauce on it," CJ said, showing Michael. "The kimchi, though, that's spicy. It's fermented cabbage with spices on it, basically."

Despite being born and raised in the US, CJ's mom quickly learned to cook Korean food when Don's family spent time with them while CJ was very little. Mara picked up cooking quickly from her mother-in-law and had fixed Korean food about once a week ever since CJ could remember. She even learned to read some Korean, enough to go to the Asian markets and buy what she needed. CJ, of course, spoke fluent Korean and learned to read and write it early on.

"I've never eaten Korean," Michael said as CJ helped with his plate.

"We should go to one of those Korean BBQ places," CJ said with a grin. "Don't worry, I'll read the menu to you."

"You can read Korean? You say stuff sometimes, but I wasn't sure if you could read and write it."

"When's he say things in Korean?" CJ's dad asked.

CJ's eyes went wide, and he flushed red immediately. "Just sometimes."

Don looked at him with a confused look on his face, but when Mara locked eyes on him, she turned back to the food. "CJ learned Korean as a child," Don said instead.

"That's cool. Teach me something," Michael said, smiling.

CJ looked at him. "Well, *namja* is the word for guy. And *yujah* is the word for girl."

"*Namja* and *yujah*. Okay, that's easy enough to remember. I guess you know all the bad words, huh?" he teased him.

CJ glanced at his dad. "Uh, I know a few."

Don cleared his throat. "So, Michael, you're working at the psychiatric center?"

Michael nodded, taking a tentative bite of the noodles. "Yeah, I got my psychology degree, graduated summa cum laude. So, it was pretty easy to get on. I'm a psychiatric technician right now, but they're going to reimburse me for my master's program as long as I pass. I'm going to take a year to save money and get our place set up, and then start next year."

Mara wasn't really looking at him. Instead, she glanced at CJ now and then, but mostly, she concentrated on her food. The twins were uncharacteristically quiet as they ate their noodles, but it was like they knew things were different with Michael there.

"So, you intend to get a master's in psychology, then?" Don asked.

"Doctorate, actually, but I'll tackle that once I finish the master's." He nodded.

There was a short silence; then Don looked at CJ. "You went back for the fall semester, CJ?"

"Yeah, I've got three more semesters after this. But I've been doing well, though it's been tough with one car," he admitted.

Of course, the unspoken question was about the car. CJ wanted to come out and asked if he could use it, but he couldn't bring himself to do it. The car was in his dad's name, unlike Michael's. Michael owned his car outright and had bought it with the money from his part-time jobs. His family had no claim to his car, but CJ's car was a different story. He wasn't sure if his father would give it to him, though, as unhappy with Michael and him being together as he obviously still was.

"I can imagine, but that's the problem when you live outside of home."

And there was the answer to the question, CJ thought, sighing a little. His dad was going to hold the car, even though he and his mom had a car of their own each, so no one could even drive CJ's car right now. He swallowed and let the silence stretch while he ate the noodles.

"It works, though," Michael said, putting down his fork and turning to Don. "I take CJ before I go to work and pick him up after I get off. He gets a chance to do homework and study or use the computer lab while I'm at work. Luckily, I've got a day shift, so I don't usually have to work late. We sometimes have to stay over, but CJ's in a safe place, and the computer lab is open twenty-four hours."

Don didn't comment but stared at Michael. CJ realized that Michael wasn't flinching at all. CJ knew his dad could be intimidating, which was odd considering the small man's stature. He had a powerful personality, though. CJ looked between them and felt the tension.

"You're a lot like Randy," Don said finally, breaking eye contact and eating some of the vegetables on his plate.

"I've heard that before," Michael said. "I think my sister took after him more, but people say I act like him."

There was another silence, and Mara broke it this time. "You've been seeing a therapist, right CJ?"

CJ nodded, looking over at her. "Yeah, she's wonderful. Her name's Nadia."

"What was wrong with Dr. Thompson?" Don asked. "He came highly recommended."

CJ shifted uncomfortably. "He wasn't what I needed."

"What's that mean? You needed a good therapist. Not one that will coddle you," Don said.

"I don't think that's fair," Michael said. "CJ needed a therapist that matched his needs, not the needs someone else thinks he has."

Don turned back to Michael. "What business is it of yours what his therapist is like?"

"I know therapists," Michael said, looking at him. "You're a doctor, not a therapist. I work with them every day, and I see what they do first hand. None of us know what goes on in CJ's therapy sessions, and none of us should know. That's between him and his therapist."

"We need to know how to help CJ," Don insisted.

Michael wasn't letting up, though. "That's fine. So, learn a little bit about PTSD and you'll understand a lot more."

"You're telling me to learn about PTSD? I was in the military. I've seen more than you can imagine," Don said through clenched teeth.

Michael still didn't flinch. "Not the kind that CJ has. Unless you were raped by several men, then you can't know what he's going through."

CJ swallowed, staring at his hands. He didn't know what to do. Should he say something? Should he stop the conversation? He didn't want to upset anyone, least of all Michael. And what Michael said was true. His dad couldn't understand what he went through.

Finally, he looked up. "Look, I have a therapist I trust, and that's what matters. All I need from everyone else is support."

"How are we supposed to support you in St. Louis?" Mara said quietly. "You're not here to support, CJ."

CJ felt everything snap, then. Something about that just sat wrong with him, and his father thinking he knew everything didn't help.

"Look, you don't get it. You can never get it," he said, looking between them. "Michael can't get it, either, and he's my boyfriend, and lover. Yes, we're lovers, and have been since we were kidnapped together. That's not your business, though. Your job as my parents is to support me in my decisions and not guilt me for making them. If they're mistakes, they are mine to make." CJ reached over and took Michael's hand. "I know this is hard for you. You wanted to protect me, and you couldn't. I get that you're guilty because of that. But it's not my fault, none of it, not me being raped, not being kidnapped, not your feelings over it."

Michael didn't say anything, only held his hand as he continued. "I've learned a lot from this therapist. She's opened my eyes to a lot of things, and I've come to realize I've never truly lived my own life. I have to find myself, not your son, Michael's boyfriend, but myself. You can't understand, and you will never understand what went on. And no, I'm not going to tell you about it." He licked his lips and sighed. "I just love you both, and I want you to know that."

He stood up and looked at Michael. "We should go."

Michael got up, pushing his chair in, and followed CJ out the door to his car. CJ leaned against it and breathed heavily. He'd done it. He'd admitted it out loud. Even said the very word that sent his heart to his throat to even think. He'd owned what happened to him. Yes, he had been raped, that was the fact, and there was no getting around it.

"You okay?" Michael asked, rubbing his back.

"No, but I did what I had to do." CJ squeezed his hand. "Let's go to your parents' place."

"You sure you don't want to go home after that?" Michael asked.

"Yeah, let's get this over with."

They got into the car and drove in silence. CJ wanted to cry, but he didn't. He'd said what he had to say. Nadia had warned him this might happen, and she'd been right. His parents had tried to guilt him into coming back to them. They tried to "understand" him when it was impossible. They'd blamed everything on Michael and treated him like it was his fault. He just hoped that the visit to Michael's family went better.

They parked and waited. "We're early," Michael said. They were supposed to be there at four.

"Want to call and make sure they're okay with us being early?" CJ asked.

"Yeah, guess I should," he said, leaning over and punching their number in the SUV's system.

"Michael?" his mother answered.

"Hey, is it okay if we're early?" Michael asked.

"Uh, yeah, why are you early? I thought you were with the Kims?" she asked.

"Stuff happened and we left," Michael said. "I can explain more if you want."

"Are you here?" she asked, and Michael saw the curtains move.

Michael waved. "Yeah."

"Then come in!" she said.

Michael turned off the car and looked over at CJ. "Okay, you ready?"

CJ nodded. "As I'll ever be. Can't be worse than my parents."

Michael wasn't sure about that, but he had high hopes. He got out and let CJ out, taking his hand and leading him to the door. Opening it, they went into the house. He looked around and noted nothing had changed since he'd left that Sunday. They walked into the dining room to see his dad and mom sitting at the table.

"Michael!" his mom said, standing up and coming around. She grabbed him in a hug. "You must be CJ," she said as she let him go and looked at CJ. "I'm Terri, and that's Michael's dad, Randy."

"Hi," CJ said a little meekly, looking between them.

"What's wrong?" Terri said, reaching out and taking CJ by the hand. "You look like you could cry at any minute!"

"Like I said, we left his parents' house. Things got a little... Tense." Michael sighed, seeing CJ wasn't really okay at all.

Randy stood up and came over. "What happened?"

"My parents, they just don't understand. They want me to stay with them, and I'm happy with Michael in our life. It's not a lot, but it's ours." CJ still was staring down.

Terri kneeled in front of CJ and looked up at him. "Oh, honey," she said.

Randy sighed. "Don was always a stubborn bastard," he said. "He'll come around, though. I did, with Rich's help. I'm sure he thinks he's doing what's best, when it's what he thinks is best, not what really is the best."

"Come, sit down, both of you," Terri said, still holding CJ's hand.

She sat CJ down beside Michael and then sat down on the other side. "Tell me what happened."

"He didn't like that CJ got a different therapist. One that actually works with people who have gone through what he's gone through, not a military specialist like the last guy," Michael explained. "I'm sure he thought the military man would be better, but he doesn't know the kind of PTSD that CJ is going through. Mr. Kim thought he knew better than anyone since he'd been around PTSD. I kind of told him unless he'd been raped, he didn't get it."

Terri covered her mouth. "Michael, you didn't."

Michael nodded. "I couldn't help it. The way he was acting, like he knew more than CJ, I just couldn't stand it."

Randy leaned over and patted Michael on the back. "Son, you're my boy, that's for sure."

Michael cracked a smile and looked at him. "Well, he did say I reminded him of you."

CJ took a shuddering breath, and Michael's attention snapped to him. He had tears running down his cheeks, and he was trying very hard not to sob out loud. Michael reacted before he thought, not caring that he was in front of his parents.

"Baby!" he gasped out and grabbed him, pulling him close. "It's okay, baby," he whispered, tucking his head into him and hugging him tight.

CJ grabbed him tight with both arms and let out a shaky sob against his chest. Michael looked over at his parents, who were staring at them with wide eyes. He stroked CJ's hair softly and talked to him quietly. His parents were silent, letting Michael handle it.

"I'll make tea," his mom said suddenly and got up and headed to the kitchen.

"CJ likes honey, if you have it," Michael said, still holding CJ against him.

Terri stopped and looked at them for a moment, then turned and went into the kitchen. Michael didn't know what to do except to be there for him. He knew the day would be hard, but he'd expected his parents to be the more difficult ones. Instead of a repeat session of past arguments and ultimatums, they were starting to accept.

"You really care a lot for him," Randy said at length. "I can see that now."

Michael turned to him and nodded. "I love him, Dad. He's everything to me."

After a few minutes, CJ pulled back, wiping his eyes. "I'm sorry," he said softly.

"Don't be sorry," Michael said, taking his glasses gently off his face. He had ridges on his nose where he'd been pressed into Michael's chest. Michael took his T-shirt and carefully wiped the tears off them and put them back on him.

Terri came in with a tray holding four teacups and a teapot. With it was a container of honey and a sugar bowl. She sat the cups in front of everyone and poured the hot tea in each cup. She pushed the sugar toward Michael after she put some in her tea and sat the honey beside CJ's teacup.

CJ took the honey and mechanically poured some in and stirred it with the silver spoon. He was sniffling a little, and Michael's shirt had a large wet spot from his tears. Michael dipped out some sugar for his tea and passed it to his dad.

"CJ, your dad will come around," Randy said. "I had someone open my eyes recently, and I came to realize that standing between Michael and you was a mistake. Your father is stubborn, and it may take him longer to make that realization, but he'll get there."

"Are you sure?" CJ asked, looking up with a forlorn look in his eyes. "He doesn't seem like he will."

"I'm sure. I'll talk to him," Randy nodded. "Just give him some time."

"He won't even let CJ have the car CJ was driving to school," Michael said, draping his arm around CJ's shoulders. "CJ mentioned not having two cars, and he just said that was too bad."

Terri shook her head. "He needs to get his head out of his ass."

"Terri!" Randy frowned.

"It's true!" Terri said. "His son is at a stranger's dinner table crying because he can't be a decent father."

"I love them," CJ said, staring at his hands. "But I can't go back. I love Michael too much to leave. And that's not going to change."

"What's going on?" Aileen stepped into the dining room and her eyes landed on her brother, growing wide. "Michael!"

"Hey, sis," Michael said, not moving. "Let me introduce you. CJ, this is my sister, Aileen," he said.

CJ turned his head and nodded at her. "Hi," he said, still sounding meek.

Aileen sat down across from him. "What's wrong?" she said, eyeing CJ's tear-stained face.

"CJ had a little trouble with his parents," Terri explained. "They aren't as accepting of the relationship as they should be."

Aileen frowned. "Well, if Michael wants to be with CJ, what's the problem? Aren't they both grownups?"

"They are, and it isn't anyone else's decision but theirs," Randy agreed.

"CJ, want to hear about Michael?" Terri asked, smiling a little.

CJ looked up and nodded. "Sure."

"Well, you know Michael plays baseball. He's a pitcher. He started playing when he was four years old. I still have pictures of him playing t-ball. He loved sports from the time he was able to walk and talk. I can remember throwing a little ball back and forth when he was two." Terri smiled. "It was no wonder he became a college player."

"Well, it helped that you put me in little league every year," Michael said. "I might not have gotten as far as I did without all that practice."

"Yeah, that's true." Randy smiled. "Were you ever into sports, CJ?"

CJ shook his head. "I was never coordinated enough. I fell too often. Dyspraxia, they call it. I do okay now, but every once in a while, I trip and fall. I broke my arm once, but it healed well, so it doesn't bother me." He paused. "I didn't even like sports, but I'd go watch Michael play. I had no idea what was going on, like the rules or anything. I just liked to watch him."

Michael felt his face heat. "I didn't even know."

"What did you do growing up?" Aileen asked.

CJ looked thoughtful. "I read a lot. Still do, but I want to be a novelist. I've got all kinds of ideas for books, and I want to write them one of these days. That's why I'm in creative writing."

"See, he's perfect to play Dungeons and Dragons with me," Michael said proudly.

"Oh, of course, you'd get him into that game," Terri said, shaking her head with a smile. "Michael is addicted to playing that game! How have you gone without playing since you've been in St. Louis?"

"It's been tough," Michael said.

CJ turned to him. "How'd you get into it, anyway?"

"Jeremy. He was into it. He and his friends used to play when they were little kids and when I became friends with him, he got me into it. I mean, my favorite movies and books were fantasies, so it just made sense that I'd like the game."

"I like what I've seen," CJ said with a slight smile. "I mean, I know what we did in that basement wasn't the real game, but it was fun."

"Oh, what'd you do?" Aileen asked.

"We got some paper and drew up characters and then he did some solo adventuring I led," Michael explained. "I mean, no dice, but we did some role playing. It was something to keep us busy other than poker."

"You played poker?" Aileen said with a sour face. "That's dumb."

"We had fun, didn't we, CJ?" He grinned and looked at CJ.

CJ reddened and shook his head a little. "Yeah, was fun."

Aileen looked confused, but Terri spoke up. "Well, at least you kept busy."

The rest of the afternoon and early evening they spent talking about different things. Mostly, Terri and Randy talked about things Michael had done, how school had been, and who his friends had been. By the end of the evening, CJ was feeling much better, and they left on a good note after eating lasagna and garlic bread.

As they drove back, Michael took CJ's hand and held it between them as he drove. "Hey, you okay baby?" he asked.

"I'm better now," he said, nodding with a smile. "I'm glad we did this, even with the bad parts of the day. It was necessary."

"I'm glad, baby. Now, if you don't mind, I think when we get home, I'm going to fuck you until you can't stand," Michael said seriously.

CJ giggled a little, and Michael completely intended to follow through on that.

Chapter Nineteen

No Longer Pieces

Time had passed. CJ was about to start his last year, and his family had still not come around. It was painful, but CJ spent a lot of time with Michael's family instead. He and Aileen went clothes shopping on more than one occasion, and he started feeling more comfortable dressing like he wanted. With his therapist, he worked through his gender identity issues and got past what Joe had said about him. He kept growing his hair out and started wearing skirts. He especially enjoyed wearing broomstick skirts with sandals. He'd been mistaken for a girl many times, and he didn't mind. Some days he felt like a girl, and others he dressed in sweats and a hoodie. It depended on the day; some days he'd wear a skirt with a hoodie.

Tonight was special. It was the anniversary of the day Michael and CJ had met. As strange as it sounded, they counted that as the day they started dating. Michael was taking CJ to dinner, a nice Italian place called Vienna. They'd never been, but their menu online looked amazing. Despite his love of home cooked Korean food, he loved all kinds of food, and Italian was one of them.

"Here's to a year!" Michael said, picking up his glass.

CJ picked his glass up and smiled as they tinged together.

"And to many more!" CJ added.

"This time next year, we'll celebrate your upcoming graduation!" Michael told him as he sat his glass down.

CJ nodded. "Won't that be strange?"

"I can't wait for that celebration with you, and every other one we have," Michael said.

The waiter came by and refilled their glasses as they waited for their food. Michael had ordered the carbonara and CJ had stuck with spaghetti. They continued to chat about school for a few minutes, and then the food arrived.

"Oh, this looks amazing," CJ said.

"Only you would come to a fancy Italian place and order spaghetti," Michael shook his head as he ate.

"It's what I like best." CJ frowned but dove into his food.

They had plans to go to the movies after dinner and see if something good was playing. Then, who knew where the evening would go?

"Desert?" Michael asked, looking at him with a smile.

CJ frowned, not sure he could eat dessert, but the waiter came by with a tiramisu and sat it down in front of him. He was a bit surprised, but something was off. There was something on it. He looked closer.

It was a ring.

CJ gasped, picking the frosting covered object out and held it up, wiping it with the napkin. "Michael, what is this?"

"Just figured it was time to ask you. You think you could marry me?" he said with a smile.

CJ stared at the ring. It was a gorgeous silver ring studded with diamonds across the band. "How'd you manage this? You didn't spend a bunch of money!"

"My dad helped me," Michael admitted. "I have to pay him back, but he's letting me pay him some every month. But make sure it fits. It's platinum and can be resized if we need."

CJ nodded, pulling off the cheap band he'd worn for the last year. It slipped on and fit perfectly. He held his hand up and smiled. "I love it!"

"So, is that a yes?" Michael asked, still grinning.

"Oh! Yes, that's a yes!" CJ said, reaching across the table to grab Michael's hand.

After they ate, they ended up at the movie theater, and found an action movie they both wanted to see. It ended up being less watching and more kissing in the dark of the nearly empty theater. They sat in the back, and about a quarter of the way through, after the popcorn was finished, Michael reached over and grabbed CJ and pulled him in for a kiss. This led to more kissing and heavy petting. When the movie finished, they were both flushed with desire and ready to go home.

As they entered the duplex, they could barely keep their hands off each other. They quickly passed the now updated living room for the stairs. They'd gotten a new sofa and chair, and a TV stand so that it looked really nice now. They got to the bedroom before Michael began stripping CJ's clothes off of him.

"CJ, I love the clothes you've been wearing. They're beautiful," Michael said, pulling his shirt over his head. It was a very feminine piece.

"Aileen helped me pick out what to wear tonight." CJ leaned up for a kiss as Michael tossed the shirt aside.

Michael's hands rested on CJ's hips as he leaned in and kissed him deeply. He then slipped his fingers under the waistband of the skirt and slipped it over his hips. He paused, sliding hands over CJ's ass and the satin panties he was wearing. They were light pink and had lace at the edges. CJ's breath heaved in his chest because tonight, he had plans to do something he had yet to try with Michael.

"I can't be the only one naked," CJ muttered against another kiss.

Michael chuckled, and quickly got out of his shirt and tossed it aside with CJ's clothes. CJ's hands went for the button on his jeans, and a few seconds later, they both stood nude in the room, kissing.

CJ took a breath. "Get on the bed and lay down," he said.

Michael paused. "Huh?"

"I think I'm ready to do something." He smiled gently at him.

Michael blinked, face lined with confusion for a moment, then it seemed to dawn on him. "You want to get on top?"

CJ nodded, blushing to his roots. He had done a lot since he started therapy, but being on top had been something he had yet to try. He'd been working up to it. Even vibrators were a fun part of their sex life, and now he was ready for the last hurdle. It seemed silly to him to have such a hangup, but his therapist assured him it wasn't unusual to have difficulty with positions like that. He wanted to get past it, though.

Michael nodded, running a gentle hand over CJ's head. "Only do it if you're ready."

CJ had made sure, after the toy incident, that he told Michael everything he wasn't ready to do. Michael had been understanding and hadn't pressed the issue at all. He had only done the things CJ was ready for. Michael had been so very patient, and CJ loved him for that.

Michael climbed into bed, laying on his back, stroking himself as he waited for CJ. CJ grabbed the lube bottle and climbed in beside him. He opened it and put some on Michael's cock. He didn't really need to be fingered much anymore because they slept together most nights. He enjoyed it, though, so Michael usually did anyway. But tonight, he just wanted to feel Michael inside him entirely.

He straddled him, his own arousal high, and Michael reached out and gripped him, making him moan in response. He swallowed and moved, gripping Michael to guide his cock to his entrance. Michael's hips bucked beneath him, and he took a breath and slipped down slowly on him.

"Oh, ah," he gasped out as Michael's cock filled him.

"That good, baby? I know you like my cock in your boy-pussy," he said.

"Yeah, feels good, Mikey, feels so good," CJ confirmed, adjusting himself so he was sitting flat on Michael's lap, his cock deep inside him.

CJ took a few steadying breaths as the memories from last year tried to assault him. Walter's face floated in front of him for a moment, but he forced it away. He wasn't going to let them ruin this moment with Michael. He braced his feet and worked up and down on him. Michael groaned and reached out, grabbing his thighs.

"That's it, baby, work that cock."

CJ nodded, concentrating as he worked his body up and down, searching for the right position to rub against his prostate. It took a bit, but he eventually felt the jolting sensation of stroking his sweet spot. He let out a low moan.

"There you are, baby. Found the good spot, did you?" Michael kept stroking him and the inside of his thighs.

"Yeah, it feels so, so good," CJ said, eyes half closed as he concentrated on that spot.

"Keep going, baby. I'm going to paint your insides white, got it? Then when we're done, I'm going to do it again. Maybe fuck you from behind and see your pretty ass while I do it."

CJ blushed hard, as he did anytime Michael called him pretty. He enjoyed it a great deal, and Michael knew it. He increased his pace as he pushed up and dropped down on Michael's cock. It felt amazing, just feeling him inside him, pressing against every sensitive spot in his body. He couldn't get enough of the sensations Michael gave him. At times, his mind betrayed him and started comparing Michael to Joe or Walter, but he'd been better able to control those moments lately. Inevitably, he'd remember the worst moments of his life during the best, he supposed, but he tried not to. He didn't want anything to spoil his time with Michael.

"That's it, baby, keep going. You think you can make me come like this?" Michael asked, rubbing his hands along the inside of his thighs and kneading the flesh there.

"I don't know," CJ managed between gasping breaths. "It's a lot of work," he added.

"Yeah, but you're doing beautifully." Michael smiled and let out a little groan.

"Oh, I think I might go soon," CJ said, leaning forward and pausing in his motions to kiss Michael's lips.

"Hmm, baby, you come when you can. If you can't finish me, I'll turn you over and fuck you from behind until I go off," Michael said. "Here, I'll help." He started stroking CJ's cock gently and slowly.

CJ sat back up and rolled his hips, finding his own sweet spot again and moaning out loud. It felt good like that, he decided, and Michael's hand firmly stroking him made it hard to hold off. He kept angling to stroke himself on Michael's thick cock and moaned louder, breathing hard.

"Ah, I'm gonna come," he whined out, bouncing harder to get to his own end.

"That's it, baby, just come on my cock. Let me feel you squeeze me tight like I love." He firmly continued the stroking.

CJ gasped out as he held on tightly to Michael, feeling his cock throb in release. Michael continued to stroke him through the orgasm and CJ melted down onto him after it was done, knowing Michael had his come all over his belly now. Michael didn't wait. He moved, sliding out and flipping CJ over on the bed and slamming back in. CJ gasped again, oversensitive to touch as he began pounding into him hard, seeking his own orgasm. CJ didn't mind, though, but he had to admit it didn't feel the best right after he'd come like that. He thrust in a few more times, then he could feel the sensation of Michael's cock throbbing inside him. No matter what, he loved that sensation, that throbbing and thrusting sensation as he shot his load into him.

After he was done, Michael pulled out and CJ fell onto the sheets on his belly. "I'm a mess," he muttered.

"Why don't you take a shower and I'll change the sheets? We made a mess of them," Michael said, stroking his hair gently.

CJ nodded, crawling off the bed and heading into the bathroom. He was proud of himself. He'd gotten past something else and now he could do that with Michael. He smiled as he got under the spray.

They were having dinner at Michael's parents' place the next Sunday and when they were seated, another knock came at the door. Michael and CJ both looked up, confused as Terri headed to the door and Randy stayed at the table. Aileen was over at a friend's house, so she wasn't home, and she wouldn't knock anyway.

"CJ?" they heard, and CJ's head whipped around.

"Mom?" he said, watching as his parents entered the room. "Dad?"

CJ's heart was pounding. A year had passed since everything began, and many months since he last talked to them. They were both standing there, and his dad looked them over.

"Come on, Don, Mara, sit down. I think there's some talk to be had," Terri said, moving around and sitting at the end of the table.

Don and Mara sat down across from CJ and Michael, and CJ could sense Michael's trepidation about this already. He reached over and grabbed his hand, and Michael gripped it in return.

"It's been a while, CJ," Don said, looking over the table at him. "I guess we have a few things to talk about."

CJ nodded. "It seems so. Michael and I are getting married after I graduate," he came out and said immediately.

Neither of his parents said anything at first. Of course, they'd already told Terri and Randy they had agreed to marry the next year. They'd helped Michael buy the ring he gave CJ after all, so they'd known all along.

"Don and I have been talking," Randy said. "And I think we've come to a few agreements about things."

Michael looked over at his dad. "You failed to mention that."

"I know. I wanted things to happen when the time was right. With the announcement of the wedding, I thought now would be a good time to mend some fences between CJ and his parents. I'd like us all to celebrate the wedding next year," Randy said, glancing over at Don. "I think Don has come to a few conclusions on his own."

Don nodded. "I'm sorry for a lot of things, CJ," Don started. "I guess the biggest part of the whole situation was me feeling guilty. It was my fault Joe came after you, and I felt like I should have protected you better. I thought I could make up for that after the fact, but I had to realize that wasn't the case. I was blaming myself for something someone else did, and it wasn't my place to do that." He paused, looking down at his hands. "I regret the way I reacted. Trying to keep you and Michael apart was a mistake."

"A mistake?" CJ frowned. "It was more than a mistake. It was you trying to control me, and it wasn't fair."

"I had a lot of things to get through with this, you have to understand. It's traditional for the first-born son to marry a Korean woman. And I thought maybe your friend Jeena might get together, after all, you spent so much time together. I just had it in my mind that you'd end up marrying her. I realize now that I was making a lot of assumptions and being an overly controlling father. I can't hold you to traditions I was raised on, because you're not only Korean, you're also American." He paused. "I did realize you might be gay, though. I just didn't want to admit it because it would destroy those preconceived notions I had."

"I've always been gay, Dad," CJ said with a deep, long-suffering sigh. "Jeena was always just my friend. There was never anything more between us. There couldn't be."

"You never told us that, though, CJ," Mara said softly. "We didn't know."

"I'm not a boy either," CJ went on.

His parents both looked at him, confused expressions on their faces. "What do you mean?"

"I'm gender-queer," CJ said, looking down at his own hand where it interconnected with Michael's. "That means I'm not a boy, and I'm not a girl. I'm kind of both at the same time. I don't claim either as my gender. You can also say I'm non-binary."

Michael squeezed his hands, and CJ knew that he was aware of what a big deal this was for him. "It's always been that way since I've known him," Michael added.

"I'm not sure what to say about that," Don said. "I've had experience in my practice with non-binary people, but I never imagined one of my children might identify as such."

"Well, it's what I am." CJ chewed on his lip. "And I've worked through a lot of things with my therapist, including my gender and sexuality. I've processed my trauma a lot, and although it will always be with me, I've come to accept what happened to me and move through it."

"I understand," Don said. "I know I said before I knew what PTSD was, but you were both right. I don't understand what you went through, CJ. It's different from what I went through in the military, both the American one and the Korean one. I know I tried to apply what I knew to your situation, but I get now that you can't do that." Don sighed, looking over at Randy. "Randy and I talked a lot about it, and I think I understand a lot better now."

"What you know when it comes to PTSD is valid," Michael said evenly. He locked eyes on Don. "But what CJ experienced is different, and he has a different set of symptoms. Some are the same, but some are different. Some things he's been able to process and work through, while others we're still working on."

"I don't like to be touched, even now," CJ spoke up. "Not by strangers or even friends. I tolerate it from people I know well, but I'd rather not be touched. I don't mind from Michael, but from others, I can't really stand it. I had a lot of trauma around sex that I had to work through, of course. And I've been able to work through most of that."

"I'm glad, CJ," Mara said, her voice a little soft.

"I'll fix tea," Terri said, standing and going to the kitchen.

"I'll help," Mara commented. She stood and followed her into the kitchen.

Don still looked a bit chastised.

"I love you, Dad," CJ said. "And not seeing you hurt a lot. You not allowing me to be myself was really hard, and I tried so hard to conform. It just wasn't me, though, you have to understand that. I didn't want to lose you over this, but I had to make a choice. Michael is my future, and he's going to be the man I spend my life with."

"What if it doesn't last?" Don asked.

"Then it doesn't last," CJ said, smiling at Michael. "But for now, we're with each other, and we're happy with that. I want you to be happy for us."

"We want you to be a grandfather," Michael added.

Don frowned, staring at him. "What?"

"We have found a surrogate," CJ explained. "She's willing to carry a baby for each of us after we're married. We've already started setting aside money every month for her payment. That's why at the wedding, we're asking for donations instead of gifts, to help pay for the surrogacy."

"That's a big responsibility," Don said. "Are you sure you'll be able to handle that?"

"By the time we're married, I'll have my master's degree and be in a counselor position at my job," Michael said. "It pays a lot better, and I'll be working on my license, so that will pay even more. CJ will be a freelance writer after he graduates and already has a few jobs lined up to work on from home."

A silence fell on them as Don thought over what they'd said. Mara and Terri came in with the tea tray and cups for everyone. She even remembered the honey for CJ to use. Everyone fixed their tea and Don looked over at Mara.

"Did Terri tell you their plans?" he asked.

"She did," she said as she sat down. "I think it's going to be a good thing for them."

Don didn't speak for a moment. "I think it's awful fast."

"I know, but we want the children to grow up and be able to enjoy them as they grow. I feel like it will be a good plan for us, so we're still young when they're older. That way CJ can stay home while they're young. I'll be making enough to support our little family, though we'll need a bigger place." Michael glanced at his father. "But Dad said he'll help."

Don looked at Randy. "He did?"

"Michael has a fund we've been putting money into for a few years. It's not a lot, but it would be enough for a down payment on a home for them. He's taken out loans for his graduate school, so he'll need to pay them back, but this would reduce their debt some." Randy sipped his tea and nodded. "So far, they have decent credit, so I don't think there will be any problem with them getting a house."

"Where will you live?" Mara asked.

"We were thinking here in St. Charles or St. Peters. It would be better for the kids to be in a smaller school," Michael said.

Mara and Don exchanged a glance. Don spoke next. "I do know a realtor for the area," he admitted. "I could put them in contact."

"Wonderful!" Terri said with a grin. "That'll make things easier."

"Ah, one thing, CJ. As part of our apology," Mara said, reaching into her purse. She pulled out a set of keys CJ recognized and a piece of paper. "We brought it with us," she said, pushing the keys and paper across the table.

CJ picked it up, seeing it was a signed title for his car. "Really?" he said, looking at them.

"Yeah, it was wrong of me to take away something I'd given you already. It was spite and bitterness that drove my hand. Take this as my way of apologizing to you about it," Don said with a sheepish grin.

"Thank you," CJ said, feeling tears welling in his eyes. He wiped them away. "I appreciate the gesture, I do."

"I'm sorry I kept it from you before. It was selfish of me to do so," Don said. "I realize that now, even though you never asked for it, it was my responsibility to take care of your needs. You're still my son. Wait, can I still call you my son?" he asked, brows scrunching together.

CJ nodded. "It's fine, son works. It's not like there's a word for non-binary offspring. And I don't mind when you call me that."

Michael squeezed CJ's hand. "Mr. Kim, I want you to know that I love CJ more than anything in my life. I'll never do anything to make him sad, and I only want to see him happy," he said, smiling over at CJ.

CJ returned the smile. "I'm glad," CJ said.

Don nodded. "I want to be a part of your lives," he said. "And I want you to see Alex and Allie grow up, and we want to be a part of your children's lives as well when they arrive. We'll help you with the house, too, and I want to help with the surrogacy costs. CJ has a fund that's been set up since he was a baby, and by now it has quite a bit in it." Don looked at Mara. "And I think it's time to let him have it."

CJ blinked in surprise. "I have a fund? Why didn't you ever tell me?" he asked.

"It was going to be a surprise when you graduated," Mara explained. "But I think now is the time to tell you about it."

"Between the house and the babies, you'll need the money," Don continued. "I want my son's family to have a good start."

CJ got up and walked around the table. "I'm glad to have you back, Dad," CJ whispered and hugged him.

Don hugged him back and CJ heard the slight catch to his voice. "I've missed you, CJ. And I'm so sorry for so many things."

"It's okay, Dad, I love you," CJ muttered against him.

CJ let go and turned around, embracing his mom. Mara was crying and sniffed loudly. "I should have said something sooner, CJ. You're always my baby, you always will be. You're my first baby, and I'll always be your mama."

"Of course, Mom," CJ said, holding her against him.

CJ was overcome and didn't know how to express it. So much had changed in one day, and he had Michael's parents to thank for that. After he finished hugging his mom, he walked over and hugged Terri, whispering thanks in her ear, and then he hugged Randy as well.

He had his family back.

Chapter Twenty

A Union of Hearts

CJ was more nervous than he had ever been in his life. Jeena stood beside him and fluffed the skirt on his specially tailored white dress. It had a jacket top that almost looked like a white tuxedo and a flared white tulle skirt that flowed out from his waist. Michael had no idea what he was wearing, so it would be a complete surprise. He looked at Jeena.

"You think he'll like it?" he said, spinning again, making the dress flare.

"Oh, he's going to love it, CJ!" She smiled at him.

After CJ's graduation in May, they decided to marry in June. They wanted a small ceremony, with only close friends and family present. CJ had Jeena standing with him, and Michael had Jeremy.

"I'm nervous!" CJ gasped out. "I want to cry, but I don't want to mess up the makeup you put on me!"

"Don't be nervous! You're beautiful, and Michael is going to be stunned!" Jeena hugged him gently. She was one of the few people who could still.

CJ had come so far from over two years ago. He still had nightmares, though. He wasn't sure they'd ever go away. He'd wake in the middle of the night, choking with sobs, and Michael would hold him tight until he fell asleep again. They never talked about the nightmares afterward. That was mostly CJ's preference, because he didn't want to talk about them. He was still with Nadia, and they worked through the nightmares every time they came up.

He still didn't like to be touched. His family, Michael's family, Jeena, and Michael were really as far as he could tolerate, and anyone beyond that he shied away from. With his freelance work, he'd be able to work from home. It would be for the best once they decided to have the babies.

His father had come around totally and actually helped pay for a house. He'd completely transferred the fund over to CJ, and they'd put a nice down payment on a house in St. Charles. It had three bedrooms, two bathrooms, and both a family room and a living room. There was a large backyard, and as a housewarming present, Michael had gotten CJ a kitten. It was a little black kitten he named Midnight. So far, he'd been sleeping in the bed with CJ and Michael, so CJ hoped that it would be a great cat to have for the kids when they came along.

"Okay, how long have we got?" CJ asked, glancing around the room for a clock. There wasn't one.

"Fifteen minutes," Jeena said, checking her watch. "I'll stick my head out and make sure everything's ready."

She opened the door, and the sounds of soft music and murmuring spilled in. He smiled when she came back. She nodded and took his hands.

"CJ, this is so amazing! To think you'd marry the guy you were crushing on so hard!"

"I know! I mean, we went through hell to get here, but everything really worked out for me in the end!" He smiled at her and looked over as a side door opened, and his dad entered.

"Dad!" he said. "I was wondering where you were."

"Just making sure everything was ready. Jeena, if you want to go to the entry, Jeremy is ready to walk up when everything starts. Alex and Allie are going to walk down first, of course, so hopefully, Alex doesn't run out of petals after a couple of feet." He chuckled at that and patted CJ on the shoulder.

"Even if she does, it'll be fine. Did you get Allie the pillow for the rings?" CJ asked.

"She's ready to walk. All you have to do is concentrate on not tripping yourself!" Don said, hugging CJ against him. "You look beautiful, my dear."

Even though CJ hadn't asked him to, his dad had stopped calling him "my son" and had started saying "my dear" when he talked to him. It was a seemingly minor thing, but to CJ, it meant a lot. It meant he was understanding what CJ's gender was, and he was accepting it.

"Thanks, Dad. Oh! It's starting," he said, peeking out.

First, Michael walked down to the front wearing his suit. CJ smiled because he looked so dapper with the suit on. He wore a green vest under it and a purple boutonniere. Their colors had been purple and green, with CJ's bouquet being made of purple flowers. He'd actually made it himself, with Terri's help.

Then, Allie walked down, wearing a purple dress that matched her twin, Alex. She was holding a green satin pillow with the rings tied on a silken ribbon so they wouldn't fall off. She went up and stood by Michael. Jeena and Jeremy were both well dressed, with Jeena in a purple dress to match the twins, and Jeremy in a suit with a purple boutonniere. They were at ease as they talked quietly and walked down the aisle, then separated to stand on opposite sides. Anticipation was like butterfly nest inside CJ's stomach as he watched the wedding party finished their walk. Little Alex spread purple flower petals on the ground, giggling a little as she did so before taking her place next to Allie. Then the music shifted.

CJ turned to his dad and nodded. "Ready," he whispered.

CJ stepped out with his dad and Michael laid eyes on him. His eyes went wide first, then a smile spread across his face. Jeena had done his makeup and did his long black hair up on top of his head. He wore a veil, too, one that Aileen had helped him pick out. It was studded with a design of crystals and hung down over his face. He held the flowers in front of him in sweaty hands as he took measured steps down the aisle with his arm linked in his father's. They came to the front, and the officiant, a friend of Michael's family named Eric, nodded and smiled as Don placed CJ's hand in Michael's and left to sit down by his mom.

Michael's eyes were still wide, and he had a half-grin on his face. He didn't say anything, but it was obvious he was pleased with how CJ looked.

Eric looked around. "Welcome, all, to the wedding of Cameron Jae Kim and Michael James Heights. I'd like to extend my deepest congratulations to our happy couple, and the two families who will be united into one today."

CJ was so nervous he could barely pay attention. "First, CJ and Michael, you have come here today to pledge your love to each other." Eric looked between them.

Eric then looked out over the room and read an excerpt from a piece called "The Bridge Across Forever" by Richard Bach. It was lovely and made everyone smile as he read it. He finished the reading and turned the page in the book he had laid in front of him.

"Michael, please take your love's hand in yours."

Michael took CJ's hand gently in his. CJ tried his best to keep it from shaking. It wasn't quite working.

"Michael, do you take CJ to be your lawfully wedded partner, in sickness and in health, in good times and bad, and in the light of the sun as well as the shadows of the world?" Eric nodded at him.

Michael cleared his throat. "I do."

"And CJ, do you take Michael to be your lawfully wedded partner, in sickness and in health, in good times and bad, and in the light of the sun as well as the shadows of the world?"

CJ was afraid his voice would fail him, but he managed, "I do."

Eric nodded again. "Now, we'll have each of you speak your vows. They've each written their own vows to share. Michael?" he said, looking at him.

Michael nodded, taking a breath. "CJ, I am vowing to be your one and only forever. I'm vowing to take you through all the storms that may lie ahead, and all the beautiful days we will share. I vow to be there for you no matter what, no matter who attempts to come between us. I have found with you something I never thought possible, a love that binds us together like nothing else. I vow this to you."

"CJ?" Eric turned to him now.

CJ swallowed hard. "Michael, you've been with me through some of the worst moments of my life, and you've stayed true to me and who I am. You've reminded me what it's like to love even when it's hard to do so. Everything started with me sneaking pictures of you at baseball practice, and I never imagined I'd be standing up here with you back then. Now, I can't imagine being without you. I vow to stand beside you and be with you through anything and everything. I vow to always be yours."

Eric looked out and gestured to Jeremy. He reached over and plucked the rings off the pillow and passed them to Michael and CJ. Jeena took the flowers and patted CJ on the back. He was glad of her support.

"A ring is an unbroken circle. It represents the circle of love that binds two people in an unbreakable bond. Please, take the rings, and you will place them on your partner's finger." He looked at Michael. "Michael, place the ring on CJ's finger and repeat after me. With this ring, we are wed. It is a symbol of love and commitment. With all my heart, I place it on your finger."

Michael slipped the ring on CJ's finger and smiled. He repeated the words, letting them roll off his tongue easily, ingraining themselves into CJ's heart.

When CJ's turn came, he took a deep breath and slipped the ring on Michael's finger, trying to remember the words Eric said. "With this ring, we are wed. It is a symbol of love and commitment. With all my heart, I place it on your finger," he managed, remembering them all.

Eric looked out at the crowd and back to CJ and Michael. "CJ and Michael, you have pledged your love to each other today, and for that, we celebrate with great joy. It is with the greatest of pleasure that by the power of the State of Missouri, I now pronounce you partners in marriage. You may now kiss if you wish!"

Michael smiled and leaned forward, just gently brushing lips with CJ's, and there was a click of a camera nearby. They pulled apart, hands entwined, and looked at their family and friends. Everyone stood up and clapped for them. CJ blushed in embarrassment, but he and Michael walked back down the aisle to the back of the venue.

CJ turned to Michael as soon as they were in the back room and hugged him tightly. "Oh my God, we did it."

"Yes, we did," Michael answered, hugging him back tightly. "You look amazing, by the way. I love the outfit. It was perfect."

CJ leaned back and kissed Michael on the lips softly. "It was Aileen and Jeena who helped me get it. They don't make a lot of wedding outfits for men like this. It cost a little, but mom helped pay for it."

"Well, it was worth it."

CJ's dad opened the door. "Picture time!" he announced.

"Let's go!" Michael said and led CJ into the other room again for the wedding party photos.

* * *

The reception was a lot of fun for everyone. It was kid friendly, and there were activities to keep the little ones busy. The cake was strawberry with cream cheese icing, which was CJ's favorite kind of all, and everyone ate their fill of the catered food CJ's dad had provided. It wasn't a very big event, maybe fifty people, but it was more than enough for CJ.

He sat at the head table beside Michael and talked with family friends as they came and went. He met some more of Michael's family, and Michael met some of his. Of course, his Korean relatives weren't in attendance, but that was to be expected. It was a long flight and there were some issues with him being a first-born son not marrying a Korean woman. Something about traditional roles. CJ certainly didn't fit those roles, and his dad was working on that side of the family to make things a little smoother.

About halfway through, Michael grabbed his hand and kissed the back of it. "You doing okay? I know this is a lot of people."

Despite therapy and going through school, CJ still preferred to stay out of crowded places. It was such a problem some days that he refused to even leave the house out of fear of encountering a busy store or eatery.

"Yeah, it's okay. I'm reaching my limit, though. I don't know if I'll make it much later," he admitted.

"It's okay. We've got a honeymoon to go on!" Michael smiled.

CJ frowned. "What do you mean? Honeymoon? Since when?"

Michael smiled slyly and winked. "Give it a minute," he said as he waved at his dad.

CJ was curious. They hadn't planned a honeymoon. Michael had taken the week off from work, but CJ had just assumed that it was because of the wedding. He didn't know there were any plans to do anything.

Randy came over with Don and talked to Michael in whispers, and then they went to the center of the room. They had yet to do any speeches and toasts, so CJ assumed that's what this was. He wasn't wrong.

"Attention!" Don said. "As CJ's dad, I'm going to give a little speech and then let Randy have a say, as well. Then Jeremy and Jeena are going to say a few words. But before we get started, Randy and I want to give our wedding present to CJ and Michael."

He reached behind him and picked up an envelope. "We racked our brains to decide what to give them. It needed to be something they would never buy for themselves, and it had to be special," Don began. "So, this is what we all decided on."

He handed the envelope to CJ. CJ frowned and opened it, pulling out a folder. In it were tickets, several of them. "What's this?" he said.

"It's a European trip," Randy said with a grin. "For one week, there are tickets to take you to London to start with, with an oyster card for each of you. Then, a trip to Paris via the chunnel. You've got about three days in each city."

CJ looked up, and his eyes were bright with tears. "I never thought... What..." he stammered.

Michael squeezed him tightly. "Don't worry; there's plenty of stuff to do! I'll take you to the Globe Theater!"

CJ looked at Michael in disbelief. "This is amazing!"

"Now, for the speeches," Don said. He looked around. "So, we've got family and friends from all over here, and you mostly know me. I'm Donald Kim, CJ's father. I've got to admit to a few mistakes I made, especially with CJ and Michael. I didn't think their love could be real, as they fell in love quickly. And with CJ's experiences, I didn't think he was ready for such a thing. I was wrong, though, and I'm happy to see them today make this union official. Randy and I never thought our kids would end up married, but who really thinks something like that? But we were good friends for many years, so it's just as well that we officially become family."

Randy smiled and nodded. "Michael has been a joy to us and a great big brother. I've always wondered where he would end up, so I was surprised a bit when he brought CJ to meet us for the first time. But in that moment, I saw the truth in my son's eyes. He was as in love as his mother and I had been when we met and married. It was something he couldn't hide, and I found myself smitten by CJ as well. He's a good kid, sweet and beautiful inside and out."

Don and Randy gestured to Jeremy to come up. He smiled, brushing his brown hair back. He stood up beside them. "Ah, well, as the best man, I guess I am supposed to have something to say, right?" Everyone chuckled a little. "Ah, well, Michael's been my friend for a while, and we've played a lot of Dungeons and Dragons together over the years. Never was into baseball, as I know some of you are from his team. Just to let you know, don't let his athleticism fool you. He's a huge nerd and geek." Again, there was laughter. "But I never expected him to marry someone. Really, I thought he'd play the field forever. Just goes to show how special CJ is to make Michael decide to settle down for good. I think what they have is special, and I don't think anything will ever come between them again." He smiled. "Um, okay, that's it. Jeena?" he said, pointing at her.

She got up and came to the front. "I didn't know what to think when CJ had this monster crush on a baseball player. I'd known he was gay for years, you know, one of the few that knew. And when he started hoarding pictures on his phone, I said, CJ, you've got it bad." There was a little chuckle from the audience. "I never expected what happened, after all, what are the chances he'd get kidnapped, and then with his crush? It was fate, and I'll swear to that from this day forward." She looked over at CJ. "CJ has always been such a gentle soul. I was happy to see how great Michael made him feel. It was obvious there was something very special between them, and even before I met Michael, I knew that to get CJ's attention, he had to be a great guy." She paused, taking a breath. "CJ's been through a lot, and it's been my pleasure to help him, but Michael's really been there for him like no one else. I don't think there is a better match."

There was a round of applause when the last speech ended, and the music started. "First dance!" Michael said, standing up and reaching a hand out for CJ.

CJ blushed and stood up, walking out in the middle of the floor as the song they'd chosen began playing. It was a haunting melody with meaningful lyrics sung along with it. Michael turned him around the floor, holding him close as they danced, everyone watching them intently. When it was over, CJ's dad came out, and Michael's mom and they each danced with their children. Then CJ's mom came and danced with him, and then Jeena. Jeremy even took a turn dancing with CJ, while Michael danced with both Allie and Alex.

By the time the night was done, CJ was exhausted, and they bid everyone goodbye and headed out to Michael's car. CJ had changed into a regular skirt and T-shirt, and Michael had switched to jeans and a T-shirt. Their plane left early the next morning, and they still had to pack. For a moment, Michael didn't turn on the car and just sat there.

"Are you okay, Mikey?" CJ asked, curious.

Michael turned, his eyes teary. "I can't believe we're married. CJ, I love you so much."

"I love you too, so very much!" CJ said and leaned over and grabbed him in a hug

[A place unknown—A time unknown]

Ecstasy didn't describe the feelings of Brishna as her arms embraced Krineshaw. For once, they were together. There was no one between them. They were as one once again. Iman would not come between them ever again.

The Curse was broken.

Tears fell of pure bliss and happiness, and the feelings could not be described by mortal words. Thousands of years had passed, and hundreds of lives. There were so many things that could be said, but the moment of the union had come, and it was the destiny that the two forgotten gods desired.

No humans worshipped them. Few even remembered their names, but they still existed in the shadows of the world. Their curse had been a terrible one and one that they had carried around their souls for so very long. But no more. Now, when these lives ended, they would be together in the heavens, and there would be no mortal that could come between them again.

Twining, spirits uniting and separating again and again, the two would never be without each other again. Despite the many years that had come between them, it was like the day they met on the River Nile. Two people of eternity and simply avatars of what was within them. Gods and goddesses came and went; it was true. But sometimes the memory existed in one person, and that was enough to keep them alive.

Epilogue

The Embrace of Destiny

"Cindy!" CJ gasped. "Get down from there. You're going to fall!"

Cindy, a dark-haired little girl with vivid blue eyes, was four years old and more than a handful. She wanted to get into everything and was intent on giving her Appa a heart attack as she tried to climb up on top of the chest of drawers again. She just wanted to fly, after all.

CJ sighed, the one-year-old, Nick, on his hip. This little boy was as blond as his daddy and had light blue eyes.

Cindy did as asked and ran into the next room where Michael was playing on the game system. "Daddy! Appa yelled at me!" CJ heard her say.

"What were you doing?" Michael asked.

"Nothing!" she answered.

"I doubt that. Don't be climbing on everything, little girl!" he said.

She came running back into the room with CJ. "I told Daddy, Appa."

"I heard you," CJ said. "I'm going to say it again, don't climb up on things!"

Cindy frowned and ran over to her dollhouse to play in it. CJ shook his head. That girl was going to be the death of him, he knew. He wandered with Nick, who was happily pulling CJ's long black hair, into the living room and sat down beside Michael.

"She still trying to fly?" Michael asked.

"Of course. I don't think those superhero movies are very good for her," CJ mused.

"Ah, don't blame it on that. She's got your spirit." Michael grinned at him.

"I suppose," he said.

The bell rang on the door. "Here, take Nick for a minute."

"Babe, I've got a boss battle coming up!" Michael complained but paused the game and took the baby anyway.

"It can wait. I think that's your mom, anyway. Remember, we're going out tonight for our anniversary?"

"Yeah, I didn't forget, don't worry," he said, making faces at Nick to get the baby to giggle.

CJ went to the door to find Terri and Aileen standing there. "Oh, I didn't expect you both," he said.

"Aileen wanted to see the kids," Terri said with a grin. "So, I thought she could come while I babysit."

"That's fine. Cindy's in her room, and Nick's in the living room with Michael." CJ smiled and shut the door behind them.

Midnight came running to greet them. He'd gotten big over the years and was quite a good cat with the kids. He slept with CJ, though, and was completely his cat. He was fine with the kids, but when it came down to it, he knew who his preferred person in the house was.

Terri went into the living room and came back with Nick. She was playing with him and he was grabbing at her fingers. Aileen went to find Cindy.

"Okay, I should get ready," CJ said with a smirk. "I bought a new outfit for tonight."

"Ooh, can't wait to see!" Terri said.

CJ went into the bedroom and stripped down, grabbing a pair of the satiny thongs that he wore on special occasions. He paired it with a matching bralette. Then he grabbed the black dress he'd bought. It came from a drag shop, meaning it fit well everywhere. He slid into it, staring at himself in the mirror.

Seven years ago, he wouldn't have dreamed of wearing a little black dress like this. He ran his hands over his slightly curving hips. He'd started taking hormones in the last couple years, just to get a more feminine shape. He'd grown a little in the chest, not a lot, but he hadn't expected much breast growth. He wasn't interested in any surgeries, just the hormone replacement therapy. So far, he'd stopped a lot of the hair growth on his face, and he had acquired more shape. He was more often accepted as a woman than a man, and with his name being CJ when he wrote, no one knew his gender. He still chose to use he/him pronouns, but he didn't mind she/her or even they/them.

All in all, he'd become much more comfortable in his own skin. He went to the bathroom and did his makeup and hair, brushing it out as it fell down to his mid-back. It was lush and shiny and he took great care of it. He smiled and came out to see Michael must have finished his boss fight because he was changing. He stopped and stared at him.

"Goddamn, you're gonna be turning all the heads tonight, baby," Michael said with awe in his voice.

"The only head I care about is yours." CJ smiled.

"Well, you got both my heads' attention," he muttered.

CJ chuckled. "That's for after we get home!"

He went out past him and Terri looked up from the kitchen table, where she was feeding Nick some mashed bananas. "Oh, you look beautiful, darling!"

"Damn, CJ," Aileen said as she came into the kitchen. "You're looking good these days. Those hormones really make a difference." She shook her head.

"Yeah, I'm happy with it," he said as Michael came down.

He was wearing dark slacks and a button-up shirt. He smiled. "Before we go, I got you something."

CJ grinned. "Well, how about that? I got you something, too!"

Michael went to the living room and brought a bag into the room and CJ retrieved a bag from under the kitchen cabinet where he'd hidden it the day before.

"Let's exchange," CJ said, smiling at Michael.

They each got into their bags, Aileen and Terri watching with grins as they did so. CJ pulled out a book. He gasped as he turned it over in his hands. It was a wood bound journal with the word for love written in Korean on it. He smiled and watched as Michael pulled out the wooden plaque he'd gotten him for his office that said, "Michael Heights, Counselor."

"We both followed the tradition!" Michael said, smiling at CJ. "I love it!"

They hugged and then headed out to dinner. It was a Korean BBQ place they loved to visit in St. Louis, and they had a great night. CJ felt more confident than ever in himself, and Michael proudly made it known that CJ was with him.

Seven years had made a lot of changes for CJ and Michael, and there were more years ahead than behind. Whether it was fate or destiny, or whatever you wanted to call it, something had bound them together. Fate may have had one thing written for them, but they had escaped it, and had managed to embrace their destiny.

Autism Women's Network

- https://autismwomensnetwork.org/

Identity First Autistic

- identityfirstautistic@gmail.com
- https://www.identityfirstautistic.org

Mental Health and Mental Health Resources

National Alliance on Mental Health

- 1-800-950-6264
- http://www.nami.org/

Depression and Bipolar Support Alliance

- 1-800-826-3632
- http://www.dbsalliance.org/

National Mental Health Association

- 800-969-6642
-

Trauma/PTSD/Anxiety

Anxiety Disorders of America

- 301-231-8368

National Center for PTSD

- 802-296-5232
- https://www.ncptsd.org

National Victim Center Infolink

- 800-FYI-CALL

Eating Disorder Resources

National Eating Disorders Association

- 800-931-2237 (M-F, 11:30 am-7:30 pm EST)
- http://www.nationaleatingdisorders.org/

ANAD: National Association of Anorexia Nervosa and Associated Disorders

- 630-577-1330 (M-F,12 pm-8 pm EST)
- http://www.anad.org/

Substance Use Disorder/Addiction Assistance

Substance Abuse and Mental Health Services Administration

- 1-877-SAMHSA-7
- https://www.samhsa.gov/

AL Anon Family Groups

- 800-344-2666
- 800-356-9996
- https://alanon.org/

American Council for Drug Education

- 800-488-DRUG
- https://www.acde.org

American Council on Alcoholism

- 800-527-5344

- https://assistedrecovery.com

Harm Reduction Coalition

- 212-213-6376
- https://harmreduction.org

National Institute on Drug Abuse (NIDA)

- https://www.nid.nih.gov

Anonymous Groups

Alcoholics Anonymous

- 212-870-3400
- https://www.aa.org

Cocaine Anonymous

- 310-559-5833
- https://www.ca.org

Co-Dependence Anonymous

- 602-277-7991

- https://www.coda.org

Families Anonymous

- 800-736-9805
- https://www.familiesanonymous.org

Gamblers Anonymous

- 213-386-8789
- https://gamblersanonymous.org

Narcotics Anonymous

- 818-733-9999
- https://na.org

Sexaholics Anonymous

- 866-424-8777
- https://sa.org

Transgender Assistance and Equality

Transgender Youth Equality Foundation

- 207-478-4087
- http://www.transyouthequality.org/

Trans Student Educational Resources

- TSER@transstudent.org
- http://www.transstudent.org/

Bullying Prevention Assistance

Stopbullying.gov

- https://www.stopbullying.gov/

PACERS National Bullying Prevention Center

- 1-800-537-2237
- http://www.pacer.org/bullying/

Suicide Prevention Hotlines and Help

National Suicide Prevention Hotline

- 1-800-273-8255
- https://suicidepreventionlifeline.org/

Crisis Text Line

- Text "Start" 741-741
- http://www.crisistextline.org/

Trans Lifeline

- US: 1-877-565-8860
- Canada: 1-877-330-6366
- https://www.translifeline.org/

Suicide Prevention Resources

- http://www.sprc.org/

The American Association of Suicidology

- http://www.suicidology.org/

American Foundation of Suicide Prevention

- https://www.afsp.org/

GLBT National Youth Talk

- 1-800-246-7743 (M-F, 4pm-12 am EST/Sat, 12 pm-5

pm EST)

The Trevor Project

- 1-866-488-7386 (24/7)
- Text "Trevor" 1-202-304-1200 (F 4 pm - 8 pm EST)
- http://www.thetrevorproject.org/

Warm Ear Line

- 1-866-WARM EAR (927-6327)
- http://warmline.org/

Self-Injury Assistance

S.A.F.E. Alternatives

- 1-800-DONTCUT
- http://www.selfinjury.com/

Human-Created Disaster Helpline

Disaster Distress Helpline

- 1-800-985-5990

- Text "TalkWithUs" 66746

Sexual Violence and Abuse Resources

National Sexual Violence Resource Center

- 1-877-739-3895
- http://www.nsvrc.org/

RAINN- Rape, Abuse, and Incest National Network

- 1-800-656-4673 (National Sexual Assault Hotline)
- https://www.rainn.org/

Domestic and Intimate Partner Violence Resources

The National Coalition Against Domestic Violence

- 303-839-1852
- http://www.ncadv.org/

The National Domestic Violence Hotline

- 1-800-799-SAFE
- http://www.thehotline.org/

The National Resource Center on Domestic Violence

- 1-800-537-2238
- http://www.nrcdv.org/

Human Trafficking Resources

National Human Trafficking Resource Center

- 1-888-373-7888
- Text BeFree (233733)

Runaway and Child Abuse Resources

National Runaway Safeline

- 1-800-RUNAWAY (786-2929) (24/7)
- http://www.1800runaway.org/

USA National Child Abuse Hotline

- 1-800-422-4453 (24/7)

National Safe Place

- Text SAFE and your current location to the number 69866 (24/7)
- http://nationalsafeplace.org/

Beverly L. Anderson started writing at eleven, and when they did, it was apparent they would stick to something other than the every day. Her first story, written in spiral notebooks, was about a kidnapping. There were endless story ideas featuring fantastic places, monstrous creatures, and forbidden love in her mind even then. There's no surprise that these days, they favor the dark corners of the psyche over the happy and fluffy parts. Enamored with the mind, she studied extensively in psychology and related fields. She spends most of her days dreaming about stories and deciding how to make the unruly characters do as they tell them. As everyone knows, sometimes the characters take off and do what they want, no matter what the author has planned.

Beverly's other hobbies include gaming of all types, including a great love of tabletop, transgender and autism advocacy, and writing fanfiction when she can. Their interest in the BDSM community began as a simple curiosity but has led her to the road to finding a place for herself there as a Domme. She has gone on the journey of self-discovery in the last few years, finally pinning down their identity after nearly thirty years of searching. Coming out as bigender, asexual, panromantic, and polyamorous was one of the hardest things they've ever done, but it gave them the confidence to become themselves even more. An autistic person and an eclectic pagan, Beverly finds themself at odds with a lot of what society calls "normal." They don't mind, though, because they find that they are uniquely queer in every aspect of her life, and she's just fine with that.

Beverly started their writing journey seriously in 2013 when she found their way to fanfiction. She spent several years writing over three million words in various fandoms. In the last few years, they have been drawn to making those stories into original pieces and publishing them for a wider audience. Finding her publishing home helped make that dream a reality, one that they try to help others find.

Visit online: https://www.phoenixreal.net/

phoenixreal.net
Queer Love

Crimson
Hunt
Behind the
Red
Part One
Beverly L Anderson
J Foster

and he can finally relax. At least, that's what he believes. Then, a dress arrives, seemingly an apology for a bit of bigotry from a shop clerk. No one thinks a dress can cause any harm, so he wears it under the stage lights. Things go awry, though, and Kerry wonders what could possibly be happening. A bounty hunter named Martin swoops in, convinced that he can be of aid in the situation. Along with Martin, there's an intrepid FBI agent named Zak on the trail of a pair of sadistic serial killers who target and manipulate young, attractive, feminine men like Kerry.

Kerry doesn't believe it at first. Can he be targeted by these people? Then, things start happening, and his phone and email is full of messages with horrible images of what these people plan to do to him. He's frightened but staunch in living his life. He is adamant that he won't let them win, no matter what they do to him. Still, as the manipulation and gaslighting continue from afar, he starts to doubt everything he's ever known. He begins to lose purchase on reality but finds that Martin and Zak ground him. He refuses to give in to their sadistic games, but in the end, he begins to wonder if his willpower is enough to keep these people away from him.

Stolen Innocence - Doctor's Training Part One

When desperate criminals find an easy target in the autistic neurosurgeon Kieran Sung, the young doctor is soon at the mercy of a local Irish mob boss with perverse desires. Despite suffering at his hands, rescue finds him with relative quickness. Pulled unwillingly into circumstances that bring his world crashing down around him and destroying the carefully laid routines and structure he desires; Kieran must find a new way to live. He discovers comfort in ways he never imagined, within sensations of pressure and binding. Taking the hand of a childhood friend who desires nothing else but to help him, Kieran realizes his heart aches for more in his life. Circumstances bind him to a tattoo artist named Varick Jaeger, an actor named Carmine DeAngelo, and a bartender named Devan Sullivan. With this unlikely trio, Kieran must learn how to handle the upheaval in a life he sees desperately needs change.

Stolen Innocence, part one of the Doctor's Training Trilogy, is a story of healing that examines D/s culture, the complexities of polyamory, and how people often deal with mental and physical trauma. Follow Kieran, Devan, Varick, Carmine, and the rest of their pack; they navigate a world that rarely accepts people who do not fit in with expectations.

Dark and the Sword – Legacy of the Phoenix Book One

The world of Avern has moved on. It has been almost a thousand years since the day the entire pantheon disappeared. Since the Abandonment, the mortals have learned to live without gods and goddesses. The world became mundane, with little magic and even less hope. Tyrants have risen, and those able to wield what is left of magic are powerful. Forces surge in the darkness that threaten to topple the already fragile world. However, the plight of the world of Avern is not unknown, and those who watch from a distance have decided to intervene. The mortals are sleeping, however, unknowing that two great powers will soon be vying for control.

Then something happens that changes things. A young princess makes a bid for power by murdering her father. She then attempts to murder her sister, the crown princess of Lineria, Keiara. Despite a true strike aided by dark powers, Keiara doesn't die. Instead, the strike pierces the barrier between her human soul and the soul sleeping within her, the soul of the

Dark Phoenix. More than a goddess, the Dark Phoenix is the legendary mother of the gods. She is a part of the Eternal Phoenix that brought life to their world eons ago, one of the primal forces of the cosmos.

Chasing the Silver Dragon – Part One Disconnect, Book One of the Dragon Trinity Cycle

Silver Dragon has become a bane to the werewolf community in recent years. Designer heroin, one that actually affects were creatures where normal drugs are simply a passing fancy, has infiltrated the St. Louis werewolves. One of these, a young woman named Anna Maddox, wants her brother back somehow from the brink he's standing at. To do this, she reaches out to the ancient order, the Children of Asclepius. Duncan Powell hears her plea and pledges to help her rescue her brother from the streets of St Louis.

He goes to Detective Sebastian Pearce, a member of Unit Zero, the law enforcement agency that deals with supernatural creatures that pose a threat to the peace in the world. Sebastian implores him to leave things to Unit Zero, but Duncan is stubborn and goes down to the Red District to find the young Were. Sebastian and his partner follow and then begin the mission that will either save Kacey Maddox or doom all of them.

Let Sparks Fly – Short Story Compilation

Romance can come from the most unexpected places. Sometimes, two people meet, and the sparks just fly between them. Then, sometimes, two people see each other every day, and don't realize the spark that exists between them.

In this volume, you will find stories of many kinds. You'll meet a pair of fellows just looking for a sub to share when they ask out two people, and a secret is revealed. A young man is pining for his very best (straight) friend when a strange entity shows him pleasures beyond imagining, along with some truth. Join a guy who secretly harbors a taboo wish he thinks will never come true. Watch the sparks as a pair of swimming rivals find themselves in a compromising position. A demon on a mountain demands a sacrifice and receives something he isn't expecting. And finally, a man finds his bliss in a woman who can completely own him.

Journey through these pages and enjoy short erotic stories of love found in some quite unusual ways.

Whispered Shadows – A Poetry Anthology

The twisting paths of a poet's mind lead to intriguing places, there can be little doubt of this. These places contain whispers of the writer's soul. Some paths show desired sights; others uncover unforeseen knowledge and, at times, unwanted things. The shadows conceal unknown discoveries on well-lit paths through the poet's mind. Travelers, beware: uncertain destinations await along these paths. Tread carefully. Becoming lost in the pages of the poet's thoughts may be a very real danger to these travelers.

So, come along and visit this place of shadows. Here, there be dragons, monsters, truth, and more to enjoy. Fantasy, Reality, and Truths form one hundred and fifty poems by Beverly L. Anderson. The first path is one of fantasy with mythic beasts of yore and darkness that creeps into the very bone. Fairies may fly, and dragons may soar. The second path is one of reality and perhaps questions of what is and is not within that reality. Questions of existence and what the world shows us daily are spoken here. And the final path is one of truths. These truths may be surprisingly uncomfortable or may not be the truth expected. In any case, travel the paths at your own risk.

Open these pages and see if something draws you into the whispered shadows of the very soul.

Reflections of the Shadow Dancer

In an abandoned dance studio, there's music and dancing unheard and unseen by anyone. The whispers in the shadows laud praises upon the figure who spins around the room, her body translucent and flickering in the night. Nothing is in motion, and yet everything moves around the room. Darkness and light intertwine and dance to cast the shadows of the world. The Shadow Dancer performs a dance that crosses the borders between the world and other surprising places within flickering shadows.

The Shadow Dancer knows the truth. Without the darkness, there can be no light. Without the light, there can be no darkness. Between them lies the shadow in which the Shadow Dancer twirls.

Enter the world of the Shadow Dancer and immerse yourself in 150 poems, living in the light, the dark, and the shadow.

Coming Next: The Chains of Blood Trilogy

Confined by Heave – Chains of Blood Book One

The day started as any other day would. Bellamy Delacroix was shopping with his brother, and then he headed home to the inevitable discussion about his future with his mother. A woman who still cooks despite technology that doesn't require her to, his mother is an old-fashioned type in a future world.

Then, his world explodes quite literally, and he's swept up into a world beyond his imagination. A war between extraplanar creatures who call themselves angels and demons draws him in because of what he is. And what he is, no one has ever seen before—a Nephilim. He is the child of an angelic mother and a demonic father and is thus capable of channeling both the positive and negative energies of the planes. This makes him dangerous and a target for both the minions of heaven and hell.

An angel named Saniel takes him under her wing and helps him adjust as he is brought to the underground city of heaven, Elysium. He learns about what he is, who they are, and their enemies in Zion, the demons. A warning from an ally of his mother, though, rings in his head, and he wonders who he should really be trusting. Things begin to spiral in ways he doesn't understand, and the world is changing before his very eyes.

Released by Hell – Chains of Blood Book Two

Driven insane by the very people he trusted, Bellamy is caught between worlds in a way like never before. He's in the hands of Addariel, the angel both at fault for his fall from grace and the current King of Hell. His mind is only clear when he is inside his own head and his world is spinning out of control. A terrible experiment that went wrong has left him on the verge of death, and it is up to the Codex of Hell and Addariel to save him.

Then, the strangest things happen among the demons. They devote themselves to his salvation, claiming him as their mate and, more than that, dedicating the hearts they didn't know they had to him. In his madness, he captures their very souls and changes the nature of the beasts around him. Even Addariel, once only interested in power, shifts his focus to taking care of the mentally fragile Bellamy. For the first time in Zion's history, the King of Hell cares more for something other than power and conquest.

Elysium, though, is not letting go of him easily. In a misguided attempt to help him, they make a move that could destroy the fragile peace between Zion and Elysium.

Transcended by Earth – Chains of Blood Book Three

Rescuing Bellamy has become a priority for both Elysium and Zion. Adding to the mix are the Arcadians, who will stand to fight for Bellamy. Held by the angel Usiel in a location no one knows, Bellamy fights for his survival and the survival of his unborn child. Usiel wants to breed an army of angels capable of fighting demons without fearing their use of negative energy, and by doing that, he needs to rid Bellamy of the demon's child within him.

A human woman senses something off with a strange neighbor and investigates the situation. What she finds shocks her, and she knows what she must do. Taking Bellamy, unstable as he is, she flees, unsure what to do with what she thinks is a young girl pregnant with her a child her captor wishes to kill.

Meanwhile, in Arcadia, angels from Elysium and demons from Zion work together with a pirate radio station to try and find the missing Nephilim. The world is unsure, but they know they must find him before Usiel captures him again.

Confined by
Heaven
Chains of Blood
Book One
Beverly L. Anderson
J. Foster

Confined by Heaven – Chains of Blood Book One

The day started as any other day would. Bellamy Delacroix was shopping with his brother, and then he headed home to the inevitable discussion about his future with his mother. A woman who still cooks despite technology that doesn't require her to, his mother is an old-fashioned type in a future world.

Then, his world explodes quite literally, and he's swept up into a world beyond his imagination. A war between extraplanar creatures who call themselves angels and demons draws him in because of what he is. And what he is, no one has ever seen before—a Nephilim. He is the child of an angelic mother and a demonic father and is thus capable of channeling both the positive and negative energies of the planes. This makes him dangerous and a target for both the minions of heaven and hell.

An angel named Saniel takes him under her wing and helps him adjust as he is brought to the underground city of heaven, Elysium. He learns about what he is, who they are, and their enemies in Zion, the demons. A warning from an ally of his mother, though, rings in his head, and he wonders who he should really be trusting. Things begin to spiral in ways he doesn't understand, and the world is changing before his very eyes.

Released by Hell – Chains of Blood Book Two

Driven insane by the very people he trusted, Bellamy is caught between worlds in a way like never before. He's in the hands of Addariel, the angel both at fault for his fall from grace and the current King of Hell. His mind is only clear when he is inside his own head and his world is spinning out of control. A terrible experiment that went wrong has left him on the verge of death, and it is up to the Codex of Hell and Addariel to save him.

Then, the strangest things happen among the demons. They devote themselves to his salvation, claiming him as their mate and, more than that, dedicating the hearts they didn't know they had to him. In his madness, he captures their very souls and changes the nature of the beasts around him. Even Addariel, once only interested in power, shifts his focus to taking care of the mentally fragile Bellamy. For the first time in Zion's history, the King of Hell cares more for something other than power and conquest.

Elysium, though, is not letting go of him easily. In a misguided attempt to help him, they make a move that could destroy the fragile peace between Zion and Elysium.

Transcended by Earth – Chains of Blood Book Three

Rescuing Bellamy has become a priority for both Elysium and Zion. Adding to the mix are the Arcadians, who will stand to fight for Bellamy. Held by the angel Usiel in a location no one knows, Bellamy fights for his survival and the survival of his unborn child. Usiel wants to breed an army of angels capable of fighting demons without fearing their use of negative energy, and by doing that, he needs to rid Bellamy of the demon's child within him.

A human woman senses something off with a strange neighbor and investigates the situation. What she finds shocks her, and she knows what she must do. Taking Bellamy, unstable as he is, she flees, unsure what to do with what she thinks is a young girl pregnant with her a child her captor wishes to kill.

Meanwhile, in Arcadia, angels from Elysium and demons from Zion work together with a pirate radio station to try and find the missing Nephilim. The world is unsure, but they know they must find him before Usiel captures him again.

Milton Keynes UK
Ingram Content Group UK Ltd.
UKHW041628240924
448733UK00002B/44